VAGABLONDE

A NOVEL

ANNA DORN

The Unnamed Press
Los Angeles, CA

AN UNNAMED PRESS BOOK

Copyright © 2020 Anna Dorn

www.unnamedpress.com

Unnamed Press, and the colophon, are registered trademarks of Unnamed Media LLC.

ISBN: 978-1951213008
eISBN: 978-1951213015
Library of Congress Control Number: 2019956583

This book is a work of fiction. Names, characters, places and incidents are wholly
fictional or are used fictitiously. Any resemblance to actual events or persons,
living or dead, is entirely coincidental.

Designed and Typeset by Jaya Nicely

Manufactured in the United States of America by Versa Press, Inc.
Distributed by Publishers Group West
First Edition

They see me as… You know, you don't see me as I see myself.

—Little Edie Beale

I always misspell genius SMH! The irony!

—Kanye West

VAGABLONDE

ONE

I'm still clinging to the memory of those twinks on Sunset telling me I was beautiful as I stare at my reflection in the mirrors above the pharmacy section of Walgreens. Turning so my ass faces the mirror, I fixate on the bulging line of fat that curls out around my underwear. I'm wearing those Kappa track pants that were popular when I was a kid—you know, the design with the naked bodies back-to-back. But they aren't flattering, and I don't play soccer anymore. I'm a thirty-year-old attorney. Wearing track pants at 3:00 P.M. on a Tuesday.

Two nights ago I was smoking a cigarette outside a neighborhood dive bar. There was a Dodgers game, so traffic was flowing. Two pretty boys in matching Mariah Carey tank tops approached begging for cigs, and I offered up two Parliaments. As one was lighting up, the other called me beautiful. The memory comforts me, although I know I shouldn't attach too much weight to it. I bend the truth constantly when I want something. I once told a cheesy lesbian in a fedora that I adored her Pink Floyd T-shirt—a bold and reckless lie, but at least I got the Marlboro.

The Walgreens fluorescents burn my eyes. I cover my face as though I'm being hounded by paparazzi, a game I like to play when I'm alone, which is most of the time. The line is long as hell. Pharmacists are the slowest people on earth. I pull my phone out of my purse. A text from Ellie, my perfect girlfriend. I'm a Virgo, so I don't take perfection lightly.

Guess who just announced a secret show tomorrow night, my love?

My heart does a little flutter. Not much excites me these days, but a charismatic woman onstage still does it for me. Ellie does PR for musicians, so she's constantly getting us into shows no one else knows about.

I tap my foot on the linoleum, scratch my head, contort my expression into something cartoonish, pretending I'm in a sitcom. Another game I like to play when I'm alone.

The typing bubbles appear. She's not going to wait for me to guess. That's okay. I'm coming up blank.

Dead Stars.

I gasp. I guess audibly, because the woman in front of me turns around and shoots me a look. I raise my eyebrows at her with an expression that says, *Nothing to see here, honey.* Once she turns back around, I return to my private excitement, try not to make another noise that draws attention.

Dead Stars is my absolute favorite band of the past year, but I've yet to see them live. It's the project of Wyatt Walcott. She was on this reality TV show about her family, *What's Up with the Walcotts*, which I pretended to watch ironically but really I cried during at least four episodes. After it ended, Wyatt left Calabasas for Echo Park—my neighborhood—and started a synth-pop band with her friend Agnes, this MIT dropout and total babe. I pray I run into them, like, every day.

My phone lights up with another text from Ellie, snatching me from my hyperlooped thoughts.

At Mirror Box!!

Mirror Box is a strip club, one of those LA establishments (rumor has it Tarantino wrote *Pulp Fiction* there). The only time Ellie and I got into a fight was when I was too tired to see her favorite dancer (Cinnamon? Saffron?). I haven't been able to break it to Ellie, but I don't care for strip clubs. I go for her, but honestly, I hate drinking in a place where everyone's gaze is directed at something other than *moi*. Also, feminism, whatever. But I'll go for Wyatt.

I look up from my phone and my gaze meets the mirrors again. Jesus, isn't there anywhere else to look? If I was that type of person, I'd write a letter to Walgreens explaining that if they want to sell things to discerning Virgos such as myself, they must make a better effort to make the lighting conditions more flattering.

I'm here to pick up my Celexa. I've been thinking of going off my SSRIs lately, but this lighting is making me feel crazy as hell, like I couldn't fathom facing the harsh world without chemical assistance. I watch the pharmacist, who is slightly too pretty to be a pharmacist, move as though she is walking through jelly. The line hasn't budged. Fuck it. My pills don't run out for a few days anyway. I just like to be prepared.

I ditch the line and slide my B-complex vitamins and Maybelline Great Lash mascara into my purse while avoiding eye contact with the too-pretty pharmacist. My energy lightens as I leave the pharmacy area, and I smile at the security guard on my way out, unconcerned about the two "stolen" items in my purse. There are lots of things I'm guilty about, but stealing roughly fifteen dollars' worth of necessary products from an objectively evil corporation is not one of them. It's more political activism than anything.

In the parking lot, I think I'll finally ask Dr. Kim about getting off my SSRIs.

Why? Because I'm thriving.

I hop in my Saab and rev the ignition, then pull onto Sunset, heading toward Dr. Kim's office on the West Side. The sun is blazing that frightening Los Angeles yellow, the type that makes palm fronds resemble shiny strips of plastic about to burst into flames. As I drive, I listen to a guided meditation from my Insight Timer app and wonder whether Dr. Kim has ever been to Echo Park. He probably thinks it's still gang territory.

My mind wanders when I meditate. I attended meditation class once after it was recommended to me by a number of medical professionals. I told my teacher that I sometimes love my mind's crazy thoughts, and she told me I was inviting delusions.

I never went back after that. I don't need a teacher to meditate. Sit there, breathe. It's not rocket science.

I've been thinking about psychotropic medication a lot lately. I've had a ten-year reliance on SSRIs—first Lexapro, now Celexa. A lot of people say, "If you were a diabetic, you wouldn't hesitate to take your insulin," but I don't care for this metaphor. Doctors seem to understand diabetes much better than they understand the human brain. I worry the pills are doing nothing at best, poisoning me at worst. What if I have some amazing personality or hidden creative genius that's being suppressed? And then there's the fact that the stuff is relatively new, meaning they don't know much about long-term effects. I'm not trying to grow an extra limb anytime soon.

I refocus my attention on the audio: *Visualize your energy shining brightly like the sun.*

I roll my eyes and shut off the meditation. This one sucks. I have zero tolerance for cheese. I just need someone with a soft, monotone voice to say, over and over again, *Everything is just perfect.*

Tupac blasts from KDAY, glaring in its contrast: *All eyez on me.*

Per usual, Dr. Kim greets me with a handshake. He's very formal—stoic, bordering on robotic. I love this about him.

"Hello, Prudence," he says, and I jump a little. No one calls me Prudence, not even my parents. It's Prue, unless it's an official document. My name is hilarious because I'm kind of a slut, at least historically.

Dr. Kim takes me into his office and I sit across from him on a stiff gray couch. I briefly take in the view of tall palm trees reflected in shiny windows. I feel grateful I left the East Coast. Whoever says they value brick buildings can go jump off one in my opinion.

"How is it going?" he asks.

"Good," I say. "Great, actually." I gather my freshly dyed platinum-blond hair into a bun on top of my head. It feels straw-like, but that's to be expected after a new dye job. "My caseload is picking up, which means more money."

For work, I write court-appointed criminal appeals for the State of California from the comfort of my bedroom. I don't make much, but it's enough until my inheritance.

"I've been writing a lot," I say.

"Great," says Dr. Kim. "Short stories or what?"

"Oh god, no." I giggle. "I was born in the eighties. I write raps."

Dr. Kim cocks his head to the ceiling. I don't blame him for being confused, but really rap and the law aren't as different as you'd think. They're both adversarial, rooted in social unrest. I'm right, you're wrong, here's why. (The law uses more roman numerals.) I wasn't the only rapper in law school, but I was definitely the best. There was this corny bitch who wore hoop earrings that said MEAGHAN in the center and rapped in a Queens accent despite being from Connecticut. When Sotomayor came to speak to our class, Meaghan cornered her with her awkward bars, necessitating Secret Service intervention. We're on different levels. I was written up on *Stereogum* once.

"I don't expect much time to pass before I start popping—" I pause, realizing I'm talking to a fifty-something-year-old man and not one of my friends. "—err, before my music career takes off." Ellie got me in the studio to feature on her friend Micah's upcoming album. He's about to blow up, and I only imagine I will with him.

"That sounds great," he says. "And your love life?"

I stifle a giggle. Dr. Kim always asks me about my love life and it always makes me want to laugh.

"My relationship is great," I say.

"That's wonderful," says Dr. Kim. He straightens his tie.

"I know," I say. I let my hair out of the bun and it falls onto my shoulders, dancing in waves illuminated by light from the windows. I imagine I look sexy as hell and wonder whether Dr. Kim ever thinks about fucking me. I can't exactly pinpoint his sexuality, but sexuality isn't real anyway.

"I like the new 'do, by the way," he says.

Again, I stifle a laugh, then give my head a little shake. "Thank you," I say. "It's for the music." My rap name has always been Vagablonde, but Ellie recently sat me down and broke the news to me that I'm really a dirty blonde. If I want to keep the name, she told me, I should have the hair to back it up.

"It's very... striking," Dr. Kim says. Definite homo. "How are things with your therapist..." He pauses, looks down at the legal pad on his lap. "Ms.... Lumpkin?"

"Oh, I hardly go to her anymore," I say.

Dr. Kim just handles my meds. Barbara Lumpkin (she has the personality to match the name) is seven dollars a session on my insurance, and I go to her for cognitive behavioral therapy on an as-needed basis. We don't really "connect"—I get the strong sense that she hates me, which in turn makes me think, *Who can blame her?* and I'm no expert but I'm pretty sure that's not how your therapist should make you feel. But seven dollars a session! And besides, I'm thriving. "But she's fine." I don't want to alarm Dr. Kim.

He nods, looks up from his legal pad. "Is everything good medication-wise?"

"Well, that's something I wanted to talk to you about." I pause, looking down at my dusty Converse sneakers. Then I look up, right in Dr. Kim's eyes. "I'm thinking of going off my Celexa."

"Oh?" His face is calm. He probably doesn't give a fuck whether I'm on my medication. It's just work to him. It's like when someone asks me for legal advice. My reaction is always: *Cool, tell me less.* Also, people are always trying to talk to me about a contract, and frankly, I've never read one.

"Why's that?" Dr. Kim asks.

"Because I'm doing great!" Then I take a breath to steady myself. I probably shouldn't appear manic while asking my doctor to go off my meds. "I've been on SSRIs since college," I say with my steady lawyer voice. "I'm thirty now, so that's about ten years. It scares me, the idea of being on it for life. Now seems like a good time as any to try living without it."

Dr. Kim says nothing, then looks down at the legal pad again. "So you're on forty milligrams now?"

I nod.

"Why don't we first try going down a bit—say, twenty milligrams—and see how that makes you feel?"

For a second, I'm defeated. I wanted to be off—to have the confidence that I can handle the world without potent and mostly unstudied chemicals. Almost all my friends are on SSRIs, so I'm not exactly ashamed, but I would feel a lot better if I was off them. I'd feel powerful and tough and superior, three of my favorite feelings. But going cold turkey might be extreme. Dr. Kim is highly credentialed and very rational. I decide to trust him. "That sounds reasonable," I finally say. Then I think about the pharmacy section of Walgreens and feel ill.

"Great," he says, "I'll write it out now." He begins scribbling in his lap. "Alternatively, you can just break your current dosage in half."

I nod, excited by the potential theatrics of this situation.

"Let's follow up in a few weeks to see if you notice any changes."

Dr. Kim hands me the script and I hand him a check and I'm out of there. He's very efficient, and that's why I pay him the big bucks.

The next morning I go on a hike with Jake Perez, my best friend from UC Berkeley (where I went for college and law school, which makes me something they call a "Double Bear"). He picks me up in his vintage black BMW, which is by far the sexiest thing about Jake Perez. He inherited it when his dad passed away in college. This was a few weeks after we became friends. I was drawn to how callous Jake was about the whole thing. He referred to his dead dad as a "charmless bigot," but he felt blessed to inherit his sexy car and enough money to start his own business. I'm not entirely sure what Jake does. Something to do with computers. The nice thing is that we both can make our own schedules, and he gets me out of my apartment during the day.

Soon we're ascending the dusty trails of Griffith Park, talking about SSRIs while weaving around packs of tourists.

"I think it's a terrible idea," he says when I tell him my news about weaning off.

"My psychiatrist, a medical doctor"—I pause for dramatic effect—"disagrees." Our friendship mostly revolves around theatrical pauses.

"Please," says Jake Perez. "Never trust a psychiatrist. You know the whole field was invented by a cokehead."

"Well, if not Freud, then who should I trust?" I ask.

"Me!" he yells. A hawk swoops overhead.

"But I'm thriving," I say.

"Are you?" he asks.

"Yes," I say. "I have a great girlfriend. My career is about to pop off."

"Defending criminals?" Jake asks as we turn the corner. He has difficulty grasping my job, that I'm a selfless crusader against injustice. Jake isn't one for nuance.

"My music career." I frown.

"Oh," says Jake. "You're still rapping?" He also has trouble comprehending my compulsion to create. He's left-brained.

"Yes, bitch," I say.

"Typical Leo rising," Jake says. Our tendency to want to make sense of a random world by trying to put people into neat astrological boxes is among our primary bonds. We're also obsessed with sociopaths and pretty movies where nothing happens. "Our generation is plagued by prolonged adolescence." He pauses. "That's not a value judgment. Just a fact."

Jake loves to qualify obvious value judgments as not value judgments. I know what he's getting at, that you're supposed to have your "rapper phase" at seventeen.

"Speaking of prolonged adolescence," I say, brushing off his barely couched denunciation, "wanna come to a show tonight?"

"What show?" Jake asks. "Hey, can you slow down?"

I look back and he's hunched over, leaning on his knees, heaving. Jake has trouble keeping up with me, on the trails and in most other ways. I start tapping my foot on the dust as I wait for him to catch up. "Dead Stars," I say.

"Never heard of them," Jake says in between heavy breaths, and now it's my turn to heave.

"It's Wyatt Walcott!" I practically shout.

"Who?" he says. And now I know he's just trying to piss me off, which Jake Perez is very good at doing. In fact, I'd say he's an expert at it. Maybe that's why we're friends. He makes me feel something. Even if it's mostly rage, it's better than the drudgery of daily existence.

I slap him on the arm and he yelps. I like that Jake is so much bigger than me (most people are) that it's fine if I hit him. When life gives you a frail frame, weaponize it. That's what I always say.

"Oh," he says. "That reality TV girl. That teenager you worship."

"She isn't a teenager," I say. "She's twenty-four. And Dead Stars is her newish band. You'd like it."

Jake's taste in music isn't exactly "on trend." It isn't bad, I mean, we're friends, after all. But it's not really party music, more like the type of thing you would hear in an '80s horror movie, synthy and ominous and all that. It's fun for writing and feeling terrified, less for drinking. But Dead Stars is bizarre enough that there might be some overlap.

"They use a Buchla," I say.

"Huh?" Jake asks.

I grin a little. "It was one of the first synths. It was created in Berkeley in the sixties, around the same time the Moog was invented in New York."

"Oh yeah," says Jake, "the Moog."

I knew this would get him because Jake is pretentious and he hates when I know things he doesn't.

"I think I had a class with Buchla's son my freshman year."

I'm pretty sure he's lying to overcompensate for his ignorance, which I love. "They're blowing up," I say.

"You say that about everyone," Jake says as he kicks a beige rock. I watch the rock skip, thinking its color reminds me of Kanye's forays into fashion.

"No, I don't." I peer back at the city below us. Various clusters of nondescript buildings, the ocean sparkling in the distance. "Our city is perfect," I say.

"Are you serious?" Jake says. "Don't you see all that nasty smog?"

"It's pretty," I say. I gaze into the gooey band between the buildings and the clouds. "The way the colors get caught in it."

"Prue," Jake Perez says, getting all in my face. "It's killing you."

The sky is turning neon pink outside my window as Ellie cuts lines on a photo of Mary-Kate's face from the Olsen coffee table book, *Influence*. My angel is no cokehead, okay, but she indulges on special occasions, and Dead Stars at the Mirror Box is one. I'm not really a cocaine enthusiast myself—I'm too old for street drugs—but I enjoy the ritual.

My one-bedroom apartment holds the usual suspects: Jake Perez, Ellie, my two perfect black cats, Missy and Ennui (confession: I can't tell them apart), and a twenty-four-year-old PR girl whose name I can't recall. Chantal? Ashton? Mackenzie? Suddenly it's dark. I stand up and flick on my neon sign of a palm tree, which casts the room in a turquoise glow—Vagablonde Blue—and makes the sky out the windows appear reddish pink.

"You look... amazing," Jake Perez says, eyeing me up and down. He tells this to everyone after a glass of wine. Literally everyone.

"Thank you," I say while looking at my dusty black Timberlands. LA is covered in dust. "I think my eyeliner looks decent tonight." I'm bad at drawing straight lines. But today I watched a YouTube tutorial that prompted me to put Scotch tape on my face, and I think it worked.

Jake Perez raises a thick black eyebrow at me. It's all eyebrow talk in this town, I swear.

Chantal(?) sits on the carpet chipping at her black nailpolish. One of the cats seemingly notices her boredom and circles her theatrically, like, *Look at me.*

"Who is this little guy?" she asks, stroking Missy or Ennui. The other cat hops out from under the couch. Thank god. I prefer to introduce them in tandem as to not reveal my ignorance as to which is which. One cat paws the other in the face.

"These girls," I say, "or *women*, are Missy and Ennui."

Chantal(?) scrunches up her face. "Ennui?"

"It's French," I say.

"Je sais," she says. "But 'ennui' means 'boredom.' Why would you name your cat 'boredom'?"

I roll my eyes. Twenty-four-year-olds understand nothing. Except for Wyatt Walcott, of course. But she's been prematurely aged by superstardom.

"Cigarette?" she asks. I follow the boring pretty girl to my tree-lined balcony and flick on the periwinkle string lights. A warm Santa Ana wind hits and the moon peeks through the leaves. Through the trees boasts a stunning view of the Chevron station.

"It's so nice out here," says Chantal. She's wearing a sheer white shirt that parades her obnoxious twenty-four-year-old nipples.

"I'll be right back," I say. I go into my room and take off my bra.

"Cig for *moi*?" I ask—again, rhetorically—when I return. I remember that we're about to see Wyatt Walcott with a microphone onstage and my blood starts swimming freestyle through my veins.

A cigarette emerges, as if by magic, from its carton. I position it in my lips in a way that begs a light. Chantal(?) giggles, then lights. Her laugh is high-pitched and breathy, a noise that exudes insecurity.

After listening to Chantal(?) complain about her non-relationship with some philosophy major barista fuccboi, I pull out the power move I tend to use around younger and more attractive women. "Oh, but you haven't even had your Saturn's Return!"

"Huh?"

The girl eyes me with concern while I explain that the universe is about to beat the shit out of her. In my return, I explain, I fell in love with a straight woman who strung me along like a fish on a hook. I also got poison oak all over my body. Twice. But I emerged wiser and more elegant—just look at me! I flip my bright blonde hair.

"Smoking without me?" Ellie emerges from inside. For the first time I realize her hair is tied back in two French braids.

"Celeste did them," she says, clocking my gaze. Ah, Celeste. I was close!

"Nice." I drop my cigarette in the ashtray, flip my hair again, and return inside.

Jake Perez is sitting on an armchair with crossed legs and a full glass of bloodred wine, refreshing Tumblr on his phone. He's dressed like a vampire. Jake's a Scorpio, so he's very morbid.

Ellie tilts her head toward the ceiling and sucks air into her nostrils with the grace of Uma Thurman in *Pulp Fiction*. Turquoise light bounces off her blonde curls. (Yes, I'm a blonde girl dating a blonde girl—imagine what Kanye would think!). No one seems to notice as I head into my bathroom, remembering it's time to take my medication.

I return to the room with a salmon-colored forty-milligram pill in my palm. For the sake of dramatic gesture, I lay it on Mary-Kate's eyelash, beside the white powdery vestige of a line. I take Ellie's AmEx and chop the pill in half.

"I just cut my SSRI dosage in half," I announce proudly, then place the pill on my tongue. Celeste is back, eyeing me with a blank expression. She probably doesn't even know what an SSRI is; she's on something newer and hipper.

I chug down the pill with my Lagunitas IPA, wondering what Dr. Kim would think.

"Mazel," says Celeste.

"I love you," says Ellie.

"Prue," says Jake Perez, finally looking up from his phone. "I cannot emphasize my disapproval enough."

Often when I see a show, I'm overcome with envy. I stand frustrated and fuming, chugging Bud Light and thinking about how I could have done a better job. But with Dead Stars, I'm just... happy. Wyatt and Agnes deserve to be there, glowing under soft neon pinks and oozing charm. Sitting at a small table toward the front and surrounded by mirrors, I'm shocked to find I'm not even tempted to look at my reflection.

The girls are wearing outfits that evoke lingerie, I suppose to cater to the fact that we're at a strip club. Agnes wears neon-pink lace; Wyatt, a black silk robe. Wyatt flips her flowing dirty-blonde hair from side to side as she croons about millennial malaise. The girls take turns slinking around the gold pole in the stage's center, less in the manner of strippers and more like eleven-year-olds at recess.

But the main star is the Buchla, this huge machine with primary-colored wires sticking out in all different directions. I can tell Jake Perez is mesmerized by the machine, which is reflected in the mirrors surrounding the stage. For a second I become panicked looking at all the wires, become afraid that the singularity is here, that the robots are taking over. But then I see Agnes manipulate them around with such confidence and grace, creating soothing sounds from the chaos. Agnes can conquer the machines. She will protect us. She went to MIT, and I read online that she's a Mensan.

Afterward, Ellie gets us backstage, where she immediately dives into the fray, floating around and chatting with other industry people in her typical self-assured manner. Celeste does the same, but it seems less sexy and more sycophantic. Jake and I plop awkwardly on a black leather couch in the corner of the room and watch Agnes and Wyatt entertain a revolving circle of admirers. Ellie keeps coming over and urging me to go talk to Wyatt, but I'm too scared. I don't want to seem like a crazed fan. But standing fifteen feet away clutching a Bud Light and staring at her probably doesn't look any better.

"Can we head?" I ask Ellie the next time she comes over to me. I can only spend so long ogling the life of someone more successful before I need to peace out. Jake's already left. He hates people even more than I do.

"Already?!" she exclaims. She always likes to stay out longer than I do. A real extrovert. I wonder what that's like.

"I'm depressed," I say, trying to make my face cute.

"Hold on," she says. "I just need to introduce you to someone real quick."

She disappears for a second and I tap my boot on the floor.

"Cigarette?" Celeste asks. I'm not sure whether she's just now appearing or if she was standing there the whole time and I just didn't notice. I'm socially tapped.

"Sure," I say. She grabs my hand and we weave through the crowd of sweaty bodies. The air in the parking lot is cool and dry. Cars fly by on Hollywood Boulevard. As Celeste hands me a cigarette from her pack, I notice a body I don't want to see.

"Sorry, girl," I say. "Bad ex at six o'clock. Must escape."

I'm sort of lying. "Ex" is a stretch. It's a Tinder date from a few years ago. Hot, but certifiable.

"Why are crazy people always so good in bed?" I'm talking about my Tinder date, but I'm also talking about myself.

Celeste just shrugs.

Inside, I approach Ellie standing with a man wearing a dress. Maybe not a dress, but more of a tunic or a muumuu. It's tribal patterned and mesh. A large crystal pendant suspended on a gold chain hangs around his neck. He has large hazel eyes, wide and aggressive in the manner of someone who has been doing cocaine all night. He scares me a little, but there is also something intriguing about him. *A Scorpio?* I wonder. Guessing people's astrological signs always makes socializing a bit more tolerable. It gives me a concrete task, a system of organization. And as a Virgo, I live to organize.

"This is Jax Jameson," Ellie says, "the producer I was telling you about."

I don't recall Ellie telling me about this person. But she's loquacious. I don't catch everything she says.

"Nice shoes," he says. I look down and see we're wearing the same Timberlands.

I smile, and then he hands me a tiny plastic bag of white powder.

TWO

I wake up feeling like a foot: sweaty, hot, swollen. One of the cats paws at my face and I shove her off. I'm pretty rough with my cats but I think they can handle it. I mean, they're descended from lions! I roll over and reach for Ellie, but she's gone. Career girls wake up early. I grab my phone: 7:30 A.M. Time to start typing.

I go to the kitchen and put on water for coffee. While it heats, I look out onto the balcony and a tree shifts and a blade of sun hits me in the eyeball. The night starts coming back.

I broke my no-cocaine rule, which explains the sniffles. Fucking cocaine. It's fun for, like, a second and then I'm no longer producing memories.

What I remember: Jax and I got along like a house on fire. We discussed Kanye's *Yeezus* as an academic text over Marlboro Reds, a cigarette I told him I respect because Mary-Kate Olsen smokes them. He unleashed a hearty laugh and responded, "Hashtag same."

Oh god, I think, *I spoke too much.* I always get paranoid like this after a morning of uppers, but right now it feels especially justified (it always does). I told Jax about going to my dad's house in Montana just after Kanye started recording there. My dad's house is near Yellowstone, and I'd never been because I'm never trying to interact too much with nature. But when I heard *Ye* was recording in Jackson Hole, I told my dad I wanted to go on a father-daughter trip. He was super excited and started talking about all the things we could do outside.

"There are, like, cute cowgirl bars there, right?" I'd asked.

He hung up.

I flew into Bozeman a few weeks later. My dad picked me up in a matte-black Chevy Tahoe. He had on a classic rock station and was wearing a cowboy hat, both of which I typically find embarrassing, but neither bothered me at the moment. I think it was the mountain air. In LA, we're breathing polluted air 24/7, which probably fucks with our serotonin receptors or something. But the mountain air made me feel high. *Maybe this is how Kanye got manic,* I thought.

The radio played Neil Young and Fleetwood Mac and the Rolling Stones—not that obnoxious honky-tonk shit but the dreamy ballads. The roads were open and people smiled at you. We drove a hundred miles per hour through these lush mountains. The landscape was dramatic and grand; snow-capped peaks pointed toward the heavens. It looked like Switzerland, but also most people drove pickup trucks and smoked cigarettes out their windows in a way that felt uniquely American Trash.

"I can see why Kanye loves it so much," I told Jax on the street.

Jax laughed really hard. He laughed super hard at all my jokes. I've always thought I'm funnier than people give me credit for. The cocaine gave me the confidence to perform a few bars for him, prewritten, of course. (I do not and will not ever freestyle, for the same reason I'm an appellate and not a trial lawyer: I need time to think.) Jax told me I'm brilliant and beautiful and he wanted to work with me, something I've been waiting to hear my whole life from a producer who shares a last name with a liquor company. We exchanged numbers to plan a recording session (he has an in-home studio, a setup that I'm confident beats GarageBand on my laptop).

Before I knew it, we were back in the main room of the Mirror Box, where Agnes and Wyatt were DJing the perfect combination of late '90s slow jams and timeless freak pop. Oh, and Kanye. Jax and I shrieked when the horns dropped on "Blood on the Leaves," and I remembered blasting it on the open Wyoming roads, smoking a cigarette out the window and pondering the existence of a higher power for the first time. Jax and I had great dance chemistry—he made me feel like a video girl, something I've always wanted to feel like. "I knew you all would hit it off," Ellie shouted at us from a few feet away.

Soon Jax and I were throwing ones at Wyatt while she slid down the pole to the beat of Lil' Kim's "Drugs." It was the first time I've thrown money at a woman, which made me feel alienated from previous versions of myself.

I suppose that's what they call "growing up."

I open up the thick brown envelope that contains the record in my new case. I always get anxious when opening a new record: all this information I must learn and synthesize. First I read the memo from my supervisor. My supervisors work in offices throughout California and I know them only via email or sometimes the phone, only when they make me. I don't love to speak, unless I'm in therapy or drinking. Otherwise I much prefer to type.

My new client is named Rachel Taften, but she's "known on the streets" as "Yumiko Houndstooth." Many of my clients have aliases, but this is by far the best I've heard. She was charged with carrying a loaded gun in a public place. My supervisor suggests we challenge the search under the Fourth Amendment, which is what I do in most of my cases. My clients are pretty much always guilty, and the cops pretty much always violated their Fourth Amendment rights in discovering that. Yumiko was leaving a liquor store with bare feet, her shoes in one hand and a bottle of Jack Daniel's in the other. A cop thought this looked suspicious and went up and grabbed her. She whipped around and struck him in the face with her shoes. The cop arrested her for assault on a police officer, during which he found a gun in her parka. The DA dropped the assault charge pursuant to her plea.

I hunch over my laptop typing for hours, composing arguments and listening to ambient music from Berlin. My fingers find a rhythm and my brain starts to quiet and I lose track of time. I stop when my eyes start to burn and it's dark out.

I check my phone, hoping no one died while I was in my writing hole. Lots of missed calls, lots of texts. Jake Perez. Ellie. Jax. Nothing from my parents, who really contact me only when something horrible has happened. I ring up Ellie.

"Hi, stranger," she says, voice all sexy and wine-soothed.

"Hi, babygirl."

"I thought you'd forgotten about me."

"I was working."

"I admire your discipline." Ellie is so supportive. How did I get so lucky?

"Where are you drinking?" I ask.

"Just leaving a work happy hour... Dinner?"

"I thought you'd never ask. Nora's?" It's our spot. Ellie and I are the only couple in LA that lives within walking distance of each other; Nora's is equidistant between us.

"See you there."

On the walk to Nora's, I remember the twenty milligrams. The nice thing about the new dosage is that it'll last twice as long, meaning half the trips to Walgreens. I text Ellie, *Gotta drop off a script real quick, order me an IPA?*

No worries, see you soon!!!

Soon I'm back under the fluorescent lights, feeling ugly as hell. I book it to the pharmacy section, not even stopping to gaze idly at the shampoos as I'm so often tempted. When I catch my reflection in those terrible mirrors, I feel hideous—haggard, puffy, mannish. Horrified, I look away quickly.

At least there isn't much of a line this time, praise be.

I check my texts as I wait.

Jake Perez: *You were faded af last night. You alive?*

Jax: *Last night was perfection. I can't wait to get in the studio. I'll text you soon with a time.*

I smile and think of that smaltzy line from *Almost Famous*—"It's all happening"—then open Wyatt Walcott's Instagram. I scroll through at least thirty photos I've already seen before, ogling her mermaid waves and nonplussed expression, until the pharmacist lady calls, "Next." I hand her the script. "Anything else?" she asks, and I say, "God no," and jet. Pharmacists are always trying to drag you into their sick, sad world.

Ellie looks sexy staring at her phone at a tiny table in the corner. She's wearing a tattered red Bulls T-shirt and her normal large black-framed glasses. The food at Nora's is just okay; we go for the ambience: wood paneling, leather booths, soft red glow. Burgundy light bounces off Ellie's dirty-blonde curls. I don't really care about food—my favorite food is cereal—but lighting is everything. I feel worlds away from the harsh fluorescents of the pharmacy.

"Oh, hi," I say. "I hope I'm not being too forward"—I put my forearm on the edge of the booth behind her—"but I noticed you from across the room." This is a game we play sometimes.

"Oh, not at all," she says, batting her lashes. "I must confess I noticed you too. I was hoping you would say something." She bites the edge of her lip. "Have a seat?"

"Are you sure I wouldn't be imposing?" I ask. We both turn our voices into something soft and breathy. This restaurant is especially conducive to roleplay. It reminds me of the first date in *Carol*, which Ellie and I watched on our first date. (Screening *Carol* is my only foreplay.) Cate Blanchett in her fur and Hermès head scarf, smoking a cigarette in her oyster-colored convertible, white gloves on, intimidating the shit out of Rooney Mara. Is there anything hotter?

"Of course not," she says.

The waiter arrives with a sauvignon blanc for Ellie, a Stone IPA for *moi*.

"Perfect timing," I say, morphing back into my normal self, or a version of it. I have many selves, everyone does.

Ellie flashes a warm smile. "How are you?"

"Jax and I are going to work together, I think." I feel a little weird and shaky. This happens when I've been holed up working all day and am then expected to act like a normal person. Every day, basically. But Ellie puts me at ease.

The waiter comes and I order a Caesar salad and Ellie orders the roasted chicken.

"I'm so happy," Ellie says. "I can't wait to hear what you geniuses come up with." She sips her wine. "How is the brief?"

"My draft isn't due for another week," I say. I feel a swell of anxiety. But I always get my work done on time, I remind myself. Besides, my upcoming meeting with Jax should take precedent. I don't have much time before my career simply must take off. "When inspiration hits, I need to obey."

Ellie smiles. "Amen."

When our food comes, Ellie's gaze seems to catch something behind me and her body stiffens.

"You okay?" I ask as a I stab a crouton, which crumbles into a bunch of tiny pieces on my plate.

She nods, without looking at me, then smiles weakly at whoever she's looking at.

Several figures march by our table: an androgynous person in all black, arm wrapped around the waist of a curvy blonde; the hostess in front of them. The androgynous person, who I can now tell is a butch lesbian, has severe features and looks mean. She quickly turns toward our table and nods her head up and to the side at Ellie. The diagonal head nod is a vile gesture and lesbians are always doing it. As she passes, I glare at her back. Her shoulder blades jut from her black T-shirt in a way that makes her look sickly. She and her lover are seated behind a large ficus, meaning they're removed from my view—thank god.

"Who's that?" I whisper to Ellie once they're a safe distance away.

She just shakes her head. I understand and zip it.

Ellie then starts speaking rapidly about one of her needy clients, pulling apart her chicken with her fingers as she vents. I typically zone out when Ellie rants about work, but now I'm particularly removed. My gaze remains casually focused on the ficus, trying to catch a glimpse of this mysterious butch, who I'm convinced is an ex. Ellie doesn't talk much about her exes, because she's a kind person, but I remember once when we were drunk after a show, early in our relationship, she told me that she's historically dated masculine women. Or men. This offended me at first, then frightened me. Masculine is the last thing I am or want to be. She must have noticed the panic on my face—she's very intuitive—and told me not to worry. Ellie found me very sexy, she assured me, and feminine. A first for her! I liked the idea that I somehow transcended her typical taste.

As I stab a piece of lettuce, another memory from that night appears. Ellie leaning in close to my ear, whiskey on her breath.

"I have a bit of a savior complex," she'd said.

In the morning I'm pouring my coffee when this Dead Stars song comes on and something just comes over me. It's like I'm possessed. My hands lift to the ceiling. My body starts curling like a wave. The cats start circling around me, tails in the air. The beat drops and my ass drops to the floor. My eye hits the clock on the TV. It's 9:30 A.M.

Fuck, I have a call. I run to my phone. I've missed it. I hate when work tries to call me. I'm not a phone person. I never know when it's my turn to talk. There's nothing that can be accomplished on a phone call and not on an email. I call back and it goes to voice mail. Thank god. I email him—David (one-third of lawyers are named David)—and say I'm sorry I missed his call and ask him what he wanted to talk about. He responds with one sentence about formatting. The California Rules of Court recently changed regarding margins. Formerly 1.5 inches, now 1.25. Why this news would require a phone call is beyond me.

Afterwards I go to pick up my prescription and try my best to avoid those terrible mirrors. I would love to curate my life so that I never have to go inside a Walgreens again. I wonder if Wyatt Walcott has ever been inside a Walgreens. I need an assistant. I think about hiring an unpaid intern from USC law school. "Scintillating opportunity to practice criminal law with quirky solo practitioner," my Craigslist ad would read. I consider this almost every day, but I never get around to doing it. The fact is no one can do my work as efficiently as I do it myself.

I check my email while I wait in line. A new message from the LA County Juvenile Hall records clerk, who writes in purple Comic Sans. Coupled with the fluorescent lights, the email is visual assault. The content doesn't help. Apparently, I filed the wrong brief in my last case. The courts use an online filing system, which is good for me because it minimizes physical labor and human contact. The bad side is I'm spacy. Tabitha is telling me I have to petition the court to allow me to resubmit the brief. I filed it over a month ago, weeks before the deadline. But this Tabitha bitch is just now telling me I did it wrong. As I tap my sneaker on the floor and watch the pharmacists move very slowly, I wonder whether the California government staffs Walgreens.

I reorganize my day in my head, figuring out how I'll make time to write this application to refile the correct brief. Do I have to tell my supervisor?

"Van Teesen," says the pharmacist lady in a suicidal-sounding voice. These people are so depressing. I hope Walgreens gives them good mental health options. "Do you have any questions about your medication?" she asks.

"Are you kidding?" I ask. "I've been on this shi—err, medication for ten years. Shouldn't you know that? Don't you, like, have that in your system?" I realize my tone is aggressive, but I don't care.

"It's a question I'm required to ask," the pharmacist says flatly.

"What if I had cancer?" I say a little too loud. I hear someone groan behind me.

"I'm sorry," the pharmacist says.

"I don't have cancer," I say. "At least not to my knowledge. But I hope with people who have serious health conditions, you are more diligent with your records. I hope you don't make them wait and jump through draconian bureaucratic hoops to get the medicine they need to stay alive." I'm remembering that time it took me a month to get my Celexa refill because of various issues out of my control: insurance delay, medicine out of stock, needs doctor approval... press repeat.

"We take the health of our customers very seriously here at Walgreens."

"Whatever," I say, like a teenager. As I slide my card into the machine, I realize a major part of being a woman is yelling at corporate customer service reps when you really want to yell at your father.

As soon as the card machine reads APPROVED, I jet. "No receipt, thanks!" I call over my shoulder.

That afternoon I'm formatting the dumb petition when Jax texts me asking if I want to record. I try not to say yes too quickly. It's almost four P.M. now, so I decide to work on Yumiko's brief until five P.M., a reasonable quitting time. I expect to lose. I always expect to lose. This is the only option when your clients are poor people accused of crimes. As an appellate lawyer, I get them after a judge or jury has found them guilty, when the chances of winning are microscopic. I guess I like a challenge. Or maybe I just like that the stakes are low.

I type hastily, filling the page with as many words as time will allow. I don't concern myself with grammar or sentence structure, instead relaxing into the mind-numbing act of typing. In between sentences, I refresh Twitter. Occasionally I peep @WYATTLOOK and become inspired by the lines her body makes in space.

When the clock hits five, I hit my vape pen—Maui Wowie, my new favorite strain (high euphoria, low panic)—and spend roughly thirty minutes shopping my own closet. I blast Tinashe's *Aquarius* and pull crumpled T-shirts and dresses out from corners. I try to sing but invariably become disappointed with my voice.

I used to want to be a singer. Mariah Carey, Aaliyah, Amy Winehouse, that type of thing. The problem is I can't sing anymore. I was decent when I was younger, then I started getting panic attacks onstage. It took SSRIs for me to get back onstage, at which point my voice was gone.

I decide to wear all black.

Jax lives in Koreatown, which is about fifteen minutes from me by Lyft, which I take instead of driving when there is any type of illegal substance inside me. I'm a party girl in control.

On the ride, I shift restlessly in my seat and stare out the window. Neon lights blur and fade. I just hope I can be "on" tonight. I wrote some raps on Maui that I was into at the time, but marijuana can cloud judgment just as easily as it sharpens it.

The Lyft pulls up to a tall white art deco building. Skinny palm trees almost reach the top floor and sway slightly in the wind. I press the buzzer and the gate screams at me. Flicking open the door, I take the elevator to Jax's apartment on the twelfth floor and stand nervously outside. I secretly hope he isn't there and I can just go home and watch YouTube videos on my laptop. As the door begins to open, thoughts race through my Maui-addled brain: *I hope I can impress him, I hope he records with booze.*

"Vagaaaaaaa," Jax says when he opens the door. His apartment glows blue just like mine, which makes me feel safe. Blue is the most relaxing color. According to feng shui, blue environments can slow down your heart rate and lower your blood pressure.

I smile. Love to be greeted by my rap name.

Jax is wearing a long tan T-shirt over tan joggers, leopard-print socks, Adidas slide sandals. His nearly black hair is braided in cornrows that look professional. He's reaching out to hug me, not my favorite activity. But the hug isn't so bad. I feel comfortable somehow, and I lean into the long embrace. Jax turns me into a different person—someone affectionate and extroverted, a video girl, the star I've always wanted to be.

Jax leads me down a neon lit hallway with tin ceilings that sparkle blue. I consider pulling out my iPhone and snapping pictures with this new Korean photo-editing app I bought, but that would be tacky. As we near the end of the hallway, I notice Jax's blue light is darker than mine, more cobalt than turquoise. *Jaxy Blue*, I think, then smile at my shoes.

The main room is expansive: tall ceilings, floor-to-ceiling windows revealing the tips of trees and other art deco buildings with windows lit in various colors. I briefly wonder how Jax affords this place. His appearance and general demeanor do not suggest a day job. Maybe he bartends, but I can't imagine him waiting on people.

The room is littered with more humans than I'd like, but I'm not surprised. Hip-hop musicians tend to crew up. I'm more of a lone wolf. But I can tolerate humans when necessary. Anything to get my voice out there.

I pull back my shoulders and try to get into social mode. "First off, PBR?" Jax asks, and relief washes over me. I try not to say yes too quickly.

While he darts into the kitchen, I scan the room. A woman with wide green eyes lounges on a navy-blue chaise longue. She's smoking a skinny blue cigarette, apparently unconcerned with the ash it's sprinkling on the concrete floor. A woman with the perfect smattering of nose freckles rolls a joint on the center table, which is entirely made of glass. The sky outside the windows looks reddish orange, just like it does in my apartment. Kelela's *Take Me Apart* bumps on the speakers.

Jax returns with two PBRs under both arms.

"My apartment does the same thing," I say, then feel embarrassed that he won't understand me. I'm constantly forgetting to provide context. The same way kids think they're invisible when they cover their eyes, I assume everyone is inside my brain. Maybe that's why I hate everyone.

"The red afterglow?" Jax hands me an ice-cold PBR tallboy.

I nod, smiling, thinking Jax gets it. I take a sip of the beer and the bubbles soothe my tongue.

"I'm so excited to introduce you to my Kingdom," he says. I stare at him blankly for a second, then figure out what he's saying. Jax, the king; his friends, his Kingdom. I admire his assumption of power and sense Leo in his chart. Scorpio rising and Leo sun? I hope I don't have any issues with Jax; I'm not great at submitting to authority. And Leos really want nothing more than submission.

"This is my queen, Pilar," he says. He points to the woman on the couch with the blue cigarettes. She doesn't say hi but instead simply blinks, then exhales toward the cracked-open window. A cool breeze hits me. Unsure of what else to do, I blink back at her.

"She has the voice of a goddess angel and Tinashe is about to wish she never met her."

My nerves from earlier quickly transform into excitement. In the corner of the room, I make out faint outlines of computer monitors and mics and wires behind translucent shoji panes. I don't know too much about the technical stuff, but the setup appears legitimate.

"I think it's good that your names are alliterative," says the girl on the couch, still meticulously rolling the joint. "Prue and Pilar."

"Exactly," says Jax. "And this is my other queen, Nina." The woman looks up from her joint and her freckles sparkle under the ceiling lights. She has perfect curls like Ellie's, but black instead of blonde. I've always thought curly hair was a sign of genius. "She's the best music writer there is right now." He pulls a Marlboro Red from his pocket and lights it. "Eat your heart out, Chuck Klosterman." Jax coughs, then unleashes a hearty laugh. "Is he even a music writer? I don't even know. I was just trying to hype you up."

"He's written about music," Nina says with a soft voice, then begins licking the joint to seal it closed.

"We got a Colombian, an Iraqi, and a Mexican," Jax says, now pointing at himself.

"I thought Jameson was Irish," Nina says. For some reason this turns me on.

"Scottish, actually," he says. "But my mom's from Albuquerque."

Everyone looks confused, but no one says anything.

"Anyways," he says, "we need a WASP."

"Do we?" Nina asks. And I'm turned on again.

"Yes," says Jax. "Everyone hates white people right now, and Prue, aka Vagablonde, has the coloring of a Nazi." I frown. "It's ironic and perfect for the Kingdom."

That's not ironic, I think but don't say. Irony is when a situation is the opposite of what you'd expect, and given that white women are everywhere, the fact that Jax met and befriended one of us in the wild is not remotely unexpected. The majority of my peers use "ironic" frequently and incorrectly. Then I think about it more. Maybe it is ironic. Because one would expect Jax to have better taste than to cling to someone as genetically passé as *moi.*

"Beau is a WASP," says Pilar. I wonder who Beau is.

"Yeah," says Jax. "But he's not the talent."

I try to suppress a smile.

We don't ever record that night, which doesn't concern me. Rap is about creating a vibe. And a vibe, we create.

Albums we listen to: M.I.A.'s *Arular,* Beyoncé's *B'Day* (for the turnup), and FKA Twigs's *LP1* (for the turndown).

Things I learn: Jax produces music for *Grand Theft Auto,* which is how he affords this apartment, and I was right, he's a Leo. Nina's first love was German electronic music, and her second was her college English professor, a woman (turned on again). Pilar gets chatty once she starts doing cocaine, but it seems like she mainly hums to herself. Everyone has had their Saturn's Return, thank motherfucking god.

Crushes I develop: one.

I firmly believe that regular flirtation is crucial to maintaining a healthy relationship, an idea I haven't explicitly discussed with Ellie, but one I'm fairly confident she understands. Nina curls up to me almost immediately. She speaks softly, sometimes whispering in my ear. During "Two Weeks" she squeezes my hand, then releases, leaving a bright blue Adderall pill in my palm. I don't do amphetamines often, but all my best friends from college are gay party boys, so I'm offered them all the time. Let it be known: I don't do drugs; I'm offered them.

I leave as the sky outside the windows turns a hazy blue: 4:30 A.M.

"I should dip," I say as Jax does a line off Kanye's *Calabasas* zine.

Pilar blinks at me again. Nina plants a damp kiss on my cheek and I feel myself blush.

On Monday I receive the court's ruling in a case I apparently worked on. I don't recall the case when I see the name: *People v. Williams*. It's not exactly a memorable name, but I never think about my cases unless I'm working on them.

I don't read the opinion, just flip to the back for the final order: reversed and remanded. I won, but I feel nothing. I throw away the paper and go online to file my final claim through the court payment system. When a case is over, I get paid, whether I win or lose.

While I'm filling in my hours, in which I just always fill in the max time allowed and wait for them to challenge me, which they're normally too lazy to do (perks of government work), a text floats in from Ellie.

Bad news bb, I heard from Micah, she writes.

Uh-oh. Micah is the rapper whose album I was supposed to feature on.

His producer says your verse isn't quite the right fit for the album, so they're cutting it.

Ugh. I fucked up. I knew I was off that day. It was too hot in that studio. I made the mistake of wearing gray, which I never wear because I'm a sweater. I knew I was supposed to be focusing on my bars, but all I could think about was the rapidly darkening spots of fabric under my arms, on my lower back and sternum. And Micah is this wholesome sober vegan, so he had nary a drop of alcohol in the studio to take the edge off. Also he is beautiful. I get very nervous around such perfect bone structure. Like, how is this man out here having better cheekbones than me? And I'm behind the glass feeling like a monkey at the zoo, and he is just staring at me with those perfect feline eyes. He is this gorgeous panther, and I am just a chimp sweating all over his studio like a real joke.

I see Ellie is calling me and I ignore it.

She texts again. *Please don't think this reflects on you or your talent as an artist*, she says. *It's a subjective business. Besides, Micah's style is very different from yours.*

Talent doesn't exist, I type back, then shut my laptop and grab my keys. I go on a walk to quiet my brain, but it doesn't work. I'm so mad at myself. I have so many opportunities just handed to me, and I fuck them all up. The only thing I'm good at is stupid law, which I don't even care about. Besides, I need to stop practicing after Yumiko Houndstooth's case. I'm way too unstable to have indigent people's liberty in my hands. As my brain spins, I wonder if I made a mistake in going off my medicine. Then I think I'm having emotions for the right reasons, because I experienced a genuine disappointment.

When I get home, I take an Adderall Nina gave me and start crafting rhymes to prepare for my next session with Jax. I don't come up with much, but I like the following: *all my cars imported / all my thoughts distorted.*

When I enter the Kingdom that night, I feel like I'm being strangled by a ghost. I can't tell if this is a side effect from my lowered dosage of Celexa or my disappointment about Micah or the Adderall I took earlier, so I decide to stop thinking about it. Pilar is there, but I interact only with Jax. We head straight to his studio in the corner of the main room. While we sip beers and listen to some beats, I think about how I fucked up with Micah and how I'll probably fuck up again and be stuck practicing law in my bedroom for the rest of my life. But "Bedroom Lawyer" might be a good song title.

The fourth beat is absolute gold, Timbaland-esque, and I know it's the one. I try out the bar about my distorted thoughts and some others I wrote a while ago about being vegan, which I'm not. *It's satire,* I think. I can never tell if what I'm doing is satire. When I get into a flow I feel like Jax's Missy Elliott. When I've hit my creative max and can't record any more without sounding scratchy and feeling stiff—approximately one hour after beginning to flow—I excuse myself. I need to get enough sleep to work on my brief.

At home, I head straight to my bedroom to get my eight hours, organizing arguments in my head as I brush my teeth. I plan to argue that the prosecution failed to prove beyond a reasonable doubt that Yumiko willfully hit the officer with her shoe (an intentional *mens rea* [state of mind] is required under the statute). Here is my version of events: the cop grabbed Yumiko's arm without reasonable suspicion, and—as an involuntary reflex— her arm (which happened to be holding a shoe) swung and hit him in the face. Unfortunate situation, really, but not criminal. As finding the gun was a fruit of the Fourth Amendment violation, the law says it must be suppressed. And without the gun, there's no charge.

Before nodding off, I call Ellie. I like to hear her voice before I go to bed and when I wake up. When I tell her about my recording session, she gets all giddy. I typically don't attach much weight to her support because she's obviously looking at me through rose-colored glasses, but this time I can tell she's serious. I wonder whether she's considering representing me or at least finding me representation. They say not to mix business and pleasure, but I've always disregarded that rule. Every job I've gotten is from someone I know. Business is pleasure is art is business, I always say, or maybe that was Andy Warhol.

Instead of asking to represent me, Ellie asks the name of my current weed strain. Marijuana isn't Ellie's drug of choice, but her clients are stoners.

"Blue Dream," I tell her.

THREE

The next morning I'm typing and listening to Kari Faux's *Lost En Los Angeles* when I think I feel an earthquake. But it's really just my iPhone buzzing against my desk. It's Ellie.

"I'm being sent to New York Shitty for three months against my will," she whines. Ellie hates New York, and so do I. Dirty, boring, overrated. "The people there are so pale," she once said, "like they're dying."

"What?" is all I can manage. It comes out froggy. My throat tightens; the ghost strangler is back. I take a deep breath and do a neck roll.

"I know, baby," she says. "When I come back I'm going to buy you something real nice. A Benz. Black, vintage, tan interior—just like you like."

"Thanks," I say. I smile and my eyes feel wet, a rare sensation. I really only cry in movies or at concerts—art moves me more than life. "Promise you won't forget about me?" I ask.

"Never," she says.

I'm silent, and after a brief pause, she says she has to go.

She hangs up and I realize I forgot to ask her why she's going to New York. I lie facedown on the bed and try to cry into my pillow, like they do on TV, but nothing happens. So I jump up, shake my limbs around, and return to the keyboard.

The law is very tedious. Lots of long, excessively complicated citations designed for a pre-Google era. I kind of freestyle the formatting part, which my less smart supervisors always harp on about because what else do they have? I really need an intern. Law students are wet for formatting.

I finish promptly at COB and feel high from pushing up against the deadline. This is very unlike me. Maybe this is the new, less medicated me: impulsive and exciting, always running on adrenaline.

Afterward I meet Ellie at Nora's. When I see the sign, the name Nora reminds me of Nina and I push the thought out of my head. I should be focusing on Ellie right now. She's leaving this weekend and we've decided to spend every night together before the wretched East Coast steals her from me.

Once inside, I remember that scary butch from the last time we were here. I'd forgotten to ask her about it afterward, or maybe I was just too afraid. The truth terrifies me. That's probably why I'm a good lawyer.

I sit down across from Ellie and we quickly settle into a nice conversational rhythm, which is mostly me talking. Ellie loves to listen to me monologue and I love to monologue. I tell her about Yumiko Houndstooth and the "shoe incident," as I'm now calling it. I tell her there is a strong Fourth Amendment claim, but the issue is that Rachel was a real psycho on the stand. At the hearing on the motion to suppress, she admitted to threatening the cop on the scene, and then she threatened the judge. I tell her about the Kingdom and about Nina and Pilar and about my being the Missy to Jax's Timbaland.

"Oh my god, I'm so jealous you got to hang out with Pilar."

"Why?" I ask.

"Have you heard her voice?" Ellie asks.

I shake my head.

"Just look her up," says Ellie.

"Fine," I say. I'm still not sure about Pilar. It's very difficult for me to like a girl who is that beautiful.

Just as my jealousy starts brewing, the alarm on Ellie's phone goes off—loud, raucous, strident, nightmarish. It's the sound I hate most in the world, and it's always going off at inopportune moments—when I'm midsentence, already having an unpleasant feeling, or, worst of all, mid-REM cycle. It's funny, Ellie is so competent in certain ways. She understands the stock market and was on *Forbes*'s "30 under 30" list in entertainment. But in other ways, she has total absentminded professor vibes, which I mostly like because I've always wanted to fuck a professor. She's always being surprised by her schedule, like we'll be having this nice, normal conversation and then her god-awful alarm will go off and she'll yell, "FUCK!" and realize she has an important meeting with the next big thing in thirty minutes. If I had an important meeting of any sort, I'd be spiraling about it for weeks. I can't imagine something important just popping up on me in the form of that terrible alarm. I'd say that alarm is the biggest hurdle in our relationship at the moment.

"And I think Celeste is friends with that Nina girl," Ellie says once she turns her alarm off. "She works with some music writers." The way Ellie says "Nina girl" suggests she's threatened. Probably because they both have curly hair and capture my attention.

"Cool," I say.

Then we stop talking about the Kingdom and Ellie starts talking about New York. I focus on my Niçoise salad and start crafting rhymes in my head.

> *Got something?*
> *do nothing*
> *you like me?*
> *that's touching*
> *I keep it chill & breezy*
> *so it's cute that you be lusting.*

Before I know it, Ellie is signing the check. The East Coast, ruining my life again. I imagine her meeting a needy butch there—or worse, a man.

Back at my apartment, we put on Pilar's SoundCloud and I suck hard on my vape pen. Ellie starts playing Candy Crush on her phone and I stare at the streetlights dancing on my wall. I think about how nice it is, the way Ellie and I can just sit in silence and inhabit our own special worlds, together, united by Pilar's spooky voice.

Eventually Ellie starts to drift off and I admire her ability to fall asleep without trying. I need to toss and turn and craft, like, twenty-seven raps or related fantasies in my head before my mind lets me sleep. This time, I imagine being onstage with the charm of Wyatt and Agnes. There is pink smoke and the crowd is screaming and my hair is longer and thicker and silkier than ever.

I wake up with bars dancing around my head. Ellie is gone. The sun pours through the palm fronds that curl over my bed. Gucci Mane once described his home, which has indoor trees, as "like living in a forest," which inspired me. The cats scream outside my bedroom door. I've started locking them out because they're getting on my nerves.

I'm waiting for my supervisor to get back to me on brief edits and I have no new cases, so I decide to spend the morning writing rhymes. I walk in circles around Echo Park Lake listening to MF Doom and typing bars in my Notes app:

> *discipline and punish, no pomo*
> *like Foucault, no homo, like Zuko, Travolta*
> *no pistol, no holster*
> *I'm winning, I told ya*
> *but y'all already know, duh.*

When I'm tired I go home, eat lunch, and take a nap. When I wake up the sky out my windows is turning pink. I reach for my phone and have two texts from Jax and two from Jake Perez.

From Jake Perez: *Hi stranger. Library sesh tomorrow?* Jake and I often work together at the Silver Lake Library, which has spacious desks and a very hot librarian. Also, there is normally someone having a very public mental breakdown, which always makes me feel better about myself. Jake says I have schadenfreude. He's not wrong.

From Jax: *Come over. The Kingdom is ablaze.* I'm not entirely sure what that means but very interested in finding out.

Calling a Lyft, I text Jax.

I'll text Jake tomorrow.

When I arrive at the Kingdom it's glowing red. I prefer the blue. The red makes me feel like something bad is about to happen, but to be fair I always feel like something bad is about to happen. It's why I was medicated for ten years.

Jax puts me at ease, as does Missy Elliott's *Supa Dupa Fly* blasting through the speakers, which was playing when I named my cat. Jax pulls my body close to his and breathes in my hair, which for some reason doesn't creep me out at all. He hands me a tiny plastic bag in a handshake and I give it back to him.

"I'm good," I whisper in his ear. I get high off abstaining.

"Perfect," he says. "More for *moi*." He flicks his head around, grabs my hand, and pulls me through the hallway, which is littered with skinny men and women with gold hoop earrings. People carry Solo cups and PBR cans. A hipster frat party.

Jax takes my hand and pulls me down the hall. In the main room, Pilar chats at someone while her cigarette ash drifts to the floor like rain. As I scan the room for Nina, my gaze hits something unpleasant. Another ex-lover. My slutty past is always coming back to haunt me.

"You okay, Vaga?" Jax asks.

At first, I can only manage a sigh. "An irritating ex is here," I finally say.

"Fuck, you want me to kick her out?"

"Him," I say. Thomas is this clinger I dated about a year ago. Whoever says that only women cling has not dated a beta male. Thomas was one of those aggressively sensitive men who uses his "kindness" as a weapon. *"But I had such a nice time with you,"* he pleaded when I called it off. Well, that's wonderful—most people enjoy my company—but it doesn't mean I have to keep dating you.

"Oh," Jax says. "I thought Vaga was strictly... vag-a."

He laughs and I laugh too even though I'm annoyed. I want to say, *Are you strictly dickly?* But instead I say, "Dearly queerly." I am coming up with this on the spot. It cracks me up, the word "queer." It's a very alienating way to identify, and I think that's why I'm drawn to it, especially now. The only other option was "mostly vaga" and that doesn't rhyme. I wanted to rhyme more than I wanted to be factually accurate. There is no spoon anyway.

He laughs again. "All right, all right," he says. I realize for the first time that I don't know Jax's sexuality and I haven't even tried to guess. He gives me post-sexuality vibes, like a god. Or Rihanna.

"That might be a song," he says, and at first I'm not sure what he's talking about. "'Dearly Queerly.' Maybe we can record it tonight, you know, once the plebes filter out."

I nod. The room is crazy crowded. I definitely don't have this many friends. Sweaty arms brush up against me on all sides and I don't love it.

"So who am I kicking out?" Jax asks. He hands me a perspiring Tecate. I have no idea where it came from.

"No, no," I say. "It's not that big of a deal."

He wipes some Tecate from his lip. "You're a better woman than I." More laughter, and I feel compelled to join. Before I know it, there is an arm around me.

"Didn't mean to scare you, kitty cat." Pilar laughs.

"Sorry," I say. "I'm on edge."

"I know," she says. "That's what we love about you."

I meant at this moment, but now I'm concerned I always come off like a nervous wreck. Also, I had no idea Pilar "loved" me. The last time I saw her she seemed aggressively indifferent to my existence.

As soon as I'm about to say thanks, she's gone, and her arm is around someone else.

"Dina train," Jax says.

"Dina?" I ask.

"Oh," he says. "Dina as in Dina Lohan." He must clock my confused expression and laughs, then lowers his voice, leans in to whisper in my ear. "As in cocaine."

This time I let out a genuine laugh. I've heard a lot of euphemisms for cocaine but this is my favorite. A floating hand holds out a blunt and I grab it eagerly. I love blunts. I just lack the dexterity to roll them so I'm at others' mercy. This is typically the case. I'd be the first to die in an apocalypse.

I pass Jax the blunt and he shakes his head. "Not until after hours," he says. Then he disappears to the couch. I'm alone and I'm high and I don't know who to talk to. Feeling paranoid, I gulp my beer to even out. This is how I like to do. Beer, weed, beer, weed, until I'm basically comatose.

I eventually walk over to Jax, who is sitting on the couch next to a bony, pale man I don't recognize. I get a weird vibe from him, like he isn't at all embarrassed to exist. Also, he seems sick.

As I walk, I'm very aware of my body and how stiff it feels when it moves. I wish I knew who rolled the blunt so I could inquire about the strain. I'm having a moment of paranoia, but I look forward to the other side. This is how it works. Euphoria, terror, euphoria, terror, until I need to smoke more.

"Hi," I say. I sit down on the ledge of the couch.

"I'm so happy you get to finally meet Beau!" Jax shouts with big Dina eyes.

"Oh, the famous Beau," I say, then become embarrassed. Is he famous? I've heard of him once. He looks at me strangely and my body language starts to fold in on itself.

"He wishes he were famous." Jax laughs. Beau just narrows his eyes, like he hates me.

I laugh at Jax's joke slightly too late.

"Something funny, new girl?" Beau asks me, I think. He's staring at his phone.

"Pardon?" I say with a French accent. I'm suddenly confident, embracing the extroverted edges of my high. "New girl?"

He looks up from his phone and I see his face for the first time, which is sunken and translucent in a way that suggests hard drug use. His hair is jet black, and his face borders on handsome but falls on the side of frightening. "Aren't you a lesbian?" he asks.

Objection: Relevance? Ten minutes at this party and I've already been interrogated about my sexuality twice. Thank god I'm not sober. "I'm queer." I hate myself as soon as the words leave my mouth. I wish there was a better word for when you feel uncomfortable identifying as a lesbian because you've seriously dated men and you don't want to cheapen those relationships, but you will likely never date a man again, and you're also an obnoxious pseudo-intellectual who believes gender and sexuality labels are a prison. Jax's gender presentation is way more confusing than mine—how come he never has to announce his sexuality? Oh right, his Y chromosome. Also, he's a Leo.

Beau looks at me blankly.

Forget it. "I have a girlfriend," I say.

He leans over and picks up a glass of dark liquor with a melting ice cube, then scoots over closer to me. "Is your girlfriend as hot as you?" he asks.

This is the nice thing about having two X chromosomes. The ability to turn men into drooling animals, utterly immobilized and at our mercy.

I sip my Tecate, then lick my lips a little. "Hotter," I say.

Beau quickly ditches me for a girl with *come on my face* face, as Jake Perez and I call it, and I don't think it needs much explanation, but Audrina Patridge is a perfect example. I talk to a guy named Tony, who tells me that he has an unusually large penis, to which

I respond that I have an abnormally beautiful vagina. Then I notice Jax under a disco ball on the dance floor and I practically run to meet him. Tamia's "So Into You" is playing, which reminds me of Ellie—we both love '90s slow jams. I consider texting her, then decide to do it after I dance a bit.

Jax grabs my hand and I'm transported to that night at the Mirror Box. "We need to play Kanye," I whisper in his ear.

"Duh," he says. He twirls me in a circle. "Dina?" he whispers in my ear.

I pause. "Sure," I say. I'm lit enough to break my own rules.

He hands me the bag. I dip my hips, then dip my finger in the bag. I rub the residue on my gums and it tastes like gasoline. My mouth feels numb and the lights seem brighter, sharper. The sound, crisper. "So Into You" ends and I recognize a familiar beat. DJ Mustard, for sure. Rihanna's voice comes in and Jax and I begin to dance in sync.

"If we record our single tonight," he says, "I'm going to put it on a zip drive and take it to DJ Mustard's house. Or Metro Boomin." His eyes are really big and I feel like mine are too. "Yeah, Metro Boomin. I'll just go to his house and drop off our track like in the olden days of hip-hop."

"How are you going to get his address?" I ask like a fucking idiot.

Jax ignores me, as he should, and starts belting Rihanna. "Youuu neeeeeeeeeeeded me."

By the time we're recording, the light outside the windows is periwinkle. I'm normally not awake at this time and now I'm mad about that. It's gorgeous and Zen. I should always create at this hour.

Jax and I are behind the shoji panels, joints lit, periwinkle everywhere. Tonight's beat reminds me of *Yeezus*-era Kanye.

I record some bars about my cats.

Missy, Ennui
I smoke, you pee
You paw, my face
I want, to kill you.

It doesn't really rhyme and feels objectively stupid but also right somehow.

"I like how you resist a traditional rhyme structure," says a female voice. I thought it was just Jax and me, but Nina is sitting on a pillow on the floor, writing in her Moleskine. How long has she been sitting there?

I take a sip of my Tecate. "Thank you."

I peek around the shoji panels to see if anyone else is still here. The disco ball is spinning and Pilar is dancing with a woman who is nearly as glamorous and beautiful as she is.

"I love your dress," the beautiful girl says to Pilar, who is wearing a blue sequined cocktail dress that makes her look like a mermaid. "Shiny af."

I start laughing and so does Jax.

"You heard that?" he asks.

"Shiny af," I say.

Nina lets out a tiny laugh and then puts her hand over her mouth, like she's embarrassed, which is adorable.

"I think that's what we should call ourselves," Jax says.

"Perfect," I say. The first hint of pink appears in the sky. "Shiny AF."

I wake up in Jax's bed, basically falling off the side. As I get up, I realize there are three people in this bed with me, none of whom is Jax. I scan the room for my belongings. I spot my purse and grab it, slide my feet into my Sambas. One of the figures in the bed rolls over and sighs. I spot Nina's bridge of freckles, then Pilar's blue sequins peek out from the white comforter. The light outside the window is yellow and harsh. I'm guessing it's about

8:30 A.M. In the main room, Jax is still behind the shoji panels. The bass shakes the tin ceilings. I guess he never went to bed.

"Heading out, Vaga?" he calls.

"Yeah," I say softly. I'm shy in the harsh brights of the morning. "Still working?" I ask as I peek awkwardly around the shoji panel. There is a violent-looking video game on his largest monitor. I remember he produces for *Grand Theft Auto*.

"Yup," he says. "Gotta pay the bills." He spreads out his arms to signify his sprawling apartment. He's wearing a floral silk kimono and, it seems, nothing underneath. Curly black chest hair pours out of the collar.

"Ah," I say. "Cool."

"Not really." He laughs. "But it's fine for now." That's exactly how I feel about my legal career.

"Well, good luck with it," I say as I back out toward the door.

"Hey," he says, rising from his leather chair. He reaches out his arms and pulls me into a warm embrace. Again, I'm less uncomfortable than I would expect given my immense fear of physical contact. "You spit fire last night."

"Did I?" I can't help but crack a smile. "My memory is pretty fuzzy, to be honest."

"Well, let's keep it fuzzy then," he says. An ambient scream from the street floats in the open window. We both ignore it. "Because you were golden."

In my Lyft on the way home, my phone lights up. It's my dad. He calls me, like, once a month to "check in." Our conversations are very forced. We don't really "connect." I mostly feel like I'm talking to a distant uncle rather than the man who provided half my genetic code and, according to him, "raised me." Let's be honest, I raised myself.

"Hello?" I say. I don't know why I still answer my phone like it's the landline era, when people truly didn't know who was calling.

"Prue," he says in a serious voice. "It's your father." My dad always greets me as though he's about to deliver terrible news.

"Hi," I say, and wait for him to tell me someone has died.

"Your mother and I are in Los Angeles," he says. My heartbeat quickens. "We had an unexpected layover on our way to Phuket. We've booked a room at this funky place called the Chateau Marmont that I think you might enjoy."

"Oh yeah," I say. "The Chateau. I'm familiar." I swallow. "Very funky."

"Wonderful," he says. "I know it's short notice, but I was hoping you could meet your mother and me for lunch."

I check the clock in the front of the Lyft. It's 9:01. I can shower and get presentable in time.

"Of course!" I say. I don't think my parents have ever come to LA before. They certainly haven't seen my apartment, and I'm happy they don't seem to want to.

Before lunch I go to Ellie's. I completely forgot to tell her where I went last night so she's mad at me, all sulky and cute. She's puttering around her apartment in a floral silk robe, totally sheer, rearranging candles and crystals. She refuses to talk to me for the first fifteen minutes, so I pick up a book and pretend to read it. After flipping through a few pages, she snatches it from my hands.

"I leave in two days, you know," Ellie says. The light from the window hits her curls and creates a halo effect.

"Are you going to leave me for a man?" I try hard to make my face all pouty, then put my hair up in a bun slowly and artfully. I know she loves to watch my hairography. Everyone does. If there's one thing I've learned from Wyatt Walcott, it's the power of hairography.

But this time it fails, because she just frowns at me.

"Or a butch woman?" I ask. "Like that girl from Nora's. The one that made you get all weird."

"I wasn't weird," she says. Her cheeks redden a little, just like they did that night.

I look out at the Citibank building sparkling gold outside her window.

"It's not important!" Ellie pulls on one of her curls—my favorite of her mannerisms. There's a lot of great hairography in this relationship.

Maybe I don't want to know about this mysterious butch.

"I'm sorry. I'm a piece of shit." I walk over and kiss her, grab the small of her back. She's stiff, so I back off. I'd rather die than have to convince someone to hook up with me. I turn around and walk back over to the bed.

As soon as I lie down, she pounces on top of me.

I spot my parents at a table under a leafy fern as soon as I enter the courtyard. I weave through tables of men with slicked-back hair and expensive-looking watches. I've never been to the Chateau during the day. It seems less chic, somehow, but it might just be the presence of my parents.

I feel very aware of my bones as I walk toward the table. I'm wearing my most parent-friendly outfit, a black DVF shift dress I found at a vintage store and camel-colored quilted flats.

"Prue," my father says when he spots me, rising. My mom remains seated. My dad gives me a stiff hug.

"Prue," my mom says, taking my clammy hand in her icy, bony one as though we're just meeting for the first time. My hands are always sweaty, but they seem worse recently. I wonder if it's Celexa withdrawal.

"Hi, Mom," I say, then sit down.

"Your dress..." she says, voice trailing off midsentence as it always does. "It looks... old."

"It's vintage," I say.

My mom says nothing, just purses her lips together. She's wearing a navy pantsuit and an expensive-looking crystal necklace. My mom always dresses like she's running for office, even though as far as I know she's never had a job.

"I'm glad we are getting to see you," my dad says.

"How is work going?" my mom asks. My heartbeat quickens. Work is one of many subjects that is tense with my parents. See also: my sexuality, my politics, my opinion on essentially anything. I prefer neutral and unemotional topics, like blockbuster movies or the weather.

"It's good!" I overcompensate. Like Jake Perez, my parents don't understand why I would represent criminals for a living. But more than that, they don't understand why I make so little money. "How are you all? I didn't realize you were going to Phuket."

"It wasn't really our choice," my mom says. She takes a sip of white wine. God bless. We're drinking.

"Kip's daughter is getting married," my dad says. My dad is from the South, so all his friends have crazy names like Kip and Granger and Buck.

"Nice," I say. I have no idea who Kip is.

"We're living vicariously through him," my mom says. The implication is obviously that she wishes I were getting married, as if that would make her happy, as if anything would make her happy. I scan the garden for the waitress. I need an IPA. My hangover is starting to kick in.

The waitress comes over and my dad orders a Manhattan and my mom orders another glass of sauvignon blanc, yet when I order an IPA they both look at me like I'm a degenerate.

"What are you all thinking of eating?" I ask.

"I'm not hungry," my mom says. She doesn't eat.

"How is the law practice, Prue?" my dad asks, ignoring me.

The waitress brings our drinks, and I take a big gulp of my IPA and my mom looks at me like I just committed a felony.

"I'll have the *steak-frites*," my dad says. "Hold the *frites*." He laughs but the waitress doesn't. We're in the land of movie and television writers, and my dad's stale frat-boy humor just doesn't cut it.

"I'll have the Niçoise salad," I say.

The waitress looks at my mom and she just closes her lips. For a second I'm reminded of Pilar. I wonder if my mom ever did cocaine in her thirties, got chatty and effusive. The waitress takes the hint and leaves our table.

"The law practice is good," I lie. "Fine" would be more accurate, but I tend to play a character with my parents—with everyone, really, but especially with them. I'm their only child and was once very good at being exactly who they wanted me to be. I got good grades, excelled at sports, had lots of friends. I was thin and blonde and unobtrusive. I went to an elite law school and dated a guy in the top of my class, now a corporate lawyer in New York. But in recent years, I've become increasingly disappointing in their eyes. I took a job with the government instead of big law. I moved to LA and started dressing "peculiar" and dabbling in "the arts." That side of me was always there, but I used to do a better job of hiding it.

"I have a pretty strong Fourth Amendment argument on my latest case," I say, and my mom looks up, mildly interested. I can still charm my parents with legalese. My dad sips his Manhattan as I go into the nitty gritty, failing to mention that I plan for it to be my last case, that I'm fully preparing to embark on my "artist life" and the daughter they once loved will be gone.

"Hey, Prue," my dad says when I finish my monologue. I hate how he says my name so much. He used to get mad at me for this when I was a kid, for not adequately addressing people by their names. He thinks it is polite; I find it oppressive. "Did you ever call up my friend Dick Caldwell at Latham & Watkins?"

I take a cool sip of my beer. The fern above my head sways in the wind and a beam of light hits my shoulders. I find strength in the warmth of the Los Angeles sun and think about my other life, the one with Shiny AF, in which I'll soon be a star. "Not yet," I say. "I will first thing Monday morning." My dad is always trying to "connect" me with his friends at big law firms. My dad works at a law firm called Gibson Dunn, which has questionable politics (they notoriously convinced the Supreme Court that corporations are constitutionally entitled to give unlimited contributions to political campaigns). I'm convinced he's never used his connections to get me a job there because I embarrass him. And I guess he embarrasses me too.

"How is work for you, Dad?" I ask.

"Oh, it's thrilling," he says. My dad is one of those rare freaks who enjoys being a lawyer. I look up at the sky and think about how my parents are space aliens. I wish they would ask me about Ellie or my music career, but they never would.

When our food comes, we all eat in silence and look at our phones. I first go to Wyatt Walcott's Instagram feed, but I'm nervous my mom will see and judge me, so I switch to the *New York Times* homepage. About halfway through pretending to read an article on North Korea, I get a text from Jake. I'll read it later.

"Well, Prue," my dad says when the check comes. "It's been great seeing you." He's staring at his phone.

"Yeah," I say. "Thanks for taking the time to meet me. Enjoy Phuket, I've heard it's beautiful."

"Thanks," my dad says. My mom looks up at me as though she's eaten something sour.

We all exchange bony hugs, and in the car on the way back to the East Side I want to cry but nothing happens. Instead I stare out the window and swallow compulsively.

The first thing I do when I get to Ellie's is collapse onto her bed. She plants a kiss on my forehead and then returns to answering emails at her desk. SZA's *Ctrl* plays from her Bluetooth speaker. Ellie makes her concentrating face while she types. It's so cute. I can't believe this perfect creature is leaving me for New York, where she might fall for a woman who wears a sports bra to the club.

As SZA sings about wanting more attention from her lover, I pull out my cell phone and open the text from Jake.

Why are u ignoring me cunt?

Suddenly I miss him.

Sorry my parents are in town, I say. I feel momentarily grateful for my parents' visit, simply for the fact that I was able to use it as an excuse for being a bad friend.

I hope you're eating enough, he writes.

Jake has always been very obsessed with my calorie intake and I assume it's because he's jealous of my discipline.

I'm stuffing bread in my face as we speak, I lie, then throw my phone to the other side of the bed, but I overshoot and it hits the floor with a thud. Ellie looks over at me with a jokey, wide-eyed expression. Her glasses fall to the end of her nose and I have the sudden urge to kiss her. She must either notice that I want her on top of me or feel the same way, because she struts over and jumps on me. Her lips are soft and full and instantly make me feel safe.

"Sorry I was in my work hole," she says.

"I love it," I say. "Work, bitch!"

She smiles and tugs a lock of my hair. "So are you going to tell me why you abused your phone?"

"I saw it as a friendly toss," I say, then kiss her.

When I finally get back to my apartment, the sun is setting over the Chevron and my cats are screaming bloody murder. I lock them in the bathroom while I put some food in their bowls. They're too annoying otherwise. I open the bathroom door and they charge into me. Once they get past me I go into the bathroom for my Celexa. It's been a few days since I've taken it, I think. It's hard to remember. Often I think I've just taken it and I can't tell whether it actually happened or it's déjà vu or some kind of weird memory inserting itself. On those occasions I decide not to take it because I feel like it's better to take it not at all than take it twice. I open the cap, stare at the salmon-colored pills inside, and then throw away the bottle. I think I feel better without it. Nina gave me a handful of Adderall last night and I take one of those instead. The bright blue pill is sweet on my tongue. I swallow it down with metallic sink water.

My phone buzzes in the other room. I skip over and pick it up. Jax is calling.

"VAGA," Jax basically screams before I say anything.

"Speaking," I say.

"I just listened to what we recorded last night and it's..." It sounds like his voice is shaking and the pause makes me nervous. "...*flames*." He pauses again, and I realize he's probably smoking a cigarette. I decide to go out on the balcony and light one myself. The cats follow me and I feel bad for shitting on them in my rhymes. They are annoying, though. One of them rubs up against my leg as I light up a Parliament from a pack I keep in a flowerpot.

"It's fire, Vaga," he says again. I inhale. "I haven't felt this way about something I've worked on in... I can't even remember. I mean it's obviously not finished, but I'm freaking the fuck out."

I exhale into a tree and instantly feel bad about it. My existence is terrible for the environment. One of the cats jumps into the tree and I remember why I like these things. They're beautiful wild animals. The other cat follows and they look like panthers in the jungle.

Jax is still talking but I've zoned out. It hits me that this big-time producer of video game music thinks I'm hot shit and I have amphetamines in my system and I begin to feel good. "When can I hear it?" I ask.

"I just emailed it to you," he says. "Vaga, I need you to stop whatever you're doing and listen to this immediately. Call me back once you do."

One of the cats charges at a squirrel. I put out my cigarette on the edge of the flowerpot. "Okay," I say.

In my bedroom, I connect my speakers to my computer and refresh my email. I lock the cats out because I can't have them bothering me right now. This is an important moment. I have two new emails: one from Jax, one from Dr. Kim. For some reason, I open Dr. Kim's first.

> Hello Prudence,
> I'm writing to check in about how the 20mg dosage is working for you. Have you noticed any shifts in your mood? Regardless, I'd like to see you in the next few weeks to check in.
>
> Best,
> Dr. Kim

I close the email and decide to answer it later. I open Jax's email and start to download the file. It says it's going to take five minutes. That's a long time to wait. I go into my kitchen and get a beer, crack it open, take a long and grateful sip. I return to my bedroom. Four minutes left in the download. This is torture. I open Instagram and look to see if Wyatt Walcott has posted anything new. Nothing.

After refreshing various websites for a few minutes, a woozy sound emerges from my speakers. The track is open in iTunes and it's playing. It's called "Dearly Queerly." To be honest, I have no memory of recording this.

The bass drops and ASMR hits. That stands for autonomous sensory meridian response, which is when you get a tingling sensation in your neck when you hear certain sounds. When I was younger, I called it "eargasm," and I thought it was something only I experienced. But then I was talking to one of Ellie's clients and she told me it's a real scientific thing. I love to find out what I think are personality quirks are attributable to science. No one is unique.

My voice comes in and I hardly recognize myself. My flow is awkward, landing on the offbeats in just the right way. Jax autotuned the shit out of my voice, which I appreciate. I have no desire to sound authentic. I aspire to be a robot. And Jax made me sound like a sexy one. I can't believe I recorded this in a blackout. And it wasn't prewritten, which means I either wrote it on the spot or freestyled. My bars here aren't as clever or as tight as they normally are, but it's working. I'm letting go.

My mind starts to drift into fantasy. My idiot meditation teacher would disapprove, but it feels amazing. I imagine myself onstage, draped in fur. Not a blue one, like Pilar typically wears, but something more Olsen. My hair is long and white and wild. Under the coat I wear a T-shirt as a dress. Black boots.

When the song is over, I call Jax and try my best to sound excited, which I am, but enthusiasm is difficult for me to convey, even when it's genuine. Ellie screams when I play it for her, then she compares me to Uffie, a Parisian rapper I once idolized. I recall shimmying around my bedroom shouting her lyrics.

After hanging up with Ellie, I lie on my bed and listen to Lana Del Rey while making a Pinterest board called "stage wear" until my eyes start to feel raw and then I fall asleep.

The next morning I write a reply brief, feeling worlds away from the previous day. The weird lunch with my parents, popping an amphetamine and listening to myself rap.

The reply brief is for my sexual assault case. My friends think it's problematic that I defend sexual offenders, but I have zero moral qualms. My client, who is seventeen, is just the victim of a society that convinced him from a young age that women are property to which he's entitled. Besides, I'm not arguing that he was innocent, just that he should have gotten sex offender treatment and probation instead of being incarcerated. This is the better option for society, trust.

I refresh my email and see one from my supervisor about my first draft in Yumiko's case. Adrenaline rushes through me. This always happens when I'm about to get feedback. The way I felt getting tests back in high school is how I would imagine a normal teen would feel walking into Six Flags. I open the email and I'm frightened by its length. I always kind of expect my supervisors to be like, *This is the worst piece of trash I've ever read. You clearly don't deserve to be a lawyer and I'm having you disbarred immediately.* Imposter syndrome, whatever. I begin to skim and feel relief. Nothing new or surprising here. My legal feedback is always along the lines of "formally sloppy; rhetorically impressive."

I decide to address the feedback later, once I finish up the annoying formalities on my rape brief. I guess I shouldn't call it that, a rape brief.

I get back to the table of authorities and one of the cats screams and I again fantasize about an assistant. I want a twink. A beautiful boy I can objectify.

FOUR

On Ellie's last night, we go to Nora's. We've already gotten into three small arguments and we haven't even ordered yet. It's tense because of her impending departure, that's obvious. But she's still annoying the shit out of me. The sound of her voice hurts my head and her energy puts me on edge. Why must she talk so loudly and emphatically? Can't she just, like, chill?

"Do you know what you all would like to drink?" the waitress asks.

"Stone IPA," I say, then look at Ellie.

"Ummm," Ellie says.

Ugh. She always takes forever to order. I find it rude to the waitress and disrespectful of her time. If you don't know what you want, just say you need a second.

"Do you have, like..." There is tension in her voice, I think because she knows I'm annoyed. "...a good dry rosé?" Just as the waitress begins to answer, Ellie cuts her off. "Or like, do you have a cucumber-based gin drink?" The menu is in front of you, bitch! The waitress again begins to respond and Ellie again cuts her off. "You know what, I'll just have a glass of the Cab."

The waitress says, "Great," and as she's walking away, Ellie's phone alarm goes off—*RAAGHH-RAAGGH-RAAGGH-RAAGGH.* The nightmarish sound echoes and heads turn. I want to pick up the phone and throw it against the wall. But instead, I take a deep breath and open Instagram on my phone. I scroll with a ninja-like focus. The alarm stops, but I don't look up from my phone. I try to render my facial expression as neutral as possible.

"Anything good on the 'Gram?" Ellie asks, trying to get my attention.

I shrug. I hate that she calls it "the 'Gram" like some kind of third-tier influencer. "Wyatt did a middle part," I say in a monotone voice.

"Rad," says Ellie. I also hate when she says "rad." Does she own a skateboard?

"Very rad," I say without looking up, tone clear that I'm mocking her.

"Why are you being such a bitch?" she asks.

"I didn't do nothing!" I say in a jokey voice without looking up from my phone. I know I'm being impossible. I comfort myself by remembering that I'm just a bunch of molecules doing their own thing, utterly out of my control.

"You're acting like my presence disgusts you," she says.

"Well, right now," I say, "it does."

Later that night in Ellie's apartment we have amazing makeup sex. We use this chic French vibrator Ellie brought home from a work trip in Paris. We orgasm at the same time and it's beautiful and disgusting.

In the morning we kiss in the yellow light and then I drive her to LAX. My car is in the shop so I use hers—a Honda Fit that is almost as cute as she is. We blast Kanye's *College Dropout* and rap all the words as we zoom past billboards advertising bad action movies. When I drop her at the terminal it's all hurried and unemotional. Cars zoom past and we kiss quickly, and then I have to drive off because someone is honking at me and I'm afraid they're going to get violent. LAX terrifies me.

On the way home I play Syd's *Fin*, and when "Body" comes on and I have that feeling again where I want to cry but instead I just swallow a lot.

Luckily that night Jax invites me to Pilar's show. I'm really excited to hear her sing. I've become a low-key superfan over the past week. Ellie was right, the EP on her SoundCloud is very good.

I spend most of the day editing my brief and refreshing Twitter. Since most of my edits are citation-based, they are very tedious. But today I don't mind. It's nice to have something mindless to do while I listen to music and stare at the @WYATTLOOK Instagram. She keeps wearing Louis Vuitton fanny packs, and I never thought I'd say this but now I want a fanny pack. But Louis Vuitton, obviously.

When my eyes start to hurt I put on my headphones and run around Echo Park Lake. Sadness hits me in the gut when I run past Ellie's. I remember a time early in our relationship when I got awful cramps running and I was worried I couldn't make it home without collapsing. I normally hate nothing more than to rely on other people, particularly when I'm in pain, but I was right outside of her house and delirious. I buzzed her apartment and her voice instantly soothed me, like painkillers had been injected into my veins. I explained my situation, and instead of buzzing me up, she came downstairs with two Motrin and a glass of cold water. After I swallowed the pills, she invited me up and we lay in bed watching *Friends* until I felt better. That was the only time I've watched *Friends* as an adult, but I remember laughing. I like Phoebe.

When I get tired of running I start walking and texting. Something about walking in circles while staring only at my phone is incredibly soothing. On this walk I text Ellie, Jax, and Jake Perez. Ellie tells me she's arrived in New York and it's freezing and she misses me and LA with all her heart. Jax and I just rap lyrics to each other; we've decided to communicate over text exclusively in rhymes today. Jake Perez tells me he's worried about me and I tell him to fuck off.

When I finally look up the sky has turned a royal blue and the buildings downtown are starting to sparkle. It's only 4:45 P.M.

An image of fire flashes in front of me, then I blink and it goes away.

I'm standing in my bathroom belting Mariah Carey through a cloud of marijuana smoke and steam from the shower and wishing my voice sounded better. It's around 6:00 P.M. and I'm meeting Jax and his crew at the venue at 9:00. I'm not really sure what to do until then. Sadly, it doesn't take me three hours to get ready (just swipe on some eyeliner and throw on a black dress).

When I polish off my IPA, I pace around my apartment with indecision and the cats follow. I think about time and how it rules me. My life is scheduled, rigid, broken up into discrete, compartmentalized sections. Brief and coffee time. Walking in circles time. Time to feed the cats, time to shower, time to orgasm—because I read it's healthy. Time to drink beer, smoke marijuana, eat carbs. Time to sleep. I'm always jealous of those people who "lose track of time." I'm time's bitch.

By the time I get to the venue I'm pretty buzzed. I order two PBRs in the front room (I figure someone else will want one, and if not, I can easily drink two) and then make my way to the back room where there is a small stage. Per usual, Jax is standing in the center of the room, at the spot where your gaze naturally hits when relaxing your eyes.

I approach the group self-consciously. Pilar is standing on Jax's left, Beau on his right.

"Hi," I say.

Jax's eyes get big and he spreads out his arms, embraces me. I can't ever remember anyone being this excited to see me.

"Hey, girl," says Pilar. She slaps my ass and I jump a little, then everyone laughs. I recall Pilar telling me she loves how on edge I am, and shame washes over me, briefly, until I turn my attention to Pilar's outfit. She's wearing a long ice-blue coat, a light pink slip dress underneath. She looks like candy.

I offer up my extra PBR and Beau snatches it. Soon Pilar disappears, and next thing I know the lights are dim and everyone is getting quiet.

Pilar seems to float toward the saturated blue lights. Her coat creates a dramatic silhouette; her face is shrouded in darkness. Her edges sparkle. She holds an almost empty martini in one hand, the mic in the other. Behind her is a tatted pale man, her DJ, who I assume handles the technical. The harsh lighting on him seems unfair in comparison to Pilar's. She looks like an angel; him, a clingy former lover. I understand wanting to create that type of power imbalance onstage.

Jax puts his arm around me and we start to sway. Our bodies create complementary lines in space, like the beat was written for our bodies. Pilar's lips approach the mic and I brace myself to be jealous. And I am. She sounds exactly as she looks: charming and elusive. It's like Lana Del Rey meets Thai spa music. Jax and I put our arms over our heads and spin our hands in wavy circles. Beau clinks his PBR against mine.

Pilar's voice hypnotizes me and I enter a trance, and it seems like everyone is under it.

An arm sweeps around my waist. It's Nina. Her hair is wild and her freckles are lit. She's wearing a black silk blouse and a pencil skirt and white Doc Martens. I move my hips toward hers and whisper, "Hey, girl," in her ear.

"Hey, freak," she says, which makes me feel bad about myself. Then: "You okay?" which makes me feel worse. My nightmare is someone asking me if I'm okay. All of my energy goes into appearing okay.

"Of course," I say, and my voice snags, defensive. "I took one of the Adderalls you gave me," I add.

She raises her eyebrows, then wraps her arm tighter around my torso. "Okay," she says into my ear.

The next morning I'm nursing my hangover with some @WYAT-TLOOK in bed when I notice my split ends are a bit crispy. I've had bad experiences with trendy Hollywood salons—they get too "creative"—so I decide to go to this cheap walk-in place called Rudy's on Sunset. I tell the receptionist I need a trim and within minutes a smiley gay appears.

"What can I do for you?" he asks, beaming like a lunatic.

"Just a trim," I say. "I like all my hair the same length. No layers, no angles."

He looks at me with an inscrutable expression in the mirror and says, "Okay!"

While he cuts, we talk about books and his recent decision to get a foster child with his husband, which has all sorts of weird requirements, like that he get a landline for tracking purposes and have screens on his windows so the kid doesn't escape. Regarding books, he tells me he "didn't read for twenty years."

He keeps spritzing this tea tree oil and peppermint formula into my hair as he snips, and I fall into a sort of meditative trance. Also I'm still a little drunk. Soon, he's done, and I thank him and tell him to "keep reading," then feel embarrassed for being patronizing and classist. Then I pay and leave.

Once I'm in the car I take a few selfies and realize something horrible. He gave me layers. Horrible layers. Choppy, artsy, mental patient layers. There is a terrible layer of hair that is three to four inches from the bottom that just sort of sits like a shelf.

It is my nightmare haircut.

I can't believe he did this to me now, right before I'm about to be famous. My hair is my entire brand. Does the universe hate me? Mercury must be in retrograde.

I begin to spiral, hard and fast. I drive home in a rage, tears streaming down my face. I think about options. I could cut it all to the shortest layer, but having long hair is the only thing that makes me feel good. Also, how am I supposed to ever trust anyone again? Could I have been any clearer? No angles, no layers. And he did the exact opposite. This man, all men, the patriarchy!

While I'm stopped at a light outside Sunset Junction, my cell lights up with a call. Without thinking, I answer.

"Vaggaaaa," Jax coos. "I'll be at your house in twenty."

Fuck. After the show last night we went to some warehouse party downtown, then back to the Kingdom. I took an Adderall from Nina's palm, maybe a bump or two. Before I left at around sunrise, Jax invited me to Palm Springs and I said of course because I always say yes when I'm fucked up. But at this moment, bawling on Sunset, the idea could not be less appealing. But it's too late to say no.

"Sounds good," I say with difficulty.

FIVE

I'm just exiting the shower when Jax calls me to say he's outside.

Be right there, I text back, then run into the kitchen and pour some bourbon into a glass with ice. I'm still kind of drunk from last night and a general emotional wreck over my hair, and I figure I'll start feeling good again soon if I start drinking again. I'll be fine, I tell myself. I just have to keep a steady buzz.

Going through my thongs, I try to remember how long Jax said we're going. I think he just said a night, maybe two. I grab four thongs just in case. Two black T-shirts, one white. Black jean shorts. A black T-shirt dress. A black one-piece bathing suit. Two pairs of Birkenstocks and one pair of Nike sneakers, in case I decide to exercise, which I won't.

I put out some extra food for the cats and chug the remainder of my bourbon and run outside. As my sandals flap against the pavement, I remind myself that my caseload is chill right now and it's good to be spontaneous and experience life. Also, it will be good to get my mind off the nightmare on my noggin.

A black G-Wagen shakes on Echo Park Avenue. Nicki Minaj's flow is loud enough that some bougie pedestrians with designer dog breeds stare. Jax's cigarette dangles out the passenger-side window.

"Beau's driving," Jax says. I wonder how Beau can afford a G-Wagen but don't ask any questions.

"Just throw your stuff in the back," Beau says.

I do as ordered and hop in the back seat. "You chill with Mimi's entire discography?" Jax asks, fiddling with his iPhone.

I'm waiting for him to say something about my hair, but he doesn't. Maybe it's not as bad as I think. Then I feel those awful choppy layers on my cheek and become ill.

"Yeah, but once we get to the desert"—I lean back in my seat, a little buzzed—"I'm going to need to hear Lana."

Before I know it, we're cruising to "Video Games" among the windmills. The desert feels like I would imagine the moon, which makes me think of space, which frightens me.

Ellie finds my fear of space "confounding." She's the type of person who loves roller coasters and turbulence on airplanes. She talks about wanting to go to Mars and watches a lot of documentaries about aliens. She once called herself a "UFOlogist" and said that it comforted her to think about the vastness of the universe and how small she was in comparison.

"I'm just, like, a speck of matter," she'd said with wide eyes.

I shudder at the memory and bring my gaze into the car. I focus on my legs, which always look the same. Just as I begin to dissociate, Jax hands me a joint. I wave it away and try to focus on my breath.

"Got any alcohol?" I ask when my breath freaks me out. I need to take the edge off. Weed will just cause more anxiety, more dissociation. I have to be in a good place, a drunk place, to enjoy cannabis.

Beau hands me a flask. I know I should be concerned because it's half empty and he's driving, but I only feel relief.

No one tells me whose house it is, a sparse, minimalist midcentury modern. Nina greets us with a gold tray filled with champagne flutes. I lean over to air-kiss her and she kind of laughs at me. I shrug and take a glass.

Nina says, finally, "Hi, freak."

I roll my eyes.

She seems to like this and she kisses me on the cheek. I wipe my cheek theatrically and she hits me on the arm.

Lil' Kim fills the room and I begin moving my hips. Jax appears and pulls me into the center of the room. People surround us. Most people here I don't recognize.

"You guys," Jax says in a sort of affected MC voice, interrupting my racing thoughts. "I want to introduce my girl Vaga, aka Vagablonde, and our new project, Shiny AF, aka Must Love Dina"—he pauses, laughs—"aka we met like a week ago."

I chew a little on my nail. People are looking at me and I force a smile. I can do this, be around people all weekend, as long as I'm properly medicated. I have to keep a steady stream of substances going and I'll be fine.

"Whose house is this?" I ask, and everyone just laughs.

We play *Truth or Dare?* by the pool as the sky pinkens.

I dare Jax to jump off the roof into the pool, and then I worry he might die and it will be my fault. My heart quickens as I watch him climb out of the second-floor window and onto the roof. But as soon as he leaps, I become mesmerized by how beautiful it looks, his pale tattooed body against the steel-gray mountains (I ate a weed mint). At some point he seems to freeze, suspended in midair for several seconds (my sense of time expands due to the edible). Then he falls quickly, like gravity is mad at him. A turquoise splash.

I pick truth every time because I'm scared of action and I'm a good liar. Jax asks me to name my first concert, which I'm embarrassed to say was Britney Spears. I was a Christina girl, but I was invited by a girl with a senator father, so my mom made me go. But Jax loves Britney, so he squeals and claps his hands, making his silver bangles clink together. His "desert look" is very retired-art-teacher-discovers-streetwear.

A girl I've never met before asks me about my first kiss. She looks very Coachella, with body glitter on her shoulders and sparkly ribbons braided into her hair. Her appearance bugs me, and I become angry that she zeroed in on me. But then I remember I get to talk about myself and ease back into the moment.

"Dante Mendoza," I say. He was hot as hell. We met at soccer camp and then he invited me to a movie over AIM. We Frenched during *Men in Black*. Afterward, he told me he was high, and after we broke up, he told everyone I was a bad kisser. But I don't tell any of this to the group. I just say that he was the best soccer player I'd ever seen.

When Nina targets me, my cheeks heat. Luckily it's darker, so I don't think anyone notices. I look up and watch palms sway against a navy-blue sky.

"Prue," she says, a plume of smoke billowing around her mouth. The smoke swirls up and dances around a pool light. "When's the last time you were vulnerable?"

God, how annoying. I take a cigarette out of the pack by my bare thigh, light it, inhale.

"Never," I say.

Soon we're in the pool house, crowded around a few monitors and speakers, sipping PBRs as Jax plays us beats. He's wearing a midthigh-length bedazzled Aaliyah T-shirt and fishnet stockings, white Nike Huaraches.

The next beat is the one; I immediately imagine my voice on it. I feel good right now. Nina gave me an Adderall to make up for her annoying question in *Truth or Dare?* I have the perfect buzz. I'm not even thinking about Yumiko's case or my vile haircut.

"This is it," I say, and everyone starts getting rowdy.

"Our magnum opus," Jax says as he squeezes my shoulder.

Jax ushers me into the booth. He closes the door and I put on the headphones and feel completely alone. This is my favorite thing about the booth, the way it shuts out the rest of the world. The beat drops and adrenaline hits. I open my mouth and start flowing.

I've been drinking for about seventeen beers
Been spittin' for about two years
DGAF about a fixed gear
That tattoo on my cheek
I wish it were a tear
I wish Wyatt were here
I wish I was her—brrrrrrrrrrr

When I exit the booth, everyone is shouting and my heart is racing. I sip my PBR and smile.

"Shots!" Jax says as Beau walks through with a tray of tiny glasses filled with clear liquid. These people and their trays of alcohol.

We all take glasses and clink, shoot. The tequila burns and I shiver.

After Pilar records a few angelic bars, we go back to the main house. Jax puts on Cardi B and Beau starts cutting lines on a gold tray, and I can tell it's going to be a long night. I'm starting to feel a little out of it, not a blackout, but graying. I worry about being a bad lawyer, then remind myself that this is all part of the plan. After Yumiko's case, I'm quitting. To be an artist.

"You okay?" Pilar asks, putting her arm around my shoulders.

"I hate my hair," I say.

"*Quelle* blasphemy!" she shouts.

"What's blasphemy?" Jax asks, then leans over to snort a line to the beat of "Bodak Yellow."

"Prue says she doesn't like her hair," Pilar says.

Jax's eyes get huge, which I attribute mostly to the cocaine. "Vagablonde!" he shouts. "Your hair is your everything."

I become uncomfortable. Everyone is looking at me, people I don't even know. Beau scowls and Nina looks bored.

"It's nothing," I say quietly. "I just got a bad haircut."

"I can cut hair!" Pilar says.

"Pilar is a beauty queen," says Jax. "She cuts my hair all the time."

Jax does have nice hair, but it's very different from mine—black and thick and coarse. Mine is fine and nearly white.

"Tell me what you don't like," Pilar says. She's now sitting in front of me cross-legged and I feel like I'm in a salon.

I grab the gross choppy layers with my hands.

"You don't like layers," she says. "You want a blunt cut."

"Exactly," I say. "And no one will give it to me."

"I will!" She grins.

I let Pilar cut my hair. She does it quickly in the bathroom. She's very focused and we don't speak, the only sounds are the scissors clipping and the crickets chirping outside the window and 2000s party rap floating in the bathroom door. Afterward, she pulls me up to look in the mirror. It's blunt like I asked but it's really short. I've never had short hair in my life, not since I was a baby. Having long blonde hair has always been my thing. Now I have a platinum bob. Since I'm still pleasantly buzzed, I smile and say, "I love it," then think, *This is the new me.*

When I emerge from the bathroom, everyone squeals. I know they're high on cocaine, but the support feels good. They all love my new hair, they love me. I bask in the glory of revising myself. Then I take another shot.

I black in and we're in a crowded bar. There are a billion red string lights and I'm surrounded by older gay men wearing leis.

"I love Toucans," Jax whispers in my ear. Oh yeah, I've heard of this place. Some legendary gay bar. I still haven't figured out Jax's sexuality, but I'm leaning toward post-sexual.

We're in the corner of the bar in a roped-off area. I scan my periphery. Beau is seated on my left; Nina on my right. I feel a hand on my ass and realize it's Nina. I swat her hand away and she laughs.

I look back up at Jax and his eyes are nearly popping out of his head. Everyone's head is turning toward a figure on the other side of the rope. Someone is removing the rope for her. She's illuminated from behind and the first thing I see is her hair. It's wild and messy and familiar. She has Wyatt Walcott hair. Oh my god.

"My god," Jax says right at her. "If it isn't the royal goddess of the flat screen."

My heart races. Wyatt Walcott is standing in front of me. She's in the same bar as me.

"Jax," she says. Her face leans over to air-kiss him. Oh my god, Wyatt knows my producer's name. We're running in the same circles and basically living the same life.

I still can't quite see Wyatt's face; it's shadowed. But I can see the golden tips of her hair in the light. Her lips move and sound emerges.

Jax pulls me close to him and my heart flaps wildly. "Wyatt, this is my girl, Vaga."

"Hi," she says. I want to ask her what's up with *What's Up*. I miss watching her on television. She was so effortlessly cool in a way no reality TV star is, it was as if she was trolling the genre.

Wyatt doesn't appear to be looking at me.

"I'm a huge fan of *What's Up*," I say under my breath, then regret it, because I know from interviews that she isn't proud of the show. I read that she didn't feel like her real self until she quit TV and started Dead Stars.

She looks back at me blankly, then moves on to air-kiss someone else. I blew it, fumbled the ball. Behind her is a girl with nearly buzzed platinum-blonde hair. It must be Agnes, her bandmate. They both look sparkly and far away.

Jax must clock my excited expression. "I know," he says.

"She knows your name!" I shout.

"We met in a treatment facility," he says. I look at him with a kind of unsure expression. "I need to tell her about Shiny AF."

My body feels warm. I'm in the hot tub. It's me and Beau, the man I still think is mentally unstable, the one I declared my enemy just one day ago. His pale skin looks blue under the silver light of the moon, and I think I see his bones. I scan my surroundings for other bodies but see no one.

"How do you know Jax?" he asks. Surely he's figured this out before now. We've been together for almost twenty-four hours.

"Through my girlfriend," I say.

His expression is hard to decipher. I feel a pang of guilt. I should call Ellie. I wonder what happened to Nina.

I grab my Tecate.

"You're hotter than I thought you were," he says.

I know he's negging me but I still feel flattered. I reach for my hair and there is nothing to grab. I'm going to need to develop a new set of mannerisms.

"Thank you," I say.

Soon Nina appears from inside, tiptoeing in a black one-piece, her freckles popping against fair skin. She hops in the tub next to me. Guilt hits, and then my brain stops making memories.

I wake up naked in a bed alone. I sit up and expect my head to hurt, but it doesn't. Instead I feel upbeat and alive. I scan my surroundings. The room is sparse. Just a white mattress on the floor, white walls, no closet or bedside table or lamp or books. Beside the bed is a clothing rack filled with black and white tunics. A wall-length mirror faces me. My nearly white hair sticks up in varying directions. I still think it's too short, but I have to admit that it looks cool right now. I feel like Andy Warhol.

I hop out of bed and massage my feet into the off-white carpet, then walk up to the mirror to check out my neck. No hickies. Good. I look down and I briefly examine my body. No bruises. No blood. Good.

There's a knock on the door and I jump, then scan the room for my clothes. Nothing in sight—not the best sign, but I decide there is an innocent explanation.

"Hold on," I say, then grab a tunic from the rack. I'm sure it's fine. My desire to feel less exposed at the moment trumps my fear of committing petty theft. I slide on the tunic and go open the door. Jax is standing there with a PBR in one hand, my duffel bag in the other. What time is it?

"Ah," I say, and take the bag.

Jax chuckles. "Sleep well, princess?" he asks, then jumps onto the bed, sprawls out, and makes himself comfortable.

"I guess?" I hold the sides of the tunic. "I took this off the rack. I hope that's okay."

Jax just shrugs. I go over to open the blinds and the room floods with yellow light. Outside the window I see only swaying palms and the gray tips of mountains in the distance. It all feels very extraterrestrial.

"Beau said he had fun with you last night," Jax says. He kicks off his Huaraches and stretches his legs.

I swallow. I'm still unsure about Beau, and I have no idea what my lizard brain got up to last night. I instinctively reach for my hair, once my fidget spinner, but there is nothing to spin.

"I had more fun in the studio," I say. I recall Nina getting in the hot tub with us and wonder why she didn't tell Jax she had fun with me too.

"O-*kayyyy*," Jax says. He rolls his tongue at the end so it's like a strange alien noise.

I feel cold and shiver.

I eat a marijuana mint with breakfast and then go lie out by the pool. Soon I'm staring at the water for several uninterrupted minutes, noting the intensity of the turquoise. My gaze meets the edge of the mountains in the distance, and I think about how I've known Jax for only about ten days, and I don't know whose house we're at, and last night I showed a man a "good time" and I have no specific memory of it.

I tell myself everything is okay. I always bender a bit on vacation, especially in Palm Springs. It's best to lean into it. I won't make this type of thing a habit.

Water hits my face. I whip my head toward the pool and Nina is sitting there, treading water and laughing. She dunks under the water and the pool lights flick on almost simultaneously. She's illuminated, like an angel. When she emerges, she squirts water through her teeth at my face. I wipe it off, annoyed. I want to ask her about last night, what happened in the hot tub, after the hot tub, but I'm afraid to ask. I'm still alive, I'm not injured, it's probably best not to know.

"You ready to hit the road, Vaga?" Jax asks from across the pool, and I want to scream with relief.

Soon we're back in the G-Wagen and I'm staring at the windmills and feeling uneasy.

Jax hands me my phone when it's fully charged. First, I go to my text chain with Ellie. It seems my lizard brain was nice and normal. It's been strange going from being in each other's physical space every day to only being able to communicate digitally. I'm not great at keeping in touch with people I don't see. The seamlessness with which I can transition from being fully obsessed with someone to hardly thinking about them has always concerned me a bit. Whenever a relationship ends, or someone leaves, I'm sad for a second, but then I start to revel in not having to deal with another human's wants and needs. I make a mental note to unpack this if I ever go back to therapy.

Then I open a text from Jake Perez.

Are you okay? Your Instagram story is scaring me.

A new text from Nina pops up.

Safe drive, freak.

The text annoys me. All she does is make fun of me. I decide she's toxic, as is Beau, who is now driving. I shut off my phone and stare at the windmills, spinning to the beat of Lana, and dream of my bed—soft and safe.

The few days after Palm Springs are dark. I'm coming down, hard. Worse, I get a reply brief, and my hair is gone. My Virgoian rigidity forces me to write it immediately. I spend two days in a writing hole, alternating between Silver Lake Library and my apartment. The cats get on my nerves and I leave the door to the balcony open, secretly hoping they won't return. The hot librarian wears a cropped leather jacket with a velour scrunchie.

At night I lie in my bed and alternate between checking Wyatt Walcott's Instagram on my phone and YouTube clips of celebrities on talk shows. I don't know why but I love watching talk show clips. It just seems like the most unnatural thing in the world, going on TV to have a conversation with a stranger, hot lights on your face and a judgy audience staring. The host is always cheesy as hell. The celebrities are expected to both be natural and entertain. It's a confusing expectation.

I watch a video of Lana Del Rey's "most awkward interview" while "In My Feelings" plays in the background. I open my Notes app on my iPhone and the first note is "in a dark place." Then my phone lights up with a text from Nina.

Hi.

So annoying. She's so paralyzed by her pathological need to appear cool she can't even put together a sentence. I turn my phone off and watch a YouTube video on my laptop of Wyatt Walcott telling Ellen DeGeneres about her sleep paralysis, and then I fall asleep.

The next morning I'm working on formatting the opening brief in my client Yumiko's case when I decide to google her. First, I enter "Rachel Taften." A few LinkedIn and Facebook profiles pop up, none of whom seem to be her. I guess it's a common name.

Then I type in "Yumiko Houndstooth." The search reveals several articles: profiles in artsy online publications. There is a piece in *Philadelphia Weekly* announcing her as the "Queen of the Philly Underground." All the articles connect her to Philadelphia. How did she end up in California?

I come across Yumiko's "contact info" and am surprised to see it includes a telephone number. I'm supposed to write my clients and be like, "What's up, I'm your lawyer." In, like, lawyer-speak. But ever since my first few clients didn't respond, I stopped doing it. Most of my cases are misdemeanors and my clients aren't in jail. So they don't seem to have much interest in their appeal. Following her guilty plea, Yumiko got four months, which she's apparently already served. Soon, without realizing why, I'm calling her.

"Hello?" she answers after just one ring. Her voice is husky and she sounds annoyed. I guess no one wants an unexpected phone call.

I hesitate for a second, wondering how to address her. "Rachel?" I finally say, and regret calling her.

"Who is this?"

"This is your lawyer," I say.

"I didn't hire any lawyer," she says.

"You didn't hire me. The state appointed me"—I swallow— "for your appeal."

"Oh," she says. I think I hear a cigarette light. "Do I have a shot?"

Fuck, I haven't even finished reading the record. Why did I call her? I'm an idiot. "I think so," I say.

"Good," she says. "I feel like I was fucked."

"You were," I say. "I just wanted to introduce myself. I'm Prue Van Teesen." Introducing myself with my full name always feels awkward, but it's expected in the law.

"Cool name," she says, and I feel myself smile.

"Thanks," I say. "I like Yumiko."

"I studied abroad in Tokyo," she says. I don't think I've ever had a client who studied abroad, let alone went to college.

"Cool," I say. "I've always wanted to go."

She's silent for a second. I imagine her dragging a cigarette on a dirty street. "You don't sound like a lawyer," she says.

"I know," I say. "But don't worry, I'm good." I don't know why I say this.

"I can tell," she says. "Is that it?"

"For now," I say. "I'll be in touch soon."

As soon as I hang up, Ellie calls.

"Hi," I say.

"My word," she says in a cute, dramatic voice. "Do you even remember me?"

"Sorta," I joke. "Curly hair? Ass for days?"

"Pretty much," she says. "I can't believe how long it's been since I've heard your voice."

I collapse onto my bed and reach for my vape pen. Has it been that long? The last week has been a blur. "The last week has been a blur," I say.

"I know," she says. "I've seen your Instagram Stories."

My cheeks heat.

Ellie starts talking about New York and how depressed she is, like everyone in New York is, like everyone everywhere is. I zone out after a few seconds and stare at the shadow my palm plant casts on the wall, thinking about the Buddhism book I read that said humans are biologically wired to be perpetually dissatisfied and there is simply no way around it.

When Ellie asks me about myself, I tell her I don't have the energy to talk right now and not to take it personally. I tell her I still love her, which I'm pretty sure is true.

"Love you to the moon," she says, then hangs up.

I think about Palm Springs and feel empty and haunted. For mental health reasons, I decide to pretend Palm Springs actually is the moon, another celestial body with its own set of special rules inapplicable to life on Earth. I did nothing wrong. No hickies, no bruises, no blood. Just "a nice time."

SIX

Jax calls me Friday morning and tells me he's throwing a "soirée" at the Chateau Marmont. "You must come," he says. "I just got a big check from *GTA*."

For a second, I'm confused. Then I remember: *Grand Theft Auto*.

I wear a black silk tunic I bought after feeling inspired in Palm Springs, Adidas Gazelles. I watch another makeup tutorial and my wings look nearly perfect. I deliver for the Chateau. Especially when it's nighttime and my parents aren't there.

When I arrive at the front desk they say, "Who are you here to see?" and I say, "Jax Jameson." Two men whisper and then one takes me to the elevator, which takes me straight into a suite. I can hear noise before the elevator opens.

The room is jam-packed and the Fugees are blasting: *Fu-la-la-la*. Less of a "soirée" and more of a full-blown rager.

"*GTA* MONEY," Jax yells over the music. "Invite whoever."

I scan the room first for alcohol, then for friends. I get a weird sinking feeling, like I'm super tired and something is pressing down on my shoulders. Pilar appears through the crowd in a floor-length blue silk kimono. She kisses me on the cheek, then slips a pill in my hand. It's the same color as her kimono: Adderall Blue.

The room empties out and I take stock of who is here: Jax, Pilar, Nina, Beau, and a generic girl on Beau's lap. Mariah Carey is playing and I feel better than when I entered, not because I don't like the Fugees—I love the Fugees—but I don't care for crowds.

Pilar's arm links through mine. She's shed the kimono and is just wearing a slip, also Adderall Blue. Her skin is crazy soft and seems to sparkle; mine feels patchy and ashy in comparison. "Prue was so fun in PS," she says.

Nina, who is rolling a joint on the coffee table before us, just laughs. "That's one way of putting it."

"Nina," Pilar says, "just because Prue doesn't have a stick up her ass like you do doesn't mean you have to ridicule her."

I'm shocked she's defending me.

Nina rolls her eyes and Pilar pulls a skinny blue cigarette out of nowhere.

"You should probably smoke that outside," Nina says. "We don't want Jax to be fined."

"Oh yes," Pilar says, voice nearing a hiss. "We must go outside, but you can smoke your endless supply of empathy-numbing hippie crack in here."

Damn.

"Pilar's got bars," Beau says without looking up from his phone. The generic girl giggles breathily in a way that makes it clear her Saturn has not returned.

"Come on, Prue," Pilar says, her arm still linked with mine. "Let's go have a cig outside. The artists are being banished. It's like the McCarthy era in here."

Soon we're in the courtyard, the same place where I had lunch with my parents just over a week ago. It's weird being back under such different circumstances. That sinking feeling hits again and I quickly light a cigarette. I exhale toward a massive, backlit leaf.

"You know she's only a cunt to you because she has a crush," Pilar says. She waves to someone in the distance.

I feel a little flutter in my chest that I want to go away. I had an inkling this was true, but also I never think anyone has a crush on me. They have to be on top of me before I realize it, and even then I'm like, *Maybe they fell?*

"No, I think she really finds my existence repulsive," I say.

"Bullllllshit," says Pilar. Then she disappears to go say hi to someone and I'm happy to have a moment alone.

I smoke my cigarette and stare at the moon. This is exactly why I started smoking cigarettes to begin with, to leave the party and stare at the moon. After a few puffs, I remove my phone from my tunic pocket. It's only 10:05 P.M. Wow. I thought it was much later. Just as I'm about to check my texts, my phone lights up with an incoming call. Holy shit, it's Yumiko.

"Hello," I say. I should have let it go to voice mail.

"Why hello, Miss Esquire Extraordinaire," she says. Her voice is a bit slurry.

"What's up?" I say. Then I curse myself for not being more formal.

"You know," she says. "*Faded Friday*." Then she lets out an unhinged cackle, which reminds me of all the texts from Jake Perez I haven't responded to.

"Yeah," I say.

"So a brief Google search earlier led me to your SoundCloud," she says.

I swallow. I've had a vague, underlying paranoia since I passed the bar that someone from my law world would find my internet persona and I would be disbarred. But Yumiko doesn't sound like she's about to report me.

"Girl, you got bars!"

Relief hits. She's just a fan. "Oh, thank you," I say. "That means a lot from the Queen of the Philly Underground."

She cackles again. "What are you doing tonight?" she asks.

"At the Chateau," I say, "for a friend's party."

"Oh my god, I love the Chateau!" She's screaming to the point that I have to remove the phone from my ear. Pilar walks by and motions that she's going back to the room. "I'm actually housesitting right by there—I could be there in, like, five minutes!"

Oh god. I cannot be partying with my client. But Yumiko isn't my average client. She's young and hip and gets it. And she's a fan!

"Great!" I say. I hang up and swallow hard.

I wait nervously outside the Chateau and watch rich people valet their Bentleys. Yumiko said she's biking, which is insane to me. I had no idea people biked in LA.

My phone lights up with a text from Nina. *Did I scare you away?*

No, I write back. She's so annoying, like an elementary school boy firing spitballs at his crush. Then I remember her tiptoeing toward the hot tub in her one-piece and feel an uncharacteristic wave of horniness. SSRIs murdered my sex drive, but I guess it's coming back. I don't feel great about this. Desire is annoying, particularly when it's hard to control. Best to avoid it.

As I put my phone back in my tunic, a bike comes barreling around the corner. The valet people look afraid as she slams the brakes and nearly falls off. She's wearing a tattered leopard-print coat and holding a plastic bottle of whiskey. She's going to fit in.

"Yumiko?" I say.

She smiles to reveal a gold tooth. "Miss Lawyer Biddy, what's goooooood?"

By the time we arrive back in the suite, Jax has set up a makeshift studio. He's cornered it off with the shoji panes and it's glowing blue, making the rest of the room appear red. Nina is in the same position rolling a joint, and Pilar is leaning on her. I guess they made up, or maybe they were never fighting. Maybe they just enjoy bickering for sport, which I absolutely cannot fault.

"Guys," I say, not totally sure where to look. I'm horrible at introducing people. Also, there are a few more people in the room now, none of whom I recognize. "This is Yumiko."

Yumiko curtsies and some whiskey drips from the bottle in her pocket and splashes onto the floor.

"Hi," Pilar and Nina say in unison, unenthusiastic. Beau just shoots a look of disgust. I guess I've never brought anyone around the Kingdom before.

"Fun crowd," Yumiko says. Her accent sounds British and I'm wondering whether I'm mishearing it now or I missed it before. "What's over there?" she asks, pointing at the studio. Her accent is definitely British, definitely for the first time at this moment, and I realize this woman is mentally unwell and I've done something horribly insane by inviting her here.

Jax appears from behind the panes, then looks Yumiko up and down. I'm terrified. He's going to yell at me for bringing this psychotic criminal to his suite at the Chateau. I want to disappear. "Who is this treat?"

Thank god.

Everyone looks at Yumiko, who is actually kind of beautiful. She has fair skin and big marshmallowy blue eyes with thick lashes. Her exaggerated facial features and oversized coat make her resemble a cartoon character or the "bad girl" in a video game. Jax seems taken. Probably because she is striking and un-hinged in the precise way he seems to find attractive.

Yumiko quickly charms Pilar and Nina by smoking them up with some "medical-grade hash" and reading their birth charts, which is great for me because now I know their charts without seeming nosy. Nina's chart is predominantly water, which means she isn't as disinterested as she seems. Pilar is a triple Gemini. No surprise there. This explains why she's simultaneously inviting and im-penetrable. It also explains her musical ability. I've always been envious of Geminis; they're the musical geniuses of the zodiac. Kanye West, Tupac Shakur, Lauryn Hill, Lana Del Rey, Wyatt Walcott. I'm a Virgo, the less fun Mercury-ruled planet. We have Amy Winehouse and Beyoncé, who represent opposite reactions to the Virgoian need for control—Beyoncé embodying it; Amy setting it on fire. But Geminis have always seemed cooler.

Yumiko also collects some important backstory on the King-dom, information I'm frankly embarrassed I don't know at this point. Jax and Pilar met when they were paired for a group project in a freshman seminar at Cal State Northridge. Instead of completing the project, they decided to drop out of school and focus on music. Their "Goth spiritual" project got some buzz at first, but Jax stopped taking it seriously when he got hired by

Grand Theft Auto, which caused a several-year rift between the two. Without a right-hand woman, Jax befriended Nina at an industry event, where he was taken by her perfectly rolled joints and encyclopedic knowledge of '90s R&B. Jax and Pilar finally made up, and the Kingdom was born.

"I don't want you to think I'm using you to further my professional goals," Yumiko says after blowing a cloud of hash smoke toward the window, "but I can freestyle quite well." She's jumped back into the British accent.

"Are you British or not?" Beau finally asks, and I must say I'm relieved I don't have to be the one to ask it.

"Do not interrogate our guest," says Pilar. She's really into defending people tonight.

"She talks in a British accent one second and working-class Philly the next," Beau almost grunts. The skinny girl with the big breasts is asleep on his lap.

"Good ear," says Yumiko.

Jax appears out from behind the panes in the corner. "Hold up," he says, looking at Yumiko. "Did you say you can freestyle?"

Soon, I'm behind the panes with Yumiko and Jax and Pilar. Beau is lurking with a DSLR. My discomfort must be obvious, because Yumiko looks at me and then looks at him and says, "Hey, beat it, Annie Leibovitz." I mouth her a "thank you."

"So," Jax says. He's in full Leo mode, ruling his pride, his Kingdom. "Our band, Shiny AF—which consists of Prue, Pilar, and myself—has this fire single we've been working on called 'Dearly Queerly.'"

"Dig it, dig it," Yumiko says, then swigs some whiskey.

"We have two dope verses from Prue," Jax continues, "and Pilar slays the hooks. But I know it's missing something, and I think if we could get a quick freestyle from you... I'm thinking like Chance on 'Ultralight Beam.'"

"Nobody else speaks!" shouts Yumiko.

"Exactly," Jax says, then looks at me. "Where did you find this bitch?"

I panic. Just as Yumiko starts to open her mouth I blurt out, "Camp friends."

Yumiko looks skeptical for a second, then nods. "Camp Wana-tonka," she says, and does a faux salute, which I try to mimic. "Bunk Eleven for life."

"Bunk Eleven for life," I echo.

Yumiko asks that everyone go to the other side of the room while she records, which makes me nervous—I hope she can deliver. I sit beside Nina so I can avoid thinking about this insane situation I've put myself in. I've just invited my client to a party and now she's going to be on my first single with my new rap group.

"Oh, so you like me again?" Nina asks as soon as I sit down.

"You're all water," I say in reference to her birth chart. My anger evaporates like water in the desert.

She shrugs. "And?"

"You're sensitive," I say, and I place my finger lightly on her leg, then start tracing circles around her kneecap.

"And you're a freak."

She pushes my finger away, then looks out the window and drags her joint. She ashes it and then looks at me. I wonder how many freckles she has. Probably billions.

"Why didn't you respond to my text the other night?"

She looks vulnerable for a second and I feel bad. Not just about not responding to her text, but about flirting so flippantly with Nina when Ellie "loves me to the moon." God, the moon. I feel dizzy.

"I'm trash," I say.

Yumiko and Jax are still behind the panes when I duck out. Nina says she wants to go too and asks if we can share an Uber back to the East Side. I shrug and say fine.

It's twilight when the Uber arrives. Nina opens the door for me, and like the little brat I am I go around and get in the other door. She frowns at me, then puts her head on my shoulder. I feel stiff, like my skin has turned to metal.

"You can sleep over if you don't feel like going all the way to Echo Park," she says. Nina lives in Silver Lake, which is only about two minutes closer.

"I'll be fine," I say.

Nina yanks her head off my shoulder and pulls out her phone, begins scrolling through Instagram with determination.

My own phone starts to buzz in my tunic pocket. I pull it out and answer. "Merry Christmas, angel," Ellie says.

"Merry Christmas," I say. I had no idea it was Christmas. Nina starts coughing theatrically like a ten-year-old throwing a tantrum. "Can I call you back in a few?"

"Of course," she says.

I hang up. "What is your issue?" I say to Nina.

She shrugs. "I know you have a girlfriend," she says. I don't really get why she's saying this and don't quite know what to say back.

"Did you know it was Christmas?" I ask.

Jake and I have a tradition of eating Christmas dinner in Thai Town. I try to cancel on him—my hangover is deadly—but he doesn't allow it. Feeling unable to drive, I force Jake to pick me up.

It's not that I'm afraid I can't operate a car or that I'll get sick inside. I just don't want to. This is how my hangovers manifest. Not illness, but disinterest. Like disinterested in being alive, everything it entails, other than aimlessly scrolling Instagram, in a soft bed, in a dark room, Lana Del Rey on repeat.

I feel a little better by the time I spot Jake's BMW outside my window.

Sucking in a deep vape hit, I head outside, where it's cooler than I expected.

Deep synths blast from Jake's car. The neon lights from the Chevron station splash onto the street and I think about an '80s horror movie. Is Jake going to kill me tonight? Hopefully.

"How high are you?" is the first thing Jake says to me when I get in.

"It's Christmas, bitch," I say, then laugh again to myself.

Jake presses his foot to the pedal. "You're going to hell."

Jake and I are seated in a cozy corner of the restaurant, behind a big Buddha statue, bathed in green and red lights, which feels oddly festive.

"To Jesus," I say, lifting my water glass at him.

"You can't cheers water," he says, "especially not to Jesus... Jesus, Prue."

"Hey!" I start bobbing to the Thai prayer music. "Where is your Christmas cheer?" I dance some more.

"You're so annoying," he says. "I should have gone home to hang out with my Libertarian mother in La Jolla." He tries to make eyes with the waiter. "At least she's a good conversationalist."

After we order, Jake asks, "How are things with the old ball and chain?"

"You know Ellie is perfect," I say. I tear a piece of my napkin in my lap. "Minus the fact that she wants to have sex with a man." Another tear. "Or someone who looks like one."

"Pardon?" Jake sips his water.

I sigh. "Okay," I say. "Once we were at Nora's."

Jake raises his eyebrows, excited for gossip.

"Calm down," I say, which only causes him to exaggerate his response. I continue. "So this mannish woman comes marching in, fully stomping."

Jake's brows rise a half inch as the waitress puts a Thai iced tea in front of me and a beer in front of Jake. We switch them and sip.

"I saw Ellie smile at her, and the butch gave her that weird lesbian diagonal head nod."

"I have no idea what that means," he says.

I try to mimic it and Jake laughs into his straw, causing milky red liquid to bubble up in the glass. I bring the beer to my lips and the carbonation tickles my tongue, and for a second I'm grateful for this weird Christmas tradition.

"You people are twisted," he says.

"By 'people'... do you mean lesbians?"

"Yes!" Jake yells.

"I can't believe you're hate-criming me on Christmas," I say with a grin.

"You wish," he says. "Anyways, so who cares about this butch?"

"Thanks for understanding," I say just as the waitress arrives with our orders. Jake's, a steaming hot plate of brown noodles; mine, two sterile spring rolls, which for the first time I realize are incredibly phallic.

"Robot penises," I say, picking up one of the rolls.

Jake shakes his head. "Can you please finish your fucking story? Actually, you know what? I don't care anymore. You are beyond lucky to have an angel like Ellie even look at you."

"She is an angel!" I say. My high turns on me, and sadness washes over me for a second. I recall Ellie whispering to me about her savior complex. "Do you think she just wants to save me?"

"One thousand percent," Jake says, then stuffs a bunch of noodles in his face.

I say nothing at the time, but I spiral later that night. I stand on the balcony and light a joint and think about how Jake Perez is a piece of shit, a thought that quickly shifts into how I'm a piece of shit. Ellie trying to save me, just like she saved that corny lesbian stomping into Nora's. As my cats begin to circle around my shins, I think about how Ellie is drawn to toxic masculine energy. This means one of two things, neither of which is good: she'll leave me, or—worse—I'm that bony butch.

I remember my reflection in those freaky mirrors at Walgreens and become disinterested in being alive.

It's Wednesday and I'm working on the reply brief—I can't bring myself to touch the "Taften File"—when a text from Jake Perez floats in on iMessage. My body feels shaky and off-balance. I've felt like this for the past few days—guilty and strange, also a bit dissociative, like I'm watching myself from the ceiling. I ignore the text and open Gmail.

I have a new email from Dr. Kim. I open it.

> Hi Prudence,
> Just following up about your medication change. I haven't heard from you in a couple weeks. I hope everything is okay. Please let me know if you need anything.
>
> Best,
> Dr. Kim

I "mark as unread" and tell myself I'll respond later. Then I open iMessage.

Um Prue.

I can see that Jake's still typing.

I came across something alarming last night on one of my Tumblr benders.

Yeah? I type back while refreshing my own Tumblr. A photo of Wyatt Walcott looking swaggy onstage in a plaid miniskirt soothes me.

Are you alone?

My shaking intensifies. *Yes,* I type back.

I debated whether or not to show you this, but I think it's best you know.

I want to jump up and run away from the computer, but my body is too heavy. The next text is a Tumblr link leading me to a set of three images on a page called Ixland Prinxexxa. The photos are bluish and hazy and atmospheric. A thin, pale naked body contorted in various abstract positions against a twilight background, a pool the same dreamy color as the sky reflected in it. I click the link again, refresh it, to ensure I'm looking at the right photos.

Then I see something familiar: a tattoo of the roman numerals XXVII on the rib cage, just like mine (I got it to symbolize the start of my Saturn's Return). I stare closer at the body, which is slightly blurred around the edges. On photo two, I can see the neck and I zoom in. I see a familiar chain, which reads in tiny gold script VAGABLONDE.

Fuck. It's me.

In Palm Springs.

And I look good.

I'm pacing in circles around Echo Park Lake, holding my phone and thinking about texting people. But I don't know who to text. Jake Perez wants me to call the police. Yeah, right. I'm a criminal defense attorney, I would never prosecute anyone—especially not for something this small. Honestly, the photos are beautiful. I look classy and hardly recognizable. What concerns me is that I don't remember it, and I don't know who took them.

It has to be Beau, I think as I watch two ducks fight over a piece of bread in the lake. The air is cooling and the sky is darkening, and I decide I can be in my house again. There are a lot of people in groups, circles of friends talking and laughing. They sicken me.

I clutch my phone and notice a text from Jax.

Omg Yumiko bitcchhhhhhhh

My stomach tightens. I'll respond later.

When I return to my apartment, I turn off my phone. I'm scared to go back to my laptop. Without electronics, I'm unsure what to do.

I walk over to the bookshelf and stare at it. I pick up *Middlesex* and put it back: too earnest. I pick up *Play It As It Lays* and put it back: too bleak. I pick up *My Brilliant Friend* and put it back: too universally beloved. I pick up *The Queer Art of Failure* and put it back: too close to home.

I've always loved the idea of reading but I've never actually enjoyed it. It's hard for me to sit still. I get antsy and think about my own ideas. The narrative in my head quickly becomes bigger and more intense than the one on the page. Next thing I know I'm braiding my hair and staring out the window and writing a screenplay in my head. When I tell people I don't like to read, they always say, "How did you get through law school?" And I say, "Control-F, babe."

My phone rings, which is bizarre because I'm almost positive I turned it off. It's Ellie. I remember I never called her back the other morning.

"Hi, angel," I say, feeling terrible about myself.

"Hi," she says. Her voice is hesitant and she sounds sad. "Are you okay?"

For a second, I become paranoid she somehow saw the photos. But that's unlikely, right? I mean, it's not like the post went viral. It has 2,356 notes on Tumblr. That's like a small college in New England. How did Jake find it anyway? I guess he spends a lot of time on the computer, doing god knows what. I make a mental note to find out what his job is.

"I'm great!" I say. One of the cats smashes into the glass door from the balcony and I jump.

"Okay," she says.

I've never heard her be this quiet. She's my tough power betch. Surely she's furious with me.

"It seems like you need space?"

She's doing that thing girls do when everything they say sounds like a question. "Uptalk" is the technical term, and I can't stand it. Like, at least *pretend* to be confident.

"Why do you say that?" I ask.

"Because you haven't been calling or texting me," she says. "I've made every single attempt at contacting you since I left. It's like if I stopped you wouldn't even notice."

I say nothing.

"And work fucking sucks right now," she says. It sounds like she's crying and I hate myself. I still don't even know what she's doing in New York. I've been too preoccupied with my own dumb brain. "And on Christmas I was so sad and alone and I called you thinking you'd perk me up and you acted like you hardly knew who I was."

She blows her nose. The other cat comes in and jumps at the other cat.

"And it sounded like there was a girl with you," she says. "Are you cheating on me?"

I swallow. What scares me is that I'm not even sure. Explanations start to pour out of my mouth. "I feel like I'm falling apart." I can't tell whether I'm saying this because it's true or because I just don't want to lose her. "Going off Celexa has been harder than I thought."

"Wait," says Ellie. "I thought you just went down a dose."

"Right," I say. "That's what I meant." I don't know why I lie. I guess I don't want her to know I went completely off my meds without psychiatrist supervision. "It's been rough. I've been having lots of unusual feelings," I say, recalling my unexpected horniness the other day. "I think I've been self-medicating, to cope with the Celexa withdrawal and with the fact that I'm expected to be 'on' and around people all the time. Jax is always with a crew of a billion people. He records late at night and he's always on cocaine and his friends scare me." My voice is shaky and I'm not crying exactly, but I think it might sound like I am. "There's this really creepy pale man and I think he tried to take advantage of me in Palm Springs." I don't tell her about the nude photos.

But she responds well because Ellie is a Cancer and Cancers love effusive emotional displays. "Aw, honey," she says. "I'm so sorry."

We talk a bit more and she tells me it's normal to feel over-whelmed right now, that I shouldn't be so hard on myself, and that she'll send someone to beat up Beau for me. For a second I feel like she's my mom. Not my actual mom, but the mom I always wanted. Someone who would acknowledge my emotions and protect me from danger. Someone I could be vulnerable to without feeling mortified.

The words "savior complex" pop into my head and I push them away.

When we finally hang up, I look at my phone and have seven-teen unread texts. Jax put me on a group thread with Nina and Pilar and Yumiko and an unknown number, which I assume is Beau's and which fills me with disgust. I'm not really a group chat gal, but it would be inappropriate to remove myself. I scroll to the top of the thread to the first text from Jax.

Guyz, I'm almost done with "Dearly Queerly." It's FIRE. Come over tonight at 9 for a listening party/workshop (if needed, which tbh I don't think so bc like I said... FLAMES).

I don't read the other texts in the thread. I guess I have to show up. I mean, this is my career. I'm thirty and I don't have a hit single. No manager. No agent. I've never played a live show. All I have is a low-paying legal job and a girlfriend I treat like crap. I need to take this seriously, but I really just want to go to bed.

It's 7:00 now. I squash my anxiety with amphetamines and beer, put on Frank Ocean's *Blonde*, and draw pink circles in between sips. When it's time to leave, I'm in good spirits. And by that I mean I feel almost nothing.

SEVEN

I'm the first person to arrive at Jax's but it doesn't bother me.
I've never cared about being fashionably late. I'm always fashionable; time has nothing to do with it.

"Vagaaaa," Jax says when he answers the door, embracing me. "I've missed you." I think this is a crazy thing to say because I just saw him five days ago. But Jax likes to feel connected to people in a way I don't think I'll ever understand.

He's dressed like a Kardashian: beige joggers and a long beige shirt and a beige Supreme hat. All beige from head to toe.

"Very Yeezy," I say.

"I'm so happy," Jax says. He seems to be shaking. I remember his comment about knowing Wyatt Walcott from some sort of treatment center and wonder if he's manic. "I really want to get this track in some important hands," he says. "I wish I knew where Metro Boomin lived." He cocks his head back down the hallway. "Beau!" he shouts. "Get me Metro Boomin's address—STAT!" His cackles fill the hallway.

"I don't know where he lives," I say. "But I do know we share a birthday." I just found this out today.

Jax does that weird tongue click that always frightens me, then leads me to the kitchen.

"Oh," he says, cracking open two beers. "So Nina has a lot of clout in the music journalism world. I want this track to get *Pitchfork*'s Best New Music. Nina could make that happen. But we have to charm her." He hands me a beer. "And luckily she's charmed by you."

My stomach tightens. I think about the nude photos from Palm Springs and wonder if Nina was there.

"You okay, Vaga?" Jax asks.

I'm staring vacantly and blink, then do a little jump. "I'm great!" I say. I sip my beer. "I'll turn up the flirt."

Nina is the last to arrive. She's wearing gold-framed glasses and carrying a Moleskine. Her presence seems to put Jax and Pilar on edge.

"Hello, darling," Jax says, hugging Nina deeply. He puts a joint behind her ear. She gives it back.

"I'm going clearheaded tonight," she says.

I try to count how many beers I've had tonight. Four, I think. That's fine. I can operate a car after four slowly consumed beers. At least according to my strange personal rule system.

"You look ravishing," Pilar says as she kisses Nina's cheek. "Like a sexy Susan Sontag."

Everyone else hugs Nina and compliments her. When it's my turn, Jax gives me a look that says, *Pressure's on.*

"You look nice," I whisper in Nina's ear as I give her a with-holding hug designed to tease. I worry I miscalculated, fumbled the ball, until Nina smiles at her shoes and turns slightly pink. Jax gives me another look, one that says, *Nailed it.*

"Shall we convene in the salon?" Jax asks. He lights a cigarette and puffs with intensity. When he exhales, he unleashes a hacking cough.

Nina just nods, and the rest of us follow.

Soon we're gathered around the monitors. Nina and Jax sit in chairs, everyone else on the floor. Pilar leans on me and I lean back on her, feeling momentarily safe. I take a moment to thank the nonexistent higher power that Beau is not here. For a second I hope something horrible has happened to him. He overdosed or got hit by a bus. But then I feel bad. I don't want the boy to die, but I would like him to disappear. Couldn't he get fucked up and take advantage of people just as easily in New York?

The beat drops in. It's minimalist and stripped down, just like I like it. Yumiko is on the intro, speaking in a Cockney accent. *Yumiko Houndstooth is shiny af. Jax Jameson is shiny. Pilar, shiny. Vagablonde. Shiny af.* Then she unleashes this little scream that sounds unhinged and perfect. *AHHH.*

Everyone is gripped and Yumiko laughs to herself on the floor. She's wearing the same outfit as the other night. Her hair is greasy and matted in a way that makes clear she hasn't showered or changed.

This weird vibrating machine comes in that makes the beat that much more haunting. It's hot. Experimental and industrial. *Yeezus*-esque.

I hear my voice and I want to close my ears, but I force myself to appear cool and pretend to listen. I think I sound annoying and stupid, but I always feel this way. I close my eyes and try to pretend I'm on a beach. Pilar squeezes my knee. Then Yumiko punches me lightly on the arm. Nina eyes me with a blank expression, and wind comes in from the crack in the window and I shiver.

Nina leaves almost immediately after we listen to the song. We're all on edge and decide to drink it off.

"She liked it, right?" Jax says after about an hour.

"Obviously," Pilar says coolly as she leans over a white line on a gold tray, an image that gives me déjà vu at this point, and likely for the foreseeable future.

"It's proper *fire*, mate!" Yumiko shouts in her Cockney accent, then swigs from her mini whiskey bottle.

I don't take them too seriously. They're coked up and high on themselves. It's impossible to judge your own work. I learned this at an early age. I had a minor panic attack onstage while performing Annie's "Tomorrow" at my third grade talent show. Afterward, I locked myself in the handicapped bathroom to brood and no one understood why. "I was perfect," they said.

"Put it on again," Pilar says. She rubs some cocaine on her gums.

Jax hardly waits for her to finish before the minimalist beat fills the apartment. We're all bouncing, filled with excitement and nervous energy.

Shiny af.

Yumiko asks me to come outside with her to smoke a cigarette, which is bizarre because I've never seen her smoke one. I follow her to the elevator. On the sidewalk, she lights what must be her fifth blunt of the evening. "So are you actually my lawyer or what?"

"Of course I am," I say.

"Then why did you lie to your friends the other night?"

A man bikes slowly beside us making kissing noises and Yumiko spits at him. "Crazy cunt!" he shouts as he bikes off.

I recall telling the Kingdom that we met at summer camp. "Oh," I say. "I just didn't want things to get complicated. These are all fairly new friends. I don't know them that well, and I can't say I entirely trust them all."

Yumiko is looking at me and nodding.

"I think—" I look at the moon, a shimmering crescent, for strength. "It might be perceived as unethical, us hanging out like this. But I don't have any doubt that I can give you the best representation possible while also hanging out occasionally and collaborating on this track." I want Yumiko to know that this is a sole collaboration. She is not part of this band. At least not until after her case is complete, which could be a year given how slow California moves.

Yumiko blows some smoke toward the street. "I get it," she says. "Completely."

"I knew you were cool," I say. But I'm lying. I couldn't possibly know this. I still don't.

"I got your back, Miss Lawyer Bitty," she says. Then she does a sealing of the lips motion. "Your esquire status is safe with me."

"Oh, they know I'm a lawyer," I say. I'm actually not sure they do. But they could. "They just don't know I'm yours. For the reasons stated before." I hate myself when I start talking like this. But there is still that part of me—that very small, but not insignificant, part—that feels powerful.

"Roger," she says.

I put out my cigarette on the street and we head back toward Jax's building. "How did you get the name Yumiko, by the way?" I ask. "You said on the phone that you studied abroad in Tokyo?"

"I did, but that's not really how I got the name." Yumiko licks her gold tooth, which flickers under the streetlight. "I was living in East London at the time."

I nod. So this is where the accent comes from.

"I was getting into the business and needed an alias." She transitions into the accent. "This wanker thought I looked like this anime character he was into, I don't even know." She ashes her blunt on a lamppost and puts the remaining portion behind her ear.

"What business?" I ask.

She just laughs, then dives back into Jax's building.

The next morning I wake up on edge. I grab my phone and refresh *Pitchfork*. Then *Complex*. Then *Billboard*. All the places Nina has regular bylines. Nothing. Nothing. Nothing.

I have an errand today, thank god. I need to get out of the house. The court sent me the wrong file and I have to send it back. It's huge. Normally I'd find this type of task to be a huge pain, but today I'm grateful for it.

I put on my best celebrity-goes-outside outfit—black leggings, oversized black cashmere sweater, Doc Martens, huge sunglasses—and lug the file into the car. I again think about hiring an assistant.

The post office has a huge line, which fills me with a soft rage. Securing a spot, I reach into my purse for my phone and realize

I left it in the car. A few more people enter and I don't want to lose my spot. I guess I'll have to just occupy my mind for the next ten minutes or so.

I look at the woman in front of me and imagine what her life is like. This is a game I've played since I was little. I got yelled at for staring a lot as a kid. Sometimes I forget people can see me.

This woman is about my age, plus or minus a few years. Twenty-eight to thirty-two, I'd say. She's at the post office at ten A.M. on a Thursday in athleisure, so she's likely a freelancer. Everyone in my neighborhood is a freelancer, it seems. Editors, screenwriters, journalists. The attention paid to her daytime eyeliner leads me to believe she has a visual profession. Freelance graphic designer. She seems sweet, sensitive. A likely Pisces. Just when I'm trying to figure out her romantic life, I feel a tap on my shoulder.

I look up, and it's Beau. What fresh hell is this? His face looks ashy and greenish under the post office fluorescents. I suddenly feel claustrophobic, like the gray concrete walls are closing in on me. Why am I wearing cashmere? Sweat breaks out on my upper lip and I worry Beau will read into it, think I'm nervous around him because I have feelings or something.

"Hi," I say, forcing my voice to be as casual and uninterested as possible. Normally I'd clutch my phone, fake a phone call. Goddamn it. What is wrong with me? Trapped in a scalding-hot post office, wearing cashmere, no phone.

He says nothing in response, just stands there looking pale, tugging at the bottom of his dirty T-shirt. I have no idea what Beau does with his days, where he's from, or even how old he is. I think of him as cocaine in human form—fun for, like, three seconds but mostly very dark. And way too cheap for my taste.

Finally the line moves and I shift my focus to lugging the box. Beau just watches me slide it along the floor, more sweat developing on my face. I wouldn't want him to help me, but I'm mad he isn't offering.

"Looks heavy," he says, then laughs, as if he's being funny instead of being a royal dick. He seems to be waiting for an explanation regarding the box, which I decide to withhold.

I say nothing and keep pushing.

"You coming to New Year's?" Beau asks finally.

I wish he would go away. I obviously haven't thought for one second about New Year's Eve. I don't care about holidays. Even celebrating my birthday feels gauche.

I shrug to convey my indifference, but Beau's just staring at the ceiling. I wonder what he's on and whether he's about to mail more of it in violation of federal law.

Finally he brings his gaze back to mine, his eyes glassy and red. "Well," he says, "I'll let you get to your line."

"Thanks," I say, and I really mean it.

I had plans to finish a big chunk of Yumiko's brief in the afternoon, but instead I just refresh various web pages in between sips of black coffee. *Pitchfork*. *Complex*. *Billboard*. @WYATTLOOK. Ixland Prinxexxa. Repeat. By noon, my nude photos have 5,023 notes.

In the early afternoon, Jax texts me about the New Year's Eve party I suppose Beau was referring to. It's at the Kingdom. New Year's is tomorrow. God, every day in LA is a thing. I feel like since I moved here it's been one big event. A screening. A secret show. A weekend bender in Palm Springs. A birthday. A Coachella party. A Fourth of July party. A Halloween party. A PR girl's half-birthday. A friendsgiving. Palm Springs again. A holiday party. Oh, and then there was that time Jake Perez married himself...

I need a break. But also I can't imagine not going. I would go on Instagram and feel left out. I'd get high and try to come up with a movie to watch and never decide on one because each one would have an issue. Not pretty enough. Too long. Too historical. Too earnest. Too masculine. Ugly cast. Too realistic. Seen it too many times.

I want to watch a movie that doesn't exist.

I march into my closet and try to choose which black dress to wear.

When I enter the Kingdom, I recognize everyone, which means the party hasn't really started. Pilar is dancing seductively with her glass of whiskey. Nina rolls a joint at the table. Jax is tinkering with his speaker system. The scene comforts me.

"Prueeee," they all say when they see me, and I get a warm feeling, like I finally belong.

"You look hot!" Pilar comes over and air-kisses me. I know I look the same as always. Black shift dress. Black boots. Messy white hair and black eyeliner. But white powder lines the edges of Pilar's left nostril and I know what's up.

Beau eyes me up and down in apparent concurrence. "Such a shame you like pussy."

I want to tell him that I like dick too sometimes, but I don't.

Nina turns around and slaps him and I feel protected. Then she turns and just raises her eyebrows at me in a way I think she considers a greeting.

Arms wrap around my waist, and for a second I'm paranoid. But as soon as I hear "Vaga" in my ear I relax. It's Jax. And I'm happy to see him. "Happy New Year, my star."

I sit down besides Nina and she places a blue pill in my palm. I told myself I wasn't going to do uppers tonight, but now that I'm here that rule no longer makes sense. My private rule system is rapidly shifting and every second I'm a different person. I swallow the pill dry, then go to the kitchen to grab a beer.

As I exit the fridge, Beau is just standing there in the doorway, smoking his cigarette at me. He's wearing a thin white T-shirt and dirty Levi's and work boots. His hair looks slightly less greasy than normal and I assume he must have showered.

I crack open my beer and take a sip. "Are you Ixland Prinx-exxa?" I ask, pronouncing it "Island Princessa." It's a strange moniker for a white man in California, which is not an island as far as I know, but Beau is nothing if not strange.

He half smiles, appearing amused. "Who the fuck you calling princess?" he asks.

I'm embarrassed and worry he thinks I'm flirting with him. "Never mind," I say, then go back into the main room to dance with Jax. I really don't want to know.

It's not long before the party is properly popping. I'm sitting between Beau and Pilar on a couch. Beau is angry because Pilar allegedly cockblocked him the previous night. I laugh out loud when he tells me this and he responds with, "You wouldn't understand, lesbo." Again, objection: Relevance? I say nothing.

I consider questioning Beau again about the photos, but I don't. Instead I think about how it's been reblogged tons more times. I wonder if it matters; is Tumblr even still a thing? Jake Perez likes it, which means it's probably not.

"Prue?" The vocal fry floats from above, attached to a body I vaguely recognize. Flowy silk top, shiny brown hair, symmetrical face. I immediately think: *public relations*.

"Hiii, girl!" I say, a little too excitedly because of the approximate thirty milligrams of Adderall and two small bumps of cocaine in my system. I can't remember her name, but it doesn't matter. This is why "hi, girl" exists.

She leans over to give me a bony hug, which is extra awkward considering I refuse to get up. I notice Beau eye her up and down and become repulsed by his bad taste.

"I don't think I've seen you since that iconic night at the Mirror Box," she says. "Dead Stars are so, so fun."

God, Chantal. No, that wasn't it. Celeste.

"Yeah, they're the shit," I say. Beau nudges me with a bony elbow and I ignore it.

"God, I miss your girl so much," she says. For a second I think she's still talking about Wyatt, but then I realize she's talking about Ellie. I should really call her.

"Same," I say. Beau nudges me again, this time harder.

"Ow!" I shout theatrically, then jump away. "You're going to bruise me, you invalid!"

Celeste giggles, then readjusts her hair in a self-conscious manner.

"Introduce me to your friend," Beau says.

"This is Beau," I say to Celeste. I get up and coo a "nice to see you" in her ear, then make my way to the dance floor. Lauryn Hill's "Ex-Factor" comes on and I strut over to Jax dancing in the middle of a small crowd. For a second it feels weird to be turning up to a song about pain and heartbreak, but then I remember all the great songs are tragic.

Jax pulls me close to him and I feel special, dancing to the beat of Lauryn's anguish. The disco ball showers me in tiny blue squares of light. A body swings in through the window, like a monkey. It's Yumiko.

"Now that," I whisper in Jax's ear, "is an entrance."

He eyes the window and laughs. "God, I would have given anything to go to that camp with you all."

Yumiko heads straight from the window—where I suppose she was smoking on the fire escape, but who knows—into the crowd. She's wearing a parka that resembles the trash bag Missy Elliott wore in the "Supa Dupa Fly" video.

As if timed by the universe, just as Yumiko reaches Jax and me, Mariah Carey's "Fantasy" comes on. We dance in a circle, our bodies rolling in sync. People gather around us and I feel high for a second and then that rush of adrenaline hits, which invariably renders me stiff and self-conscious, like the wind is being knocked out of me.

A new pair of arms wraps around my waist. It's not Jax, because he's in front of me. I pray it's not Beau.

"Hi, freak," I hear in my ear. Oh god. Nina. I guess I should keep up the flirt. I've yet to see a review.

"Hi, freckle face," I say. I turn toward her and start grinding my body up on hers. She's wearing high-waisted jeans. Light wash. Levi's, probably. A black silk crop top, buttoned to her neck. A thin gold chain that sparkles blue. The crowd starts getting rowdy. Bottles of champagne pop around us.

Ten... nine... eight... seven...
I look at Nina and she bites her lip.
...six... five... four... three...
Jax pours champagne into my mouth.
...two... one...

Nina's face blurs slightly. Obscured freckles. Blue feathers fly in from above. Pilar's arms around us, then Yumiko pops up from under her. The four of us put our arms around one another. Jax pours champagne into all of our mouths. Nina spits hers into my face. Then I pour a tiny bit of beer on her head.

And then she kisses me.

EIGHT

I wake up drenched in sweat. I had this freaky dream I get when partying sometimes, where the night just continues but takes on a surreal quality. One minute I'll be chatting with someone and the next we'll both float up to the ceiling. In this particular dream, Beau was photographing me. And then I turned into a unicorn.

I'm in Jax's bedroom. The bass shakes softly in the other room. There is an arm around my waist. I look down and notice it's freckled. Nina. I wriggle out of her grasp. She whines and grips harder and I continue to wriggle. Once I'm free she rolls over and sighs. On the other side of her is Yumiko, who is still wearing her puffy jacket. It is a little cold in here. The windows are open and the sky over K-town sparkles periwinkle.

I slide into my boots and go into the main room. In the morning light, everything looks less magical. Once shiny and decadent, the tin ceiling looks rusty and cracked. The floor is covered in boot prints. Dust balls gather in the corners. The space is cavernous and depressing, like a dirt hole.

Beau, Jax, and Pilar are sitting in a circle on the floor around a glass tray peppered with white residue. Pilar leans on Jax, and she's crying. I feel bad for barging in on this emotional outpouring. I tend to leave before the drugs take the party here, to crying while discussing past trauma as the sun rises. Oh god, is Radiohead playing? No, it's Mazzy Star. "In the Kingdom." I smile a little.

"Hi, Vaga," Jax says in a sad voice.

"Hi," I say. "Didn't mean to interrupt. Just going to slip out."

"No, no," says Jax. He gestures for me to come over. He's wearing a tribal-patterned mesh robe and stacks of crystal necklaces he wasn't wearing earlier. He looks like some sort of urban shaman. Beau lies down with his head on Jax's lap and gives me a look that makes me queasy. Pilar sits up and wipes the mascara from under her eyes.

"I should go," I say.

Yumiko walks in with a lit blunt in her mouth. "Happy New Year, bitches," she says when she takes it out.

"Yassss, bish," says Jax, turning his gaze to her.

I take this opportunity to slip out. When I'm on the street, a text floats in from Nina.

I had a nice time with you, Freak.

And then I see a blonde girl vomit on the street.

That afternoon, I'm lying in bed blasting Grimes, drinking a Diet Coke, and looking at @WYATTLOOK when I receive a text from Jax. It's a link.

My browser opens to *Pitchfork* and my heartrate quickens. I put down the Diet Coke.

"Best New Music: Shiny AF's 'Dearly Queerly,'" by Nina Nazari.

Fuck.

> For the sake of full disclosure, I was there the night Shiny AF formed. The phrase was uttered by an after-hours partier when Jax Jameson and Prue Van Teesen locked eyes and laughed; they knew this was their project. Jax and Prue met only about a month ago at an exclusive Dead Stars show at the cult strip club Mirror Box. Their chemistry appeared immediate. They draw from the same references. '90s R&B. Goth electro-scuzz. The industrial minimalism of *Yeezus*. An appreciation for camp that would be easy to dismiss as satire or parody,

but there is too much affection for their subjects—cheap fame, tragic glamour, frivolity, escapism. There is also an element of cultural vulturism that is impossible to ignore. Prue has, in Jax's own words, "the coloring of a Nazi." Yet she feels comfortable expressing herself in hip-hop, an art form born from systematic oppression. (Blurring matters, she is also a state-appointed criminal defense attorney for the indigent.) But unlike some of her white counterparts, Prue—who raps as Vagablonde—does not affect an urban New York accent or detail a life on the streets she couldn't possibly understand. Rather, she catalogs her own bourgeois experience in her authentic (albeit autotuned) voice—monotone and vocal fried, with the occasional dip into vocal registers that resemble a seductive alien. In "Dearly Queerly," Prue tackles queer erasure with a tongue-in-cheek swagger. Jax adds sparkly synths, low bass shudders, and crashing percussion. Pilar Vera coos the song's title in the hook, her voice chopped up and processed past humankind. The chorus is pierced by the primal screams of hype woman Yumiko Houndstooth (neither Asian nor British), pixelated outbursts that symbolize a postapocalyptic urgency. In the end, "Dearly Queerly" sounds like the future, and it's time we catch the fuck up.

I compose a text to Nina on iMessage. *So you think I'm seductive?* Typing bubbles appear immediately. This bitch has no chill. *You're welcome, freak.* I smile and then I worry if she actually thinks the song is good or if she was just doing me a favor.

Then a text from Ellie. *BNM BITCH!!!!!! <3 <3 <3*

I almost call her but I don't. I imagine a life where I have a private jet and surprise Ellie with a room at the Plaza. I prefer my daydreams because I can't cheat on them.

It's very anticlimactic that I have to go get my smog checked that afternoon. This is my last day to do it before my registration expires. When I start the car, my whole body is shaking, mostly with excitement, but also anxiety because I remember that Celeste might have been at that party and might have seen me and Nina kiss.

But it's hard to be anxious when the best thing just happened to me ever. I mean, Best New Music. I've been dreaming about this since I was seventeen. I want to go back and shake that girl who had to quit choir because of her panic attacks and say, *"Girl, just you wait."*

It's 2:15 when I turn onto Sunset. The only place that's open today is on the West Side, which I tend to take great pains to avoid during the day. Once I merge from the 110 onto the 10, everything looks shiny and harsh, like the highway might catch on fire. I look out at the San Gabriel Mountains in the distance and wonder how they look from space. Then I feel dizzy and my stomach clenches.

A car cuts in front of me and I feel like I'm on a battlefield. The walls on the edges of the highway resemble a slate fortress. I'm trapped in between. I'm in a death field. My peripheral vision zooms out, dissociates, and suddenly I'm viewing myself from above. A tiny car winding, twisting, through a maze of highways, on a rock spinning in space. My hands are sweating so hard it's difficult to clutch the wheel. My breath is doing that thing where I know I'm breathing but I don't feel any air coming in. This is a panic attack. Logically, I know this. But I still feel terrified. And also angry. I thought I was over this shit.

A car zooms past me and I think, *I'm going to die on this highway.*

A freeway sign gets bigger as I approach, then disappears. These rapidly changing signs are ominous. The sky is too bright. The concrete is too harsh. These drivers are too aggressive. The sun hurts my eyes. I watch a bird swoop across the highway with a small animal hanging from its mouth. The world is a vicious, terrifying place. Everyone is out for prey.

I reach for my Altoid tin and open it with difficulty. My hands are sweaty and shaky, but I still manage to get two into my palm, then I force them into my mouth. I hope the mints will distract me. But my heart just starts beating even harder.

I think about pulling over but that terrifies me. I don't think I can handle it. I just need to stay on the highway until I get to my exit. Driving isn't hard, I tell myself. Drunk people do it all the time. Then I worry about losing consciousness. I attempt to focus on a calming image, a palm tree. A healthy one. But I can't find one. These leaves look like plastic. They're too bright. They're going to catch on fire, I'm sure of it.

A text from Ellie pops up on my phone. Almost simultaneously, another one from Nina.

I'm going to die, I think.

And I deserve it.

I somehow make it to the smog place alive. I'm still shaking when I get there, breathing shallow. I'm terrified about driving back to the East Side. I never want to drive again. I think about calling Barbara Lumpkin, my therapist, but I know she'll only make me feel terrible about myself. Ellie can normally calm me down, but I can't call her now. I can't even bring myself to check her text. I consider calling my mom for some reason, then I remember how hard it was to get her to let me see a psychiatrist when I got those panic attacks as a kid. "I don't understand why you can't just calm down," she'd always say. I mean, me neither. That's why I needed help.

I walk with difficulty to the front desk and tell the man I need my smog checked. He makes me feel the way I always feel in any type of car place: like a fucking idiot. I'm a great candidate for being taken advantage of. A mechanic could be like, *You need a new set of wings,* and I'd be like swipe.

"Your car is really dirty," he says.

Normally I'd say something sassy, but at the moment I can't manage anything but focusing on staying conscious. It's really hot in here and there's a water cooler in the corner. I practically lunge at it. I fill my cup, chug, refill. I do this a few times.

"Thirsty?" the idiot man asks.

"Always," I say. I think about Nina's review to calm myself down. I'm a seductive alien. This doesn't help and instead makes me think of outer space. At least I'm inside and can't see Earth. Maybe this is all a computer simulation. That's what Elon Musk thinks and it comforts me. I'd rather be a computer than a human.

"So you need a smog check," he says.

Did I stutter the first time? I wonder for a second if the man notices that I feel death is imminent, but no one ever notices my panic. The last time I had a panic attack I was driving to Vegas with Jake Perez for his birthday. I will never do that again. Nevada is all one color, a dusty brown. We were in bumper-to-bumper traffic and I felt trapped and there was nowhere to look. I quietly told Jake to hand me a Klonopin, which thank god I had in my purse. Later he told me it was "the most elegant panic attack he'd ever seen."

The man walks over to my car. He's very slow-moving, like a pharmacist, and he smells like stale coffee. "It'll take about twenty minutes. You're welcome to hang out here." He points to a single leather chair in front of a coffee table with some car magazines on it. Yuck.

I sit and pull out my phone. Two more texts from Ellie. I can't bring myself to check them. Instead I go on Twitter and scroll through @WYATTLOOK until the man calls my name.

"Your cylinder needs to be replaced," he says.

I look at him blankly. "Okay," I say. "I thought you were just checking the smog."

"I was," he says. "You passed, but I noticed your cylinder is shot."

"Okay," I say. "Can I still drive it?"

"Not for very long," he says. "You need to get it fixed as soon as possible."

Jesus Christ. I was already terrified to drive home and now this. I'm going to expect death the entire way. But I push forward.

On the drive I alternate between being furious at myself and thinking I'm about to die.

You should not have stopped taking your medication, you fucking idiot.

Your cylinder is going to explode and an aggressive driver is going to run you over.

You're going to pass out at the wheel.

You're having a panic attack and it's all your fault.

You're having a panic attack and you are a weak individual.

You aren't getting any air to your brain and you'll probably have a stroke.

You sabotaged things with the one person in the world who makes you feel safe.

Something is about to implode.

It's either your cylinder or your brain or the universe.

You're going to die in this car.

And you deserve it.

At home, I consider taking a Klonopin but I don't. I just hold it in my hand for a few seconds and then put it back in the bottle. I have a weird relationship with Klonopin. It's the one drug I actually need and I won't take it unless the situation is dire. Adderall I'll take with abandon because it's purely recreational and therefore seems safer. I don't know.

I lie on my bed and the cats comfort me for once. One lies on each side of my stomach and our breathing starts to sync up. I wonder if they sense my fear. Cats are smarter than humans, especially when it comes to emotions.

I put on Lana Del Rey and finally feel ready to check my texts from Ellie, which are as bad as I expected. Comically bad. They are the worst texts I could possibly receive from her.

Celeste saw you kiss Nina last night.

I don't want to speak to you until I'm back.

I call Jake Perez when I get the news.

"I don't blame her," he says. "Something is up with you."

"What do you mean?" I ask. One of the cats pounces on my stomach. The afternoon light casts a shadow of my plant on my wall.

"Prue," he says. I imagine him furrowing his brow. "You're my best friend and I can hardly get ahold of you."

"Oh," I say. I pet my hair to self-soothe.

"Are you okay?" he asks.

"I'm great," I say. "Did you see I got Best New Music?"

"I meant about Ellie," he says. "I thought she was the one." He coughs. It borders on a laugh. "Or whatever."

I've never been great at accessing my emotions at the moment of a breakup, or at any moment really. The last time someone I cared about broke up with me I was twenty-six. My law school boyfriend. I was madly in love with him, although I've lost touch with that version of myself. The one who wanted to marry a Silicon Valley lawyer whom my parents would love. He told me I wasn't "marriage material." He was right.

"There is no such thing as the one," I say.

Jake Perez and I go to Taix, a restaurant that's been around since the 1920s or something. It looks like a dingy ski lodge in the French Alps. We sit by a fire and under a TV playing some sport. Jake Perez orders the roasted chicken and I order a Caesar salad and we both order martinis—dry, Bombay Sapphire.

"Congratulations," Jake Perez says once we get our drinks.

This is the first time tonight he's said something nice to me. On the drive over, he mainly ripped into me, told me I was "self-sabotaging with abandon." I didn't object.

"This is your dream, right?" he asks. "How does it feel?"

I sip my martini and my body shakes as it goes down. "Normal," I say.

"So you expected it?" he asks, and this feels like a trap.

"You didn't?!" I shake his biceps playfully.

He shrugs me off. "No," he says. "I really didn't."

I roll my eyes and pull out my phone. There's a text from Jax. I can feel Jake Perez's judgmental eyes on me.

Pitchfork party tonight!!! Kingdom @ 9.

Lord. Another party. It's New Year's Day! And I've had a panic attack and been broken up with. I can't possibly attend another party at the Kingdom.

"Your new degenerate friends?" Jake Perez asks.

I roll my eyes. "We're artists," I say, then immediately hate myself.

Our food arrives and Jake Perez grabs his knife to cut the chicken in a way that scares me for a moment. I remember being on the highway, convinced I was going to die. I shouldn't be out, I think. I should be resting.

I take a bite of my Caesar, and the salty, creamy dressing provides a brief moment of ease. I sip my martini. Everything is going to be okay.

I text Jax back. *Wouldn't miss it!*

I bring Jake Perez along because he said we need to "work on our friendship." But really I think he just wants to keep an eye on me. We walk into the Kingdom to the sound of my voice.

"Wow," Jake says to me as Jax leads us down the hallway. I can't tell if he's talking about my seductive alien rapping or Jax's cavernous apartment or the fact that he's wearing a dress. Jake is conservative, at least aesthetically. He's from San Diego.

I get déjà vu as we enter the main room. "This is Jake," I say to the group. Everyone looks at him confused and makes vague attempts at smiles.

"Jake," Jax says finally. "Like Jax... but more simple." He chuckles, and then Beau chuckles, and then Jake glares at both of them. I'm embarrassed that I brought him here. Jake won't be able to charm them like Yumiko could. He isn't messy enough.

"Yes, I'm aware my name is common," says Jake, and everyone just stares at him blankly.

Yumiko enters through the window, crawling in from the fire escape. Last time I thought she'd just been smoking on the fire escape, but now I think this is just how she enters. She's so extra.

Jake eyes Yumiko like she's from outer space. Yumiko opens her mouth at the same time her shriek comes in from the song and it gives me chills.

Jax walks in with an armful of PBRs and begins doling them out.

"Oh, no thanks," says Jake. "I don't drink beer."

Jax shrugs. "I have tequila."

Yumiko says, "I have whiskey."

"I'm okay," says Jake Perez. Then he gives me a weird look.

Once Jax has handed out the beers, the song restarts. He lights a cigarette.

"I'll take one of those," Jake says. This is Jake Perez's worst habit. He's a smoker who refuses to buy cigarettes.

Jake walks over toward the window and smokes while watching Shiny AF dance like maniacs under the disco ball. We scream and howl and grunt and grind. Nina and Jake, the Scorpios, stand in the corner watching us with judgmental expressions. I haven't spoken to Nina yet, and her presence makes me uneasy. I try not to look at her or think about the fact that Pilar was right about her being a sexy Susan Sontag. I mean, Susan Sontag was already sexy. But Nina has that vibe, like she's thinking about something really important and she'd be running intellectual laps around you if she wasn't so withholding.

After about the fifth playing of "Dearly Queerly," Jake Perez announces he has to go. I'm torn. I don't want to stay in the Kingdom. I can't be left alone with drugs and Nina right now.

In an unusual moment of strength, I say, "Me too."

In the car I start to cry.

"Thank god," says Jake Perez. "You're a human being."

I ask Jake if I can sleep over at his house and he says yes. We crawl into his bed with a bowl of popcorn and small glasses of fancy scotch. He projects *Call Me by Your Name* onto the wall. We saw it in theaters when it first came out and were both obsessed, along with the rest of the coastal elite.

During one of many scenes in which the boys are flirting about classical music, I pick up my phone. Jake Perez raises his eyebrows at me when I check it. He believes in "unplugging" during films. I refresh Twitter and I have a hundred new followers. My phone lights up with a text from Nina. *Why did you leave?*

I need a night off, I text back.

I was hoping we could celebrate, she texts back. I feel Jake's eyes on me and I turn off my phone.

I know the movie is about the boys, but I have a crush on the mom. She's always smoking cigarettes in all denim and speaking a thousand different languages and being sexy as hell. When her son gets sad because "the American" boy has to go home, she just pets his hair. Then the dad gives this horrible speech that Jake Perez and most people seem to love. I find it gratuitous.

The last scene always gets me. Elio, the younger and more beautiful boy, is crying in front of the fire while Sufjan Stevens plays. This is a few months after the love affair and he's really started to lean into his gay identity. Oliver, "the American," calls to announce that he's engaged. To a woman, probably. The fucker. I've been there. I can't tell you how many times a woman has left me to be hetero.

The cool thing about this movie is that it perfectly shows how with your first gay experience, it can really be with anyone. It's not really about the other person—Oliver is just kind of a blank slate with a nice ass. My first girlfriend was this horrible masculine woman named Sam. This was around the time Lindsay Lohan was dating Sam Ronson, which was pretty much the only thing that gave me the courage to do it. My Sam was mean as hell and didn't have a job and was always calling me at work to yell at me. I put up with it because I was infatuated, less with her than with the fact that she was my girlfriend and she had huge breasts—something I'd never experienced given my own are, like, nonexistent. And I think it was the same with Elio. Not that he didn't have some nice memories. Oliver was confident and charming; Sam was funny as hell when she wanted to be. But mostly Oliver was a tight ass and Sam was big breasts, which she unfortunately kept contained in a sports bra.

Anyway, in the last scene, Elio just cries for what feels like ten minutes. The movie is superlong and you'd think I'd be like, *When is this going to fucking end?* but instead I'm cool with watching him cry and cry. The fire casts a golden glow on Elio's face and he keeps biting his lip to keep from losing it. In the background, his hot mom sets the table. And at the very end, Elio does this little smile and it's just the most precious thing I've ever seen. That is love, that is life. Mostly pain, punctuated by tiny moments of pleasure, normally based on random synapses firing in our brains.

In the morning I decide to really bite the bullet and finish Yumiko's brief. The argument is pretty simple. The police lacked reasonable suspicion for the pat-down. The officer's "hunch" that she looked "suspicious" was insufficient to justify the detention under the law. The only issue is Yumiko's outbursts on the stand, but that shouldn't have any legal relevance. Unfortunately judges are human beings, and the fact that this white girl was threatening everyone will make the court less likely to see our side. I write, "That Ms. Taften was agitated on the stand—an apparent response to the stressful courtroom atmosphere—has zero relevance to the legal issues at hand." In between sentences I check Twitter and watch my followers gradually increase, a drug that feels not unlike amphetamines. I have 738. Not exactly Lindsay Lohan, but it's a noticeable increase from the 245 I had before. Intermittently, I type "Dearly Queerly" into the search field to see what the people are saying. The responses vary.

Dearly queerly is straight up fire.

Dearly queerly is aural assault.

It's only been one day but I can already tell Dearly Queerly is the best track of 2018.

Dearly Queerly is the dumbest fucking name I've ever heard.

That's the point you cretin! I type in the reply box, then take a screenshot and close the browser without uploading.

I think about the scene in *Grey Gardens* when Edie Beale is sifting through a pile of trash and tells the Maysleses, "This is all art."

At around noon the Kingdom group chat starts popping off.

Wicked Ice wants to meet with us, Beau writes. I'm kind of surprised he writes "us," as if he's part of Shiny AF. I thought he was just our drug guy. How does he know people at Wicked Ice? The indie LA label. Kelela, Yaeji... fuck, I'm pretty sure they signed Dead Stars. I cannot believe this is happening.

When? I write.

Tomorrow.

Good lorddddd!

NINE

Wicked Ice's office is in Chinatown, right across from this place I used to go dancing in my twenties with Jake Perez called Hop Louie. It's a weird dive bar with a jukebox and the bartenders are mean as hell. Chinatown looks very different during the day, sterile and cartoonish.

The office is crisp and white and minimalist. Paintings of cool ocean scenes decorate canvases on the walls. A woman with hair the shade of her bright red lipstick takes us into the back room. Two heavyset white men dressed like rappers are seated at the edge of a white table.

The men introduce themselves as Max and Ezra. We introduce ourselves and sit down. I'm wearing a black tunic and my hair is tied up in a velvet scrunchie on top of my head. I think I look pretty great. But I don't really feel great. *Looking great and feeling terrible.*

As soon as I sit down I start sweating. I force myself to take a breath. I try to talk myself into being excited. I'm about to be famous! Wicked Ice! I force a smile, which I never do, but it's supposed to do something good neurologically. Pilar gives me a strange look.

Pilar sits on my right and Jax on my left; Yumiko and Beau are on either side of them. Beau is shaking his leg and it thrashes against the table and I keep thinking it's an earthquake. Everything feels ominous in this harsh light. It's so bright in here. Outside the windows people work at massive white Mac computers. Occasionally they look in and say something to each other. I feel like a goldfish, or the food for the goldfish.

"So along with the rest of the world, we loved 'Dearly Queerly,'" says Max or Ezra. I forget which is which. They look very similar except one is slightly heavier. The heavier one was speaking. Shit, did he say "world"? For the first time, I wonder whether our song is actually good or if Nina is just a really good writer who happens to have a crush on me, then I think of Lana— *I fucked my way to the top.*

The less heavy one speaks. "But one hit single does not a career make," he says. "Just look at Kreayshawn."

Ouch. I mean, I like "Gucci Gucci," but we're obviously on a different level. I make eye contact with Jax, who is frowning angrily at the table. Good, we're on the same page.

"We ain't no Kreayshawn," Yumiko shouts at the men. I have an image of her in the courtroom, and for some reason my immediate instinct is to laugh. This moment is so strange. I watch the women outside, shuffling around behind their massive Macs. I feel like I'm one of them, watching the situation from outside the glass.

"We understand that, Yumiko," says the less heavy man. Her name sounds weird coming out of his mouth, like he's emphasizing the wrong syllable.

"Don't fuck with us," she says, and slams both hands on the table. Jax looks impressed. Yumiko pulls back her arm and shoves the speakerphone in the middle of the table. Max and Ezra jump a little and this time I actually laugh.

"We have no interest in fucking with you," says the heavier man.

The redhead who led us in is gesticulating wildly outside the glass. I think she's on the phone. I stifle a laugh and Pilar gives me a weird look again.

"Just checkin'," says Yumiko. She's using an accent I've never heard before.

"We don't want to waste anyone's time," says the less heavy one. He adjusts his black fitted cap. "We want to put out your first EP on Wicked Ice."

"Okay," says Jax.

I'm staring at the ceiling, which is so white and bright I begin to feel dizzy. I wipe my wet palms on my dress. I look out the windows and it's equally terrifying somehow. The redhead seems manic. She's moving too much. Everyone outside the room is moving around like a maniac, and everyone in this room is paralyzed with fear. The tension reminds me of our song, at least how Nina described it. Maximalism meets minimalism; everything cloaked in panic.

I check my reflection in the glass and I look calm somehow. *Try to be that person in the reflection,* I tell myself. But soon I'm looking at that maniac redhead again screaming into her cell phone. She reminds me of Beau, who is speaking right now. He's talking numbers, which I don't understand. I try to focus on the in and out of my breath. I'm an artist.

I am not getting air in.

I am dying.

I fantasize about jumping out of my chair and leaving the room, but I can't imagine it. I can't walk. I'd collapse.

Just then, Max and Ezra start to stand. They reach out their hands. We stand and everyone reaches out a hand except Yumiko, who walks straight toward the door. I'm impressed by her erratic behavior. I'd love to be that uninhibited. I guess that's why I'm always dosing myself.

I'm mad at Beau for being here, and he has no qualities I want to emulate.

The redhead comes over and walks us out of the office, gesturing more than she needs toward the door. Soon, we're outside. I take a big breath of hot exhaust and somehow feel okay.

I file Yumiko's brief the next morning. I realize it might be the last opening brief I ever file and have a little private celebration in my head. I got a fair amount of money from the Wicked Ice deal, enough to not need to rely on appeals for a while. Plus, I'll still have money coming in from the California government as my lingering cases are decided. I get my inheritance at thirty-five as long as I can maintain the right image for my parents. (Luckily, they are internet illiterate.) I stopped taking the Big Pharma medication that was stifling my creative power and causing me to write mindless legal briefs for the government. Now I'm self-medicating to maximize my creative potential. It's all happening.

Yumiko's parka flashes through my brain, then exits as fast.

I go meet Jake Perez for lunch to celebrate my independence from government servitude. We bring our laptops to this place called Subtropical, where people go to day drink and pretend to work. Jake and I open our laptops and begin performatively clicking our keyboards.

"So, your dreams are coming true," says Jake Perez after we've ordered. "How does it feel?"

My chest tightens a little and I sip some beer. "It feels great."

A text from Nina slides across my iMessage.

Hi.

God, she's so annoying. I can't believe I ruined my perfect relationship with Ellie for someone who communicates like a middle school boy.

"Who's texting you?" asks Jake. I don't respond. "This is your Venus conjunct Pluto issue."

"Excuse me?" I ask. I know Jake Perez has told me about this aspect of my chart before, but I've taken care to avoid preserving it in my memory. I know my sun, moon, and rising, but I don't fuck with the aspects. I respect that Jake is into it, but for me, it's a line that cannot be crossed. The last thing I need is more minutiae to obsess over.

"How many times do I have to explain it to you, Prue?" Jake Perez asks. He sips his wine and his lips are red. "You attract stalkers."

I text Nina back. *I admire your brevity.*

"Nina isn't a stalker," I say. "She hardly even likes me."

"Remember Thomas?" Jake asks.

"Gawd," I say. Jake set me up with Thomas, so he was dragged into his post-breakup cling. For several months, Thomas just "happened" to be everywhere I was—every party, every yoga class... I even saw him at my therapist's office. Once Thomas cornered Jake in a 7-Eleven demanding an explanation for the demise of our barely relationship. I really can't imagine dating a man again. Too needy. Also not pretty enough.

Annoying as it was, a part of me secretly enjoyed Thomas's obsession. For a few desperate months, his entire world revolved around *moi*. As I sip my beer, I feel a strange sense of loss at the fact that Thomas has likely moved on.

"I like being stalked," I say. "Stalk me, bitch."

"You're unwell," Jake says.

I sip my beer again, then grin at Jake Perez. "Oh, wait," I say. "You already did."

"Pardon?"

Once Jake told me that he decided to befriend me after seeing a photo of me on a mutual friend's Facebook page and thinking I looked cool. I like to bring it up constantly. Mostly because it embarrasses him, but also because it makes me feel good. I guess you could say it was my first experience being recognized.

"Why did you decide to be my friend?" I ask.

Jake rolls his eyes, then his entire head. "Not a day goes by that I don't regret telling you that."

Dinner? Nina texts back.

"I can't believe you're going on a date right now," Jake Perez says to me when we leave the restaurant. "You were, like, just dumped."

"It's not a date," I say. "And I wasn't dumped. In the words of Ross Geller, I'd call it a break."

"She said she doesn't want to hear from you," says Jake Perez.

"Until she gets back," I say.

"You're delusional," he says. He takes my cigarette from my fingers, drags it. "But I'm glad Nina's a Scorpio." After an exhale: "There's no way you can handle one of us."

I meet up with Nina at a Mexican restaurant with flaming margaritas. They ask if we want to sit outside or inside. The patio is really cute, but I have horrible circulation. "Inside," I say, and Nina looks at me kind of strange. She looks good in her normal uniform: a silk crop top, high-waisted Levi's, a black braided belt, a thin gold chain. If she were to DJ, her name could be DJ High-Wasted, although she isn't really ever wasted.

"Do you have any siblings?" she asks when we're seated.

"Is this a date?" I ask.

Nina laughs, thankfully. I need her to loosen up.

"Do you want it to be?" She bites her lip and her freckles scrunch.

"I'm not in the mood to be interviewed," I say.

"I'm a journalist," she says. "I'm curious. I like getting to know people."

"And I'm an artist," I say. "I love to deflect."

She laughs.

"Do you have siblings?" I ask.

"Nope," she says.

I light up. I never meet only children. This is exciting. "Me neither!"

"Shocker," she says.

"I never learned to share." I dunk a chip in guacamole mainly for something to do with my hands. I'm not hungry. I place the chip on my plate.

"Do you get jealous when people talk about their siblings?" Nina asks.

"No," I say.

"You don't want them?"

"No."

"Why?"

"Lack of interest."

"What do you want?"

I decide to quote Lana. "Money, power, glory."

She frowns. "You're pretty fame-obsessed."

A rebuttal comes quickly. "Yes, I'd like to be noticed." I pick up the previously discarded chip on my plate. "As a queer woman, my story has been erased by the canon." I'm trying my absolute hardest to say this with a straight face.

"A white woman with a law degree," Nina says. "I'd hardly call your kind erased... You basically invented the canon." This turns me on.

"Which makes me the perfect person to subvert it," I say, then bite the chip.

After two drinks Nina asks me if I want to go to a show downtown. Some DJ she likes. In the Lyft, she puts an Adderall in my hand. Now this is a date.

I swallow it while Nina asks the driver for his auxiliary cable. She puts on Drake. Interesting choice.

"So are you going to write about all this?" I ask.

"Depends," she says. Then she starts rolling her body to Drake. She looks good, though.

"Did you really like the track?" I ask. The Adderall has already given me courage.

"Prudence," she says.

"No one calls me that," I say.

She jabs me in the rib cage. "You really care about my approval, don't you?"

"Only because Jax does," I say. "I don't really care about the people who read *Pitchfork*." I can't tell if I'm lying. "I want to win over the red states."

"Yes, 'Dearly Queerly' definitely has that alt-right appeal," Nina jokes. She reaches for her iPhone and switches the song.

"Oh god," I say.

Nina rolls down the windows and starts chanting along with Yumiko's voice on the speaker.

"Oh, this song," says the driver.

I try to hold back my smile.

The driver drops us in a parking lot in front of an enormous millennial-pink warehouse.

"Oh," I say. "This is near where American Apparel was invented."

Nina says nothing. I don't know many people who are as good at keeping their thoughts in their head as I am. I light a cigarette outside and she shares it with me. In between drags, she gushes about this DJ we're about to see and I can't help but feel a bit jealous.

As we walk up the stairway, she grabs my hand and I feel a little flutter. I remember when I felt this way with Ellie. On our first date, she took me to an indie rock show at the Teragram Ballroom downtown. Neither of us is really into rock music, but the band is a client of hers and I think she was trying to impress me. We got to stand in the VIP section and smoke a blunt with the band afterward. During the show, we danced the way we thought we were supposed to dance at rock shows, kind of thrashing against each other, jokey and playful. I'm pretty sure I did an air guitar and she laughed. The memory gives me a little pang. I consider texting her, but I want to respect her wishes that I don't contact her. I'm toxic, and she's an angel. If nothing else, she deserves for me to leave her alone.

"I need another cigarette," I say when I spot some people smoking out the stairwell windows. I practically run over there and light up. Looking out at the shimmery buildings as smoke burns my lungs, I feel a brief sense of peace.

"You have an oral fixation," Nina says.

"Thanks, Sigmund," I say. She raises an eyebrow like she's impressed I know who Freud is, which, frankly, is sad.

I put it out after only a few puffs. It's really that first drag I'm after. The theatrics of lighting the cigarette and that pensive first drag. I take one more look at the moon and then grab her hand. She leads me up the stairwell and down a pink-lit hallway, then into a steamy room filled with people who look like they belong in the Kingdom. I wonder if any of them will be here.

As soon as Nina and I are in the middle of the morass, I feel an arm on my shoulder and jump.

"Ohhh, Vaga is out." It's Beau. His energy immediately shatters the romance I was feeling with Nina. I feel his beady eyes all over my body.

"Shut up," I say, as he pulls me into a bony hug. My least favorite thing about the Kingdom is all the hugging; it's barbaric. Beau brushes his bony knuckles along my skull and teases my hair. The sociopathic brother I never wanted. I slap him on the arm.

The lines shift and, yay, the bar is open; I leap toward it. As I order, I hope Nina isn't talking to Beau. I'm thrilled when she swoops her arm around my waist. "Grab me a Tecate?" After handing her a drink, I recognize a familiar figure edging toward the stage. Holy shit. It's Wyatt. Agnes is behind her. I squeeze Nina's arm.

"I wanted to surprise you," she says. I kick my Timberland boot and do a little scream.

Next thing I know I'm at the Kingdom. I don't remember many details from the show, but I assume my lizard brain enjoyed it. Jax is in front of me cutting lines, and I wonder if he was at the show too. I look around the twilit loft, watching artsy weirdos with whom I have varying degrees of familiarity snort white powder off gold trays and exchange pills in elusive handshakes, and it makes me think of Andy Warhol's Factory. Jax is Andy; I'm his Edie Sedgwick. I guess that would make me dead for two years (I'm pretty sure she overdosed at twenty-eight), which, given the combination of drugs in my system at this moment, makes me laugh for some reason.

A puffy parka swings through the window from the fire escape, pulls me from my thoughts.

"Yumiiiii," Jax says. I've never heard him call her this.

Instead of looking at Jax, Yumiko looks me right in the eye. Her eyes are huge and round and watery—sweet, with an underlying tinge of scary. "You gonna win my case, bitch?"

Jax looks at her confused, and I immediately grab Yumiko by the parka collar. I'm self-conscious for a second, but Beau, Pilar, and Nina are all in their private drug zones. Beau screams "fuck" at his phone. Pilar is braiding Nina's hair. Jax turns to them, his eyes glassy and vacant.

On the fire escape, Yumiko just laughs in my face—haunting, unhinged. I imagine myself in Palm Springs, lying out by the pool at twilight, naked and exposed, but also feeling myself.

"Of course I'm going to win your case," I say, then I laugh back in her face.

I think about 1950s housewives on benzos, or quaaludes I guess. Downers keep women passive and in the home, unable to do anything but vacuum rugs and suck dick. Uppers make women participate in the marketplace. We talk a lot, unafraid of what people will think, like men all the time. Women on Adderall are magazine editors and CEOs and doctors and, apparently, lawyers. Girl bosses. I lick my lips.

"Vaga doesn't lose."

Back inside, Nina clutches a Budweiser in the corner of the room, her skin glowing blue, and I move toward her almost without thinking. She's fiddling with her jean jacket pocket. I swing my hip toward hers, but she doesn't seem to notice, or maybe she's ignoring me. Something cold hits my shoulder.

"Thanks," I say, taking a cold beer from her hand. I pop it open and it fizzles. "How do you know Beau?" I ask. He's sitting on the couch and I glare at him a little. I'm feeling unlike myself. Confident, assertive, aggressive. I've only really ever felt this way while writing, but this is the new me. Amphetamine feminist.

Nina just shakes her head and laughs.

I glare at Beau a little harder, squinting my eyes to the point I almost can't see. He's staring blankly at the smoke floating up from Pilar's cigarette, a thin gray snake weaving up to the tin ceiling. I momentarily become transfixed, plucked from my rage. Suddenly Beau pokes Pilar on the shoulder like a twelve-year-old boy and I start glaring again.

"I think he's bad news," I say.

Nina just laughs again.

"I'm glad I'm just one big joke to you," I say.

"Oh please," she says. She adjusts her jean jacket and reminds me of James Dean somehow. Like if he were a hot girl. "You aren't serious, are you?"

"How can I be serious when I'm such a joke?"

"Where is this coming from?"

"I asked you a question and you laughed," I say.

"I'm sorry," she says. "I'm high." She licks her upper lip and I want to bite it, half in a sexual way and half in a violent way. "Beau and I went to high school together."

"Was he your weed dealer?"

She laughs and licks her lip again. "Yes, actually."

Jax appears out of nowhere with a tray of shot glasses. I'm sick of shots at this point but I do one anyway.

"Fuck, I love this game." I'm on a skateboard, soaring through the air.

Beau laughs. "You've said that, like, twelve times." He flips his bangs and the light from the TV makes his hair shine and it looks kind of cool.

I'm in an unfamiliar apartment now. It's high up; we're looking at the tops of buildings. Big windows, but it's not the Kingdom. I don't remember leaving.

One of the windows flies open. A hand hits my thigh. I look to my right. It's Nina. I try to smile at her and she says, "Freak." Then she wraps her arm around my waist and pulls me close to her. Her body is warm and soft, and for a second I feel safe.

"Sup, bitches," says Yumiko. She looks me in the eye again. "My little esquire bitch."

"I told you, babygirl," I say while looking in Yumiko's eyes. It must be the uppers, or maybe my new outlook on life, induced by the uppers. "I got you."

"Hey!" Beau shouts at me. "Focus on the game."

I redirect my eyes to the screen and the Xbox controller in my hand, try to avoid hitting trees and other obstacles. I guess I'm racing Beau, who is also holding a controller. His thigh is shaking against mine.

"What do you mean, 'you got her'?" Nina asks. I'm nervous for a second that she knows Yumiko is my client. I haven't said anything, but maybe she's done some digging.

"The game!" Beau says again, and when I return my gaze to the screen it says I've "died." Oh well.

"Too literal," I say. As I put down my controller, Yumiko opens her parka and my eye is drawn to something in her inside jacket pocket.

Nina grabs my thigh and whispers in my ear: "She's packing heat."

For a second I think Nina is joking and I laugh. Also, I'm relieved we've moved on from the esquire bit. Then I realize Yumiko is really carrying a gun. It has a shiny gold handle and it's actually really pretty. The parka swings closed. Yumiko is delivering an enthusiastic interpretive dance, and I look outside the window again. The streetlights outside hurt my eyes. I look back at Yumiko, her jacket open again, my eye hitting the gold handle.

"What the *fuck*?" Pilar screams as she comes out of the bathroom with Jax. I didn't even know they were here. "Is that a *gun*?"

Yumiko looks embarrassed, like her mom just walked in on her masturbating.

"Dude, chill," Beau says.

"Is it, though?" Jax asks. "You know I don't fuck with weapons or violence." He holds up two peace signs. "Namaste." He laughs a little.

"This isn't funny," Pilar says, grabbing her purse from the table. She heads for the door.

Yumiko runs to stop her and grabs her arm. "Wait," she says.

Pilar freezes, looking legitimately afraid.

Yumiko reveals the gun and puts it on the floor. A slow and theatrical surrender. A Tarantino movie.

Jax runs over to Pilar and wraps her in his arms, and—to my shock—Pilar begins weeping.

"I'm sorry," Yumiko says.

Pilar looks right at me. "I knew your friend was sketch," she says. "Everything has been sketch since she got here." She frees herself from Jax's grasp. "I'm done." She slams the door on the way out.

Jax looks like he wants to run after her, then he shifts his focus to Yumiko. "What the fuck?" he asks.

"I'm sorry," Yumiko says. "I had no idea you would freak out like that." She's using a voice I haven't heard, kind of soft and sincere. Maybe it's her actual, god-given voice.

"Toting a gun at four A.M. when we're all on drugs isn't chill at all," says Jax. "I mean, toting a gun is never chill."

"I'm just a little confused," says Yumiko. "I thought you all would be into it, honestly. You blast 'Paper Planes,' like, every night, and I've seen Pilar do fake gunshots with her hands on the chorus. You all do!"

"Emphasis on 'fake,'" says Jax.

"You work for *Grand Theft Auto*!" Yumiko says.

"It's a game," says Jax. "And frankly I'm very conflicted about the message it sends." He looks like he might cry for a second. "I've lost sleep over it."

"I understand," says Yumiko. "Listen, I don't like violence either. But I believe in protecting myself. And I really didn't think it would be a big deal."

"Well, it is," he says. "I'm going to talk to Pilar."

TEN

I wake up in my bed, alone, and feel accomplished. I roll around, take up as much room as possible. I sprawl and thrash and make imaginary snow angels. The light peeking in through the curtains hits my palm plant and casts a pretty shadow on the wall. I feel giddy.

Then I grab my phone, and there's a lot to take in.

First, a text from Jax. *Love you Vaga.*

It makes me uncomfortable, but I type back, *love you too,* because female conditioning.

Then Jake Perez: *Call Me By Your Dealer's Name. That's my new name for you. LOL.*

I type, *LOL.*

Then a new text from Jax. *But we need to talk.* Last night floats into my head. The gun in Yumiko's parka, glinting. Pilar's freakout, the Tarantino movie. Shame and embarrassment and some other things fill my stomach. Pilar looked me in the eyes, called me "sketch," and blamed me.

There's also a text from Nina. *Do you hate me?* I don't know why I'd hate her.

Why would I hate you? I type back. Then I realize I do hate her. Just a little bit. But revulsion is a crucial component of attraction. And she obviously doesn't respect me. Actually, I have no idea what she thinks, which only intensifies my stirrings.

I see those typing bubbles and then they disappear.

I meet Jax and Pilar at the Kingdom that afternoon. Everything looks dirty in the harsh afternoon light. I notice tufts of dust and scratches on the ceiling and beer cans everywhere. My instinct is to turn back toward the door, drive home or maybe to the ocean. But the traffic would be terrible and I'm a little high and would probably have a panic attack.

Pilar is sitting on the edge of the couch, smoking and staring out the window. Jax leads me over and I sit on the floor. For a second I imagine Nina rolling her joint on the table in front of me. I should probably text her. I know Jax and Pilar want me to play up the flirt for the sake of Shiny AF, about which I have no real ethical qualms (this is Hollywood), but I do feel momentarily confused. I mean, they are best friends with her. Shouldn't that be enough? Shouldn't our music be enough? I laugh a little at that thought.

Jax dips a tea bag in and out of a steaming mug. No one is saying anything, and I feel saliva building in my throat and it quickly becomes all I can think about. Eventually I swallow so loudly it seems to echo against the tin ceilings and then my cheeks get hot. I regret vaping on the way over.

"Last night was really not cool," Pilar says finally. She's still looking out the window. Jax is looking at his teacup and I'm looking all around.

"I'm so sorry," I say, looking toward Pilar. I feel her head shifting toward mine. *Make normal eye contact,* my inner voice says. *Kind and sympathetic. NOT creepy.* But I'm so high. I know my eyes are crazy. I try to focus on my breath, like they recommend in the guided meditations I don't listen to.

"I like you, Prue," she says, "but I don't know you that well. And last night you put us in an incredibly dangerous situation."

I nod. As my chin bobs up and down I feel like a doll. "I know," I said. "I had no idea that would happen. I was just as surprised as you." I mean, I am representing Yumiko for gun possession. I should have known that this could happen.

"Like, you said you know her from summer camp," Pilar says. "I trusted that we were in a safe space." She looks deep in my eyes and I swallow again. "And she—and you by association—betrayed that trust."

Pilar lights another cigarette and I swallow twice more. Jax just bobs the tea bag up and down, seemingly transfixed, and I realize he's higher than I am. I want to laugh at that, but instead I swallow one more time.

"She pulled a gun on us," Pilar says suddenly.

"Okay, okay," I say. "I wouldn't say she 'pulled a gun.'" My criminal defense brain steps in automatically. "She was showing us." I was pretty drunk, and I still haven't talked to Yumiko about it. But I'm pretty confident she wouldn't threaten anyone. "I really think she thought you would be into it. Like she said, because you act in a certain way—"

"It's an aesthetic," she says. "We don't like guns, weapons, or violence."

Jax looks up from his tea and nods furiously. I can tell he's trying as hard as I am to come up with the right facial expressions, and we share a brief and knowing smile.

"I get that," I say. "I can have a talk with her. Let her know that kind of thing is completely unacceptable."

"Yes," Pilar says. "That's what I was going to say."

"Same," says Jax.

"If Yumiko is going to stay on with us," Pilar continues, and something about the way she says "us" makes me feel happy, like everything is going to be okay, "she's going to have to promise not to do anything like that again."

I nod. "Of course." I'm proud of myself for saying the right things and not letting Pilar know how high I am.

"Also, why the fuck does she have a gun?" Pilar asks.

"For protection," I say. "Like she said."

"She's a white girl from Pennsylvania," Pilar retorts. "What on earth does she need protection from?" She steps toward me and grabs a chunk of my hair with an unsettling mix of aggression and tenderness. "I mean, she went to summer camp with you." She releases my hair and I get her point.

I want to tell Pilar that Yumiko has a fairly lengthy criminal record (mostly misdemeanors, but probably just due to her baby-blue eyes), that she's been involved—romantically and professionally—with some of the biggest arms dealers on each coast.

But I can't, so I don't.

"Everyone needs protection," I say instead.

The next morning I'm petting one of the cats when I notice a missed call and voice mail from my dad. He also texted me, thank god. I'm a millennial. I don't check voice mail. So much listening. Hopefully no one has died. I open the text.

Hello Prue. Your mother and I are in LA on the way back from Phuket. Would you like to get lunch?

He sent it only an hour ago. What time is it now? I check my clock: 9:13 A.M.

Of course, I type back. *Tell me when and where* ☺

Then I call Yumiko. It rings and rings and she doesn't answer. As I reach for my laptop to put on music, she calls back.

"Hi," I say.

"Hey." Her voice is distant and withdrawn.

"I talked to Pilar and Jax yesterday," I say. "They said you need to promise not to pull anything like the other night again." In this moment I feel like her lawyer. And she reminds me of one of my clients, just waiting for me to tell her what to do, as if I'm at all qualified to ever do that to anyone ever.

"I'm pretty embarrassed," she says.

"Don't be," I say.

"I mean," she says, her voice perking up, "I'm pretty shocked they were so bourgeois about it."

I laugh.

"Like, it's a gorgeous gold glock."

I remember the light dancing off it. "It was pretty," I say. "But unfortunately it's a deal breaker for them."

"It's no issue," Yumiko says. "I've left most of that behind."

I'm interested in her use of "most" for a second, then I decided to forget about it. "So you promise?"

"I promise."

This time my parents are staying at the Beverly Hills Hotel. I've never been, but I've seen the pink building in films and know it's famous for its wallpaper. My dad greets me outside. "Did you know it's thirty dollars for a hot dog here?" he whispers in my ear as though this is impressive.

My dad takes me into the garden restaurant. We pass many different variations of pink-and-green wallpaper. I vaped earlier, so I'm mesmerized. I'm grateful that my dad doesn't try to make small talk.

My mom is sitting at a table under an umbrella, half in the sun, stirring what appears to be an espresso with a tiny spoon. The restaurant is mostly empty and the sound of stirring reverberates.

"Hi, Mom," I say. I force a smile.

My mom nods with a hesitant expression. She's wearing a stiff gray suit, completely at odds with the aggressively casual surroundings.

"Your mother is very tired," says my dad.

When I was five years old, I came home from school with a drawing for my mom. I never had great motor skills. Doing my makeup presents a challenge to this day. But I tried my best. It was a portrait of her in a black dress with a tiny pearl necklace, and underneath it said I LOVE MY MOM. I gave it to her when she was smoking a cigarette in the sunroom, staring at a plant. She didn't say anything. My dad walked in and said, "Your mother is very tired."

"How was the trip?" I ask as I take a seat. I put my sunglasses on and instantly feel more comfortable.

Soon my parents and I are all on our phones again. I'm pretending to look at the *New York Times* home page while my thoughts start running. My dad is looking at his email and I feel like my mom is spying on me. Sometimes I think she's a literal spy. She doesn't emote. Wears only gray. Always "very tired." Why? It's not like she has a job. I literally have no idea how she fills her time.

Nina texts me and I'm grateful for the distraction.

Hi.

Ugh. Such a Scorpio.

Chatty Cathy, I type back. I look up and my mom is raising her eyebrow at me. I don't think she saw what I wrote, but she's always judging me, and this time she happens to be correct. It was a dumb thing to say.

"Prue," my mom says, addressing me for the first time this afternoon. "What are you wearing?"

Honestly, I've forgotten. I try to look down at myself without being obvious about it. "A tunic," I say. "It's modern."

She frowns at me.

"The style is different in LA," I say. "It's not as formal."

"'Style,'" she says, "is generous." Even though this hurts my feelings, a small part of me feels proud to be descended from such a scathing critic.

A text pops up on my phone. I hope it's Nina, but unfortunately it's from Walgreens. My refill is due. Suckers. I don't need it anymore! *Thriving,* I almost type as a wet Cobb salad burp rises up in my throat.

The next day I hang out with Jake Perez at Echo Park Lake. We bring a bottle of wine and a joint and a loaf of bread and chill.

A large bird approaches us, making weird sounds and frightening me, when a text from Nina pops up.

Jake Perez lets out a dramatic sigh. "Venus conjunct Pluto problems," he says, then throws some bread at the bird. I'm mad at him for encouraging the bird to approach. More birds follow.

I scoot back, feeling paranoid. Birds really scare me, as do most living things.

"You've been single for like a day and you already have a new girlfriend," says Jake. He puts the rest of the piece of bread in his mouth. I'm scared for him, worried that the birds will lunge at his mouth.

"I do not," I say. I look at my phone and see a text from Jax, calling a meeting for the EP that evening at the Kingdom. I look up at a tall palm tree swaying in the wind and feel lucky I live in California and my parents are gone, far away on the other side of the country.

"Your Aquarius moon gives you strong powers of rationalization," he says. "Strong defense mechanisms."

"I never should have given you my birth time," I say, and I mean it. I don't think Jake Perez actually believes in astrology, nor does he understand it. He uses it only to read people to their faces, to rip into my personality in particular. And who am I kidding? I love it for the same reason.

"Can we talk about something else?" I watch two birds fight over the last piece of bread and feel lucky they're focused on something other than us.

"Sure," says Jake. "I checked that Ixland Prinxexxa post again." God. Out of the flames and into the fire. "It has a lot of reblogs, Prue."

I know he wants me to feel concerned, but I'm flattered and try to suppress a smile. "How many?"

"Your lack of concern concerns me," he says.

"Why should I be concerned?" I ask. "I look good." A goose starts waddling toward me and I back up. "And they're tasteful."

"What about your bar license?"

"I'm going to quit law soon, anyway," I say. "And besides, I don't think being naked online violates any ethical rules."

"Well, you'll have to get another job, right?" he says. "Nude pictures of you plastered all over the internet doesn't exactly scream 'employ me.'"

"I don't want to scream 'employ me,'" I say. "And I wouldn't exactly say my photos are 'plastered all over the internet.' It's one dumb Tumblr."

Jake shakes his head. "Well, aren't you concerned about who took them? It's wild to me that you don't even know and don't seem remotely interested in finding out."

He's right, but I'm afraid of the truth. What if I hooked up with Beau that night? What if I did something worse?

"What you don't know can't hurt you," I say.

"Of course it can!" he shouts. "My aunt had a lump in her breast for seven months, she kept refusing to get it checked out. And guess where she is now?"

"Where?" I ask.

"Dead!" he says. "She's dead, Prue."

I want to feel sympathetic, but I'm pretty sure Jake made this up.

"Good thing these puppies are lump-free," I say, then clutch my chest.

"Please don't call your breasts 'puppies,'" he says. "It's vile."

"Please don't call my puppies 'breasts,'" I say, then shimmy up in his face.

"You're impossible," Jake says as he backs away. He turns his body completely away from me and we sit in silence for a few seconds. I stare at the geyser spewing water in the middle of the lake. The color is a bright turquoise, unnatural looking, probably dyed.

"How was seeing your parents?" Jake Perez asks finally, seeming to realize I'm not going to join him in his rage over my being exploited. I'm fine with being exploited. My entire existence screams "exploit me." I was born with so much privilege I squander, the world deserves to get something back.

"Bleak," I say.

Just as the birds are starting to waddle off, Jake throws another piece of bread in their direction and I want to slap him.

"Venus conjunct Pluto is a master of projection," he says.

And then I do slap him, hard on the leg. His squeal scares the geese and they scatter.

I go to the Kingdom that evening as ordered.

The sky outside the windows is a cool blue, which infiltrates the apartment and makes everything seem relaxed and holy.

"Vagaaaa," Jax calls from behind the panes. He comes over to give me a hug. He's wearing a black silk tunic and I'm flattered that he's jacking my style. A large crystal pendant hangs around his neck on a gold chain. Leopard-print socks. No shoes. A focused expression.

Pilar follows closely behind him. Just as she kisses the air beside my cheek, there's a knock on the door. As Jax goes to get it, Pilar and I are left alone. My stomach begins to clench and I ask about her day to fill the silence. She starts venting about something that happened at work and I try to make the appropriate facial expressions, but I'm just thinking about how stern she was the other day and how she called me "sketch."

Jax comes back into the room with Yumiko. Pilar goes silent. And I swallow.

"Can I have a quick word with you guys outside?" Yumiko asks.

"Sure," says Jax, "but make it quick. We have work to do."

Yumiko goes out to the fire escape and we all follow. It's decorated with candles and crystals, like a small shrine, and I realize I don't know if this is Jax's or Yumiko's handiwork.

A breeze hits and I watch the palms sway. It feels nice, and Jax lights a Marlboro Red and Pilar lights one of her skinny blue cigarettes. To fit in, I light a Parliament. The smoke burns my throat and I cough. I'm not used to smoking sober.

"I just wanted to apologize for the other night," Yumiko says finally. "It was a serious misjudgment on my part—"

"Misjudgment?" Pilar interrupts. "A misjudgment is driving after you've had a few drinks, not pulling a gun on your friends."

"I didn't pull a gun on you," Yumiko says, and as her lawyer, I'm proud of her careful use of language. "I was just trying to show you."

"Jesus, that's what Prue said," Pilar says. "What kind of weird camp did you go to? Was it for aspiring criminals?"

"Look, Prue has nothing to do with this," Yumiko says. "This was all me. I really thought you would think it was cool... I misju—I was really, monumentally stupid."

Pilar nods, seeming satisfied with this explanation. Jax is dragging and staring at the trees, clearly elsewhere. I feel bonded to him.

"You put us in danger," Pilar says.

"The safety was on," Yumiko says. Her expression gets serious. "I want you all to know I really value our friendship and our art."

Jax turns his gaze back to her on the word "art." I pull my cigarette to my lips and take care not to inhale this time.

"Meeting you guys has been the best thing to happen to me in a while, and I would never do anything to jeopardize that."

Pilar nods. I wonder if she still thinks I'm "sketch." Maybe she just said that in the heat of the moment. I'm no stranger to saying rude things I don't mean when emotionally charged. It's human nature. That's why I've never really vibed with "the law." It assumes we're rational, and we just aren't.

"The safety was on?" Pilar asks, tapping her cigarette on the metal ledge. "So it couldn't have gone off by accident?"

"Nope," says Yumiko. "I'm very responsible with my guns." She looks at me and I swallow. "But if you all aren't comfortable, I completely respect that."

"You have to," says Pilar. "I just can't be in a situation like that again." She ashes her cigarette. "I'm not twenty-four anymore."

"I understand." Yumiko looks up at the sky, pauses. "Also, I unexpectedly saw an ex that night. I know I have a tendency to scare people when I'm feeling powerless. I'm working on it in therapy." I'm surprised Yumiko is in therapy, then I remember it was court mandated; it's in the record. She looks at me with her big, watery blue eyes. "But that's no excuse," she says.

Soon, Yumiko and Pilar are hugging. And Jax and I are just staring at the trees, likely thinking about our art to avoid the emotional intimacy beside us. When Yumiko and Pilar release, Jax announces we need to "get cracking." Pilar follows him through the window back inside, and just when I'm about to join, Yumiko grabs my hand.

"I'm sorry again," she says. "I can't thank you enough for all you've done for me. I'm so embarrassed."

I feel guilty. Yumiko has just been this character in my mind, a manic cartoon to entertain me. I've broken ethical rules and exploited her.

"It's okay," I say. "I hardly remember it anyway."

Inside, Pilar sits beside Beau, who has just appeared, as he does. Jax is standing opposite them on the other side of the coffee table, as though he's the teacher and they're his students. Yumiko and I sit on opposite sides of the couch, perched on its edges.

"Okay," Jax says. He leans over and puts out his cigarette on the tin ashtray on the table. His crystal pendant hits the coffee table and it dings, and I notice for the first time that no music is playing. A first for the Kingdom. The silence makes me nervous. I become conscious of the fact that I'm breathing, and I try to breathe more quietly. The breath has always been a source of anxiety for me. Just like airplanes, breathing will never not be weird to me. We have to suck air in and out of us every few seconds in order to stay alive. Nothing about bodies isn't weird. Nothing about being alive isn't weird. I try not to think about it, instead focus on Jax.

"I know you all know Party Jax," he says. "But I'd like you to meet Business Jax." He taps his leopard-print sock on the floor. Pilar lets out an airy little Gemini giggle, and Jax shoots her a *not now* Leo look. She promptly shuts up, then takes a sip of clear liquid from a gold-rimmed glass.

"Wicked Ice wants an EP from us," he says with a serious tone I've never heard from him before. "This is a big deal. A huge opportunity. Something I've wanted my whole life, and I assume you feel the same."

Beau elbows me in the rib and I'm mad that he's here. I had a dream that I confronted Jax about Beau under the Kingdom's neon-lit tin ceiling. "Why is Beau getting a free ride?" I asked, grabbing the collar of his pink flannel. Jax's eyes just got really big and bulgy, and I felt like he was about to hit me and then I woke up.

As far as I can tell, Beau just provides drugs and takes questionable photos of us. I guess every musical group has someone like this. I guess I wouldn't know. I'm not used to working with others. All my other shit was just me in my bedroom on Garage-Band, my cats screaming outside the door. Actually I started making raps even before I had cats: 2007 was the year M.I.A. released *Kala* and Kanye released *Graduation* and Vagablonde created a SoundCloud page.

Jax is still talking. I nod fiercely to prove I'm paying attention. I sip my PBR.

"I want to put us on a tight deadline," he says. "It's going to be tough, but we have no choice."

I swallow. I'm starting to get a little scared.

"What's happened to us is the type of thing musicians wait their whole lives for. This is when everything changes."

I don't love change. I stare out the window and become mesmerized by a palm tree that seems to sway with the cadence of Jax's speech.

When I zone back in, Jax is asking us about our schedules. "Pilar, I know you work Tuesday and Thursday nights." He's writing things down on a notepad, very serious. Pilar complains about her manager constantly. His name is Rodger. She does the best impression of him. I have no idea where she works, but I do know her entire birth chart. "Prue, you told me you could take some time off from cases." I nod dutifully, and then I can't help but smile. "We need Beau for listening sessions, but he's always available." Jax unleashes a laugh, and everyone else laughs too, excited for a release. I worry I'm laughing too hard so I sip my PBR.

"Yumiko," he says, "I don't really know your schedule. We'll need you I'd say two to three hours a day for your vocals, but more for your energy."

"I'm all yours," Yumiko says. She smiles big and her gold tooth flickers.

Jax unleashes a warm smile, which warms me. "The most work is going to be between me and Prue," he says. "Obviously."

I inhale sharply. *I can do this,* I think. *I can handle a challenge. I passed the California Bar Exam.*

"I'm thinking like three P.M. to six A.M. for us every day for the next two weeks," he says. He's smiling like he's happy, but these hours seem insane. "The first few hours will be about getting into a vibe, getting the energy right." He clutches his crystal. "We probably won't start recording until the sun goes down"— he smiles—"as we do." Then he laughs, and I laugh too, again too hard. I inhale sharply again. I can handle this. I'll just change my sleep schedule. And no more new cases!

"Perfect," I say, then force a smile.

ELEVEN

I go to brunch with Nina the next morning. It's the first day of what Jax called "Shiny Season." I try to sleep in, but one of the cats wakes me at seven A.M. I don't know where the other one is. I try to remember the last time I saw her. A few days ago? One time one of the cats left for around seven days, pretty soon after I got them, so I'm not super concerned. Cats are tough. I decide the one with me is Missy. "Ennui" was always hard to say.

We eat at this place called Winsome on the south end of Echo Park, toward downtown, under this weird apartment building I've always wanted to live in because it's basically all glass. Nina's wearing a loose white T-shirt and vintage black Levi's.

We're seated in the back corner in a camel leather booth, beneath teal wallpaper. Our waitress looks like she's about to die, but in a pretty way. She's so thin, like she might float away. I assume she's on some kind of raw diet.

I order grains and eggs, my favorite on the menu. I'm not really a foodie, I mean my favorite food is Domino's. But this shit is good. Crispy grains covered in cool green cilantro-yogurt sauce and fried eggs with runny yolks.

Nina orders a burger, which I respect. And we both order Bloody Marys.

"I notice you rap a lot about your hair," Nina says after sipping hers.

"Sherlock Holmes," I say.

She rolls her eyes at me.

"What? You think I should be rapping about, like, global warming? Gun control? Peace in the Middle East?" I throw up a peace sign.

"You make being politically conscious sound like a bad thing," she says.

"Hair is political!" I accidentally yell, and someone in the booth beside us turns to stare. I lower my voice a bit. "Look, I have no business speaking to how countries should be governed or how to save our rapidly crumbling planet." I watch Nina's face to see if she's buying it. "Some people might find the topic of hair trivial, but I'd argue that women don't really have the luxury of not caring about our hair." I pull the celery stick from my drink and take a bite. "So I guess you could say my work is a radically honest portrayal of the crushing weight of gender performance."

Nina's expression remains inscrutable, and I don't blame her—I don't really buy what I'm saying either. I just love my hair!

"You seemed pretty fixated on your hair in Palm Springs," she says, "in a way that seemed kinda, I don't know..."

"Vain?" I attack myself before she can. "They aren't mutually exclusive. Politics and vanity, that is."

Nina picks up her burger. "When did you start rapping?" she asks, then dives in for a ravenous bite. It's sexy.

"Um," I say. "End of college."

"Where did you go?"

I poke my dish, which seems off somehow, with my fork. I normally like the sauce, but at this moment I'm just focused on how unnaturally green it is. Neon almost, like nothing anyone should ever eat. Like poison. I look up. "Wait, is this for a story?"

Nina wipes her mouth. Her freckles scrunch. "I'm getting to know you."

"Okay." I shrug. "Either way I'm cool with it."

The waitress floats over and asks if we're okay. *Everything's great.*

"I went to Cal," I say. "And, no, I did not study science."

Nina laughs, then straightens her expression. "What did you major in?"

"Rhetoric," I say. "But I believe your original question pertained to my rap career."

"Yeah," she says. She licks some burger juice from her top lip and I fantasize about biting it.

"It was my junior year of college," I say. I take a mini sip of my Bloody, try to look cute. "I had recently discovered the magical elixir that is cannabis."

Nina laughs again, sips her Bloody. "Bless," she says. "Wait. You didn't smoke weed until you were a junior in college?"

"False," I say. "I just hadn't discovered its magic." I cut into the egg and yolk pours over the grains and bleeds onto the plate. "Can I finish, writer girl?"

"Please," she says.

I force myself to take a bite, not because I want to, but because I know Nina cares about my answer, and I want to make her wait. Her dark brown eyes watch me chew with curiosity. I pretend I'm enjoying my food, but I'm not.

"I was deep in the midst of my first spiritual high, surrounded by my undergrad crew—a gaggle of beautiful gay men." I sip again for dramatic effect, then I feel a bit drunk. "We went to this party on Haste Street, where all the frat stars lived. These idiot lacrosse players started to battle rap to MF Doom."

"Doom forever," Nina says. I smile, but I'm also annoyed at her for interrupting my story.

"I was overcome with intense anger," I say. "Rage, really. How dare these idiots defame Doom? I had a good buzz on at this point, so I jumped in the circle. I started up a freestyle of my own, interrupting one of these idiots."

Now Nina is giggling. "Was it good?"

"No!" I laugh. I am drunk. I need to find some stimulants before I record tonight. I guess that's what Beau is for. "But that was my first taste," I say. "I felt adrenaline. That rush. The high."

I scoop some runny egg on my fork, then put it back on the plate. "And I've been chasing it ever since."

Nina kisses me when she drops me off at the Kingdom. It gives me a little butterfly, but I quickly suppress it. I'm being insane, getting romantic with this girl—woman, journalist—right after ending the best relationship of my life. I should be focusing on my art anyway.

No one answers when I ring the doorbell. I check my phone: 3:03 P.M. Jax said 3:00, right? I check my Google Calendar. Maybe I wrote it down wrong.

Finally Beau opens the door, almost running me over.

"Oh, hey, Vaga," he says. I don't like him calling me this.

"Where's Jax?" I ask.

"Sleeping," he says. "You can come in, though."

He lets me in. I'm annoyed at him letting me in as though it's some favor. This is my project. I am Shiny AF. But I'm impressed by what a diva I'm being. When Jake read my tarot cards a few months ago, he told me this would happen when I got famous.

I walk down the hallway and see Yumiko sitting on the couch.

"Hey, Vaga," she says. I guess this is my name now.

"Hi," I say, now shy.

She pats the space next to her on the couch. I obey. There is some music I've never heard before on the speakers—something raucous and stringent, no hints of R&B. Must be Yumiko's doing.

"So Jax said," she says, lowering her voice to a whisper, I assume because Jax is sleeping. "Jax said that you aren't taking any more cases. Does this mean you passed mine off to someone else?"

"No, no," I say. She looks so sad it breaks my heart. "I already filed your brief!" I can't remember ever having sounded this enthusiastic about law.

"Oh, good," she says, looking relieved. She puts her parka around me. I've seen Yumiko only in a parka. I've never seen her arms. "I don't normally trust lawyers," she says, and I back away slightly. "But I trust you."

I smile.

It's dark out when Jax finally emerges from his bedroom. I'm pretty drunk at this point, and whatever else. I'm French braiding Pilar's hair. I'm really good at French braiding. I used to be convinced this was the only reason I had friends. It still might be.

Jax stretches his arms and blue light hits his translucent kimono. "Okay, leggo," he says. I drop Pilar's hair and we both rise, like his loyal army. Pilar's hair falls out of the braid. Her hair is shiny and slippery, not the best for braiding. Too beautiful, almost. Yumiko appears from the fire escape. I think about checking my phone for the time, but I don't. It's best not to know.

Soon we're behind the shoji panes and Jax is playing us a bunch of beats, and rhymes start swirling through my head.

The next morning I wake up with a cat lying on my chest. I push her off and she paws my face. I push her again and she obeys. I guess I have to come to terms with the fact that one of my cats is missing. I wonder if Missy misses Ennui. Probably not. God knows I don't. Cats are selfish, and that's why I respect them.

I'm so tired. The light in my room is bright as hell. I normally wake up early, around seven. But this light suggests it's much later.

I grab my phone. 10:00 A.M. Damn. I feel an anxious pang about work emails I may have missed. But then I remember I'm an artist now.

I have a bunch of texts on my phone.

From Jax: *Flames, Vaga. Gotta keep up this momentum. Almost Famous.* Then a crying-laughing sideways-face emoji.

The night floods back to me. Last night I wrote a song making fun of that dumb "it's all happening" line. Making fun but also embracing it, just like Nina said. That's our vibe. I think about how critics can shape artists, whether that's okay, and if I even trust Nina. The cat jumps on me again and I know I have to feed her, but I'm too tired to get up.

From Jake Perez: *Just saw your ex at Gelson's. He cornered me in the produce aisle. Your Venus conjunct Pluto issues are now impacting me and this is not okay. Call me.*

From Nina: *I heard you still got it.* I get a little flicker of excitement, then paranoia. I wonder who told her that. Does she like me as a person or just as a musician to write about? These are very celebrity issues, I think, and start to feel better. These are the types of issues I've wanted since I moved to LA.

Missy is now screaming bloody murder. I sit up and my head pounds. I feel like I've been hit by a truck. I wonder if it's the alcohol and the drugs or the creative expression or the new crush or all of the above. I lie back down and fall asleep to the sound of Missy's screams.

When I wake up again, it's around twelve. I can't remember the last time I've slept until twelve. Probably college. I call Jake Perez and we decide to get lunch. Well, breakfast for me. We go to this weird diner I've never been to, for good reason. Jake is obsessed with terrible diners because they remind him of *Pulp Fiction* and his taste is very obvious. I'm not really a diner person. They never seem to have alcohol and the lighting is always unflattering and I never know what to order. I go mostly because whenever Jake Perez accuses me of being a bad friend I can say, "But I go to all those terrible diners you love."

"You need a restraining order" is the first thing Jake says when we sit down. He always took Thomas's obsession with me a little too seriously. Sure, it was annoying the way he continued to insert himself in my life after our breakup, but ultimately harmless and slightly flattering. Not that his opinion means anything.

Jake orders something called "Southern Decadence" that looks revolting.

I order a spinach omelet and Jake says, "You always have to make me look bad with your healthy-ass orders, don't you?"

"Nothing in this restaurant is healthy," I say. "I can assure you."

We both order black coffee, which cannot come soon enough.

"So what did he say?" I ask.

"He said he's worried about you."

My stomach sinks a bit, but I say nothing. I don't like when people worry about me, but I'm also flattered my lame ex is still paying attention. He must be watching my Instagram Stories. When I wake up and see that little red circle around my Instagram avatar, I immediately start deleting. I'm forced to see the first frame, which is typically me with droopy eyes singing the wrong words to a song, my arm around someone I don't know.

The coffee comes and I gulp so quickly it burns my tongue. I sip some water to soothe it.

"I mean, you've def been on one," Jake says. "But the point is that's none of his business."

"True," I say. Should I be worried about myself? Anxiety rises in my chest and wraps its grip around my throat. I swallow with difficulty.

"But get this," Jake Perez says. He wipes a droplet of coffee off his lip. "He told me he saw the nudies of you on le Tumbdizzle."

"Nudies?" is all I can manage. What year is this?

Jake lowers his volume to a whisper, but it still feels like he's screaming: "Your naked photos!"

"I got that," I say. "I was just surprised by your phrasing." I take another sip of coffee. My gaze floats toward the window and it's too bright so I look away.

"Jesus, Prue," Jake says. "The things you choose to dwell on are always so bizarre." Our food comes and both plates look disgusting, unidentifiable food substances drowned in oil. Jake looks thrilled and begins to dig in. I focus on poking my omelet with my fork. It's bouncy, like rubber.

"I mean," Jake says when he comes up for air. "Aren't you freaked out?"

"Can we talk about something else?" I ask. "Like... how are you?"

"Wow," says Jake Perez. "Prudence Van Teesen wants to discuss something other than Prudence Van Teesen. The moment I've been waiting for my entire life."

I stick out my tongue at him. Jake Perez smiles and begins to tell me, in excruciating detail, about the blow job he received the previous night in the McDonald's parking lot behind Akbar.

I quickly fall into a nice little artist routine. I start waking up at around noon. Feed the cat, make coffee, go for a walk. I normally listen to whatever we've recorded the night before. Sometimes I listen to Missy or Nicki Minaj or M.I.A. for inspiration. Sometimes I listen to MF Doom beats and make notes on my phone.

Afterward I'll eat something. I'll go to brunch with Jake Pe-rez and we'll stare at our laptops, or I'll got to brunch with Nina and I won't be able to tell whether she's flirting with me or neg-ging me or using me, and the mystery keeps me enticed.

I start arriving at the Kingdom at around five or six. (There are only so many French braids I can do.) Once there, Pilar will hand me an Adderall and I'll start writing ideas on my iPhone to the beat of Yumiko's crazy Philly noise punk. I'll go out every half hour and smoke a cigarette with Yumiko at her shrine. Jax emerges around 6:30 in a different kimono every day. I wonder how many he has.

We get behind the shoji panes at around seven or eight, crack open PBRs, and Jax plays me some beats. He scrolls through them until I hear something that excites me, and then I hop in the "booth," which is just three mattresses shoved in the corner. Jax swears he does this out of artistic preference rather than necessity. "The sound is more raw," he says.

I like it in there, alone and surrounded by cushions. Safe and not afraid at all. This is where I belong.

I spit verses about the following topics: Wyatt Walcott's hair, swallowing B vitamins with beer, killing tech bros at Burning Man, *Clarissa Explains It All* as a necessary antidote to mansplaining, and the grotesque noises men make while exercising. I know this from the notes on my phone, not from my memory.

On day four, Beau greets me at the door with a massive DSLR in my face. I'm filled with fear, then a flicker of excitement. What the fuck is wrong with me?

Jax appears behind Beau, arm around his shoulders. The hallway is illuminated with the hints of natural light. I'm confused. Why is Jax awake during the day?

"Good news, Vaga," Jax says.

Beau snaps a photo and the click seems unnaturally loud. I jump a little. The flash burns my eyes.

"We're gonna be in *FADER*," he says. "Print."

I unleash a little squeal.

In the main room, Beau is pouring shots. I'm surprised to see Nina, who hasn't joined any of our artist sessions. That's what I'm calling them now. I said that to Jake Perez and he did a full-body eye roll, so I knew it was good. I prefer laughter, but I'll take disgust. Any emotional reaction is good. Mimi Carey makes people cry every time she performs.

Beau pours Nina a shot, a big one. "Drink up, writer girl," Jax says. This makes me giggle pretty hard for some reason. Nina looks at me like I'm insane. I just realize at this point that she's probably writing the *FADER* story.

Beau thrusts a shot glass in my hand. Then a massive puffy arm is around me. Yumiko. This sneaky bitch.

Beau fills my shot glass with whiskey and I sip it.

"Did you just sip your shot?" Yumiko yells in my ear. Then she grabs my shot glass out of my hand, throws it back. "No dead soldiers," she says.

Soon it feels much later and I'm on the edge of Jax's bed in between Nina and Beau. I guess we're not getting behind the panes tonight. Beau stands up and starts snapping pictures of us. He's been taking photos all night, mostly of me and Jax. Some of Pilar and Yumiko. I wonder why he's getting photos of Nina. She's just the writer. I instinctively shift away from her. She grabs my waist, pulls me back toward her, laughs in my face. I want to be angry, but she looks cute, her freckles all scrunched. I tap her nose with my index finger, and she jabs me in the ribs.

Pilar appears in the doorframe, her feathered jacket silhouetted by baby-blue light. She floats over and pulls my hand, twirls me in a circle. Mariah Carey's "Honey" pours in from the other room.

"The sexiest song of all time," I mutter under my breath. Pilar doesn't seem to hear me. No one notices me. Everyone is in their own fucked-up world.

Pilar is looking over at the bed, giggling. I follow her gaze and am shocked by what I see.

Nina and Beau are making out.

Anger bubbles up inside me. I want to go over there and rip them apart. I thought Nina was in love with me. Isn't this the whole point, why we're blowing up on the internet, because I seduced the right person?

I'm furious, but I don't want it to show. No one will notice anyway. Nina and Beau are deep in French. Pilar is dancing around like a fairy. I take her hand and pull her into the other room. On the dance floor, Jax dances alone. He holds up a gold tray covered in white residue like Simba in *The Lion King*.

"Yasss," he says when he spots Pilar and me. "My queens."

This is good, I think. *I'll just dance it off. I'll dance myself clean.*

The song switches to M.I.A.'s "Bamboo Banga." I can do this. I chant the lyrics.

Yumiko shimmies onto the dance floor and her parka shakes on the beat. She probably thinks this song is about her. Jax's kimono quivers. Pilar's feathered coat moves like a wave. I curse myself for not wearing a statement jacket.

The image of Beau and Nina pops back into my head and my stomach churns. Why is it so upsetting to me? It's not like we're married. I didn't even think I liked the girl. But I'm angry. So I leave.

"I gotta go," I say. I air-kiss everyone on the cheek and leave. No one seems to care.

Outside the sky is a lighter blue than I expected. Four thirty A.M., I guess. I call a Lyft. While I wait for it to arrive, I smoke a cigarette and stare at the faint hint of the moon.

The next day at around noon I go to Jake's. I have no texts from Nina and that crushes me.

"You look sad," he says when he opens the front door. He's wearing a ratty bathrobe and his facial hair is wild. "And skeletal."

I can't help but feel good about this. I've always been thin, except for that two-year period when my metabolism slowed down at the end of high school without my realizing it and I was still eating Chipotle burritos as a snack. My mom snapped out of her depression enough to let me know my appearance was unacceptable. She shamed me skinny, just like she shamed me into law school: "You're terrified of blood, Prue, and you still don't understand the stock market. Law seems like the only viable option."

"Thank you," I say, then kick off my Sambas.

"It's not a compliment," he says. "You look sick."

"It's probably the stress," I say, then pause for dramatic effect, "of recording." I know very well it's the Adderall. I've been diagnosed with eating disorders a few times in my life, but I don't think it's that big of a deal. I've never been hospitalized or anything.

"I'm making us popcorn," Jake says. "With butter."

"Great," I say. I lick my lips to show him I still have an appetite. But in reality I don't. This always happens when my weight drops. It'll be fine.

We decide to watch *Vicky Cristina Barcelona*, which I kind of hate. I don't care for voice-over. I hate Vicky and Cristina. If I wanted to see two frumpy, uptight white girls with too much money gallivant around Europe, I'd go back to high school. But María Elena. When she arrives at Juan Antonio's straight from the mental hospital everything changes. The woman is my dream. Disheveled and unstable, angrily chain-smoking while screaming about being a "genius."

We lie in his bed and eat popcorn and he pets my hair, which feels nice. Jake Perez is one of the few people I allow to touch me. I guess Jax also falls into that category now.

I feel weird when María Elena comes onto Cristina in the darkroom. This is normally my favorite scene, but this time it makes my skin crawl. Because I know they're all going to have sex with that overrated man later. Throuples sicken me. They're unnatural.

I pull out my phone. And Jake rolls his eyes at me.

I have no texts from Nina, only one from Jax.

We're taking today off. See you Saturday. Xx.

I have no idea what day it is, but I assume Saturday is tomorrow. I'm glad we're taking the day off. I need it. I've been working too hard.

"I need to go home and take a nap," I tell Jake.

"Now?" Jake has a serious thing about finishing movies.

"I'm sorry," I say. I grab my purse and head toward the door, then blow him a kiss. He responds by narrowing his eyes at me.

As I start my Saab, I decide my next song will be called "Genius."

When I get home, I turn off my phone, eat a massive bowl of cereal, and then sleep for fifteen hours.

TWELVE

When I'm not dreaming about a surreal continuation of the night, I tend to be stuck on an airplane or in a faraway, nonexistent country without my benzos. But this time my dream is just a slight variation on an actual memory.

It's Christmas Eve and I'm twenty-one, home from my senior year of college. It's after midnight and can't find my phone. The house is quiet and snow falls under the streetlights outside. I slink into the kitchen, which I assume is empty. I jump when I see my mom, quietly buttering her sprouted toast in dim lighting.

"You forgot your pants," my mom says, eyeing my outfit, which is just a T-shirt. Light from the streetlamp bounces off her buttered knife, which terrifies me in dreamland.

A buzzing sound suddenly echoes through the kitchen and I jump again, but my mom remains still. She eyes my phone on the marble counter and says, "Some girl keeps texting you."

My face reddens—my shame is intense and exaggerated in the dream. I snatch the phone and read my texts. It's this girl Lara, a bisexual, my first experience with a woman.

"Is there anything you need to tell me?" my mom asks.

I start to panic. "I got into Berkeley Law," I say. It's true, but I wasn't going to tell my mom or anyone else. I was going to move to Los Angeles and pursue music. But I froze, and I told her. And she was so happy. And snow was falling. And she hugged me and cried. And for the first time I felt like I had a mother.

When I wake up I still feel horrible, like I'm lying under a pile of bricks. My room is filled with bright white light that dizzies me. Jake Perez put up these blackout curtains when I moved in four years ago that are clearly not doing their job. LA is too bright. That's my one complaint. Shiny AF. I chuckle to myself a little, and phlegm loosens in my throat. I cough, which seems to lure the cat. Missy, whom I'm now calling Ennui because she seems depressed as hell, slinks in. Just as she meows, my stomach rumbles. It's time to feed us. First I check Twitter. I now have 1,745 followers. Not exactly a celebrity yet, but I'm getting there. I decide to fire off a fresh one:

as a queer icon with academic aspirations,, i feel like,, i should at least pretend to have watched buffy

As it loads, I become insecure that my new fan base is too young to know what *Buffy* is. I delete it, out of sight out of mind.

I pour some food in Ennui's bowl and then I pour some cereal in mine. I'm happy that we're both eating. I like when someone tells me I look skeletal because I know it means I can start eating. My body may feel like shit but at least I have carbs to soothe me. When I finish the cereal, I chug the sweet milk. When I put it down, Ennui is staring at me. Judgmental bitch.

"Jake Perez said I was skeletal," I hiss at her.

Because she's a literal cat, she hisses back.

In the Lyft on the way to Jax's, I make some notes on my iPhone for "Genius." I like how María Elena made a point to distinguish talent from genius. She was furious that Juan Antonio used the word "talent," spitting it out like a slur. I feel the same way. Being talented is like being good at grammar. So you've mastered the tools arbitrarily determined by the stuffy white men in power. Mazel.

But genius. Genius is something else entirely. Genius is tapping into the collective unconscious. Genius is confronting uncomfortable truths. Genius is elusive and subversive. It's fucking the rules up against a wall.

As we near Koreatown, I remove an Adderall from the mini blue Altoid tin I keep them in. I'm running low from the last handful Pilar gave me. It's okay, I tell myself, there's always more. As I place the blue miracle pill on my tongue, the driver eyes me suspiciously in the rearview mirror and I quickly avert my eyes. "Mmmm, minty," I mutter.

I open up Instagram and see a post from some idiots I went to high school with, smiling like freaks in front of Michelangelo's *David*. They look so happy and proud of themselves you'd think they invented sculpture. I think about those frumpy idiots Vicky and Cristina. I can't believe María Elena wanted to kiss one of them.

Another idiot I went to high school with commented #*FOMO* on the photo. God, there is nothing I hate more than that hashtag. It's so tragic. Like, way to advertise your desperation. Who on earth wants to be included in anything, let alone a trip to Italy? They're in their thirties and it's 2017. They could at least be in Asia. But then I imagine these bitches making racist faces in front of a temple and feel ill.

"We're here," the driver says with an annoyed expression, like it's the second or third time he's said it.

"Thanks," I say, and hop out.

I open the app and give him two stars. Bad attitude.

I'm shocked when Nina greets me at the Kingdom. Quickly it morphs into irritation. She leans in to kiss me on the mouth and I turn my head so that she lands on my cheek. As if I'd let her touch my mouth after it's been on slimy Beau. Before I can clock her reaction, I spot Pilar in the hallway and float over to her.

"My angel," Pilar says. "Jax mastered our latest track. It sounds... delish."

"Oh?" I say. I'm surprised. As I enter the main room, a camera starts clicking and I instinctively cover my face.

"I'm not the paparazzi," Beau says.

I want to punch him in the face. I feel a weird mixture of tired and edgy and I know my chemical composition is off.

"She's practicing," I hear Pilar say, and I go into the kitchen. To my shock, there is no PBR in the fridge. I want to scream. I frantically start looking around for something else. Anything to take the edge off. I feel like a crazed alcoholic from one of those black-and-white movies from the '40s Jake Perez is always making me watch, getting the shakes and all that. I spot a bottle of scotch, almost empty, on the counter. I add an ice cube into a plastic Lakers cup and empty the scotch into it. The sound of the crackling ice drowns out my rattling thoughts. I fill the rest of the cup with water, then gulp.

The click of the camera shocks me, and I jump a little.

"You okay, Vaga?" Beau asks, slinking in the doorframe. He looks greasier than usual, like he ate cheese fries and then wiped his face, then put his hands through his hair. I'm suddenly nauseated.

"Only Jax calls me Vaga," I say. This isn't entirely true. Pilar and Yumiko call me Vaga as well, so does Ellie. Or Ellie did sometimes. Sadness hits. I wish I were back in my bed, her warm body wrapped around me. She always felt so warm and smelled so good.

Jax calls out to me from behind the panes. I take a big steadying gulp and walk over. I'm a bit calmer, but my body still feels heavy.

The sight of Jax shocks me a bit. There are empty beer cans everywhere, vestiges of white lines on magazines. His hair points out in various directions. He looks at me with eyeballs that seem to shake. "Vagaaaa," he says, then lets out a hacking cough that frightens me. He fumbles for a cigarette, which I'm pretty sure is the last thing he should be doing right now.

"Tupac made 7 Day Theory in seven days," he says to me. His hand shakes as he smokes the cigarette. There are black circles under his eyes. It's clear he hasn't slept in days. He lets out some hacking coughs again.

"I didn't know that," I say.

"We should do the same," he says. "For our fans."

I try to remember how many days it's been since we've been recording this EP. I honestly have no idea. It's been a blur. I feel like it's been more than seven, but who knows.

"Good idea," I say. I'm nervous. Is this what I look like? I take another sip of my "cocktail," and it makes me nauseated. I need something else.

"I have to play you our newest track," he says.

"Wait," I say. Jax is making me too nervous right now. "Can I record something real quick? I gotta get it off my chest."

Jax lights up. "Of course," he says. "When inspiration calls."

I head toward the mattress cave, my safe space.

"Beau, babyboi," Jax calls from behind the panes. "Can you get us more PBR?"

I decide to rap on the first beat Jax gives me. I'm not sure it's out of genuine interest or desperation. Either way, the rhymes start flowing out of me. I'm not even looking at my phone. I'm freestyling. About being a genius.

"Holy fuck, Vaga," Beau says when I exit the booth. He snaps a photo. This time, I'm feeling myself, so I'm okay with the fact that he's taking my picture, which I told him not to do, and calling me Vaga, which I told him not to call me.

"Gen-ius!" Jax shouts. "Gen-ius!"

The way he says it makes me think he knows it's a *Vicki Cristina* reference, and I'm less afraid of him. My mood has shifted. The bricks have been lifted.

"Vaga," Jax says, handing me a PBR. I snatch it with excitement. The perspiring icy can on my skin only intensifies my high. I crack it open and get ASMR. "You're the blonde María Elena."

I grin widely. I feel how I did when I first entered the Kingdom. Jax gets it. But more important, he gets me.

I make eye contact with Nina, who is eyeing me with an indiscernible expression. I quickly look away and see Yumiko's parka flying at me. She plants a big wet kiss on my cheek.

"Gen-ius!" she shouts, in a way that makes me think she doesn't get the reference, but that's okay.

Jax plays us the song he'd previously mastered. He's looking more alive, more healthy, which always seems to happen after midnight. I'm not sure if it's him or just my perception of him. The song is called "B$_{12}$" and I'm shocked by my sexy robot flow. I sound good as hell.

Pilar puts her arm around me and I whisper in her ear, "Do you have Adderall?" I'm feeling great and I don't want the feeling to go away.

She makes a sad face. "We're all out," she says.

I panic and gulp my beer. I think of those losers I saw on my Instagram in Italy. The FOMO hashtag.

"Can I get back in the booth?" I ask when "B$_{12}$" is done.

Jax's eyes widen. "We got the blonde Tupac up in here."

I go back into my mattress cave and rap a song called "FOBI."

Fear Of Being Included.

Later in the night, Pilar is recording her vocals while I sit on the couch alone, staring out the window and thinking about Adderall. My post-recording high has faded, and I need to get my next fix. Beau got more cocaine, but he said their guy is out of pharmaceuticals. I thought he could get any drug. I thought that was the whole point of him. I find myself becoming angry and sip some beer to steady myself.

Nina left. I still feel angry at her, but that anger was good for my art. At least I think it was. I have no idea whether Shiny AF is good or whether we're just charming or hot or whether everyone is just fucked up out of their minds.

A text from Nina floats in. *Wanna come over?*

I text back, *I'm recording.*

"Do you have any Adderall?" I whisper in Beau's ear.

"You keep saying that," he says.

I'm blacked out. I should probably go home.

"For the billionth time," Beau says, "our guy is out."

Click. Beau's camera is in my face. I slap it away.

"The fuck," he says. "This is a 5D, bitch."

I shrug, then laugh. Yumiko laughs along with me, although she couldn't possibly know what I'm laughing at. Her laugh is guttural and unhinged. I think she's mirroring Jax a bit.

"Don't you have a psychiatrist?" Beau whispers in my ear.

I stiffen. "Why?" I ask. My eyes dart around the room. Do I come off as crazy?

"Um," he says. He runs his fingers through his thick brown hair, and for some reason I'm jealous of his fingers. "I don't know. I feel like every girl like you has a shrink."

I relax. It's just a class thing. He doesn't think I'm crazy. "I do," I say. "But he's pretty smart." I think about Dr. Kim. He hasn't tried harder than two emails to figure out why I stopped seeing him or whether I'm even alive. He doesn't give a fuck about me. I wonder if he's pilled out himself. I think I saw a tweet earlier when I was checking my followers about how all shrinks are heavily medicated. I mean, I would be too. What type of person chooses to be a psychiatrist? A pill-head who's good at science.

"So?" Beau asks.

Do you have any more Adderall? I find myself asking Nina.

No, she types back. *I'm not a drug dispenser.*

I swallow my shame with my last sip of beer and then get up to leave. Yumiko's parka slides into my vision. She gets up in my face and frightens me. Then a smile loosens her look. Her big blue eyes are watery and dazed.

"Do you have Adderall?" I whisper into her ear.

"Daddio?" she yells back at me. "Daddddiooooo." She starts rolling her body and repeating "daddio" to the beat of a trap song I don't specifically recognize but that sounds like every other trap song. "That should be our next song!"

It annoys me how she says "our."

"I have to go," I say, and then I leave.

The next day, I'm sitting at my desk crafting and deleting sentences in an email to Dr. Kim. At the moment, it's blank. My body still feels dead but also wired. I have a weird mix of fatigue and anxiety. Actually, I'm pretty sure this is close to my natural state, but a heightened version.

I refresh Twitter. I have almost two thousand followers.

My phone lights up with a text from Jax.

Vagaaaaaaaa.

Hiiiiiii, I write back.

Come over today at 3.

My gut tightens.

We have 4 songs we can work with—dearly queerly, FOBI, B12, genius—we need 1 mo I think.

I gulp my water. Ennui paws my leg.

Yeeeee, I type back.

You got this, Vaga?

The question mark makes me nervous.

Of course!!!! I write back.

Yassssss.

I put the phone down and open my email again.

> Hi Dr. Kim,
>
> I'm writing because I feel I need to renew my Adderall prescription to treat my ADD. I was diagnosed and prescribed in law school, and now that my workload has increased substantially, I think it would be helpful to resume. My dose in school was 10mg, as needed. We can discuss at our next appointment if you prefer.
>
> Thanks,
> Prue

I click send, then put on my Nikes. I attempt a run, but my body isn't having it. I start walking, but that feels difficult too. Eventually I sit down on the curb and start to pull up my email. A crack-head-looking man tries to talk to me. His muscles are inked up. He's an inch away from a barista, but too twitchy.

"Hi, blondie," he says.

I want to ignore him, but I like the nickname. "Hi," I say, and flash a coy smile.

He smiles back. His lips are chapped and I think I spot a speckle of blood. "You Brazilian?" he asks.

Wow. This is a first. I'm like the most generically WASPy person ever. But Brazilians are notoriously hot, right? I mean, isn't Brazilian just slang for hot?

"Maybe," I say. I'm flattered but over it and go back to staring at my phone.

I refresh my email. Nothing from Dr. Kim. So irritating. I mean, what if I was having a medical emergency? He's a doctor. He should be more available.

I scan my body (something I learned in meditation class) and wonder if it's an emergency for me. My body always feels off, but right now it's intense. I need to be medicated. Get your shit together, Dr. Kim.

"You want a sandwich?" the crackhead asks.

I narrow my eyes at him.

"Eat a sandwich, bitch," he says. He starts manically laughing. He must have a trust fund. Too sociopathic to be a legitimate crackhead. "Brazilian skeleton," he adds. He starts making weird noises.

"Do you have any stimulants?" I ask.

His face becomes serious, and at this point I'm positive he has a trust fund. He narrows his eyes back at me. The twitching subsides. He means business.

"What are you looking for?"

Nina gives me a ride to Jax's. I skip to her car. The trust-fund crack-head gave me Vyvanse, which is like fancier Adderall. I drank a few light beers while I got dressed and did my makeup. I listened to Mariah Carey and thought of those quotes from '90s *Cosmopolitan* magazines about how your confidence is directly related to your physical appearance.

I don't even say hi before I light a cigarette.

"Can you not smoke in here?" Nina says. She's is such a downer. I miss Ellie, who let me do whatever I wanted and never made out with gross, greasy losers. I pull out my phone and almost text her, then decide against it.

I toss my cigarette onto the lawn beside the curb, then hop in her car.

She just raises her eyebrows at me and I imagine her and Jake Perez becoming friends and ganging up on me constantly. Dark electronic music plays on the speakers. Pretentious, like it was made in Berlin by a man who studied engineering.

"Can we change it to something more upbeat?" I ask.

She raises her brows again. They're unkempt in a way that kind of turns me on. "Are you really asking me to turn off Kraftwerk?"

I stare at her blankly, pretending I don't know who Kraftwerk is. I'm pretty much a music encyclopedia. I've been memorizing genres and key artists since I was a kid. I'm surprised I didn't recognize it immediately; must be a deep cut. I'm not a huge fan of Krautrock, but I get that it's important. I could easily monologue on this subject and impress Nina, but I get off on feigning ignorance. It's a blonde thing. And besides, I'm mad at her.

"Give me your phone," I say.

I reach for it and she pulls it away.

"You're so annoying," I say.

She smiles and licks her top lip. She's flirting!

"Oh, so you're into me again?" I ask.

She turns left with one hand, very sexy. "I wasn't aware I was over you," she says.

I stare out the window with forced apathy and think about how to play this. I could mention Beau, but instead I choose silence. This is impressive discipline, particularly considering that I'm on Vyvanse, and stimulants make me chatty as hell. I reach for her phone again. This time she doesn't object. I put on Migos's "Narcos," the song I think is most aesthetically and sonically opposed to Kraftwerk.

She seems okay with my choice and we sit in silence as she merges onto the 110. I wonder for a second whether Nina and I are too similar, whether we're just mirrors of each other. Strategic bitches. Everything is a power move. We keep mad layers between ourselves and the world. But I'm more fun. And I'm not trying to be strategic. I just come off that way.

I turn up the bass, then bob my blonde hair and stare at myself in the side view mirror as the car vibrates.

"Are you mad I made out with Beau?" Nina asks when she exits the freeway.

"Is that why you did it?" I ask.

We're approaching Jax's block and I'm happy for that. Soon I'll be back behind the cushions spitting brilliance while people give me validation. And on Vyvanse! It'll be magic. We just have one more song to make before we become famous.

"I did it because I wanted to," she says.

I light a cigarette, then remember she's a square, then continue to smoke anyway.

"Are you punishing me?"

"No," I say. "I'm smoking because I want to."

THIRTEEN

At the Kingdom I drink a few Bud Lights while sitting on Beau's lap and intermittently staring at Nina. She seems unconcerned and that concerns me.

"When is the *FADER* story coming out?" Jax asks Nina while she rolls a joint. I get a pang of nostalgia for the first night when I visited the Kingdom, when I was innocent and precious. Before I had been corrupted by Nina and her stupid games.

Nina shrugs. "Probably around the time your EP debuts," she says. "It's really up to my editor, but that's what I'll propose."

"Makes sense," says Jax. He seems more grounded today, like he's slept. Or maybe my powers of perception are just compromised. The point is I need to be brilliant today. And I'm pretty sure I can do it, but I still don't have that spark. It's okay. It's still light out. It'll be hours until we get behind the panes, until I cozy up in the cushions. I just need to keep drinking, keep talking, keep smoking. I need to open my body like a vessel. An artist is nothing more than a vessel. It's like being a medium. You just have to open your mind to the possibility, and—*boom*—ghosts are everywhere.

Soon I'm smoking a cigarette on the fire escape while Yumiko lights some candles on the portion she's turned into a makeshift altar. I look out at the slightly fading sky and announce, "I'm an artist."

I don't think she hears me, which is good because I surely sound obnoxious. But I also mean it. As I drag my cigarette and stare at the moon, I wonder how different my life would have been if my parents had encouraged me in the arts, if I hadn't gone to law school. I mean, it obviously wasn't their job to mold me or not mold me in a certain direction. My parents aren't perfect, but I'd never dare blame them for anything, particularly considering how cushy my life has been. But it's interesting to think about. DC is not a creative place. Law and politics were the only option, I felt. My mom was an artist before I was born, allegedly. She never talks about it. I only know from my grandmother. She once had a show at the Gagosian. When I tried to ask her about it, she said something along the lines of "Dreams are a very dangerous thing."

I hear the click of a camera. Beau is shooting me from inside. I didn't even realize he was here. Because I'm feeling myself, I curve my body and toss my hair, giving him a real pose. He seems to like it because he starts clicking like crazy.

Yumiko stands up behind me and flares her parka, which I'm sure creates an amazing silhouette. I'm not even mad at her for stealing my moment, because she isn't really. She's fading properly in the background, allowing me to shine. We both begin to hang off the scaffolding in various poses, hamming it up. I catch Nina's glare from inside, a slight eye roll. She begins writing something in her Moleskine and I look away. Then I start strutting inside. I swing into the room like Yumiko normally does, and she follows me.

"Jaxy," I say, standing in the window frame so that I'm physically looking down on everyone. "Do you like Kraftwerk?"

"Fuck no," he says, then unleashes one of his classic cackles.

I grin and then ask Beau to get me a beer.

Soon it's fully dark and I still haven't taken any notes. I've just been chatting. I feel the buzz of the Vyvanse wearing off, so I go into the bathroom and break a pill in half and pour a sprinkle of beads onto my tongue. I have no idea why I'm being secretive about it when I'm surrounded by drug addicts. Maybe I just want it all to myself.

When I emerge from the bathroom in Jax's room, Nina is standing right there. "Go ahead," I say, making way for her to enter.

"I don't have to go," she says. Then she lies down on the bed. She's wearing a black silk tank, lacy on the top, with her normal mom jeans. My gaze meets the freckles at the top of her breasts and I quickly look away. But she seems to have seen me. Fucking writers. They see everything.

"Okay," I say, and then start to head out back to the group. I know the Vyvanse couldn't possibly have hit yet, but I feel a little pep in my step.

"Wait," she says.

I flip my head around in a way that I hope looks dramatic and glamorous.

She pats the seat next to her on the bed. I take a second to decide whether to obey. Obedience is for people with low IQs. Dogs are obedient. So instead of sitting next to her I just pivot fully toward her and lean in the doorframe.

"What's up?" I ask.

"Why are you being weird?"

God, what an annoying question. I'm an artist. I'm always weird. That's the point. "Are you gonna put this conversation in your story?"

She shrugs, bites her lip. She does look cute. "You're very hard to read, Prue Van Teesen."

"My full name... am I in trouble?"

She slinks toward me, sexy as hell. Fuck.

"Do you want to be?" She strokes my face.

I shrug.

"I still have a crush on you, you know," she says. I'm pretty sure this is the first time she's said this to me.

"Then why did you make out with that greasy boy in front of my face?"

She laughs, but I'm embarrassed. I hope I don't sound crazed.

"You know I'm poly," she says.

Oh god. Poly. How boring. She's like fucking María Elena, storming in from the mental hospital to ruin my life. But María Elena would never call herself "poly." She's a romantic, not a New Age loser.

Oh. That's it.

"Get me behind the cushions!" I shout when I'm back in the main room.

"Here she is!" Jax yells with glee.

I strut in clutching a PBR in my hand and my cell phone in the other. I look at my phone as if I've written something down but I haven't. Soon my body is moving like a wave and I'm seeing the bass in color. A light blue fog undulates out of the speakers and into my mattress cave. The smoke surrounds me and soon the words are coming out mint green, dancing in the periwinkle. My eyes hit Jax, then Nina. And then I'm gone.

> *Popping dolls*
> *New Age molly*
> *Not my purse*
> *New age folly*
> *Nothing worse*
> *Than being obvi*
> *Nothing worse than*
> *Than being poly*
> *Someone's toy*
> *Another's dolly*

My stomach sinks as soon as I leave the cushions. Everyone is looking at me and I can't tell what they think. The Vyvanse is crashing. Beau snaps my picture and I push his camera away.

"The fuck?" he says.

"Don't snap at her," Jax says. I see him as a lion defending his pride.

"Especially after snapping me," I say, and then I click my tongue the way Jax does sometimes.

"You're such a spaz," Beau mumbles under his breath as he storms out of the panes, cradling his camera like a wounded child.

Pilar puts her arm around me. My shoulder is covered in blue feathers. "I think he's on his period," she whispers in my ear.

I shrug it off. I need more Vyvanse. But that would be crazy. I eye the time on Jax's monitor. It's after midnight. I've already had two tonight, but I want that high again. I should probably get back behind the cushions. This is supposed to be our final night of recording, our final song. I have to give Jax as much to work with as possible.

"I have a nice little hook in my head for this beat," Pilar coos toward me.

"Get in there, babygirl," Jax says.

I take this moment to sneak out. Beau is tinkering with his camera on the couch. I attempt to slink past without him noticing me. In the bathroom, I open my Altoid tin and pour my third sprinkle of Vyvanse onto my tongue. I have only two pills left. It's okay. I need them tonight.

When I open the door, I kind of hope Nina will be on the other side. But she's gone.

The next day I'm sitting at my kitchen table sipping ice water with lemon and refreshing Twitter. The sun is bright as hell and I'm still buzzing. I've had about a fifteen-year routine of waking up in the mornings and drinking coffee and working on something: writing an essay for school, studying for a test, writing a brief, composing a rap. But I have no cases and the EP is done (I think), and I'm not totally sure what to do with myself. I decide to work on some new rhymes. I mean, I'm not sure what I recorded last night will be workable. Jax and Yumiko seemed to like it, but they're always hyping me up. I open my "Raps" document and stare at it for a few seconds, then go back to Twitter.

I search for Kanye's name. He deactivated his Twitter about six months ago and I keep hoping he'll come back. Poets are amazing at Twitter. I imagine him in Wyoming, in some minimal industrial studio tucked into a mountain valley, perfect acoustics, phone locked away in some box by the powers that be. God, I can't wait for someone to lock my phone up.

A new Gmail pops up. It's from Dr. Kim. I thought he'd forgotten about me.

> Hi Prudence,
> Sorry for the late reply. I was out of town and just returned last night. Do you want to schedule an appointment to discuss the adderall?
>
> —Dr. Kim

Plot twist. I like that he didn't capitalize "adderall." Also, he didn't ask me about how I'm doing on the lowered SSRI dosage, which I stopped taking entirely. This man really doesn't give a shit about me. I can't blame him. He just wants a check. Dr. Feelgood.

I write him back.

> Hi Dr. Kim,
> Thanks for getting back to me. My schedule is pretty open right now, so I can come at earliest appointment time you have available. Afternoons are better.
>
> Best,
> Prue

After pressing send, I return to Twitter. I have three new followers. I now have more than three thousand. I type "Dearly

Queerly" in the search window and watch the results appear.
The first one makes me smile.

*still spinning dearly queerly on repeat... shiny AF GIVE US
MORE!!!!*

The next one is less positive.

the world still sux but at least we're over dearly queerly

That stings a bit. But it also feels good. The fact that this sad
individual is pleading the world to be "over" the track means
that at one point it was under it. Then I search my name.

*can someone please tell me WHO prue van teesen aka "vagablonde"
is FUCKING?!? like... who gave this bitch a mic?*

I type Nina's name in the reply box, giggle, take a screenshot, but don't upload it.

There is something refreshing about watching people talk
shit about me on the internet. I used to joke about looking forward
to this moment. I think about Kanye. "My haters are my motiva-
tors." I mean, you have to care to really hate someone. Plus, I
have so much negative self-talk, it's nice to hear an external voice
to these thoughts. Like, objective evidence. I'm right. I suck.
The point is people are thinking about me and expressing these
thoughts on a public forum. That means I'm something. I'm not
invisible. I exist. I matter.

There are lots of replies to the tweet.

*FOR REAL. homegirl disgraces the english language and the
human voice in a way i never thot (lol she looks like one) possible*

Well, I like the way he expresses himself. I guess I shouldn't
assume it's a man just because he thinks he's funnier than he is.

The next reply says, *did you see the nude photos of her???? she
look good tho.*

My face gets hot. The next tweet is a link to Ixland Prinxexxa.
I close out Twitter.

I check iMessage and am excited to see an unread message
from Nina. FKA Twigs's "Two Weeks" comes on, my favorite
song about unrequited longing, a song that sums up my twenties.
But I'm not dreaming anymore.

Am I your muse? Nina texts me.

I click to my Gmail browser. I don't need to answer right away. I'm trying to remember how the previous night ended. I see flashes. I got back in the cushions, I'm pretty sure. Probably disgraced the human voice or whatever. The word "Krautrock" jumps into my head, then fades. I see Yumiko's parka, the jab of her gun. The repetition of these images comforts me, then my stomach sinks. The darkness is coming. I need more Vyvanse. I have two left. I open my mini Altoid tin. There's only one pill. I feel worried. I normally keep better track of these things.

I have an unread email from Dr. Kim.

> Hi Prue,
> I have tomorrow and Thursday at 3 p.m. If one
> of those doesn't work, let me know and we'll
> work out another date.
>
> —DK

Oh my word! "DK." Dr. Kim is getting intimate!

> I'll see you tomorrow at 3.

I think about asking if he has anything today, but I don't want to sound too desperate.

No, I text back to Nina.

The sun is predictably bright when I drive west the next day to "DK's." I leave at 2:00, just to be safe. I'd woken up only a few hours earlier. Last night I took the last Vyvanse and tried to write. I mainly just listened to Lana Del Rey and produced several pages of ugly, obsessive scribbles. I hope I at least enjoyed myself. My memory is foggy. Neither cat was there when I left.

As I curve onto the 10, someone is honking. Someone is always honking at you on the freeway in LA. I think of *Clueless*, that scene where Cher and D accidentally end up on the freeway and start screaming, petrified by cars zooming all around them and the imposing concrete dividers between safety and danger. I feel this way whenever I go to the West Side, as soon as the 10 straightens out. It must be, like, ten lanes. Concrete walls on both sides. The palm trees that hang over look especially dry, dirty, and flammable. Massive hunks of metal zoom by in every direction.

My palms sweat on the wheel. I turn up the air conditioner and pull my face up toward it. I try to slow down my breathing. I hear the air coming in and out, but I don't feel it. I wipe my wet hands on the wheel. A car cuts in front of me, then weaves through some more cars. The traffic starts to slow down. I roll behind a Jeep with a bumper sticker that says: BEWARE OF DRIVER. I swallow.

I reach for my phone and my hand is shaking. My palms are sweating so much that I can hardly grip the phone. I go to my Insight Timer app and click "SOS Meditation for Panic" just when traffic moves. I press the gas and wonder if I really know how to drive. If I press the pedal too hard, I could crash into another car and kill us both.

The woman's voice comes on, soft and breathy. *You might be feeling very anxious right now, but that is normal given your circumstances.*

Why is it normal for me to feel anxious under these circumstances? I'm just driving to my psychiatrist's to get more pills to feel the best I can. I'm not in a war zone. I'm not about to take the bar exam or perform on *Conan*.

You may feel very scared right now, but that is only a feeling. Try not to fight it. Instead, just notice.

I notice and realize I'm freaking the fuck out. I need to get off this highway. But I can't. I have to be able to get through this. I'm just driving across town. I'm thirty years old. I need my medicine. I'm about to be a celebrity. I can't be having this kind of anxiety right now. I remind myself that I've driven across the country thrice. I can drive across town.

Notice the air coming in and out of your nose.

I notice the air, but I'm convinced I'm not breathing. My iPhone tells me I'll be at Dr. Kim's in fifteen minutes. It'll take longer to get home. I may as well stick it out. But I worry about the drive home.

I wonder if maybe this isn't a panic attack. Maybe it's a reaction to the Vyvanse, an allergic reaction that requires actual medical intervention. Maybe the pills were laced with fentanyl. A car honks and I press the pedal, as lightly as possible. The car honks again and I speed up a bit. I won't drive any quicker than necessary.

Listen to the sounds around you. Feel supported by the earth under your sit bones.

The phrase "sit bones" always makes me uneasy. I don't feel supported by the earth. Earth is spinning in space. How could I possibly feel supported by this rock that might explode at any moment or get hit by another rock? The earth under my "sit bones" is probably a fucking fault line. It could start shaking and I could fall into a sinkhole and burn alive in the earth's core. I focus on the sounds, but all I hear are strident horns and ignitions rumbling. A motorcycle zooms past my window.

Traffic starts to speed up and I relax for a brief moment. I eye my phone. Only a few minutes until the exit. I got this. The panic is probably fading. I feel silly and shut off the meditation. Kendrick's "Humble" blasts from KDAY, and it's so loud it shocks me a bit.

I look at all the lanes until the exit. I watch a hawk swoop into a tree, hungry for something. I focus on the road, but it reflects the sun and hurts my eyes. *Focus on your breath!* I yell at myself.

Another motorcycle zooms around me and I focus on making my exit.

By the time I get out of the car, I'm weak and shaky. I hope Dr. Kim has benzo samples on him, because Vaga needs one. I wipe my sweaty hands on my jeans and then pull my sunglasses closer to my face. I have my big sunglasses on, but the sun is still too bright. Everyone on the street looks like an avatar. I feel like I'm in a video game. I don't trust this neighborhood.

Dr. Kim's office is at the top of a tall and soulless building. Inside the elevator, I have the urge to sit down. I don't think my legs can carry me.

In the waiting room, I stare at a *Rolling Stone* cover from three years ago and cross and uncross my legs. I wonder if I died on the highway and this is hell.

"Prudence." Dr. Kim is in the doorway, standing rigidly, straight out of a damn computer simulation. I want to run. I want to go home and take a Klonopin and crawl into my bed and never get up. But to do that I'd have to get on the freeway, which I don't think I can ever face again. Maybe I can order a helicopter.

"Hi," I say. My voice sounds calm. I probably look elegant as hell. I got this.

As I walk over to the couch, I try not to look out his massive windows that glow neon yellow. I almost instinctively walk over to close the blinds, but that would be rude, so instead I sit down. I wipe my palms on my pants.

I look at Dr. Kim, who is already seated in the chair across from me, looking tired and sad. I wonder what's going on with him. Does he have a newborn? A book proposal due? A second family? He appears to be under some major stress, and for some reason that calms me.

"How are you?" he asks.

"I'm great," I say. My chest tightens, as though my body is calling my bullshit. I swallow. "I haven't really noticed any major difference from going off the Celexa."

Dr. Kim nods vaguely. "That's wonderful," he says, his face seeming to just now put together that he's prescribed me Celexa for two years. He then begins firing off his standard questions, seeming to read them from a clipboard on his lap.

"Exercise?"

"Still hiking." Okay, pacing. But he doesn't need to know that.

"Sleep okay?"

"Yep. I love sleep." I wish I was in my bed right now. My stomach sinks thinking about the hoops it will take to get to my bed.

"Still with your girlfriend?"

"We broke up," I say. "But it's fine. It was mutual." A white lie. No need to alarm him. "Being single is much better for me professionally."

He looks at me a little confused, and I decide to elaborate.

"I've been having a major creative Renaissance." I fumble over the phrasing, then remember it doesn't matter. I'm here for business. Also, you know, the unrelenting panic in my gut. "I've joined a, err..." I don't want to say "rap group" because that makes me sound like a '90s teen with disciplinary issues, but "band" just sounds so lame. "I started a musical project with a few others—a very talented producer and singer—and we made a track that did quite well. We got a record deal and we've been hustling—err, working very hard to finish the EP—"

"How's your legal practice?" Dr. Kim interrupts. I'm shocked, given that until this moment he didn't entirely seem to know who I was. I switch gears, imagine that he's my father.

"The advance from the record company was substantial enough that I was able to take a hiatus," I say. "I'll request more cases whenever the money gets low again, but I assume we'll be able to tour soon, which is when the money really starts flowing." I'm not totally sure about this. We've never performed, and I recall those panic attacks I got onstage as a child and think about the drive home and think about asking Dr. Kim to take me to a hospital. I look up at Dr. Kim, whose expression is hard to read.

"No dark moods? No bipolar episodes?"

"No dark moods," I say. I try to focus on my breath, but my stomach feels tight, like it's made of metal and can't contract. "Wait, bipolar?" I've never been diagnosed with bipolar disorder, just anxiety and depression. And I guess, as I'm about to convince him, mild ADD.

Dr. Kim shakes his head. "Sorry, I didn't mean to alarm you. It's a turn of phrase."

"Turn of phrase"? I wonder whether Dr. Kim is a quack. I guess no one knows what the fuck they're talking about when it comes to the human brain.

"My patients are always coming back furious, saying, 'You called me bipolar,' or something along those lines." He laughs, and I just stare at him. "See, there are various degrees of bipolar. There is bipolar one, which is the type of crazy person you see screaming on the street."

I nod, thinking this is mildly insensitive. I can tell Dr. Kim is going into lecture mode. It comforts me, makes me feel like I'm back at school, where everything was easy and I was a star.

"Then there is bipolar two, and a lot of successful people have this diagnosis. It's associated with high intelligence and creativity."

I perk up a bit.

"It's also associated with inflated self-esteem." He pauses and looks toward me, narrowly missing eye contact in a way that makes me think he's an avatar again. "I'm not going to say that everyone who tries to be an actor is bipolar two, but it's common out here. Like, you're from Middle America and you're good-looking and you decide to come out to LA to make it as an actress. Well, there are a lot of good-looking people out here. To live in Ohio and move out here thinking you're going to be the next Jennifer Lawrence, I don't know, it involves a degree of, well—never mind, I'm getting off track."

My entire body feels hot and tingly. I examine the freckles on my arms and start to wonder whether they belong to me.

"Then there is bipolar three, which is not really a diagnosis, more an idea. It's a useful framework for explaining moods." He runs his fingers through his hair in a way that makes me certain he's a homosexual. "Anyway, what was the Adderall dosage you were prescribed in law school?"

"Ten milligrams," I say, thrilled to have a concrete question to focus on instead of my finicky breath. I spent the morning googling and reading about various dosages. The ones Nina gave me were tens, and those seem perfect for me. A person can be prescribed up to sixty milligrams a day, so popping a few a night shouldn't cause any issues. In fact, it's reasonable and moderate.

"Okay," says Dr. Kim. "I can start out with prescribing thirty?"

My heart starts racing just thinking about it. Thirty pills! That should last me a while.

Dr. Kim starts writing out the prescription, and in the silence I can hear my shallow breath and I remember that I'm about to get back on the highway. I should just ask him if he has any benzo samples. I'm sure he does and that would solve my problem. Just take a benzo and cruise home.

But I can't bring myself to ask him, and soon he's shaking my hand goodbye.

I feel okay until I merge onto the highway again, and then my palms start sweating like crazy. I'm in the middle lane, trapped. I force air into my stomach, but a phantom metal cage is blocking it. I wipe my sweaty hand on the wheel and reach for my phone. Before I know it, I'm making a call.

"Hi," Ellie answers on the second ring. Her voice sounds raw and soft and immediately puts me at ease. I eye the clock and do the math: 4:30 P.M. here, so 7:30 P.M. in New York. I wonder what she was doing. Maybe on her way to dinner. It's January, so it's probably freezing and her nose is probably red.

"Hi," I say. "I'm sorry to bother you—"

"Why are you calling me, Prue?" Her voice is harsher now. A car honks at me and I remember why I called.

"I'm kind of freaking out," I say. I feel dizzy and I want to just stop the car and close my eyes. "I'm having a rather serious panic attack." I don't know why I'm saying it like this, as if I'm at tea with my grandmother. I hate how in the media when someone has an anxiety attack they're always crying and hysterical. I sound like I'm delivering an oral argument before a judge.

"Are you fucking serious?"

"Yes," I say. "I know I sound normal but I'm really freaking out." Tears well up in my eyes. I don't normally tell people these things, but Ellie always makes me feel safe. I told her once when I was experiencing panic early in our relationship, actually before we even defined it. That was when I knew she was special. Ellie just looked at me with her warm green eyes and put her hand on my knee and listened to me talk until I calmed down. We became girlfriends a few days later.

"I don't mean are you serious about the panic attack, Prue," she says. "I mean are you serious that you're calling me? You cheated on me and showed zero signs of remorse. I haven't heard from you once. And now you call me to fucking calm you down? Isn't there a pill you can take for that?"

She's right. About everything. I shouldn't be calling her. I should have asked Dr. Kim for the benzos I need for my anxiety disorder instead of the stimulants I take recreationally. I'm really twisted. I probably should go back on the Celexa too, or maybe just be locked up in a psych ward. A car honks and I jump and roll forward but say nothing.

"Jesus, Prue. You know, I defended you when my friends called you a delusional narcissist." She sounds as though she's swallowing back a tear, which puts a knife in my heart. But at least I know I'm breathing and I'm feeling normal emotions. "But I was the delusional one. I cannot believe I thought there was something worthwhile behind that insane exterior."

The traffic loosens and I speed up. I still can't think of anything to say. I want Ellie to keep talking and luckily she does. I don't care that she's yelling. I just like hearing her voice.

"I haven't heard from you in almost a month, and this is when you call me. The audacity."

My fear of the freeway feels years away. It's just a freeway. Cars can pretty much drive themselves these days, anyway. I feel in control and crack open my window slightly. Cool wind rushes at my cheek. Ellie isn't speaking so I figure it's my turn to talk.

"I didn't think you wanted to hear from me," I say softly. My voice is raw like Ellie's when she answered the phone. I wait a few seconds and she says nothing.

Then I realize she's hung up.

FOURTEEN

The following afternoon I'm walking in circles around Echo Park Lake when the Kingdom text thread lights up.

Beau texts first. *A booking agent hit me up.*

I'm not sure what this means.

He wants to meet Shiny AF at CAA tomorrow at 2pm. Century City. I'll pick you up.

Everyone texts back *ok.*

When people stop texting, I start to spiral. What will I wear? And will I be able to remain composed? I'll wear that tiny fanny pack Jake Perez gave me and put a Klonopin in the pocket. I didn't like this gift when I received it, but desperate times call for desperate measures.

The next day when Beau texts to say he's outside, I'm pacing around the apartment with Ennui in my arms. I'm wearing all black, so it doesn't matter that she's shedding all over me. I got black cats for a reason. I take a nibble of the Klonopin in my hand, then run outside.

Beau's black G-Wagen is vibrating on my street.

Inside, SZA's "Doves in the Wind" is playing. *Think I caught a vibe,* she sings, and I feel okay about this meeting. Jax puts his arm around me. The seat is comfortable. Pilar turns around and squeezes my knee.

"Vaga," Jax whispers in my ear. "I think the EP is done."

"Shut up," I say in a kind of sorority-girl voice I do sometimes when I'm uncomfortable.

"I will not!" he almost yells, and I wonder if he's on cocaine. Maybe I should be on uppers for this meeting. I feel tired and uncharismatic. But at least I look good. I'm wearing a vintage black DVF shift dress, black Doc Martens, a black velvet scrunchie, and my grandmother's gold chain from the '60s. Looking great and feeling terrible.

"Vaga, that last song was fire," he says. "'Poly Folly.'"

I smile. I hardly remember recording it.

"I'm thinking we'll start with 'Dearly Queerly,' for our fans"—Jax laughs—"then close with 'Poly Folly,' for symmetry." He cracks his window and lights a Marlboro. "I'm thinking 'FOBI,' then 'Genius' in the middle because it's our second single, I think. Wind down a bit on 'B$_{12}$.' Then—*boom*—'Poly Folly.'"

"Love," I say in the sorority-girl voice again. But I'm not actually that excited. I'm never experiencing the right emotion at the right time. I should probably go to a hospital. Maybe if I got better Ellie would take me back.

"Here goes nothing," Jax says as we roll up to a shiny building that freaks me out in the same way as Dr. Kim's office, sterile and soulless. "We can tour on these songs."

He throws his cigarette out the window, and I clutch my fanny pack and feel the outline of the two Klonopin pills I put in there earlier.

I catch my reflection in the massive windows in the CAA lobby and I feel good about how I look, like even my mom would be proud. She wouldn't admit it. She'd raise her eyebrows and tell me I looked like an alien. But I'd know in her head she'd be thinking of a very chic alien.

An aggressively large orchid blocks my face, which I don't mind, because my face is my least favorite part of my appearance. But I wonder who decided to put this here and why.

A man in a suit comes up to us and says, "Shiny AF," in a robotic voice.

I jump a little bit and Pilar gives me that look she always gives me in these meetings. Well, just this one and the other one.

"Where's Yumiko?" I whisper in Jax's ear as we're escorted to the elevator.

"Beau thought she should hang back for this one," he whispers back. "Given what went down at Wicked Ice."

I frown. I thought we all agreed Yumiko was iconic at the Wicked Ice meeting. Why are we listening to Beau? What does he know about anything?

In the elevator, we watch the yellow light climb numbers, curious about when it will stop. Finally, 13. Some people think this number is lucky, and I'm not one of them.

We're led into a sprawling glass conference room that overlooks the city and some mountains. I'm not sure which part of the city or which mountains, but the view looks expensive. And I love glass.

Pilar struts into the room in a way that impresses me. This room is her stage, and I want to be more like her. I try it. I swing my hips, but I catch my reflection and realize I look spastic. I just try to focus on sitting in a chair, which I finally manage. Beads of sweat start to form on my upper lip.

Two white men in street wear sit at the other end of the large conference table. They look identical to the men at Wicked Ice. The older I get, the less I'm able to tell men apart. Especially the ones in the record industry. I need an app for this shit. Shazam, but for people named Daniel and its varietals.

"Shiny AF," one of them says in an affected Brooklyn accent. Pilar gives me that look again, and I wonder if my face did something inappropriate or if she's just disgusted by the sweat above my lip.

"Yup," says Jax. He's confident too. Why can't I be like them? This should be my stage too. But I'm thinking about an earthquake and all the glass.

The man starts talking and I'm mostly focused on my sweaty lip. I try to quiet my mind, think about my mindfulness app. It's normal to feel stressed in this situation—with two indistinguish-able men who clearly do not get it in between me and my dreams.

Then I look at the mountains and feel my stomach sink. The scenery looks surreal, fake, a computer simulation, and I wonder who is holding the controllers.

I keep trying to zone into the conversation, but mostly just pick up a lot of "totallys" and "for sures" and "on the same pages." I hear each of the Daniels say, "We gotta strike the iron while it's hot," and each time I try very hard not to laugh. This is the type of thing Jake Perez says when he thinks he's about to get his dick sucked.

Soon, everyone is shaking hands. I wipe my palm on my dress and try my best to make eye contact with the silly men I can't distinguish. And quickly I escape from the glass cage.

In the parking lot, Jax starts doing a little dance. *"We're open-ing for Dead Stars,"* he sings to the beat of his rolling hips, *"at the motherfucking Teragram."* He puts his hand on my shoulder, then leans close to my ear and begins whispering: "What if we get on @WYATTLOOK?"

I was so blacked out from anxiety, I didn't even realize what was being negotiated. I'm annoyed at myself, momentarily, and then excitement takes over.

We have rehearsal the next day at eleven A.M. This is extremely early in Shiny AF hours. But we all get up and show up, because we're about to open for motherfucking Dead Stars. As I skip to my Lyft, I thank the lord that Jax Jameson found me and made my dreams come true.

As I arrive at the rehearsal space—a nondescript warehouse beside several other nondescript warehouses—Ellie pops into my head. I recall that terrible phone call where she confirmed all my worst fears about myself.

Also, I haven't heard from Nina in a while, and I can't tell if I actually care or if my insatiable hunger for romantic validation makes me think I care. Either way, I'm annoyed. Is she over me now that the review is out? Did she meet someone else? Someone hotter, younger, more interesting... blonder?

The warehouse door swings open. It's Jax, wearing an over-sized bedazzled Tupac T-shirt as a dress.

"Vagaaaa," he says.

Yumiko arrives shortly after. "Teragram, bitches!" she shouts through a cloud of smoke, apparently not annoyed that she was excluded from the meeting, which relieves me. Pilar arrives next, looking very serious and ready for business.

Rehearsal goes better than I expected. Once I'm onstage, I'm fine. But there's no audience. Luckily, Beau shows up shortly after we begin with a cooler of various adult beverages. I scowl at him and then take a PBR. I decide I'll bring beer onstage. Musicians do this all the time.

On our first break, Jax tells me the EP is almost done. I want to trust him, but he's said the EP was "almost done" several times. This frustrates me. When I say I'm going to finish something at a certain time, I mean it. I imagine my money running out, having to move back to DC. My hometown is similar to LA in that they're both obsessed with power and status, but DC is en-tirely devoid of glamour. Aesthetically, the mid-Atlantic is pure tragedy.

"Lots of sleepless nights," Jax says. He does a little sniffing gesture with his nose, and I force a laugh but my stomach sinks.

On our second break, Nina shows up with a cigarette case filled with pre-rolled joints. Everyone lights one except me, because I worry it will interfere with my performance. But I drink more, and everyone else does, and our second break turns into a sort of party. We blast *Aquarius* as loud as possible. When the title song comes on, Nina takes my hand to dance.

"My Aquarius moon," she whispers into my ear, and I can't help but smile. I guess I've missed her, or maybe I've just missed being flirted with. She's wearing a color today, red. And I feel like an unimaginative man for thinking she looks insanely sexy.

By the time I get back onstage, I'm lit as hell. But not as lit as Yumiko, who keeps screaming and jumping in front of Pilar and me whenever we have a verse. Pilar seems annoyed, but she says nothing. Only the occasional glare, to which Yumiko seems impervious. Personally, I like that she's taking the attention off. I'm not in the mood to be looked at.

Afterward, Beau and Nina tell us we were "on fire." We all continue to party, and by the time we slide open the warehouse doors, I'm disoriented. The sky is a light blue, and for a second I think it's the late afternoon, but it's morning.

Jax, Pilar, Yumiko, and I link arms inside the dark and smoky warehouse and strut into the bright Los Angeles morning. Shiny AF.

FIFTEEN

I wake up around three P.M. with a few texts. Ennui paws my face and I push her away. She feels lighter than normal. She screeches bloody murder and I try to remember the last time I fed her. I can't recall.

Glancing at my text notifications, I'm shocked. Two texts from Ellie. There's also one from Nina. And Jax and Jake. I frantically swipe and open Ellie's.

I'm sorry for being rude to you on the phone the other day. I'm still very hurt and angry, but I don't really think you're a sociopathic narcissist. I hope you're feeling less panicked.

The next text says, *I still think we should take some space.*

I'm filled with an overwhelming need to hear her voice. It's around six P.M. in New York, so she's probably had a wine. The anti-Nina, sweet and light and chatty. I linger over her contact for a few moments, then return to my other texts. But Ellie doesn't leave my mind. She wants to take "some space," which suggests that at a certain point the space will collapse and we'll be back together. The thought fills me with warmth but also frightens me. I don't know what I want. My stomach sinks. I'm coming down from the Adderall, from the being onstage, from validation, from Nina taking me in her arms and calling me her "Aquarius moon." I respond to Ellie, *Fair,* because what else is there to say?

I open the texts from Jax.

You slayed yesterday, Vaga... we got this!

I haven't slept yet lol.

The EP is coming together... I'll def have it done by the 1.

I look at the calendar on my phone. It's January 22. I walk over to my computer and google "Dead Stars LA Teragram Ballroom." It's on February 1. Openers "not yet listed." I hope this is for real.

There is another text from Jax.

Next rehearsal on Sunday ... same place, same time.

I look at my calendar again. Today is Saturday, so that's tomorrow. My body feels like lead. I'll sleep until tomorrow.

Since I'm at my computer, I refresh Twitter. I'm approaching four thousand followers. The cat screeches again. "Hold on," I bark at her.

I refresh Gmail. There's an email from the California Court of Appeal filing system, which alarms me. The subject line reads: "REMINDER: REPLY BRIEF DUE SHORTLY."

Fuck.

I open the email and realize the reply brief in Yumiko's case is due in thirteen days. I completely forgot about the reply. I missed the government's brief, so I'll have to find that, read it, and write the reply. I try to calm myself down. The government briefs are normally shit, so it shouldn't be hard to reply to. But Yumiko is my friend. The stakes are higher. I can't let her down. Also, Nina said something about her being our "glue," mainly from a performance perspective. My head hurts. The cat screeches again. I get up to feed it, but before that, I go into the bathroom and take an Adderall, just to steady myself.

The Adderall makes me nervy, so I drink a beer and smoke a cigarette to steady myself. After that, I'm buzzed. Certainly too buzzed to read any kind of legal document. So instead, I spend the evening blasting Dead Stars, practicing my makeup, and trying on various "stage outfits," which are all variations on all black—Wednesday Addams all grown up.

After listening to *Songs for JonBenét*—their first EP, the least polished but my favorite—thrice, my phone rings, which is bizarre because I never keep my ringer on. Absentmindedly, I answer it without even looking at who it is.

"Hellooo," I coo. I put the phone on speaker because I don't like the feeling of it against my ear. Also, this way I can still put on my eyeliner. I'm experimenting with extra dramatic wings, but I hope for the show I'll have a makeup artist. Or maybe at least Pilar. I think she used to work at MAC.

"Hi." I recognize Nina's voice and my heart does a little flutter. Her voice is all husky. I imagine her sitting on her bed in her underwear listening to some obscure record. A joint hangs from her lips and smoke fills the room. Her window is open and cars on Sunset zoom past.

"What are you listening to?" I drag the liquid liner along my lid, then decide to put it down. The image of Nina listening to music got me excited and I don't want to fuck up my eyes. Instead I hop over to my bed and collapse on my stomach. I pop up my legs and put my fist under my chin.

The sound changes, and I'm hearing some ambient noise. At first I think the call dropped, but then I realize Nina wants me to guess what's playing. I put the phone closer to my ear and listen. It's kind of surfy rock. Loud and raucous. A shouty female voice. Definitely East Coast; too passionate for the West. Nina is waiting for me to answer and I feel pressure. But it's the kind of pressure I like. Not the kind where I'm expected to entertain, but rather the one where I'm expected to identify a piece of knowledge. The sweet adrenaline of taking a test.

"'JJ,'" I say without even thinking. The nice thing about drugs is that they leave things to your subconscious, the most creative and knowledgeable part of us. The conscious mind is always getting in the way. "This was my jam over the summer." The band, Priests, is from DC. But I don't want to mention that because I don't want to talk about DC because it's a major buzzkill. I don't care for the US government or blazers. When I wear something other than a T-shirt I feel like a police officer.

"Well done, my freak," she says.

"I don't like that nickname," I say.

"I'm sorry," Nina says. She sounds earnest. I wonder what her underwear is like. Probably black and lacy. I picture her lying back on her pillow, her freckled legs open to the ceiling.

"How was your day?" she asks.

"I got served with a notice about a reply brief so I'm stressing," I say. I look around my room, various items of black clothing strewn about. My laptop is conspicuously closed. "It's due in thirteen days. I meant to work on it tonight, but I just couldn't get in the zone. This is really unusual for me." Ennui slinks in, sinewy and petite. She hops on the bed and I reach down to pet her. She dives away, then leaps as though my hand were made of acid. "But it's fine," I continue. "I have thirteen days." I mentally begin planning. Thirteen days is a long time.

"I didn't realize you were a practicing lawyer," she says. "I thought you were just a rich girl who went to law school."

This upsets me and makes me feel seen at the same time. "I practice," I say. Ennui jumps back up on the bed, the little tease. I make a note not to reach for her, because I know it'll make her come over and curl up.

"Why?" she asks.

"I don't know," I say. "Can you believe we're opening for Dead Stars?"

"Of course I can," Nina says, and my cheeks heat.

"So do you practice law?" she asks. I imagine the moon pouring in through her window and casting a bluish glow on her exposed brick wall across from her bed. I don't think her apartment is earthquake safe. It's interesting that she's asking me this now for the first time. I realize we don't really know each other.

"Why are you always interrogating me?" I ask. Ennui curls up next to my rib cage just as anticipated. Our breathing quickly begins to sync up.

"Excuse me for being interested in your life," she says.

"I thought you were just interested in a story," I say, "and making out with drug addicts."

"I wouldn't call you a drug addict, exactly... " she says.

"I was talking about Beau," I say, offended.

"Don't do that," she says.

"What?"

"Imply that I'm using you," she says. "And condescend my life choices."

"Oh," I say. I feel guilty, then I wonder if she's gaslighting me. "I practice law because it's the path of least resistance."

"You don't hear many people say that."

"Well, I'm very unique."

Ennui jams her paw into my rib cage.

"Do you want to come over?"

Nina arrives at my door with a bottle of rosé under her arm. She's wearing an oversized jean jacket and her hair is extra curly, like she used a new product or something. She's wearing coral-red lipstick, which I've never seen her wear.

"Who did you get all dolled up for?" I ask when I lean over to air-kiss her.

She just rolls her eyes. "I assume you have glasses?" She saunters into my kitchen with confidence. She walks how she drives: masculine swagger with a feminine grace. It's an attractive combination.

I lie back on the couch and blow on my freshly painted nails. Aaliyah's "More Than a Woman" comes on. Nina slides in next to me on the couch and swings a wineglass by my mouth. She tips the glass to my lips and I quickly cover my mouth with my hands. She looks at me strangely.

"I don't fuck with wine," I blurt out. "It makes me ill." Also, I think it's tacky.

She laughs. "Oh god. I'm a horrible guest."

"You should drink it, though," I say. "I wanna get you good and liquored." I say this in a way that sounds more creepy than seductive by accident.

Nina shrugs, then laughs in a way that calms me. "I guess I should put this away," she says about the empty wineglass, and begins to stand up.

"No, no," I say. "I'll use it." I stand up to get my Laphroaig. This is my fancy scotch I drink only on dates. It takes me something stronger than beer to get physical with someone. But as soon as I stand, I remember my nails. I don't want to fuck them up.

"Actually, can you grab me the Laphroaig from the cabinet above the sink?" I ask. "My nails aren't dry." I blow on them. "I'm a horrible host."

"We're both horrible," she says. "Also, Laphroaig. Fancy."

"You like it?" I ask. "Someone told me they think it tastes like Band-Aids."

"Luckily I've never eaten a Band-Aid," she says, then heads toward my kitchen. Ennui prances out in front of Nina and she almost trips.

"Who is this little one?" She reaches down to pet her.

"These are my cats—" I forget that Missy, or Ennui, whichever one it is, has been missing for seven, or thirteen, or god knows how many days. "This is Ennui," I say. I place the back of my hand on my forehead in a way that I hope expresses the name.

"You said 'cats,'" she said.

"Did I?" I laugh nervously, wondering whether I should divulge the fact of my missing cat to Nina, worried she'll judge me, decide I'm a sociopath, and never speak to me again. "They're outdoor cats," I say. Technically true. They climb the tree outside my balcony, and once one of them was gone for seven days, and now... whatever. "Missy is on one of her jaunts." I try to make it sound glamorous.

Nina's stroking Ennui's back. "She's so... petite."

"She's been depressed... " I say, trailing off, realizing I sound mildly insane. A crazy cat lady, a potential animal abuser. I'm probably both of these things. "Anyways," I say, "have some."

Nina locates the bottle. "We're going to drink Laphroaig from wineglasses?"

"Yes," I say, then blow on my fingers.

Soon my nails are dry and there is a noticeable dent in the Laphroaig bottle and my legs are draped on Nina's thighs and we're talking about Yumiko.

"She's my client," I blurt out. Then I feel ashamed and stupid. I drink alcohol to let my guard down and I hate it because it lets my guard down.

"What?" Nina says, eyes open wide.

"Off the record," I say in my serious lawyer voice.

"You can trust that everything we've said tonight is off the record," she says. "I'm ethical."

"Right," I say. "Same." That's a lie. I wouldn't know an ethic if it hit me in the face.

I excuse myself to the bathroom, where I pull out my Adderall bottle from my shiny gold bag. I turn on the water in case Nina can hear me. A few days ago on the phone, Jake Perez and I were discussing smoking joints and I said I didn't care for them. "Some people enjoy the ritual of smoking joints in social settings," he'd said. "You know, like passing it in a circle."

"Yeah," I'd said, then thought, *And I enjoy the ritual of swallowing pills alone in a bathroom.*

I stare at the neon-blue ten-milligram Adderall and think about swallowing it, then I decide to break it in half. I don't know exactly what time it is but it feels late, too late to be taking a whole Adderall.

I break the pill in half, taking care not to crack my nail polish. The sides are surprisingly equal. Whenever I break a pill in half, I take the larger half. But this time I can't discern the larger half, which makes me nervous. I worry that five milligrams won't be enough. Maybe I'll take one half plus a quarter of the second half, totaling 7.5 milligrams. That seems reasonable in my head.

But just as I'm about to break the second half into a quarter I feel irrationally sad about the quarter that will be small and alone in the pill bottle. Then I mumble, "Fuck it," and swallow both halves. I flush the toilet, then swallow some water from the sink. I stick out my tongue to make sure it isn't blue. All good.

"Did you fall in?" Nina asks when I return.

I stick my tongue out at her, confident that it shows no sign of my bathroom infidelities. That should be the name of a song. I sit down and grab my phone from the table. "Hold on," I say, "I need to text myself something."

"Inspiration hit?" she asks. I guess she took off her jacket while I was in the bathroom, or maybe earlier. The freckles on her shoulder twinkle under the palm tree's neon glow.

"Yeah," I say, looking into her eyes briefly, feeling frightened, then quickly looking down to text myself.

When I look up, Nina is rolling a joint. Ennui's tail slaps me on the leg.

"Perfect," I say. "I could really use a mellow." I laugh at myself, first softly, then louder, then almost hysterically.

"You amuse yourself, don't you?" she asks.

"I work from home for a reason," I say.

"So how did Yumiko become your client?" She begins to lick the edge of the rolling paper and I feel a tiny throb between my legs.

"Well, her real name is Rachel," I say. The Adderall pulses and I prepare to unleash a monologue. I assure myself that Nina is a journalist with an apparent journalistic interest in me, so I'm sure it will appeal to her, the impending monologue. "Rachel Taften. I work for the State of California, I forget if I told you." I look at Nina and she shakes her head, then licks the rolling paper again. "Okay," I say. "So you know what a public defender is, right?"

She cracks a condescending smile. "Yeah."

"So when an indigent criminal—someone who has a public defender—loses their trial, the state is constitutionally required to pay for their appeal. *Pennsylvania v. Finley* established that right sometime in the late eighties—1987, I think... the year I was born! Anyway, California has six appellate districts and a panel of available appellate attorneys for each district. I'm on the panel for the second appellate district, where Los Angeles lies. They say it's the hardest one to be accepted to, but I don't know who determined that or how—" I pause to look at Nina, who seems mildly impressed. She begins to light her joint, shooting me an expression that says, *Is it okay to smoke in here?*

"Let's go outside," I say. "I could use a cig."

We get up and head to the balcony. Ennui follows. She's been needy as hell since her sister left. Outside the air is cold and damp, but refreshing. Nina and I light up simultaneously. When she exhales, Ennui hops into a tree of smoke. The branches shake.

I exhale and try to keep the smoke away from Ennui. "So Rachel Taften was appointed to me," I say. I'm smiling, I think because of the combination of amphetamines and nicotine and whatever else. "Gun possession," I say. "I have no idea why she has a court-appointed attorney because she seems rich. I'm surprised her parents didn't pay for an attorney or something. She always alludes to being in the 'gun trade,' which I've found alarming. I mean, you remember that night."

"Kind of," Nina says. "I was pretty faded. But I remember the gold handle."

"Right," I say.

"It's not unethical, right?" she asks. "You being friends with your client like that? Embarking on a creative and, I guess, financial endeavor separate from the case?"

I laugh nervously, then take a drag. As far as I know there is no rule about being friends with your client, but I hadn't thought about the financial part. Jesus, how do nonlawyers always know more about the law than me? So embarrassing. I attempt to reason with myself. Nina is just a journalist asking a question; she doesn't know anything. I make a note to look up the financial thing later.

"It's fine unless I sleep with her," I say. Then I do a stupid wink, and Nina makes a face of mock disgust.

Later we're back on the couch and Nina lunges at me. She grabs my breast and jams her tongue down my throat. I'm not in the mood. Adderall kills my sex drive. It turns me into a sexy robot with no desires, which I love.

"Hey," I say, scooting back. "Wanna just keep chatting for a bit?"

"We've been chatting for, like... three hours," she says. She's clearly hurt, which I understand. I'd be hurt if I were her. I know I should comfort her, but instead I go into attack mode—The Prue.

"So what?" I say. "You put in a certain amount of hours of talking and you get full access to my body?"

Nina just looks at me stunned, then laughs. "Full access to your body? Who do you think you are?" She pauses, licks her lips. For a second I want to kiss her, but the desire evaporates as quickly as it develops. "You aren't exactly a Victoria's Secret model."

I rise, belligerent. "And thank god, because Victoria's Secret models are beyond tacky!"

"Oh," she says. "You're on an upper."

I shrug.

"I never should have given you that pill," she says.

"I have agency, Nina," I say. I'm going into feminist-theory robot mode. "I can have my own drug problem." I wonder for a second whether I do, in fact, have a drug problem. I suppose the average person would say I do. But I'm very careful with my dosages. And I need to be medicated for my career and life in general. I have disorders.

"I'm going to go," she says.

"Good," I say. I spot Ennui by my foot and swipe her up. She tries to squirm away, but I hold her tighter and her body stills.

I imagine I look like an old rich lady with this sinewy black cat in my arms. An unhinged old rich lady, one whose glamour and wealth are fading. Ennui flaps her tail in a way that reads as a power move.

Nina shakes her head at me. "I don't understand what you want."

I swallow. Ennui flaps her tail again. "I want you to leave."

SIXTEEN

By the time I arrive at rehearsal the next day, I haven't even typed a sentence of the brief. Instead I've been popping Adderall like mints and drinking lemon water and organizing my Spotify playlists.

Jax greets me when the warehouse doors slide open. Today he's wearing a ripped Fugees T-shirt over black mesh shorts.

"Sporty Spice," I say, eyeing his shorts.

He laughs, and I loosen up. I'm excited to be out of my apartment to get onstage. A hand slaps my ass. I turn around to see Yumiko, hug her uneasily. I feel guilty about procrastinating on her reply brief. It's very unlike me to procrastinate, but I suppose this is being an artist. My priorities are in this warehouse.

Jax makes me practice my bars while running in place, a trick he "learned from Beyoncé." My lung strength is decent, but it's still hard. Luckily, I like a challenge. I recall studying for the bar exam, the way I studied twelve hours a day for three months, propelled by adrenaline and caffeine and pure fear. I never told anyone this, but I enjoyed the experience. I entered a fake universe filled with endless, useless knowledge and constant multiple-choice tests in which I could measurably track my progress, leaving my mundane daily worries behind. For three months, I never once spiraled about my hair.

During a cigarette break I tell Jax I have a new idea for a song.

"I wouldn't expect anything less," he says. "But do tell." His nails are painted. Half black, half gold. Diagonal lines.

"Bathroom infidelities." I say this in kind of an eccentric, rich-woman voice. I imagine holding Ennui with her tail fanning the air.

"Perfect," he says. Yumiko appears and lights a blunt.

"Jax," Beau calls from inside. He's been working on the lighting and I have to admit he's doing a decent job. Cool, minimalist blues. James Turrell vibes. Like the Kingdom, or my apartment.

Jax puts out his cigarette and rushes back in.

Yumiko and I are now alone and guilt hits. In between drags, she opens her mouth to say something and I brace myself for her to ask me about the case.

"My friend Crystal is a dope designer," she says, pulling her flip phone out of her pocket. Yumiko is the only person I know with a flip phone, and when I told her this she said, "What else would I have?" A low-res photo of a parka covered in turquoise glitter pops up on her screen. "For the show," she says.

I examine the photo, and the parka is, in fact, "dope," although I must admit I was skeptical when I heard the woman's name was Crystal. And this picture is very grainy. "I love it," I say.

She looks down and smiles, her thick lashes batting against her face.

The next morning I take two Adderall and begin reading the government's brief. It's better written and more thoroughly researched than most government briefs. (Mostly, the government's argument consists of something like "appellant's argument lacks merit because it is meritless" or "defendant's conduct was illegal because it was not legal.") The brief is also sixty-seven pages, which is certainly the longest reply brief I've ever received. This sends me into a mini-rage. Why is the government so concerned with upholding the nonviolent misdemeanor conviction of this middle-class white girl? Then I feel bad for thinking that Yumiko deserves special treatment because she's white. Really, I think she deserves special treatment because she's my friend.

As I read the brief, I rephrase all the government's arguments in bullet points in a separate Word document. I reply to each bullet point with a counterargument, or an idea of how to research a counterargument. At a certain point I find myself entering a flow state. I always forget this can happen to me with law until it happens. I imagine myself on a battlefield, coming to rescue my friend with my ability to twist language to my benefit.

Every few sentences, I refresh Twitter. I count my new followers or search @WYATTLOOK. Whenever I remember that we'll be performing on the same stage I feel giddy, then terrified, and then I go back to typing.

Soon my notes become sentences, then paragraphs. I copy and paste the boring legal portions, mildly tweaking the phrasing to avoid overt plagiarism. I fall into a nice rhythm while piano music plays. Sometimes Ennui meows in sync with the music and it seems my typing and the music and Ennui are all part of a single breathing organism. Then I remember she's meowing because I need to feed her. So I go do that.

When I return, I see a text from Yumiko. It says, *Do you want Crystal to make you something? She said she can do gold on black.*

Crystal's style is a bit flashy for me, but I don't want to hurt Yumiko's feelings, so instead I change the subject.

I'm slaying the fuck out of your reply brief, I write. At this point I'm pretty high on myself and don't even think it's an exaggeration. The government brief is so idiotic, couching its lack of legitimate arguments in pretentious language and irrelevant cases.

RIGHT ON SISTAAAAAA, she writes back, and I feel proud. Then I remember what Nina said about my possibly breaking ethical rules. I make a mental note to google this later, although I can't imagine there has been a situation in which a lawyer and client have ended up in a successful rap group before. I remind myself that Robert Kardashian was close personal friends with O.J. and then I calm down a bit.

I'd say it's a definite winner, I type, *but the sad fact is it's always an uphill battle when defending the accused in this country.*

I understand, she types back. *I already served my time anyway, and it's not like my record is squeaky clean.*

I'm kind of upset by this response. I want her to want me to win so that I will care. I close iMessage and get back to typing. I make a note to remember this exchange in a few years when someone asks me why I quit law.

The next day I'm almost done with my first draft when the Kingdom text thread lights up with a text from Jax.

YOU GUYZ. I think the EP is done. Listening party tonight?? Come over around 9?

I look at the clock on my MacBook. It's four P.M. I'll probably be done with this draft in twenty minutes. This leaves almost five hours to get ready, a chunk of time that makes me uncomfortable. Fucking time. My bête noire. I want to be semi-coherent at the listening party. I want the perfect buzz. I just want to look and feel good at all times, and I don't think this is too much to ask.

I consider texting Nina, but then I remember we aren't speaking. At least I think we aren't speaking? I haven't tried to contact her and she hasn't tried to contact me since I kicked her out the other night.

I text Jake Perez, *Hi.*

New phone, who dis, he responds.

Yeah, yeah, I'm a shit friend, I type back. *Is this a venus conjunct pluto thing?*

No, he responds.

Then it's just a sociopathic narcissist thing. Ellie's exact phrasing. I make a note to bring this up in therapy if I ever go back. I can't imagine calling Barbara Lumpkin, and finding a new therapist is hell. I'll think about it later.

Happy hour? I ask.

The typing bubbles appear, then disappear.

By the time I arrive at the Kingdom that night, I'm a tad wobbly. I handed in my draft to my supervisor at 4:30 and then from 4:30 to 8:45 did the following:

Smoked my vape pen.

Coated my hair in coconut oil and painted my nails black.

Zoned out and watched various shades of light hit the wall.

Washed my hair.

Took half an Adderall.

Brushed my teeth.

Fed Ennui.

Composed and then deleted pathetic-sounding text messages to both Ellie and Nina.

Applied eyeliner.

Drank four light beers while making a Spotify playlist called "Sad Girlz."

Took off my eyeliner because I thought it looked messy.

Took the other half of the Adderall.

I'm annoyed when Beau answers the door. I mumble hi and walk past him, then strut down the sparkly blue hallway, imagining it to be a runway. In the main room, I see Jax's silhouette behind the shoji panes, hunched over the panels. The window beside him is cracked open, and Yumiko is lighting candles in her shrine. I feel a warmth toward her, probably because I spent the past few days crafting savage sentences on her behalf.

On the couch, a forlorn-looking Pilar smokes a long, thin cigarette. Nina rolls a joint at the coffee table, and despite my confused feelings toward her at the moment, I'm comforted by the predictability of the Kingdom, our Factory. I imagine Andy Warhol joining Pilar on the couch, swallowing an Adderall with a chilled glass of bourbon, then saying, "In the future, everyone will be world-famous for fifteen minutes."

Nina looks up at me with blank eyes for a second, then returns to rolling her joint. Hatred fills my gut. Then shame.

I walk over to Pilar and give her a strategic kiss on the cheek. Not an air-kiss, but a wet one. I do the same for Beau.

Then I give Nina a condescending pat on the head, from which she recoils.

"Anyone need anything from the kitchen?" I ask, looking only at Beau and Pilar. They both shake their heads, but Beau follows me. Soon he's standing in the kitchen doorway, looking like a greasy rat.

"You sure you need another drink?" he asks.

I can't believe a drug dealer is monitoring my substance intake. "I'm just getting a water," I lie. My words are slurring a bit. "What's it to you, anyway?" I grab a plastic Lakers cup, fill it with ice, then water. My good mood is dropping, no plummeting. I plan to add a splash of bourbon when Beau leaves.

"Just looking out for you," he says. "You've been looking... kinda pale."

I point to a pot on the stove, then a kettle.

"Whatever." He shrugs.

"I thought you liked me pale and frail," I say. "Better to take advantage of?"

"Excuse me?" he says with a limp-wristed, feminine tone.

"Palm Spring her?" I say. "I hardly know her." I know I'm sounding kind of crazy. I'm also pretty fucked up.

"Drink some water," he says, then leaves the kitchen. Once he's gone, I look around for the bourbon. When I locate the bottle, it's empty. Behind it, there's an almost-empty bottle of Bombay Sapphire. I don't normally drink gin that isn't a martini, but *c'est la vie*. I empty the bottle's remaining contents into my cup.

When I return to the main room, Jax has emerged from behind the shoji panes. He's standing while everyone else sits, reigning over his loyal subjects. I wonder whether Andy Warhol was ever this tyrannical. He was a Leo too. I sit on the ledge of the couch beside Beau.

"My Kingdom," Jax says, opening his arms wide. The turquoise beads on the ends of the strands of his fringed black coat clink together and the strands make a wave. "Tonight is a big night. I imagine a lot of big nights in the near future. Tonight, the EP. Next week, the Teragram, our *FADER* cover." He winks at Nina and I can't see what face she makes back. "I haven't slept in the past three days," he adds. "And I don't know when I'm going to sleep again."

He laughs and everyone else laughs, and I become afraid. I'm not ready to give up sleep. I'm too fragile. Jax looks pale and tired, shaky. I wonder if this is how I appear to Beau. My stomach sinks and I sip my drink, which provides no relief.

"I want to first give a major shout-out to my girl Vaga," he says.

I feel everyone's eyes on me. How am I supposed to perform in front of hundreds of people if I'm embarrassed when five friends look at me?

"I've been waiting for you my entire life," Jax continues.

Yumiko lets out a little holler, which causes everyone to laugh and puts me at ease. I stick my tongue out at her and she sticks hers out back at me.

"Now," he says, "let's listen."

The listening session is very uncomfortable. Everyone keeps nudging me and looking at me, and Nina is taking frantic notes in her Moleskine. I become paranoid that I ruined Shiny AF's career by fucking it up with Nina. I keep wanting to look at what she's writing but I know that would be insane. The only parts of the listening session I enjoy are when Pilar is singing. Her voice is really angelic and makes me feel like I'm part of something good and right. By the third track, Yumiko has her arm around me and I'm nuzzling up in her parka and she's petting my hair. I imagine what my supervisors would think and try to push away the thought.

When it's finally over, I'm relieved. After a few seconds of silence, Jax asks for our permission to send it along to Wicked Ice and everyone agrees that it's ready. I'm tempted to say no, mainly because I want to get back in the booth. I don't want to be done. I want to keep creating. I don't want to be alone with my thoughts and my time.

"And now," Jax says, "we party."

Like clockwork, Beau pulls out a Ziploc bag of white powder and lays it on the gold tray on the table. He also lays down some bright blue pills and winks at me. I can't believe he had the nerve to interrogate me earlier. The doorbell rings and I jump.

"Invite whoever," Jax says as he gets up to get the door.

Soon the Kingdom is packed wall to wall. It's steamy and glows red and looks ominous, and the scariest part is I don't remember when all these people got here. I'm sitting on the couch next to Beau. He's mumbling expletives at his phone while I stare vacantly into the masses and think about what Edie Sedgwick would do right now, other than take too many drugs and die.

I feel a tap on my shoulder. A part of me hopes it's Nina, but I look behind me and it's Yumiko. "Shrine?" she asks. I can't get up fast enough.

Yumiko has to make a tent around the end of my cigarette as I light it because the wind is blowing. It's been unusually cold the past few weeks, not getting above the mid-60s—finally appropriate parka weather. The air is damp and misty and I feel nostalgic for the Bay Area, which rarely happens. LA is where the freaks are, like Lana said.

"I filed a draft to my supervisor," I say to Yumiko as she lights her blunt.

"Awesome," she says. "I'm sure it's amazing." Another wind hits and I think I smell the ocean.

"You'll see the final copy when it's filed." I say this as though it's a nice gesture, but it's legally required.

"Can't wait to bring those pigs down," she says.

"The length of their reply brief suggested they were scared," I say, then drag.

"They should be," she says. "Look at my lawyer."

It takes me a second to realize she's talking about me. Though I passed the bar four years ago, I've never really felt like a lawyer. Lawyers are rational adults, and I'm drugged out on a rickety fire escape, sharing a blunt with a former gun dealer.

"I want to be able to do you justice," I say, then realize I've said something atypically cheesy.

"I trust you," she says, and I feel terrible.

Yumiko and I exhale simultaneously and smoke dances away from the fire escape and up toward the palms.

I turn and look through the windows into the room. The dance floor is packed. I see Jax and Pilar in the center under the disco ball but don't really recognize anyone else. I spot Beau because he's so tall. His arm is around someone I can't make out. Then I see the curls. Nina.

I grab Yumiko's hand. "Let's dance!"

She throws her blunt off the ledge and I drag her inside.

The dance floor has emptied out a bit, and it's less hot. The neon is no longer red but a calm baby blue. The music isn't pulsing but rather soft and sonorous. I don't recognize the song, but when I look over at Pilar and see how she's singing it—it's her. I put my arm around her and we bump hips. Jax, Yumiko, Pilar, and I are all under the disco ball, swaying in sync, Shiny AF.

Just when I feel calm, the bedroom door opens. Beau is tugging the bottom of his T-shirt down as though it's been off. Nina emerges behind him. I want to look away, but I force myself to watch. It's emotional cutting, like looking at the Instagram pages of my enemies.

"Shrine?" I whisper in Yumiko's ear.

"But we were just there," she says.

Instead of answering, I grab her arm and start pulling it, and luckily she doesn't put up a fight. I feel the weight of Beau's presence behind me, like a slimy drugged-out ghost.

Once we're on the fire escape, I burst into tears. It's very unlike me to cry around someone. But Yumiko doesn't feel like a person.

And besides, the drugs and alcohol whirling around in my system have frayed my natural defense mechanisms. I had no idea I cared this much about Nina even. This is good. Maybe I'm finally getting to the heart of my feelings. I'll become more vulnerable and less sociopathic.

"Who do I need to pop?" she asks.

I laugh, and I lean into her parka. She wraps her arms around me. My gaze floats inside briefly and I make eye contact with Nina, who is leaning on Beau's shoulder. I quickly look away.

"Wanna get out of here?" I ask Yumiko.

"Yes," she says. "I start to feel cooped up when I'm in here for too long."

She starts walking toward the window and I grab her arm. "Wait," I say. "I can't go in there... " I eye the fire escape and then Yumiko. Her eyes light up.

I'm terrified of heights. And I'm fucked up on a potpourri of mind-altering substances. Sound judgment says this is a horrible idea. And yet I'm here, grasping a metal ladder twelve stories above the ground, wind hitting me from all sides.

Yumiko is already two platforms below me, urging me on. "You got it, Vaga," she says, using her guttural "hype woman" voice. I worry that she's waking up Jax's neighbors. I think of aborting this mission, then I imagine Nina and Beau mid-coital and I get a surge of courage. The grotesque image, combined with Yumiko's hooting, propels me to quickly scale down two stories. As soon as I reach Yumiko, I collapse into her parka, feeling wobbly and weak. She grabs both my arms and shakes me upright.

"You got this, Vaga," she says. "The closer you are to the ground, the easier it is."

She then swings down to the next ladder, moving gracefully and without fear, a trapeze artist. I take care not to look at the ground.

Yumiko yells, her voice faint from the distance: "Imagine you're onstage."

I want to yell back that, historically, I panic onstage. I want to tell her I could hardly handle five people looking at me during the listening party. I want to tell her that I've been medicating myself into near collapse just to handle the past few months. But I say nothing and grab the ladder and descend, until I'm right beside her voice.

"Almost halfway there," she says.

This is not helpful. My legs feel weak. I don't think I can make it another half. I look in the window of the apartment we're beside, wonder if anyone could let me in and escort me to the elevator. But it looks dark and very bougie. I would frighten these people. They might call the police. And Yumiko has a criminal record.

"Okay," she says. "Imagine Nina yelling from above, saying you can't do it."

"She would never do that," I yell back, and think about how much I hate Nina.

Yumiko's already hanging on the next ladder with only one hand. "Look," she says, "the more you drag it out the worse it's going to be. It'll take longer to get back up than it will to get down at this point." Then she starts swinging down the ladder, like a monkey.

I follow much less gracefully. One step at a time. Don't look down. With each step, the entire structure seems to shake and I wonder whether it will just break and I'll fall to my death. Death doesn't scare me, but the free fall does, as does hitting the pavement. *If I die*, I pray to a god I don't believe in, *I want it to be quick*. And then I'll smoke cigarettes with Edie Sedgwick in hell.

After what seems like twenty minutes, I reach Yumiko again.

"Yes, Vaga," she says. "Halfway."

"I want to die," I say matter-of-factly. I sit down cross-legged on the platform, which seems to shake. I peer into the apartment beside us, which is even darker and bougier. There is an empty growler of kombucha on the table and a baby stroller on the floor. This couple would call the cops on us, surely. I'm trapped.

"This is not the Vaga I know," Yumiko says, sitting beside me. She pulls a half-smoked blunt from her pocket and lights it. Only Yumiko would smoke a blunt while descending a twelve-story fire escape. After a hefty inhale, she passes the blunt to me. "The Vaga I know is a bad bitch."

I wave the blunt away, then say, "You don't know me."

Yumiko looks hurt, then annoyed. "Fine," she says.

She begins flying down the ladder, blunt in her mouth. The whole platform shakes. I fantasize about lying down and being lulled asleep by the steady trembling of Yumiko's descent. In the morning, the bougie couple will find me, and I'll explain that I was roofied at a strange party on the twelfth floor and only made it this far before I lost consciousness.

Just as I begin to lie down, my coat vibrates and I pull out my phone. There is a text from Nina and I feel a weird mix of anger and excitement. I open it.

It's beau, u got any addys? We running low on uppers.

I shut the phone off and stand up.

"Attagirl!" Yumiko shouts from below. I don't look down, but she sounds pretty distant. I grab the ladder and try to channel my fearless friend. I imagine her floating down the ladder without apparent effort, huffing cannabis with abandon. I start moving, quicker than before. Yumiko is shouting "go Vaga" and "almost there" intermittently in a way that keeps me motivated. Soon, I've reached her level and she wraps me in her parka and I feel both safe and accomplished.

"Look down," she says.

I look back at her with hesitance.

"Trust me," she says.

I emerge from the parka cave and slowly look down, and there is just one more ladder below us. We're almost there. I feel an immense wave of relief, like when an airplane is about to land. I'm overcome with a strange urge to kiss Yumiko, who at this moment looks particularly beautiful, a streetlamp illuminating her big blue eyes. Just as my gaze settles, she jerks away and swings back on the ladder. I follow. Soon we're on solid ground and I'm elated.

"You wanna know something?" Yumiko says.

I shrug.

"I don't really care that much about my appeal," she says. "Like I said, I already served my time, I already have a record. A clean slate isn't necessarily my brand." She giggles and so do I, but I'm also annoyed for doing all that work in vain. Yumiko looks up toward the streetlight and her long lashes light up. "I just thought you were cool and wanted an excuse to connect."

I smile and I really feel happy, like the high of completing this terrifying descent is combining with a feeling of genuine interpersonal connection—a rare experience for me—and it's, like, better than Adderall. Less chemically.

"That is so nice," I say. "I don't know what to say."

"You don't have to say anything," she says.

So I don't, and the silence of the empty street takes over the moment. A cat screams in the distance and I think about Missy.

SEVENTEEN

The next morning, Yumiko's wearing a T-shirt, which looks strange. I've never seen her without a parka. Her right arm is covered in scars; her left, a tattoo sleeve.

She sits beside me on the bed and hands me a steaming mug. "Morning, sunshine," she says. I'm in her bed, which is just a mattress on the floor with a puffy black duvet.

This is a new side of Yumiko, kind and domestic. It's bright in her apartment and oddly clean. Across from the bed is a mirror closet that takes up the entire wall. I watch us in the reflection and we look like a bad mumblecore film, all tired-eyed and unsure in the harsh sun of the morning. What happened last night?

"What time is it?" I ask. As I sit up, the heaviness descends. I feel like I need an IV drip, more amphetamines, or both. Instead, I sip the coffee. It's good, like she grinded fancy beans and used a Chemex or something.

"Threeish," she says. Sounds about right from the light, bright as can be. "Man, that party was lit." She laughs.

"Yeah," I say. "I had no idea the listening party would draw that many people."

"No," she says. "I mean the other one. After the fire escape." I have no memory of a party after that. I wonder if Yumiko and I did anything last night. The memory of the fire escape intensifies my dread.

"Jesus, I can't believe we scaled that fire escape!" I say.

Yumiko laughs. "I've done it a billion times," she says. "But I was proud of you," she adds, then touches my forearm in a way that makes me feel a bit paranoid. I'm already on shaky ethical ground with Yumiko, but if I slept with her? Case closed. I consider writing a song called "Waking Up in Strange Beds." Or "Parties I Don't Remember." Or "Did We Sleep Together?" The next album will basically write itself.

"I should probably go," I say. "My supervisor might have gotten back to me with edits on your brief."

She pushes some hair out of her face and I try not to stare at the burn scars on her arm.

"I know you don't care about the appeal," I continue, "but it's my job." I feel corny and awkward, a mumblecore side character. Not even the lead, not even close to the lead.

"Well, I won't stop you," Yumiko says.

"Thanks for saving me last night," I say.

"Vaga!" Yumiko says, jumping up, reoccupying the Yumiko I know and am familiar with. "You know I have your back, boo!"

"I know," I say, and then I leave.

When I get home, I take half a Klonopin and eat a bowl of cereal and fall asleep with Ennui on my rib cage while it's still light outside. I don't wake up until nine A.M. the next morning.

My supervisor's email is longer than I'd like, so long I want to bang my head against my desk. She says I need to "reorganize" my arguments. She also says that certain things weren't "adequately briefed" in my opening brief, but I can "correct them now." She doesn't seem to realize that she read, edited, and approved my opening brief. Everything in this job seems so random. I felt really good about this brief. I was feeling myself when I wrote it. I was in the zone. Other times I'll write a brief and feel totally detached and uninterested and just be waiting to get it done, then I hand it in and my supervisor is like, "You are a true legal talent and will one day be briefing before the Supreme Court." As if I'd want that.

I take an Adderall and start typing. I take the dissociative route, just getting through my supervisor's comments with as little effort or passion as possible. It doesn't seem to matter. In between sentences, I refresh Twitter and watch my followers increase.

At around two P.M., the Kingdom thread lights up with a text from Jax

Wicked Ice loves the EP.

A text from Nina floats in and I feel a sliver of excitement, then realize it's just to the group.

Rad. When's the rollout?

I assume she's asking because she wants to know when she can file her story, when she can cash in on our brilliance.

Jax replies, *They said they only have a few minor edits, they want it out in the next week.*

Pilar chimes in, *Yeeeeeeeeeeeee.*

Then Yumiko: *BrRRRT BrRRRT.*

I shut iMessage and continue working on my brief, feeling absolutely nothing.

That night in bed, I begin to spiral. I'm listening to my "Sad Girlz" playlist, which is mostly Lana Del Rey, and alternating between staring at the palm fronds above my bed and scrolling aimlessly through Instagram when the intrusive thoughts start. It begins with Ennui pawing her way into my room. I thought I'd closed the door, but I guess not. She looks so thin and sad and lonely, and I think about how they say pets mirror their owners. I recall Beau telling me I look pale. I recall how I sabotaged my perfect relationship by hooking up with this poly loser with no respect for me. I know I'm not always a ray of sunshine toward Nina, but at least I have the decency to avoid hooking up with someone she hates in front of her.

I got off SSRIs in part because I was worried about my physical health. Now I'm taking Adderall, a stimulant with a chemical compound almost identical to crystal meth, in an uncontrolled manner. I'm suffering obvious delusions of grandeur with my fewer than four thousand Twitter followers. People online are saying that Shiny AF is "aural assault." And when the EP inevitably bombs, I will have nothing. I will go back to writing briefs that have zero impact on anyone's life alone in my apartment and making no money and embarrassing everyone who knows me. But I might not even have that option, because I might have slept with my client. And the scariest part is I'm not even sure. *Did We Sleep Together? A Memoir.*

Ennui meows bloody murder. I throw my phone on my pillow and follow her to the kitchen. She's starving and keeps running into my legs and I accidentally kick her. I look in the cabinet and realize I'm out of cat food. My body is too heavy to go to the store. Leaving my bedroom is hard enough. I search my cabinets for something a cat might like. I nearly shout when I find a dusty can of tuna in the very back. I can't remember ever buying canned tuna, but I don't question it. I open it and put it in the bowl, ignoring its strange color and odor, and think, *What if I really am famous?*

Fame feels equally depressing to being delusional. Ellen DeGeneres is famous, and she's corny as hell. People love that Nazi-esque Victoria's Secret model Karlie Kloss, a woman so blah I couldn't pick her out of a lineup. Corrupt real estate mogul turned reality TV star Donald Trump beat out career politician Hillary Clinton for the presidency. People think Oprah should run next, just because she exploits people for their traumas and gives them cars on live television. Women with low IQs protest gender inequality by buying T-shirts with glittery slogans, ignorant to the irony that social equality is untenable under capitalism. Reese Witherspoon wore black on the red carpet as a political statement and everyone was like, *Omg, genius!* And whenever an actual genius happens to become famous, like Kanye, he is instantly demonized because we're terrified to confront our own darkness. God, everyone is so horny for mediocrity, it sickens me. I wish I could just disappear.

Once Ennui starts eating, I drag myself back to bed, where I sleep for twelve hours.

I wake up with a lot of texts. The *FADER* article is up. I don't click the link because I don't want to read it, nor do I want to look at the pictures. I ignore all my texts except the ones from Jake.

Prudence. You are a hot mess.

Emphasis on the HOT.

I roll my eyes. I don't want to see or talk to anyone, especially Jake Perez. But I know I need to get out of this funk. I look at my calendar and realize the show is in three days. I go into my bathroom and open my gold bag and count my Adderall. I have two left. Panic hits. It's only been ten days, I can't possibly ask Dr. Kim for a refill. Or maybe I could? Didn't he say something along the lines of "we'll start with thirty pills and see how it goes?" I could email him and say, "I need more," make up something about how I've realized ADD is my main issue and I need to be prescribed at least sixty milligrams a day, but I prefer to take it in ten-milligram doses. I go to my laptop and write that email, then realize how long it takes Dr. Kim to get back. I consider Yelping "lenient psychiatrist," and then I remember that trust-fund crackhead I bought Vyvanse from. I must have his number. I grab my phone and start frantically searching. Just as I find it, a text from Nina comes in.

Hi.

Classic. I ignore it and text the crackhead. *Hi, I need more V. ASAP.* I sound insane but I don't care. I'm opening for Dead Stars in three days. The thought alone makes my heart race. I become dizzy and sit down on my bed. Ennui comes over, apparently sensing my distress, and rubs up against my rib cage.

Then she throws up on my lap.

EIGHTEEN

Dr. Kim gets back to me the next morning, but he tells me that California law requires a handwritten prescription, which I must retrieve from his office. Alternatively, he could mail it. I opt for that option, mostly to avoid a panic attack on the drive. Trust-fund crackhead has only three Vyvanse, and I buy him out. I open the pills and pour the beads in a tiny Ziploc bag, then wet my finger and put some tiny salmon-colored beads on my tongue. Ennui becomes entranced by the process. I almost zone out and let her lick some beads off my finger. But I quickly remove my finger before her tongue gets to it, proving to myself that I'm not an animal abuser. Then I go to rehearsal.

Onstage, I feel stiff and awkward, despite Jax's constant assurances that I'm "slaying." I don't trust him. At one point, I snap at Beau for "laughing at me," but he tells me he was laughing at a text from Nina, which obviously infuriates me more. I remember this cultural phenomenon I read about in Indonesia, where a minor social insult launches people into a long period of brooding followed by murderous rage. During a smoke break, a woman driving by yells, "Shiny AF!" out of her car. Jax goes, "Eyyyyy," and Yumiko goes, "Brrrat brraat," and I feel an intense tightening in my neck.

During the second smoke break, I text Nina. *Can you not text our lighting guy while I'm trying to rehearse?* I sound like an insane diva, just like I probably sounded in her article, which I still haven't read.

Jax comes out and tells me he has "news." I'm annoyed. I can't handle any new information. I feel nostalgic for my old life, when I'd just write briefs in my room and go out to dinner with Ellie and do uppers once a month like a normal fucking person. Before one of my cats went missing and the other one began starving to death. I make a mental note to buy cat food.

"Wyatt texted me this morning," says Jax, "about the Teragram show." He drags, looking pleased with himself. "She said she's hyped we're opening."

I force a weak smile and say, "Cool."

"You're always so blasé," says Pilar. I want to respond, *it's the pharmaceuticals*, but instead I say nothing.

"Pinch me!" Jax screams.

I pinch him, harder than I mean. He laughs, but it looks like he's in pain. Then Nina texts back. It just says, *lol*.

The day before the show I'm out of Vyvanse, but luckily the prescription from Dr. Kim arrives in the mail. I basically run to Walgreens, the place I most hate in the world, with an enthusiasm like I'm on a pilgrimage to Mecca. I don't even care when the line is long, when the pharmacist says she's required "by law" to give a consultation. I'm just smiling and laughing periodically to myself, not caring when the pharmacist looks at me concerned.

Afterward, I get lunch with Jake Perez. "Holy shit" is the first thing he says when he sees me. He reaches for my arm and puts his fingers around it and I slap it away.

"Don't body-shame me," I say. I know his point is that I look unhealthy, but I can't help but feel flattered. It's not about vanity—well, of course it is—but it's more than that. My mom's mantra was always "humans need much less food than they think they do." Withholding food provides a strange illusion of power. I told the nutritionist I was forced to go to that I was simply a victim of late capitalism, and she said I was a "tough case." When asked point-blank I'll say I've been "diagnosed with eating disorders" (how many times is not important), but I'll never say I've "suffered from eating disorders" the way girls in those lame confessional essays in *Cosmo* do. The DMV? That's suffering. Eating disorder? That's privilege.

"Are you ready?" he asks after the waiter takes our orders. We're at Canter's. I'd demanded we sit in the bar section, where it's dimmer and hipper, where there's a full bar, where hot people go at night.

"Don't ask dumb questions," I say.

"You're very aggressive today," he says.

I shrug, then eye the room. It's hard for me to be in a room without my eyes flitting around, especially today, especially now. But luckily, there isn't much to look at in here.

When the waitress comes with our drinks, I practically snatch mine from her hand. I sip. Then I look at Jake.

"I'm terrified."

"You're confusing, Prue," he says, and I agree. "You are unconcerned about the fact that there are nude photos of you, that you cannot account for, flourishing on the internet," he continues, and I suppress a smile. "Yet getting to open for your two favorite musicians at your favorite venue, something you seem to have wanted since I've known you, throws you into despair."

"You're so fixated on my nudies." I wink and stir my drink. "Are you considering getting back into the puss?"

Jake makes a face like he's about to vomit. "I was never into 'the puss,'" he says. "And what the hell with that vile, fuccboi, antifeminist phrasing? Very uncouth."

I respond by motorboating the air. Freshman year, Jake Perez told everyone he motorboated a cheerleader at a frat party and then vomited in her cleavage. Senior year, he admitted he made it up.

"Don't be disgusting," he says. "Speaking of, did you do something to your hair?"

"Excuse me?" I instinctively reach for my ends.

The waitress puts a tray covered with various plates in front of Jake. I don't really recognize anything on there, except for pickles. I take one without asking.

"It just looks a bit"—he digs his fork into a brown hunk of mystery meat—"dry?"

A lump forms in my throat. My hair is my whole brand. I remember reading an interview with Wyatt's sister, Stella, where she said she was taking a bunch of Adderall so she could exercise more and her hair started falling out. God, that can't be happening to me. Skeletal is chill, but I need my hair to look healthy.

"You okay?" Jake asks.

I take a steadying sip of my bourbon. "Yeah," I say. My head feels pleasantly fuzzy for a moment. "Just thinking about you lying about vomiting into a woman's breasts." I start to giggle. "It's just funny you wouldn't give yourself a better edit." I stab a piece of lettuce. "Especially, you know, given that it was a lie."

"You know not everyone is pathologically obsessed with what irrelevant people think of them," he says.

I start chewing my lettuce. "Yes, they are."

On the way out of the restaurant, I spot a cool teenager and start to stare, hoping I can maybe secondhand inhale some of her youthful *je ne sais quoi*. She's wearing all black with checkered Vans and has dirty-blonde hair. Soon, she's staring back at me, which makes me embarrassed. She probably thinks I'm some kind of creep. She starts to approach on a skateboard that I didn't see before.

"Vagablondeeee," she says. She stops her skateboard and pops it up into her arm.

Jake raises his eyebrows at her, and I stand frozen.

"'Dearly Queerly' is my shit!" she says.

I force an uncomfortable smile and feel a desperate need to escape. I look around me and get that feeling I get on the freeway, like the world is too vast and I am too small and the weight of space will crush me.

"And that *FADER* article!" she says, apparently oblivious to my discomfort. "You're what's up!"

I feel a weight on my head, my shoulders, all around me. Jake puts his arm around me, which makes me jump.

"Thanks for your support," Jake says to the teen, then escorts me to the car like he's my bodyguard or something. As we walk, I notice a few other cool teens with their phones out, maybe taking photos, maybe filming. I cover my face with my hand and feel myself leave my body. I've been practicing for this moment my entire life, but it doesn't feel as cool as I thought it was. Actually I feel like I'm dying.

That evening I'm staring at the palm frond while Ennui makes hacking noises when Nina calls. I answer it.

"Hi," I say with a cool monotone. "That's my impression of you."

"I'm sorry about the article," she says.

"Didn't read it," I say.

"Are you seri—"

Another call is coming in, from Yumiko. Saved by the bell.

"I'll call you back," I say, then switch calls. "Yo, b."

"Hi, lovey," she says. She's speaking in the Cockney accent, which I haven't heard her use in a while. "I'm freaking out a bit. Having a proper breakdown, if you will."

"SAME!"

"You fucking with me?" she asks. "You're always so chillllll."

"Are you kidding?" I ask. "Did you not see me on the fire escape, boo?"

She laughs. "Yeah," she says, her accent fading. Her voice softens, and I remember the side of her from the morning I slept over. The girl with the T-shirt and the steaming coffee mug and the burn marks. I still wonder what happened to her arm. I imagine it's a good story. "But you seem so natural onstage."

"That's good," I say. "I typically feel like I'm dying."

"God," she says. "Same."

"I didn't realize fear was an emotion you experienced," I say. "You are, like... " I pet Ennui, searching for the words. "...missing an amygdala." Ennui makes a sound like she might vomit and I feel no particular way about it.

"Yeah," she says. "As a performance artist... " She pauses. "I take my art very seriously. Falling off a fire escape, I'd just die or become disfigured. Tragic, maybe, but not as tragic as fucking up my art."

My stomach churns as I imagine bones cracking on the pavement.

"I'm not that precious about my art," I say.

"Bullshit."

When she hangs up, I collapse onto the bed and my self-hate spirals out of control. Not only am I a sad thirtysomething chasing untenable delusions, but I'm so fixated on my internal drama that I alienate everyone who tries to get close to me. Besides, what do I have to be so fucking depressed about? I'm thin and well educated. People seem to like me and want to have sex with me. My parents are rich enough that I don't really ever have to worry about being homeless. I should volunteer, think about someone else for once, rather than wallowing in an endless vortex of self-loathing. Or maybe I could get a lobotomy, like a light one. Like where I'm still smart but I have a totally different personality.

I take half a Klonopin, turn off the light, and type "Wyatt Walcott hair" into the search engine on Pinterest, then begin to scroll until my brain shuts the fuck up.

My body is nearly shaking when I awake. As I reach for my phone I spot a bit of cat vomit on the edge of my bed and feel like I might throw up myself. It's only 10:30 A.M. I don't have to be at the venue until 6:00 P.M. The expanse of time scares me.

What will I do to fill it? How will I stay sober enough to perform?
I remember a time I saw Das Racist in 2012 and they were chugging vodka onstage and couldn't form a coherent bar. I finagled
my way backstage after the show, which was easy because I was
the hottest girl, maybe the only girl, in the audience (their music
is very boy). This was during the straightest period of my life,
when I used to throw myself at any boy with a cute sweater who
fancied himself clever. That night, I latched on to Heems, the
chubby one in the group. Not long after I sat on his lap, he started
smoking heroin and my square law school friend got scared and
we had to leave. Later he told me I dodged a "fat bullet." But the
point is they were signed to Sony, and they were very fucked up,
much more than I ever have been or ever will be.

U up? I text Yumiko.

Spiraling, she types back, and I'm relieved.

I begin typing *same* and then I decide to call her. "I want to
start naming your characters," I say, then put the call on speaker.
I get up to grab a cloth and wet it under the faucet, for the cat
vomit.

"Characters?"

"Yeah." I go to the bed and start wiping off the vomit. I focus on
the fact that I'm opening for my heroes tonight and try to, like, be
happy or whatever. It doesn't work. I still have no idea whether
Shiny AF is even good or whether everyone is just laughing at
us.

"They aren't characters," she says. "They're me."

I realize I've made a real friend out of Yumiko, then I wonder
whether we slept together. I typically can't get close to people until I sleep with them, which Barbara Lumpkin called a "problem."
But she was a bitch. I wonder whether anyone in the downtown
office saw my *FADER* spread. I wonder what Nina wrote. My
brain is going really quick.

"What are we going to do before the show?" I ask.

"Kill ourselves?"

I laugh. "That's Jessica," I say. "Your character."

"Actually," she says, "it's my impression of you."

I stick my tongue out, momentarily forgetting she can't see me.

"Also," she says, "Jessica is the worst name on the planet."

Ennui slinks in.

"Okay, Rachel," I say.

"Bitch!"

I laugh, and then there is a brief moment of silence. I pet Ennui and notice her coat is silky smooth. I pet the crispy hair on my head and feel envious.

"What are you doing right now?" she asks in a manic sorority-girl voice.

"Petting my cat and my own head," I say. Ennui slinks away on the word "cat" as though she is punishing me for acknowledging her.

"Okay," she says. "I'm going to pick you up in twenty."

"Okay," I say. Spontaneity is not typically my thing, but at this moment I'm desperate for anything to occupy my time.

"Wear something you can move in," she says.

"We aren't scaling anything tall, are we?" I ask when I get into Yumiko's car, a boxy black Lincoln filled with fast-food-related trash and a strong scent of marijuana. "Because I'd prefer to avoid an anxiety attack on the day of the show." I clutch my fanny pack, which contains my Altoid tin filled with four amphetamines and four benzos, depending on what I feel I need. I recall how this Altoid tin once contained actual Altoids. Now it's just a tin of drugs I use to remain upright.

"I'm going to take care of you," she says, then squeezes my knee, pounds the gas. KDAY is playing Ashanti and the sun is bright and hot. I feel like we're in a music video from the early aughts—appropriate for show day.

"I didn't know you had a car," I say.

"It's my man's," she says. The fact that she has a "man" makes me feel relieved. Maybe she's fully "heterosexual," which

I wasn't aware people were anymore, especially not people as cool as Yumiko. Maybe she's acting straight to be ironic, or maybe it's her performance art. As warm air pours in through the open windows, my imagination soothes my addled brain. I watch passing palms and imagine Yumiko's man as a hot guy with tattoos, black hair, a charming smile.

"So, wanna know what we're doing?" Yumiko asks as she turns onto San Fernando Road, the street by the dried-up river, Frogtown. Being close to the rehearsal space makes me anxious, as does Yumiko's offer to explain actual future events. I want to forever remain in timeless dreamland.

"Of course," I lie.

"So we're going to my Afro-Caribbean dance class," she says. "My girl Crystal teaches it and you're going to love it. It will loosen you up for the show, and you might even get some ideas for moves—not that you need them."

This is the fastest and most animated I've ever heard Yumiko speak, and I wonder if she's on uppers. Then I realize this is the first time I've seen her without a blunt in her mouth. Maybe she's just sober.

"Then," she says, whipping around the curved road, "we're going to eat a burger." The way she drives reminds me of the way she descended the fire escape: reckless and unfazed. It doesn't help that this car is bulky as hell and emitting weird sounds. "Because I need you well fed up there."

"I'm a vegetarian," I lie. I really don't like burgers. My mouth is too small for them.

"Veggie burger then!" She swings into a parking lot, then into a space. "Then we'll get ready."

The car is now stopped. Yumiko points to the back seat. I look back and see open duffel bags overflowing with sequined jackets and neon wigs and scuffed tubes of mascara. I feel silly that I didn't think about this. I had a vague idea of what I wanted to wear onstage at some point, but then I forgot. I pull out my phone and text Jax.

Any ideas about my look tonight?

By the time I hit send, Yumiko is already walking toward the studio with a kind of swaggy strut. I put my phone back in my fanny pack and laugh at myself walking into an Afro-Caribbean dance class with a fanny pack and neon-blonde hair.

"Vaga?" asks a girl with white braids as soon as I enter the studio. It's run-down with exposed brick. Dramatic lighting cuts in from various mysterious holes. Very *Save the Last Dance*.

"Hi," I say to the girl. The two other women in the room seem to be looking at me.

"Yumi has told me a lot about you," she says. "I'm Crystal." She's wearing a sequined bodysuit that reminds me of the jacket Yumiko showed me the other day on her flip phone.

"Ah," I say. I should have realized it was her. "Likewise."

Crystal begins with a popping dancehall track that instantly pulls me in. I'd forgotten how fun it is to dance in front of mirrors. Halfway into the track, I accidentally burst out laughing, in a normal and hopefully not rude way, at the fact that I'm taking an Afro-Caribbean dance class in a gentrified neighborhood of East Los Angeles taught by a white woman for white women— a bunch of Rachel Dolezals shaking our nonexistent asses. Afterward, I become sad, feeling guilty about my obvious role in gentrification and my voyeurism into cultures I know nothing about, but which seem "exciting" in the abstract, in comparison to my mundane and sheltered existence. I refocus on the dance moves to quiet my brain.

Dance class goes by quickly. Crystal has great energy and rhythm, and many times I find myself jumping into the air with her and moving my body in an uninhibited manner. A few times Yumiko hip-bumps me midmove, and each time I imagine her saying "my man" and feel, simultaneously, comforted and jealous. The two other women dance with very nervous and understated movements. *We teach women to shrink themselves*, I think, then I quickly refocus on my body. At the end of class, the two other white women scamper out of the room without my noticing. Either that or they never existed.

"Are you ready for tonight?" Crystal asks.

"No," I say.

"I'm excited," she says. This girl seems nice.

Yumiko pulls my arm. "Time to get this delicate flower fed," she says.

"Kill it tonight," Crystal says, and I wonder if it's time to dose.

Outside, I pull out my phone to avoid looking at the sun. The time hits me in the face: 2:30 P.M. That means I don't get to the venue for another three and a half hours, meaning I don't go on for another five hours. As my stomach begins to sink, I check my text from Jax.

LOL Vaga you always look amazing!!! Just do you <3

As cars zoom by in front of me, I try to come up with a response. My iPhone feels hot in my palm.

I'm bad at my makeup, I type back. Yumiko honks. I put my phone back in my purse and skip over to her car, propelled back into the timeless dream space.

Yumiko takes me to a gastropub on Los Feliz Boulevard. I've been here once before with Jake Perez. It's dark and feels like a cave... womblike. We sit in the corner and order big draft beers and burgers—mine, vegetarian. I decide to obey Yumiko's command to eat. I'm normally pretty regimented about my caloric intake, but today I decide I could use some lining in my stomach. I even eat the fries, which are thick and greasy, and slather them in ketchup.

When I'm full, I pull out my phone. There's a text from Jax. *Pilar can do your makeup!* ☺

Perfect, I write back. I wonder what I'm going to wear. I check the time. It's not even three P.M. Three hours until I get to the venue. I'm scared to go home, where I have abundant access to pills and alcohol and cigarettes and weed, and where I'll likely lose all self-control, then show up to the venue in a catatonic state. Ugh, time, you frustrating bitch.

"Do you wanna get ready at your place?" I ask Yumiko. I think if there is anything I need. I could shower at her house. She has great T-shirts and boots. I'm not particularly attached to anything I own. I have my pills. I clutch my fanny pack.

"I'm low on cash so I Airbnb'd it," she says. "I've been sleeping at my man's."

"Oh," I say. "That's fine." I do some math in my head. We could probably stay here another hour or so, have another beer. We could get back to my house at around 4:00, 4:30. Shower. Get ready. Leave for the venue at 5:45 P.M. It doesn't take either of us very long to get dressed.

Yumiko slaps my arm. "Calm down!"

"I'm trying," I say. Then I go to the bathroom and break one of my Adderall pills in half and crunch the five milligrams between my molars. I rinse my mouth out with water from the bathroom sink and flush the toilet for good measure. Bathroom infidelities.

Returning to the table, I feel the amphetamine jolt. I'm chatting as soon as I sit down. My mouth is on autopilot and my crazy thoughts are easily finding their way out of my head. "I'm thinking long black T-shirt, I have one I can wear as a dress. Black thigh-high socks. Black Timberlands. Maybe a thin silver or gold chain... " I'm not even looking at Yumiko as I speak. She may as well not be there. Soon I'm not even listening to myself, and then my phone rings.

It's Nina. "Hi," I say.

"You never called me back," she says. I could not be more over her in this moment.

"Sorry," I say. "Something came up."

Yumiko takes an aggressive bite of burger, then makes a funny face. I laugh.

"Do you even want me to come tonight?" she asks.

"I really don't care," I say. I put a fry into my mouth and speak while chewing. "I'm eating lunch, is there anything you need from me?"

"What do you mean?"

"Like for an article or something," I say. I know I'm being a brat. Ellie floats into my brain. I can't believe I'm about to open for Dead Stars and we aren't even speaking.

"No?" she says in a way that annoys me. I hang up.

"Nina?" Yumiko asks.

"Yeah," I say.

"What's going on with you two?"

"Nothing," I say, then put another fry into my mouth.

At home, I try my best to focus on discrete tasks. I don't want to ingest more than 10 milligrams of Adderall before I go onstage. But I also want to feel up—like a star, with charisma. I took 5 milligrams at the bar. I decide to take the other 5 milligrams before I leave the house. Maybe I'll take 2.5—a quarter—right before I go onstage. I'll bring my fanny pack in case I have an emergency. I shouldn't take uppers and downers at the same time, but it's nice knowing the benzos are there in case I need them.

Yumiko takes the first shower. While the water falls, I sip a beer very slowly and lay out various T-shirt options on the bed. I blast the EP and rap along as practice. I try to move while I'm doing it. I dim the lights in my room and sway in front of the mirror and thank god for blessing me with alienating mannerisms that translate as alluring and vulnerable onstage.

Soon the bathroom door flies open and steam fills my bedroom. Ennui meows in protest. Yumiko struts out buck naked, then starts twerking to the song. Her breasts flap wildly and her butt pops with precision. I address my discomfort by turning up my dance energy. I still feel the euphoria of the five milligrams, and with the second half I'll be in a good state by the time I get to the venue. I check the clock: 4:45 P.M. One hour.

In the shower, I wash every corner of my body, twice, then shave every hair on my body. I deep condition my hair. I sit down in the middle of the shower and take deep, steamy breaths. For several minutes, I stand aimlessly under the stream of hot water, which burns in a good way. I coat my whole body in coconut oil. When I exit the shower, I hit my vape pen. The vapor combines with the steam from the shower and I remember when we used to fill Jake Perez's old BMW with blunt smoke on the way to the movies in college.

"I was about to come check on you," Yumiko says when I finally exit—with a towel, thank you.

"It's called self-care," I say. Then I check the time: 5:10. Fuck. Time is moving at a glacial pace. I return to the bathroom and take another five milligrams. When I exit, I step directly into cat vomit.

NINETEEN

I'm more buzzed than I wanted to be when we arrive at the venue, but it could be worse. We're fifteen minutes late because Yumiko had a small "wardrobe malfunction" with an accompanying freak-out.

We're standing aimlessly outside of shut black doors when Jax and Pilar arrive. Jax runs up and puts his arms around us, pulls us all into a tight quartet that makes me feel safe. Then we spend several minutes trying to figure out how to get inside.

A large man in all black escorts us to our "green room," which is not green. It's black with chipped paint and cracked leather couches, like the break room of a shitty office. To my chagrin, there is a small fridge filled with domestic light beers. There are also bottles of bourbon and gin, which I vow not to touch. Pink cans of LaCroix. Haribo gummy bears. Two blunts.

I crack open a beer and sit down on the couch while Jax puts *The Miseducation of Lauryn Hill* on the speakers. I start rolling my shoulders and go into the nice, timeless zone. I forget that I'm about to perform and feel like I'm just at a normal party with my new friends. Then the large man returns and says "sound check" and Jax pauses Lauryn and we all head to the empty stage. Jax starts plugging things in and communicating with the venue's sound engineer in what sounds like a foreign language. I zone out and think about how I will pass the time before the performance, how many milligrams I'll consume, whether Wyatt is here yet and what she'll be wearing. The beat to "Dearly Queerly" drops and I jump a little. Jax starts going *eyyyyyy* and Yumiko does her little scream and I rap my verse vacantly into the empty ballroom.

When we return to the green room, Pilar pulls me over to a chair in front of a bulb-lined mirror and starts doing my makeup, which feels relaxing and very Old Hollywood. I ask her to do dramatic 1970s wings, like Lindsay Lohan in *The Canyons*, which is not set in the 1970s (nothing about that movie makes sense). I think about whether I should tell Wyatt that I watch YouTube videos of her sister, Stella, to figure out how to do my makeup. Then my stomach sinks a little. I wonder if we'll see her before we go on.

When my makeup is done, Jax and I dance to M.I.A. while clutching perspiring beers and everything feels good and normal.

Then the fat man peeks in and says, "Ten minutes."

And then I begin to freak out a bit. What if I freeze? When I saw Cat Power in college, Chan Marshall had a major breakdown onstage and her career could not be better. *I'm in the right profession*, I tell myself, then try to calculate how many milligrams of Adderall are in my system.

Yumiko interrupts my internal calculations. "Cigarette?"

"Please," I say.

We go outside. In the hallway I imagine Wyatt or Agnes popping up at any moment.

"How are you doing?" Yumiko looks into my eyes with a sincere expression that makes me uncomfortable.

"I'm great!"

She grabs my shoulders. "Don't fuck with me."

I grab hers. "Don't freak me out."

"I'm being a friend," she says.

"Don't!" I yell, then I light my cigarette.

As soon as we get back inside, people are yelling at us. Arms and voices urge us down the hall. Yumiko hits my butt and we both run. My heart is beating out of my chest. I can no longer make out shapes or figures. The colors and people blur together into a kaleidoscopic mess that alternates between beautiful and terrifying between seconds. I've never taken psychedelics but it feels like I'm tripping.

Soon there is noise everywhere. A screaming faceless mass. A hand caresses my back—Jax or maybe Pilar. We take our places, "blocking" like we practiced. Another wave of screams rushes at us and my body freezes. I'm paralyzed, just like I feared. I meant to bring a beer onstage, but I forgot. I clutch my fanny pack, which cuts diagonally across my black T-shirt so that I look like a crossing guard in *The Matrix*. At least that's what Yumiko said before we left.

Soon the beat drops and my mouth is opening and making sounds and people are screaming. I can't hear myself or distinguish between the sounds really, but I'm glad the audience isn't quiet. I'm also glad I can't make out faces or even distinct bodies. It's just a shiny black mass. But as soon as my inner voice latches on to that language—"shiny black mass"—I think of outer space and start to feel vertigo. I feel trapped and like I'm dying, which I am, technically. We all are, everyone in this shiny black mass.

I try to remember what I'm supposed to think about to calm myself down. My breath? It doesn't feel like I'm breathing. The present moment? Nope, too terrifying. I think about Das Racist making no sense onstage, chugging vodka. I think about Cat Power having a mental breakdown and shouting incoherent obscenities into the audience. Between bars, I briefly scan the stage for a bottle, something. As soon as I turn, Yumiko is handing me her trademark plastic bottle of Maker's. Bless her manic little heart.

I snatch the bottle and chug a big sip. The crowd goes wild and I feel dizzy. I crave silence and wonder how much longer I have to be up here. Before I know it, I'm edging toward the front of the stage, pouring drips of bourbon into the audience, trying to channel Chan Marshall. The crowd is screaming and Jax hops over to me, starts pouring his beer into the crowd.

"'Dearly Queerly'!" someone shouts at the top of his lungs.

A familiar beat drops, and I again go into autopilot. While I'm rapping, my mind is elsewhere. I think about high school choir, before I was medicated, about that desperate need to escape the stage. I think about how I was in love with my best friend, Maddy, and how I liked giving hand jobs to my boyfriend, Michael, and how I didn't know about the Kinsey scale or the word "heteroromantic." And now I'm singing a song called "Dearly Queerly" to an audience of screaming fans. Yet I still feel that same sinking incurable dread. It does not "get better."

I want to go back to being backstage, dancing with Jax. My whole body is hot and my heart is beating like crazy. I think about how I could get away with popping a benzo and the audience would probably cheer, but I'm too afraid to do anything but rap and flail my body around.

I spend the rest of the set in a state of terror, occasionally comforted by a neutral memory or the thought of returning to the green room. When the fifth beat drops, I feel a glimmer of hope, like when the airplane starts to descend or when I see a sign for my freeway exit. The light at the end of the spiral.

The final song is "Genius," and for a quick second in the final bars, I get into it. I feel present and alive, like when they say performance is a drug. But as soon as I realize that I'm enjoying myself, I've left the moment. I'm back in the terrors of my brain, afraid and paralyzed and desperate to leave.

When the crowd erupts, I feel an immense relief. We run offstage just as quickly as we entered. Once backstage, I expect to feel better, but the dread quickly returns.

"Vaga," Jax says. "You killed it."

I continue to drink and smoke weed and take pills, but the dread remains, it's simply coated in a chemical sheen of false comfort. Several times I go into the alleyway by myself to smoke a cigarette and pace while staring at the moon.

At one point we're funneled out of the green room to watch Dead Stars from the side of the stage. I mostly feel nervous watching them, remembering what it was like to be up there myself, the sensory overload and the dread. It's hard to look away from Agnes, who runs around the stage like a banshee in between moving the wires of the Buchla, which scare me again, like they did at the Mirror Box. I imagine the wires coming to life, moving toward the audience and toward the side stage, wrapping around my body and strangling me like a python. I shake my head to snap the image, refocus on Agnes's confident expression. Her tan skin is covered in a glittery sheen; her white hair sticks up in a billion directions. She doesn't look afraid at all. She's in her natural habitat, in complete control.

My gaze moves to Wyatt, whose stage presence is more understated. I've always been drawn to her for this reason, the fact that she doesn't look like she's trying. On her TV show, she would float across the screen as though she were unaware she was being filmed, as though it were reality. I watch her flip her heaps of hair to the other side of her head and wonder if she's afraid, then take a sip of my beer.

After the set, we funnel back into the green room. Our group has expanded. Beau is here, cutting lines on a gold tray. I remember watching Heems do heroin backstage and remember it could always get darker.

I look around for Nina but don't see her. Then I become filled with rage, directed only at myself. For not enjoying this moment. For being afraid onstage instead of alive like a banshee. For not being excited that at any moment Wyatt or Agnes could come into our room and talk to us like equals.

"You okay?" Yumiko asks.

I look at her big blue eyes, slightly blurred by my current chemical cocktail. My gaze floats behind her head, to avoid eye contact, when I see something that makes me think I might be hallucinating. Ellie? Jax is hugging her.

"Be right back," I say to Yumiko. I push past her and slink out of the room, down the hallway, outside into the cool night. It must be in the low 50s. I'm just wearing my T-shirt dress, but I feel neither cold nor hot. I think about how it's weird that I hate space, but the moon comforts me. Then I try not to think anything at all. After a few drags, my not-thinking is interrupted by someone asking me for a light. I look up, prepared to be annoyed, then realize it's Wyatt Walcott. The chemicals in my brain confuse me, make me think I'm looking at a screen. @WYATTLOOK.

"Ah," she says, eyeing my cigarette. "Parliament Lights." She does a little body roll. "I didn't think there were any of us left."

I want to tell her that I smoke them because of her, but I resist the urge. *We're equals,* I tell myself. I thank the chemical cocktail in my brain at this moment for preventing me from feeling a fucking thing. I glance down at my hand and it's still and clammy, not even a little bit shaky.

"You were great," I say.

She flips a mass of hair from one side of her head to the other. I should be freaking out that I'm just inches away from the primary object of my fascination over the past few years: Wyatt Walcott's hairography. Just masses of golden blonde waves. When we're big time, I could get extensions that look like hers. But this career isn't for me. I can't handle it. I'll crack under the pressure. I have nothing.

"So were you," Wyatt says as she exhales. "Agnes and I have been loving the EP. I'm so proud of Jax. He was the only person I could tolerate at that horrible... facility."

She drags and my heartbeat quickens. I suppose it's my turn to speak, but my mind is blank. I just want to watch her, like she's the northern lights and I'm a tourist in Sweden.

Luckily, she saves me: "Even my idiot sister likes 'Dearly Queerly.'"

"Stella!" The name leaps out of my mouth and I feel like a crazed fangirl.

Wyatt seems amused. She drags again, looking at me for the first time as she exhales. "I like your hair," she says.

My heart rises up into my throat. I'm suddenly hyperaware of my body in relation to the earth's core and imagine being sucked into the blazes. I wish I had something to lean on to steady myself.

The door opens and a man in all black says, "Encore time."

Wyatt drops her cigarette and stomps it, and I follow in unison. As I crush the ember, I remember that Ellie is in there. I want to escape. Did Wyatt really say she liked my hair?

Back on the side stage, it's hot and sweaty and noisy. I instantly feel dizzy and on edge. I'm surrounded by people I don't recognize, yelling and screaming and looking happy. I'm in a different world from them, a scarier and bleaker one. I focus on Wyatt, her charm and her energy. But looking at her just makes me more afraid and more sad.

The colors darken and I feel dizzier. I need to sit down. I'll be mad at myself for ditching the encore, but I have no choice. Someone screams in my ear and I turn around and then everything turns black.

When I come to, I'm moving in the back seat of an unfamiliar car. I'm terrified, more afraid than I was in the crowds of the side stage.

"Oh, thank god," a voice says. "You're awake." Jake Perez whips his head around. "Prue," he says, interrupting my scream. "It's just me. You fainted and I'm taking you to the hospital."

"I know it's you," I hiss. I'm furious. How did Jax let this happen? How did Yumiko? They're supposed to have my back. "What happened to the Beemer?" I ask. I'm sitting on gray cloth seats.

"Jesus, Prue, the things you decide to fixate on," he says as he turns the wheel. "It's a rental. You know that car is a piece of shit, you just like it because it's shiny—"

"Take me back to the Teragram or I'm calling the cops." I reach into my fanny pack and pull out my phone. I dial 911 and wave the phone in the air so he knows I'm serious.

"You need to go to the hospital," he said. "You passed out. You were out for almost ten minutes."

"Did you drug me?" I ask. My hands are shaking and I'm thinking about who to text. Before I can decide, a text from Yumiko pops up: *Where you?*

"You drugged yourself, dumbass," Jake says. "You need to go to the hospital."

I hop up and look out the window. We're on Wilshire near the Good Samaritan where I get my yearly pap smears.

"I'm fine," I say. I text Yumiko, *I fainted and my "friend" Jake kidnapped me.*

Fuckkk!!! Yumiko texts back quickly, thank god.

"Let me out," I yell. Then again: "Let me out!"

"Calm down," he says, reaching for my arm.

I swat his hand away. "I'll have someone pick me up," I say. "Just drop me here at this corner."

"Why are you acting like I'm kidnapping you?" Jake asks. "I'm your best friend, remember?" He's turns onto the hospital's street.

"You should have left me there," I say. "The venue probably had a medic."

He says nothing but does pull over. As soon as the car comes to a stop, I reach for the handle and pull, but the car is locked.

"It was the biggest night of my life," I say.

"You know I'm just trying to help you," he responds, a broken record.

"Do you have Advil?" I ask. My head is killing me.

"Are you kidding? The last thing you need is another pill."

I roll my eyes and start texting Yumiko. *Can you get me?*

How?? she texts back. I remember she doesn't have her car or a smartphone; I just recently had to describe to her what Uber is.

Fuck, I say and type at the same time, then rack my brain. I can't ask Jax, I'm too embarrassed. Anyway, he's probably snorting lines with Wyatt and Agnes right now and I couldn't possibly take that experience away from him. I don't feel comfortable enough with Pilar and I couldn't rely on her. Same with Beau.

"I think I should just take you inside," Jake says, eyeing the hospital. "You were out cold for a few minutes and that's worrisome."

He's right. I'm no stranger to a memory blackout, but typically I remain conscious. Although I guess I have fallen asleep in some foreign places and positions. But this was a unique situation. It was our first show, the pressure, the adrenaline. I overserved myself to cope. In the future, I'll do less.

"I'm fine," I say. "You're just 'concerned' because my career is taking off just the way I want it to and you can't handle it. So you're taking me to the hospital, trying to lock me up." I look him in the eye for dramatic effect. "Just like they did with all the great female artists of history. Like F. Scott did to Zelda." I turn my gaze toward the window.

"F. Scott and Zelda were lovers, you sicko," he says. For a second I feel like we're at one of our gross diner lunches, Jake stuffing some vile meat product in his mouth while I pick at a salad.

A text from Yumiko pops up. *That curly hair girl just asked if you're okay... I could ask her?*

At first I think she's talking about Nina, and I don't want to be alone with her. But Yumiko knows Nina; she wouldn't not use her name. *Blonde curls?* I type back.

Yeah! she writes back.

Ellie.

Tell her that Jake kidnapped me and I need her to pick me up at the parking lot at the Good Samaritan hospital.

"Someone is coming to get me," I announce proudly.

"I can't believe you're doing this," he says.

I quickly look away from his face, which looks genuinely hurt, and I can't face it. I open Instagram. I have a lot of notifications.

Wyatt Walcott tagged me in a photo. I can't believe Jax is probably dancing to Rihanna with Dead Stars while I'm trapped in this shitty rental car.

"Is it one of your bandmates?" he asks. "Because I don't trust them."

"Good thing you don't have to," I say. I feel dizzy, like I might pass out again, so I look out the window and watch a homeless woman peel a Band-Aid off her face. "It's Ellie."

"Ellie?!" I'm not looking at Jake, but I imagine his eyes getting all big and I fantasize about punching him. "I cannot believe you are taking advantage of her savior complex after you cheated on her."

I bring my gaze back in the car and look into his eyes, which peer right at me. He looks different, as if a layer has been peeled back. He isn't hiding behind his typical saltiness. And it scares the shit out of me.

"That's straight-up cruel, Prue," he says.

Ellie looks like an angel sent from heaven in the back of a a gray Kia Soul. I spot her hair before I see the car. It's golden and bathed in streetlights.

"Ride's here," I shout in Jake's direction, and reach for the door handle. It's still locked. "Open up, M. Night Shyamalan."

I refuse to look at him as I jangle the door handle. He says nothing.

"Open up," I say again. The door opens and I sprint toward the Kia Soul, something I never thought I'd do.

"You seem fine," Ellie says when I sit down beside her, ensuring no inch of my body touches any inch of hers, despite how badly I want it to.

"Thanks again," I say. Ellie is wearing her typical tortoiseshell glasses and oversized T-shirt over a leather skirt and black tights.

"I didn't have much of a choice," she says.

My stomach drops. I ruined our relationship, I cheated on her, and now she's back in LA and I ruined her night. I try to recall when she left, whether her time in New York is up or whether she just happened to be in town for my show. I doubt she would fly back just to see me. Maybe she came back for Dead Stars, or for work.

I remember that mean butch from Nora's, the one who made Ellie all scared and flustered.

"Did you meet someone else?" I ask.

"Prue," Ellie says. "Are you fucking kidding me?"

My body collapses in on itself. Averting my gaze from her, I stare at passing buildings on Wilshire, sparkly and empty, just like me. Turning back toward her, I try to make my face serious. For a second I think she's going to hit me.

"You have been terrible to me," she says. "And you have the nerve to rely on me in a time of crisis, when you know well that I struggle with saying no to people in need." My self-hatred flairs. "Have you ever heard of a boundary?"

I slink back. We once did this exercise in law school to see if everyone had healthy boundaries with their clients. It was this checklist, and I didn't see any real issue with anything on there, so I checked them all. I can't believe Yumiko doesn't have a smartphone.

"I'm worried about you," she says finally, the corners of her eyes becoming wet. "You don't look like yourself."

I hope she isn't talking about my hair. I reach for my split ends, give them a little tug, then turn toward her. But she's looking away again.

"I'm sorry," I say, because I don't know what else to say. The only thing I can think of is to downplay my crisis, make her feel angry again instead of sad. "I think I just overindulged... given the nerves."

She says nothing but cracks open her window a little. Wind hits my face in a cold sheet.

"I didn't know who else to call." I'm speaking without thinking, my mouth just doing its own thing, and I'm coming down too hard to protest. "Jake wouldn't let me call my own car. Yumiko doesn't have a car or a smartphone. I couldn't possibly take Jax from Wyatt."

"Nina?" she says with a pointed tone.

A feeling wells up in my chest. The pills must be wearing off.

"I'm not speaking to her," I say. I hope this makes her feel good. I want Ellie to know she's special to me, more so than Nina, more so than anyone. What I'd give to take back the past few months, to be back on my SSRIs, writing briefs alone in my bedroom, spending my nights with the sweetest girl in the world. The idea of being a viral musician was much nicer when it was just an idea. The idea of anything is nicer as an idea.

"Because of the article?" she asks. I still haven't read it.

"No," I say, bringing my head in the car. "Because she's a loser." I say this to the back of Ellie's head. Then I turn back toward the window.

The driver exits the highway, begins creeping around Echo Park Lake while Ellie and I sit in silence with our heads turned away from each other.

"Thank you," I say to the driver when he pulls in front of my building.

Then I turn to Ellie. Before I can speak, she says, "I'm glad you cheated on me with someone you consider a loser."

I have no response to that. She's right. I'm terrible. I took advantage of her savior complex, mistook it for genuine connection, then emotionally bulldozed her.

"Thank you again," I say to her before I get out, but she isn't even looking at me.

TWENTY

I wake up feeling the worst I've ever felt in my life, like a rhinoceros is lying on my chest and a sinkhole is about to suck me into the earth's core. But I won't die. There will be no release.

I grab my phone as an instinct. I have lots of texts.

From Pilar: *You KILLED it. But you're alive, right?? Haha. I hope.*

From Jax: *VAGAAA WE DID IT. I heard you fainted? You okay??? Need me to bring you some soup? Jk I would never do that... Get better soon!!!*

From Yumiko: *The curly hair girl said she got you... I hope you're feeling better my STAR!*

I stop reading and aimlessly scroll through Instagram for several minutes while Ennui screeches. When I can't take the sound anymore, I hurl myself out of bed and go into the kitchen to feed her. I remember I'm out of cat food but find a yogurt in the fridge that's only a week past the expiration date. Yogurt is basically milk, and cats love milk, right? I put it in a bowl and Ennui stares at it with confusion. Then she looks back up at me with an expression that says, *What the fuck is wrong with you?* I wish I could tell ya, kitty cat!

I walk into my bathroom and open the shiny gold pouch and take out the bottle of Adderall and throw it away, just like I did with my Celexa a few months ago. Then I decide to go on a walk, without my phone. I empty the trash in the dumpster on the way out.

Walking in circles around Echo Park Lake, I try not to think about the previous night, which inevitably makes me feel dissociated and afraid. I refocus my attention on the future, which also scares me. So then I just stare at the shifting light on the water.

On the third loop, I think about how it might be nice to go to therapy. Then I remember Barbara Lumpkin, that awful woman who looked like she wanted to kill me—or herself— whenever I spoke. I don't blame her at all, my problems are objectively annoying and hardly qualify as problems at all. Barbara Lumpkin was not my first therapist, and she will not be my last. I make a note to ask Dr. Kim for a recommendation when I get home. Then I continue to walk and stare at the geyser in the center of the lake.

"Vagablonde?"

I'm jerked from my meditation. In front of me stands a stranger. A cool teen in all black. I remember that I'm semirecognizable now and panic. I hate any kind of social interaction I'm not expecting. I think, *What would Wyatt do?* I imagine she would give a weak smile and continue walking, which is exactly what I do.

I stop at Walgreens on the way home to buy cat food. I jet in and out, head down, without taking off my sunglasses. I don't even look at the pharmacy section.

When I get home, I check the mail and there's an envelope from Wicked Ice. I open it and it's a check. The first money I've made from music. Inside, I take a picture of the check and send it to my parents.

They don't respond.

The next day, I get an email from my supervisor about my draft in Yumiko's case. She tells me that her comments are "nitpicky" because she thinks I have the "skill to be an exceptional appellate attorney," which makes me depressed as hell. I address the edits quickly to get them over with, then file the brief, taking only enough care to ensure it's the correct one.

Afterward, I listen to MF Doom and try to write raps. Not long after a few songs have played and I've written nothing, a text from Nina floats in on iMessage.

Hi.

This morning, Jax lit up the Kingdom thread about a "first show" party. I ignored it, tired about the idea of another party. I think about Kanye saying, *No more parties in LA,* and feel him deeply. I threw away my Adderall and can't fathom socializing without it. That said, someone at the party will probably have amphetamines or another upper. I decide my new rule can be my old rule: I don't do drugs; I'm offered them.

I close iMessage, ignoring the text from Nina. I pick up my phone and call Ellie.

"Hi," she answers on the third ring.

"Hi," I say. "I'd love to see you if possible."

"I'm back in New York," she says.

"Did you come to LA to see me?" I ask, then immediately want to take it back. I imagine the words being sucked back in through a tube, and in the empty space she tells me she misses me. Per usual, reality unfolds less pleasantly.

"I went because it's my job." Ellie has never been this cold with me. I'm not shocked or even surprised. She should hate me. People are typically unpredictable, but one thing you can always count on is that they'll eventually hate you. Especially when you're me.

"Right," I say. "Well, I wanted to apologize in person, but I guess the phone will have to do."

"Apologize for what?"

"For being a monster," I say.

"You aren't a monster, Prue," she says. "You're just immature." Then she hangs up.

Inside, I fire up my laptop and type "Shiny AF Fader" into the Google search bar. *Time to "face my demons,"* I think with a smirk as the article pops up. I click the link and begin reading.

It begins on the fire escape. Nina paints the scene well. The damp air, the swaying palms, the indigo sky. Yumiko is lighting candles while I stare at small gray clouds and take pensive drags of my cigarette.

> "You know, Yumi," Prue says.
> "Yes, dahling?" Yumiko turns to face Prue, parka swinging in the wind.
> "I love you," Prue says with a sincerity I had no idea she possessed. "You're the only person who doesn't need me to be a certain way."
> Yumiko walks over and plants a maternal kiss on Prue's cheek. "You're perfect as you are, doll," she says.

I stop reading and smile, then feel my eyes water slightly.
I have no memory of this conversation.
I keep reading.
Yumiko and I return to the party, where Jax and I dance to Aaliyah as though our bodies are "quantum entangled," a "mechanical phenomenon whereby when one particle is acted upon, the other necessarily reacts." Nina describes the gold tray and the white lines and the "rapid velocity at which Jax's nose can inhale things."
At the end, it's not as bad as I expected. I don't bite anyone or say anything racist. Yes, portions frighten me. Particularly those describing my "vacant drug glare" and "near-pathological need to avoid reality." But there are also good things. Nina describes me as very beautiful and very talented. And she calls my hair Warhol-esque.
The worst thing I did when I was blacked out was tell someone I loved them.
I turn on Dead Stars' first EP and pick which tunic to wear to the Kingdom and think about what I said to Yumiko on the fire escape, the tender conversation I don't remember. That's why I

dose myself. To be kind. To be vulnerable. To access my subconscious.

The only problem is it might be killing me.

The Kingdom is glowing teal when I arrive, and I recall the first time I walked down this hallway. It was a month and a half ago, which is insane. So much has changed. I have almost ten thousand Twitter followers now.

Jax wraps me in a huge hug when I enter the main room. "My star," he says. The exchange makes me uncomfortable. I think about having to go back onstage and feel ill. What am I doing?

I sit timidly on the edge of the couch beside Yumiko. Maybe sensing my discomfort, Beau hands me a beer.

"You killed it, Vaga," he says. "You all did." He holds up his camera. "I got some great shots." I think about how this very lens has maybe seen my naked body and feel no real way about it.

"Thank you," I say. I look over at Nina, who is predictably rolling a joint on the table. As she looks up, I quickly look away. No one is talking and there is no music playing. I take a very loud sip of beer. It's hard to swallow, my throat is too tight.

Yumiko puts her hand on my knee and says, "Fire escape?"

It's cold and windy out there, probably in the 50s, but the air feels good. Yumiko makes a tent with her hands over my Parliament and I make one with my hands over her blunt and we smoke in silence. After a few puffs, Erykah Badu's *But You Caint Use My Phone* mixtape floats out the window. I peek inside and see Jax dancing over a gold tray covered in white lines and blue pills. I get excited by the Adderall, then feel depressed. Can I handle one party without uppers? Do I only like these people on stimulants?

Back inside, I immediately take a blue pill from the tray and put it on my tongue without thinking. I feel it so fast it must be the placebo effect, and I immediately start chatting with Pilar about our skincare routines. I'm just yapping, making sounds, saying "marula oil" and "hyaluronic acid," words I've seen on Twitter. I'm suddenly very interested in how much things cost.

"If money runs low for me I think I'll be an escort," I'm soon telling Pilar. I've never thought this before, but at this moment it feels like the best idea. Lame straight men love my blonde hair and emotional distance. They'll pay me loads of money to be dismissive and withholding, to turn courtship into a game they'll never win. I'll have to fly to New York—on their dime, of course—because the coked-out Wall Street bro is my audience. Technocrats are too needy. They didn't get laid until they were twenty-five and therefore need to be coddled. I become nostalgic for when the banks had more power than tech. They're all evil, but at least the bankers were unapologetic about it. I'd rather be dead at Dorsia than alive at Burning Man. The possibility that I could end up murdered would make it all that more exciting.

By the time I need a cigarette, there are more people in the room. I wade through bodies to get to the fire escape.

"How are you feeling?" Yumiko asks.

"Much better," I lie. "Oh," I say. "I filed your brief. My supervisor thinks we might win."

"Cool," she says. I know I'm just talking about the case to avoid talking about my feelings, which is perhaps why I got into the law in the first place. Same with Adderall, which is doing a fantastic job of keeping my emotions nowhere near me. But I know I'll need more soon or else experience profound despair.

Unsure what to say, I offer Yumiko a sip of my beer. She shakes her head. "I gave up drinking."

I look back at her, confused.

"I only do plant-based drugs now," she says. "I've gotten really into Terence McKenna."

Yumiko is full of surprises.

"Alcohol isn't quite as bad as some other stuff, like Adderall and Xanax." She raises an eyebrow at me, and I feel ashamed. "Pharmaceuticals are made up of, like, ten different toxic compounds. Also they're created by publicly owned corporations that only care about profit."

"But they feel so good," I say as I drag my cigarette.

"Only for one to three hours," she says, "then you feel bad for the remainder of the twenty-four. Psychedelics don't have the same comedown. I'm usually happier after a trip, because I see the world as more wonderful and the future as less bleak."

Unsure what to say, I take another drag.

"Also, you should smoke organic tobacco," she says. "Those things are filled with pesticides."

"Okay, Mom," I say. I throw my cigarette on the ground. I don't feel particularly disturbed by what Yumiko is saying because the Adderall is peaking and nothing could disturb me.

Back inside, the dance floor is picking up. Future starts playing and Nina sways alone under the disco ball. She spots me and slinks up, starts grinding against me. I back up. I don't want to be sexual right now. Maybe sensing my discomfort, Nina places an Adderall in my palm. I look at the pill and note how artificially blue it is, then think about Yumiko's admonition about "toxic compounds." Sweat from Nina's hand smudges blue onto my palm. It disgusts me. She disgusts me. I give it back. And then I leave.

When I arrive at my house, there is a familiar feline figure at my doorstep. It's Missy. I start to cry, mainly because she looks significantly healthier than Ennui, which means she was better without me. And, yet, she came back.

I spend the next morning inside an internet rabbit hole about SSRIs, leading me to wonder whether I should be microdosing LSD instead. I miss a few phone calls: one from my dad and three from the downtown office. I don't listen to my dad's voice mail, but I do call him back.

"Hello, Prue." My dad's voice is robotic.

"Hi, Dad," I say.

"I have speakerphone on," he says. "Your mom is also here."

"Hi, Mom," I say. I fantasize about hanging up "accidentally."

"Hi, Prudence," she says.

Prudence? My body feels heavy, a phantom pushes down on my shoulders.

"What's up?" I ask

"I guess there is no easy way to say this," he says.

I start to wonder who died. All my grandparents are dead. I have no siblings. Maybe a cousin or family friend. A thin layer of sweat forms on my palms and I wipe them on my jeans.

"We received a letter from the California Appellate Project that was meant for you," he says.

Ugh, I keep meaning to change my address with the California Bar Association. I was living in DC when I got my bar results, and it still lists my parents' address. But I've worked at this job for three years—they should know where I fucking live! Jesus, the California government... giving a new meaning to incompetence every day.

My dad's voice yanks me from my rage. "Your mother opened it by mistake, and, well, she was frightened by what she saw."

I swallow hard.

"First, they've terminated your employment," my dad says.

"What?" I ask. I'm legitimately confused. They fired me? "My supervisor just told me my argumentation was 'exceptional.'"

"It's not for poor performance, Prue," my dad says. "We've always known you are very bright." He pauses, seems to swallow. "They wrote that they were alerted to an article in a music magazine by an intern that depicted you in a troubling light. You were fraternizing with your client and engaging in rampant illegal drug use."

My dad pauses like he's expecting me to say something, but I have no words.

"We're in shock, Prue," my dad says. "How did you hide this from us?" His volume rises like he's expecting an answer.

"I tried to tell you I'm an artist," I say quietly. I feel like I'm five years old, giving my mom a painting she's too "tired" to receive.

"We don't understand," my dad says. "You went to a top ten law school, you graduated in the top of your class. You won the National Moot Court Competition." Honestly, I'd forgotten about that awful competition; it was so embarrassing. "You were supposed to follow in my footsteps. You should be working at a top law firm making six figures, preparing to buy a house."

"I don't want a house!" I say without thinking. My rage escalates. I always knew my dad felt this way, but he's never been so explicit. Despite my difficulty catching my breath, I partly feel good. There's no longer an elephant in the room. My father is gravely disappointed with me, and he's finally being honest about it. My mom may as well be a ghost.

"Well," he says, "what do you want?"

I rack my brain for how to answer. I'm used to giving my parents an edited version of myself, one I think they want. I try to imagine Jax asking me the same, and I realize I also edit myself for him. For my parents: I'm dutiful, achieving, innocent. For Jax: I'm performative, irreverent, unhinged. But which is the real me? Is there a real me? What do I want? Surprising myself, I start to cry.

"I don't know," I say.

My dad twice threatens to send me to rehab, and I am forced to swallow my tears and jerk back into performance mode. I fall into the role fairly easily, despite the dread and rage gripping my stomach, as I've been playing it my whole life. Pretending I'm in a courtroom, I explain to my parents that my career, while not what they expected, could not be more thriving. I tell them that I've been featured in all the major music outlets, that the perfect label put out my first EP, that one of the "Big Three" agencies booked my first show. I tell them that I have enough money in my bank account to support myself for at least the next six months (I have no idea) and that I can only assume more money will be coming in soon (again, conjecture). I even at one point compare myself to my dad's hero, Bob Dylan, whom I despise, but it seems to get him on my side. I end the call with a promise to stop doing uppers and to start seeing my psychiatrist again. My mom says nothing the entire time.

The next few days I spend mostly curled up with the cats, making various depressive playlists and eating cereal and napping. The only time I feel good is just before I fall asleep, just after a carbo-load, curtains closed and fan on full blast. They say sleep is the cousin of death, which I guess makes me basically dead.

On the third day, Jax lights up the Kingdom thread about our "next steps," which frightens me. I've committed myself to avoiding uppers, and I'm nervous about handling Shiny AF without them. But I've also been restless without a purpose. Messy as it was, at least during "Shiny Season," there was a tangible goal. We've already recorded and released the EP. We got Best New Music and a *FADER* feature. We had our first show. Now, we're in limbo.

Without my old pharmaceutical cocktail, I've been filling the void with cereal.

Brazilian baile funk pours onto my street from a trembling Lincoln.

"You look good," says Yumiko when I hop in the car. "Healthy."

I shrug. "Healthy" has always felt like a euphemism for "fat" to me, but it feels okay right now. I don't have a good sense of how I appear to others, but the external consensus is that I've been skeletal, pale, near death. I needed to down a few boxes of cereal in a short time span, but I vow not to make a habit of it.

The song coming out of the speakers snatches me from my thoughts, and the drop takes me back in time: I'm a first-year in law school and I'm on Molly in a sweaty club in downtown San Francisco. Back when I did drugs exclusively on special occasions.

"Holy shit, is this *Jeffree's Volume...*" I purse my lips in thought. *Jeffree's* were the mixtapes Mad Decent used to release periodically, before Diplo got cheesy and tragic. "*Volume 4?*"

"Girl's got an ear!" Yumiko shouts, then her expression becomes serious. "I'm so sad about Tom."

"Tom?" I ask.

As Yumiko revs the ignition and starts rolling out of the parking lot, I realize she's talking about Diplo.

"Oh, you know him?" I ask, trying to sound casual, I'm not totally sure why. I remember the article about Yumiko being the "Queen of the Philly Underground." Mad Decent originated in Philly, so I quickly connect the dots.

"I more than knew him..." she says, then grins.

"Oh my god," I say. "You fucked Diplo."

She unleashes a diabolical laugh.

"And you're sad because... he sold out?" I ask.

"In the worst way!" she yells, then cuts in front of another driver.

"Yeah, I went to a Mad Decent block party a few years ago," I say. "My law school friend invited me, and there wasn't much to do in Berkeley, so I went. Diplo was so embarrassing. I just remember he kept jumping up and down and raising his hands like he was headlining Electric Daisy Carnival or something tragic like that. His backup dancers were fire, but I kept wanting Dip—*Tom*—to leave the stage."

Yumiko unleashes another laugh as she merges onto the freeway. "Oh my god, the jumping!"

My stomach tightens as I think about whether there is a tragic Diplo narrative in my future. I mean, at least he's rich as hell, but... "Do you think he's happy?" I find myself asking without thinking.

"Fuck no!" says Yumiko as she swerves around another car. We aren't late, so I guess she just wants adrenaline. "Also"—she lowers her voice to a whisper—"he's got a small dick."

We both laugh, unhinged and wild, as Yumiko speeds along the 110. For a second, I feel like I'm in Montana, safe and grandiose and enveloped by the heavens.

Jax greets us with wide, manic eyes. He's wearing a floor-length leopard-print coat over a black T-shirt dress, velour loafers on his feet.

"This look," Yumiko says as she embraces him in a big hug.

I stand, nervous for my turn. "And if it isn't my star," Jax says before pulling me into his coat. I feel trapped and wait quietly for him to release me. I recall the early days of the Kingdom, when I actually wanted him to hug me.

In the other room, Pilar and Beau are playing cards. Pilar sips a tea. I guess everyone is coming down. Except Jax, whose bloodshot eyes and dilated pupils suggest continued upper abuse and little or no sleep.

"Gather 'round, my people," he says, widening his arms.

My heartbeat quickens. I think I see Pilar roll her eyes. She lights a thin blue cigarette.

"Our next move," he says, "is crucial."

Yumiko nods furiously. I imagine she's thinking of Diplo. Tom.

"Our dominos are perfectly aligned," he says. "One wrong move, and they fall—we fade into obscurity."

I think about how dominos look pretty and peaceful when they fall.

"But if we make the right moves," he says, "we build an empire."

I look at Pilar, who is looking out the window.

Beau gets up and goes to the kitchen. I pray he's getting PBRs.

"I was at a show downtown last night," Jax says. His stamina for partying confounds me. "And I saw Kreayshawn."

Anger washes over Yumiko's face. I remember her pushing that conference table phone at the Wicked Ice meeting and try not to laugh. I don't want Pilar to roll her eyes at me.

"I have to admit it caused me to spiral a bit," Jax says. "She was with some ugly dude, looking cheap as hell. No crew, no security, no charisma."

I imagine Jax as a preacher, calling out from his pulpit: the Church of Dina.

Then I recall telling my parents that I'm thriving.

I'm thirty years old; I shouldn't care what my parents think. Did Kanye care what his parents thought? Actually, I think his dad was out of the picture and his mom was quite proud of him until she tragically passed away. Bad example. Andy Warhol? Ugh, I'm pretty sure his parents were super proud. Whatever.

Beau returns with four cold beers and I want to kiss him, then quickly become disgusted by the thought. I haven't had a drink in days, and a beer is just what I need right now. The bubbles calm me. PBR is low alcohol anyway. It's basically seltzer water. The point is to avoid uppers.

I look around the room and watch the blue light bounce off various surfaces: the tin on the ceiling, the shoji panes, the coffee table. I recall Jake's comment about "prolonged adolescence."

At the same time I crack my beer open, Pilar shoos hers away. I wonder what's going on with her.

"The time is now to go on a tour," Jax says. "The hype is high. We boost our audience, get them wanting more, then come home and record our debut album."

Listening to him talk makes me feel exhausted. Does a tour involve living on a bus? I don't think I can handle that. Is Jax going to expect me to perform for him all the time? Dance with him and listen to his sermons and laugh at his jokes? Make me hug him? I once again become nostalgic for my old life, where I just typed alone in my apartment and got paid to be salty to the

US government. Are the only lives we want the ones we aren't living?

"Beau," Jax says, "can you get us another meeting with CAA in the next few days?"

Beau shrugs his pale, bony shoulders. "Probably."

I shiver thinking about going back into that sterile building, having to talk to those indistinguishable white men inside a glass box of panic.

"Perfect. And in the meantime," Jax says, eyes lighting up, "we party."

"I have to work," says Pilar, getting up. I've never been so envious of someone for having a job before.

"You'll be missed," Jax says, an intense glint in his eye, "my love."

Pilar says nothing but blows us all kisses, then floats out of the room. I want to grab her and say, *Take me with you.*

I pull out my phone and text Yumiko, *Can we leave?* But she never checks her phone. So I get up and head toward the fire escape. Yumiko follows.

"Can we get out of here?" I ask as soon as she lights her blunt. Pink sky rises behind the palms in the distance.

Yumiko looks back at me a little confused.

"I'm trying to be, you know... " I stumble for the words. "More healthy." I pause for a second, embarrassed. "If you want to stay, I can take a Ly—"

"I got you," Yumiko says. She puts out her blunt, then puts it behind her ear.

Jax looks kind of upset when we announce that we're leaving. For a second I feel guilty. Then Beau pulls out a tiny bag of white powder and starts shaking it, and Jax quickly becomes distracted, like a cat eyeing a toy. As soon as the bag opens, we slip out.

I don't hear from Jax or anyone in the Kingdom for roughly a week, which feels like a blessing. I need some "me time," which all time once was. I'm happy to have my schedule back, to be free of "Shiny Season." I go to Crystal's dance class with Yumiko. I watch old *What's Up with the Walcotts* episodes with the cats, experiencing a newfound appreciation for having both of them together. I text Jake several times and he doesn't respond. Andy Warhol's voice loops through my brain with increasing regularity: "In the future, everyone will be world-famous for fifteen minutes."

After writing Dr. Kim a dramatic email using the phrases "minor mental breakdown" and "light addiction issues," he gets me an appointment with a therapist on the East Side who has a comforting affinity for turquoise. She quickly identifies in me a "concerning need for external validation."

"Well, where the hell else am I supposed to get it from?" I ask.

She unleashes a hearty laugh, as if I'm joking, which I'm not.

I give myself permission not to think about the future until I hear back from Jax. When he finally calls another meeting at the Kingdom, dread sinks in. I don't want to go back to that drug den and listen to him preach at us. When I tell this to Yumiko, she says, "Why don't you just quit and go solo?"

"I need Jax," I say. "I need the group."

"No, you don't," she says. "They need you."

We go to the meeting regardless but decide to meet on the fire escape if and when either of us needs to, well, escape.

Jax greets us with wider and more manic eyes than the previous week. He's wearing the same leopard-print coat over what appears to be a woman's bathing suit. I note the faint residue of white powder on the collar of his coat, which I take care to avoid when he wraps me inside a claustrophobic hug.

Pilar isn't here yet, and I realize this is the first time I've been in the Kingdom without her. It often seemed like she lived here. While we wait, we sip PBRs with Beau. Yumiko chats at Beau, and I zone out, imagine Nina rolling joints on the coffee table. I feel a weird pang, like I miss her, but then I remember how she betrayed me.

Jax keeps pacing around the apartment, ducking in and out of various areas—the kitchen, behind the shoji panes, his bedroom. Each time he emerges from his bedroom with wider eyes, and I wonder whether he's doing something harder than Dina in there. Then I decide it's none of my business.

Pilar arrives in a blue coat and a cloud of smoke. She seems annoyed. Not the unflustered Gemini fairy I've been partying with the past few months. Jax lunges at her for a hug, and Pilar deftly converts it into an air-kiss. I look at Yumiko to privately acknowledge the tension, but she's busy talking with Beau about *Grand Theft Auto*. Yumiko can talk to anyone about anything.

Jax spreads his arm wide when we're all seated before him. He's wearing more jewelry than when we arrived. "My babies. I missed my babies."

Pilar lights a fresh cigarette. "Why are we here?"

"Okay," he says, pacing toward the shoji panes. Jax gestures toward Beau, who is cutting a line of white powder with surgical precision on a gold tray in front of him.

"Wicked Ice is ghosting us," Beau says flatly.

"It's okayyyyyyyyyy," Jax says, rushing back toward us. "We just need a plan." Then he disappears back into his bedroom.

Pilar sighs. "How long is this going to take?"

Before anyone can respond, Jax charges out of the bedroom without the leopard-print coat. He's just wearing the woman's bathing suit and thigh-high socks, crystal pendants clinking as he walks—no struts—into the room. He's on a runway, nearly voguing.

"Baby Beau," Jax says, reaching his arm toward him in a way that could be read as a dance move. "Can you get us another meeting at CAA?"

"I can try to set something up in the next few weeks," Beau says.

"No, I mean like now," Jax says, then eyes us with suspicion. "What time is it?"

I jump at the opportunity for a concrete task and pull out my iPhone. "Six thirty," I say dutifully.

Beau moves a hand through his greasy hair. "Okay, so I hit up my guy at CAA," he says slowly. "He said Shiny AF needs an album before you go on tour." He leans over and sucks a line up his nose, then brushes his nostril. The whole performance is revolting. Then he continues speaking. "He was kind of... evasive."

Pilar shrugs. "So what? Agents are busy." She exhales a stream of pale smoke toward the cracked window.

I look at Yumiko to fill the silence.

"Maybe we should take some time," Yumiko says, "think about other projects."

"That makes sense," says Pilar.

I'm surprised by both of these statements, but I also feel comforted by the idea of "time," of "other projects."

Jax crouches down, puts his head in his hands, starts shaking slightly. I reach nervously for my PBR, but it's empty. Usually I'm pretty wasted around Jax and his behavior is entertaining, if not inspiring. But now, basically sober, I don't feel amused.

"It's okay!" Jax jumps up and spreads his pale, tattooed arms. "We'll go tomorrow," Jax says. "First thing tomorrow." Then he bursts into laughter, does a plié, skips off toward his bedroom. In the doorframe, he turns toward us. "If they don't respond"— he laughs again—"we'll just show up." Then he shuts the door behind him.

"Okay, what the fuck is he on?" Pilar asks Beau.

Beau shrugs.

Pilar gets up close to him, blowing smoke in his face. "What," she says, "is he on?"

"There's no snow right now," says Beau, and I think about how lame he sounds, like a coke dealer in the NYU dorms. "So we got some crystal." He smiles and his teeth are nearly gray, much like his skin. "It's really good," he says. He gestures toward the tray. "Do you want to try?"

Pilar slaps Beau right across the face, which is cathartic to watch. I've wanted to slap his dumb face so many times. I look at Yumiko and she seems similarly delighted.

Beau unleashes a high-pitched scream like a baby, then grabs his face. "Bitch, that hurt," he whines.

Pilar is now standing over Beau, who is curled up in pain on the couch. "You remember what happened last time he did meth, right?"

Beau shrugs.

Pilar hits him again, this time on the arm, slightly less hard. "I fucking can't with you," she says. "We're too old for this shit. People our age have babies, families, mortgages."

It's kind of an old-fashioned point. I had no idea Pilar was so conservative.

She grabs her purse and puts out her cigarette. "Call me if you need me to take him somewhere," she says to Beau, "but only if it's an emergency." Her heels click toward the door, echoing on the concrete floors.

"Fire escape?" Yumiko says to me when Pilar is gone.

I nod and jump up. Just then, Jax reemerges from his bedroom.

"Who wants shots?" he asks. He's holding several empty shot glasses, no liquor in sight, hips shimmying to a nonexistent beat.

Beau just laughs really hard, like it's a bit.

"We're gonna smoke a cigarette real quick," I say, grabbing Yumiko's arm. We slide out the window onto the fire escape.

"He's full-blown manic," Yumiko says.

"I want to leave," I say. "But is that irresponsible?" I pull out a cigarette and light it, but don't inhale. I'm trying to quit cigarettes, but I don't want Jax to think we're being shady. "Or, like... immoral?" I recall how Jax never so much as texted me when I fainted at the Teragram.

Yumiko shakes her head. "It's called taking care of our-selves."

The next day, I'm reading an article on "blonde privilege" when Jake finally responds to one of my text messages. We haven't spoken since I escaped his car the night of the show.

Glad you're alive, he says.

I'm sorry is all I can come up with. I can't believe this is the first time I'm saying it. Now that I'm more clearheaded, I feel insane for how I behaved that night. He was trying to help me.

Jax is doing meth, I type. *I think he's having some kind of... episode.*

Jesus Christ, he writes. The typing bubbles appear, disappear, reappear. *What are you doing right now?*

When I arrive at Echo Park Lake, Jake is sitting in a patch of shade near the paddleboat station, under some tall palms. I approach with hesitation.

"You look good," he says. I experience déjà vu, back to the time we were in my apartment before Dead Stars at the Mirror Box and a thousand times before that. I run my fingers through my hair and think about my blonde privilege and whether I should dye my hair back to its natural color, which is, like, beige. It's ugly, but less ugly, conceptually, I think, than bleaching it to resemble a Northern European child.

I shrug. "You look the same," I say.

He unleashes a laugh, and my muscles relax a bit. Then I sit down beside him on a gray fleece blanket.

"You didn't bring me anything?" Jake asks, raising his dark eyebrow in a way that might read to the average person as intimidating but that I find very comforting.

I shrug. "Still insufferable," I say.

"You know Virgos are supposed to be generous." He looks up at the sky, then back at me. "You're very atypical in that sense."

I slap him on the arm. "I'm sorry Scorpios are so predictable," I say. I await his reaction nervously, wondering if we're okay to start joking around again. When he reveals a sliver of a smile, I continue. "Brood, be salty... never stop thinking about sex."

Jake performatively attaches his gaze to a muscly twenty-something jogging around the lake.

"Latte thief?" I ask. It's an old inside joke. This cheesy gay in a rainbow-flag T-shirt stole Jake's latte once at the Peet's on Telegraph in Downtown Berkeley, and it's been our code for homo ever since. I guess we haven't used it in a while because homosexuality feels kind of passé these days. Everyone is fluid, gender is fake, blah blah blah. Being gay was so much more interesting when it was taboo.

"One thousand percent," says Jake.

I'm suddenly transported back to the Thai restaurant on Christmas, when I asked Jake if he thought Ellie just wanted to save me and he had an identical reaction. Then I remember Ellie calling me "immature," what Jake calls my "prolonged adolescence," and how I mutilate my hair to resemble both a child and a colonist. I sink into self-hatred and long for a pill to lift me out of it.

"Are you okay?" he asks. He opens his Nalgene and takes a sip of water. For a second, I'm transported back to college, to Jake and me sharing a joint in the Berkeley Hills and watching the fog roll in over the Golden Gate Bridge.

"Not really," I say. It feels refreshing to be honest. I've wanted to say this my whole life but didn't realize it was an option.

"Are you doing anything about it?" he asks.

"I'm back in therapy," I say. "My therapist loves turquoise."

"Very Berkeley," he says.

"Exactly," I say. I pick up a clump of grass, then flick it a few feet away. "Do you think I should dye my hair?" I ask. Talking about my hair, which is pretty and dead, is easier than talking about my feelings, which are ugly and alive. "You know, to make it look less... infantile?"

Jake shrugs. "You know I'm no expert on matters of aesthetics." I knew this, but I didn't know he knew it about himself. "Maybe you could ask one of your bandmates," he says.

The suggestion makes me uneasy. I recall Jax's mismatching pendants clacking to the strange beat inside his head. "I'm thinking about going back on my SSRIs," I say.

"I thought you just went down a dose," he says with a concerned tone.

I keep my focus on the grass, which I'm picking neurotically. "I threw them away," I say quietly.

"Prue, you should be medicated," he says. I'm not looking at him, but I know his eyes are big. "I say this as a friend—a concerned friend."

I sigh. "But they're poison. Yumiko told me they contain toxic compounds."

"Are you seriously taking medical advice from your gun-slinging client?"

"Former client," I say, still picking. "And yeah. She's smart."

"Did the grass do something to you?" Jake asks. "You know the planet doesn't need any extra help being destroyed by humans."

I stop picking and refocus on my shoelaces, tying and retying.

"Toxic doesn't mean anything," he says. "Water is toxic in large enough amounts."

I finally look up at him, comforted. His eyes are warm and present, a sharp opposition to the glassy glares of the Kingdom.

"I assume she's thinking they're toxic because they're synthetic," he says. "But so is most of the food you eat, and people are living longer than ever."

"But what about the fact most pharmaceuticals are produced by corporations, which only care about profit?"

"Jesus, Prue," Jake says in a way that makes me remember how much I've missed him. I think about making a T-shirt that says, JESUS, PRUE, and giving it to him for his birthday. "I thought you were over your Marxist phase," Jake continues.

"It just seems sick that the drugs provided to alleviate the drudgery of late capitalism are mediated by the capitalist profit center that is the pharmaceutical industry," I say, obscuring my feelings with pseudo-intellectual nonsense.

"Do I have to remind you again how much you've benefitted from capitalism, Miss Granny Paid for Law School?"

I'm about to launch into rebuttal mode, reminding him that capitalism has succeeded in large part with the help of the nuclear family, which functions by systematically devaluing women, but I decide to drop the intellectual façade and say what I'm really feeling. "I guess I'm worried I could be happier and healthier unmedicated," I say, "but I'll never have the courage to find out."

"I don't know," he says. "I feel about SSRIs kind of like how I feel about Diet Coke. Like maybe they're marginally bad for me but not enough to outweigh the good."

I think about the Diet Coke I drank this morning, the nice chemical burn it left in the back of my throat, the moderate high from the caffeine.

One of those freaky geese starts charging at us. Jake shoos it away, then turns toward me.

"Live your art and take your meds," he says.

The day before my appointment with Dr. Kim, LA experiences a major heat wave. My apartment doesn't have AC, so I bring my three massive fans out of the closet and keep them on full blast. Periodically, I roll ice cubes on my face, then roll them along the cats' fur. Missy likes it better than Ennui. I can tell them apart now.

As I ice, I look at pictures of snowy New York on Instagram with mild bemusement. People complain about the heat waves in LA, but I love them. The heat relaxes me. I feel like I'm a desert lizard, or at the Korean spa.

When Yumiko calls, I answer in a haze.

"Get your suit on, betch," she shrieks, "we're going to the beach!"

"Really?" I ask. I never go to the beach in LA. It's so far away. I was spoiled by my childhood, when I'd spend my summers at my grandmother's house in the Outer Banks. The ocean was her front yard, and the beach was private. The idea of sitting in traffic for an hour to get to a crowded public beach seems unappealing. The Pacific is so cold and there is too much kelp.

"Yesssss," she says.

As a bead of sweat rolls down from my armpit, I agree.

"I'm picking you up in an hour!"

When Yumiko texts to say she's outside, I'm preparing to hit my vape pen. I pause to peek out the window to look for the Lincoln, but I don't see it. Instead I see Beau's G-Wagen. I put the vape back in my tote bag without taking a drag.

I want to back out, but the car is outside, and guilt compels my legs to move down the stairs, albeit very slowly.

"Vagaaaaaa," Jax yells out the window when he sees me. He's smoking a cigarette, and his hair is not in its usual braids. Instead, it's wild and voluminous, partially dreaded. He's wearing a leop-ard-print one-piece bathing suit and maybe ten crystal prayer bead necklaces.

I force a weak smile, feeling kind of awkward as I've been ignoring his texts. He's been sending a lot of weirdly punctuated paragraphs filled with oblique references to the Illuminati. I might find them interesting if they didn't scare me so much.

My stomach sinks when Beau nods his sickly-looking head at me.

Yumiko flings open the back seat door and my heart starts to race. Am I really about to get in a car with a driver who is probably on meth?

"We don't have all day, slut!" Yumiko shouts at my slow-moving body.

I move even slower to punish her.

When Beau starts driving, I open my Notes app and write: *I can't believe you didn't tell me they were coming... This could be dangerous!*

I hand the phone to Yumiko. I know better than to text her at this point.

As Jax belts Britney Spears in the front seat, Yumiko begins typing back on the app. She hands the phone back to me, and I look down at it apprehensively. *They're sober. Stash ran out.*

I'm a little relieved but still uncomfortable. And skeptical.

Jax whips around toward us and I jump a little. He looks me in the eye, chuckles, then continues singing "Everytime."

You sure? I type on the Notes app.

Jax turns his head back around, and I notice a large chunk of his hair is missing—a spot of bright white scalp surrounded by jagged pieces of coarse black hair.

I hand the phone back to Yumiko.

"I need you, baby," Jax sings while looking directly into my eyes.

Yumiko just looks at me and shrugs.

We swerve through Topanga Canyon to a tiny beach in Malibu that Jax claims is a "Kingdom secret." Getting there involves shimmying through a bougainvillea bush onto what appears to be a private path. We're surely trespassing, but I don't care when I spot the first glimpse of water, sparkling rolls of turquoise. I hear a wave crash and genuinely start to smile, an experience so foreign to me that for a second I think I'm having a stroke.

The air is salty and the sand feels warm on my feet and the beach is practically empty.

Yumiko runs straight toward the water, and without really thinking, I follow. I can't remember the last time I ran.

The water is freezing but refreshing, like the cold plunge at a Korean spa. Yumiko dives into a crashing wave, shrieking when she emerges. Her voice seems to skip across the water like a thin rock, and for a second I remember being onstage with her. Although I thought that I was dying at the time, the memory feels pleasant at this moment.

"Oh my god," she yells. "It feels so good!" She floats up into a wave, and I dive into it just before it crashes.

We stay in the same spot for a few minutes, treading water and drifting with the tide. I stare at the line where the ocean meets the atmosphere and feel like I'm looking at a Rothko. The water rocks me like a baby, back and forth, up and down.

Yumiko jumps on my shoulders and pushes me under. When I emerge, I'm facing the boys on the beach. They look nearly translucent. I watch Jax dance like a maniac.

I stay in the water a little longer than Yumiko. I just want to be alone out here. Normally I'm just alone in my bed, and this is a more profound version of that. Because I'm, like, in the world.

When my fingers turn white, I return to the crew. They're on a big, neon-striped Mexican blanket. Jax dances in circles around its perimeter.

There is no music playing.

Beau and Yumiko are sharing a blunt and yapping about some video game. I feel a brief and intense moment of hatred for Beau, for enabling Jax, for making out with Nina in front of my face on multiple occasions, for constantly taking Yumiko's attention from me. She's just trying to be nice. He obviously has zero qualms when it comes to taking advantage of people. Everyone is just a little pawn in his twisted game.

I lie down on a patch of sand, pointedly beside, and not on, the blanket, then sink into the warm sand, an exfoliant. *I'm going to be so beautiful after this trip*, I think as I put a towel over my face so no one will talk to me.

Just as I'm fully reclined, Jax hovers over me. *"Vagaaaaa,"* he sings. Before I can respond or be annoyed, he starts monologuing. "We need to talk about our next steps, okay? We have to figure out a plan."

The towel is still on my face, but I can see his silhouette moving a lot. He's towering over me, and I start to feel afraid.

"Our boy Beau"—he chuckles—"he's getting us a meeting soon."

He moves his hands toward me quickly and I rip the towel off my face.

He laughs again. *"No need to be afraid, my dearrrr"*—singing again.

I want to ask him for some personal space, but I've never done that before, and I have no idea how.

"My phone isn't working," he says, holding it over my face. "You can see the screen is all cracked."

It's not.

"I hate that I can't communicate with you."

He can.

Jax's face drops, like he might cry, and he plops down on the patch of blanket next to me.

I want to run back into the water, but instead I put the towel back on my face. I've been ignoring Jax the way Jake was ignoring me. Modern society, I decide, is just a never-ending cycle of ignoring people for a vague illusion of control and going crazy when the same is done to you.

"Vaga," Jax whispers, lifting the towel slightly to reach my ear, "I've been seeing Pac in my dreams."

"Hey!" I yank the towel from his hands. "Whatever you're on is killing my vibe." I'm proud of myself for being firm.

Jax just starts laughing manically. "I'm sober, Vaga," he says. "I don't do drugs anymore! I want to be present." He pauses, pulling a crystal pendant off his neck and putting it around mine; we lock eyes. "Like Madonna."

If he's really sober, something else is going on. He seems fully dissociated. I recall Pilar telling the boys to call her if it becomes an emergency. Are we there yet?

"Should I dye my hair?" I ask to change the subject to something neutral and nonthreatening.

Jax shrieks and I jump a little. "Nooooooo!" he squeals. "Your hair is your everything, Vaga. You look like a doll." He reaches down to pet my hair. "My perfect little doll."

I jerk away, feeling degraded and afraid, like the blonde who dies first in a horror film. Jake always tells me I fit that archetype "to a T."

"Vaga, I'm so glad I found you," Jax continues. "I've been waiting for you my whole life. You're all I've ever wanted and needed."

I prepare to be murdered.

Jax jumps up, grabs my hand, and starts tugging it. *"I need you, baby."* He's singing again.

I try to pull my hand away and look over at Beau and Yumiko to snatch them from their idiotic gamer talk.

"Come on, Prue," he begs, still yanking my arm. "We're going to the water. I need to baptize you."

I pull back harder, but he's much stronger than me.

"We need to wash the devil off our hands," Jax says. Just as he starts lifting me off the sand, Beau appears above him and pulls him back.

"Back off her, man," Beau says.

"But I need her, baby," Jax says again as he tries to wrestle out of Beau's grip. Beau pulls back, and Jax starts to get aggressive.

"Hey," Beau says to Yumiko, while trying to restrain Jax, "can you hand me the prescription bottle in that backpack? I think he needs a Klonopin."

Jax only becomes more aggressive. "I don't take drugs!" he shouts. He tries to free himself from Beau's grasp. "I don't take drugs, I don't take drugs." He just keeps repeating it, like a mantra, each time becoming softer. Eventually, he's crying. "I don't take drugs." He falls down onto the blanket, curls up into a ball, and starts shaking, still cooing. *"I don't take drugs, I don't take drugs, I don't take drugs."*

"I think we need to call Pilar," Beau says.

TWENTY-ONE

As winter turns to spring, Jax is admitted into a residential treatment facility, my Twitter followers drop by half, and I dye my hair back to its natural color. Shiny AF fades into obscurity. Wicked Ice drops us. CAA drops us. We were "of a moment," they tell us, "and that moment is gone."

Soon I'm back under those awful fluorescents, waiting in a line that refuses to budge, staring at @WYATTLOOK to avoid the dire scene around me. My present mood could best be described as "abysmal." I'm in the pharmacy section of Walgreens to pick up my dreaded Celexa. Back to square one. The biggest mind-fuck of SRRIs is that when you go on and off them, they cause the very symptoms they're meant to cure—anxiety and depression and suicidal ideation—for up to a month. Dr. Kim prescribes me extra Klonopin to deal with the transition, which I plan to take as prescribed.

I press the home button on my phone and see a text from Nina. *Be there in 5.* Nina called me a few days ago to tell me she's writing another piece on Shiny AF.

"Shiny AF is over," I'd said when she called. This was the first time we'd talked since she tried to hand me that sweaty pill at the Kingdom a few weeks ago. But I'd be lying if I said I hadn't thought about her. Those freckles are cemented in my mind, probably forever. I know she's more than clusters of concentrated melaninized cells, but I was very fucked up during most of our interactions, and I've learned from therapy that I have a tendency to flatten what I'm looking at to make it easier to digest. In other words, I'm shallow. I remember Andy Warhol called himself "a deeply superficial person," so I don't worry too much.

"Yeah," Nina had responded awkwardly, "that's kind of what I want to talk about."

"Ah," I'd said. It was nice to hear her voice. I wanted to say that, but instead I said, "'The Rise and Fall of Shiny AF.'"

I agreed to the interview. My Shiny AF money is dwindling so I need to get a job soon. Maybe I hope Nina will have some leads, or maybe I just want closure.

Closure isn't real, Jake Perez texted me. *And you need to stop giving chances to people who are clearly using you.*

I didn't respond.

It's weird being back in Nina's Prius, watching her put her foot up on her seat as I get in.

"Hey," she says more warmly than I expected. This is maybe the first time I've been sober around Nina. Maybe she was warm all along, but that seems unlikely. I was on Adderall, not acid.

"I'm not your freak anymore?" I ask.

She grins but doesn't answer. "Do you have a place in mind?" she asks.

"Hmm," I say. "It's nice out." It's pretty much always nice out in LA, so I always feel silly when I say this, but today it's particularly true. Not too hot. There's a breeze. "We could sit outside somewhere."

"That sounds nice," she says. We're saying "nice" a lot and I'm suddenly hyperaware of my breath. The issue with being around people so lucid is that I can never figure out when to breathe or swallow.

"Barnsdall Park?" she asks.

"Perfect," I say.

We don't say much on the drive. I watch the passing palms out the window and try not to think about whether Nina is judging me or if she thinks I look pretty. My therapist keeps telling me to find validation from within, but she obviously hasn't met this cunt inside my head.

The park is fairly empty since it's a weekday. We pick a spot shaded by an olive tree and with views of buildings in the distance, maybe West Hollywood or maybe Koreatown. I squint and try to look for the Kingdom, but it's too far.

Nina lays out an oversized flannel shirt for us to sit on, then pulls out her iPhone. "Is it cool if I record this?" She opens her voice memo app.

"No Moleskine?" I ask.

She smiles. "Not today."

"Record away," I say, then I look toward the city below us, feeling like an Old Hollywood starlet. I wonder if Mrs. Barnsdall was ever interviewed here. I looked her up on Wikipedia that morning. She was an oil heiress with an experimental theater company in Chicago. She decided she "liked Los Angeles" and then commissioned Frank Lloyd Wright to build her a residence/theater compound. I don't know why I don't share this with Nina. She might find it interesting. Or maybe she'd think I'm vapid for caring so much about an heiress.

"So," Nina says, and I'm snatched from my thoughts. "What can you tell me about Shiny AF's decision to break up?"

"Are you interviewing Jax and Pilar?" I ask. "Yumiko?" This feels important. I don't want to betray them.

"I spoke to Jax last night," she says.

I picture Jax and Nina in the Kingdom's cobalt glow: Jax on his couch, legs crossed, thrilled for the audience, ecstasy in his eyes, pontificating with abandon; Nina sitting on the floor, disappearing into open-ended questions and rolling new joints as Jax's sermon unfolds.

Nina looks down at her lap. "He seems to have a nice setup there."

I swallow. I had forgotten that Jax is still at the facility. I haven't visited him yet. I've driven halfway to Malibu three times. But each time I merge onto the 1, I remember him trying to baptize me on the beach that day and my throat starts to close up and I have to pull over. I turn around, and to assuage my guilt, I blast *Yeezus* on the way home in his honor.

"You visited him?" I ask.

She nods. "How is your relationship with Jax?"

"Copacetic," I say. "I'm sure we'll see Dead Stars next time they perform in LA."

Nina picks up a blade of grass and starts tearing its edges, like Jake Perez hates when I do. "Jax really adores you." She gives the blade another tiny tear. "He couldn't stop gloating yesterday. He thinks you're, like, magical."

I feel sad and happy and annoyed at the same time. "Jax would hype up a rock," I say, just as I feel a tear rising up.

Nina bursts out laughing. Her lip quivers and I have another stirring.

"I've actually seen him do it!" I lie, just to play up the bit. "We were smoking a cigarette outside the Mirror Box, and he picked up this dirty rock on the ground and was all, 'Yasssssss, queen, slayyyy.' And he held up the rock and showed it to everyone around us and was like, 'Isn't she so chic? So petite! Ugh, I just want to dress this angelic goddess.' Then he got all frantic, like, 'Give this queen a mic, ASAP!'"

Nina is laughing so hard tears are streaming down her face, and I feel calm for the first time since I got in her car.

"What about your relationship with Pilar?" Nina asks when she finally stops laughing, and my muscles tense again.

"Same," I say. "She has a show next month in some warehouse downtown. I plan on going."

"Oh, yeah. I'm going too," says Nina. "I talk to her tomorrow."

I'm relieved she changed the subject from Jax, about whom I still have many conflicting feelings. At this point, I think he's best experienced from afar, both of us rapping *Yeezus* at the same time on separate sides of the city.

"Cool," I say. I imagine Pilar in a dramatic blue coat, smoking thin cigarettes and acting distant and forlorn. At the least appropriate time, she'll sing her answer, then giggle softly to herself. Her skin will glow like a Glossier ad.

"So," Nina says to her lap. "The breakup?"

"Our breakup was organic," I say. "What we had wasn't sustainable." I realize it sounds like I'm talking about farming, but it's best to be vague. If there's one thing I learned from my mother, it's that you never need to explain yourself.

"Expand?" Nina says.

I grin. "Remember that article you wrote?... *FADER*, I think it was?"

Nina bites her lip. "Fair enough." She touches her neck and I suddenly remember we've been intimate, that she isn't just a journalist interviewing me. Her neck is pale and delicate, sprinkled with freckles, a painting that belongs in the Met. I turn my head away, not wanting to objectify her. But also wishing she would objectify me.

"Yumiko?"

"I'm going to dance class with her later," I say. "We go every week."

We actually go every day. Sometimes twice. I even tried to use Wicked Ice money to pay Crystal to come to my apartment and give Yumiko and me a private class. She came over but she didn't take my money. Afterward, we sat in plastic chairs on my balcony taking puffs of my vape pen and bitching about capitalism, then zoning out and looking at the leaves.

"I'm grateful for dance right now," I say. "It centers me."

I worry I sound New Agey and corny, a California transplant cliché, but Nina just nods. She really seems nicer today.

"Speaking of Yumiko," Nina asks, "what happened with her case? Has it been resolved?"

This question gives me pause. My instinct is to withhold, but I also have nothing to lose. "It hasn't," I say. "The California judicial system is slow as hell." I pause. "Imagine the pharmacy section of Walgreens."

She doesn't laugh and I realize I probably told her this joke before.

"Are you still practicing law?" she asks.

A breeze hits my face. "No." I look down at the city wistfully again, twirl a blade of grass in my fingers. "I'm looking for a new job. Yumiko's 'man'... "

Nina laughs when I put up air quotes and I relax again.

I tell her about how he works at the LA Spotify office and got me an interview to be a curator, and at a certain point the conversation starts to flow, becomes less of a question-and-answer situation. I tell her I still vape cannabis a few times a week, which I call "cannabis" now because I'm in my thirties, and I take my Celexa, but I'm not drinking alcohol or doing other drugs at the moment. She tells me she is taking a break from weed because it was making her "distant" and "abrupt." I get very silent and she says, "Which you know." Then she laughs and so do I.

When the sky starts to turn a darker blue and I see the faint hint of the moon in the distance, Nina asks me about Ellie.

"Done," I say. The nicest thing I can do for Ellie right now, I've decided—and my therapist agrees—is to leave her alone.

"One last question," Nina says.

I pray it's not about Beau.

"Are you making new music?"

A day after the breakup was announced, Wyatt Walcott sent me an Instagram DM saying how sad she was. *The industry is garbage,* she wrote, *but you should put out a solo project.* I've since been writing and recording raps over other musicians' beats on GarageBand in my bedroom, just like in the old days. But I haven't had the urge to share anything yet.

Instead of answering, I just put a finger to my lips. I hope she adds this gesture in the article.

"Understood," she says. She starts to stand up and I follow. It's jarring, being plucked from the safety of our conversation, with its clear purpose, and being ejected back into the randomness of the day.

"Thanks for your time."

"So business." I laugh. "That's all we are, right? Just two girl bosses."

Nina bites her lip; her tooth pierces a freckle. "We aren't girl bosses," she says. "Neither of us has AC."

I breathe in sharply, feigning indignation. "How dare you?" For a second I miss being onstage, then remember that it almost killed me.

Nina picks up the flannel and waves it in the air, allowing bits of debris to fly into the olive grove, then starts walking toward the car. Once we're both looking ahead, she says, "I feel pretty awkward around you."

"Same," I say. It's true, and it comes out easily. Maybe the subconscious can unleash itself without chemical assistance.

We're now walking through the olive grove, our black boots marching in unison. She trips on her shoelace and I accidentally laugh, but she seems okay and she laughs too. She sits on a concrete ledge to tie her shoe and I sit down beside her. I accidentally plop down a little too close, so that our legs are touching, and I can feel her pulse in her thigh, or maybe it's mine.

Suddenly I'm speaking without thinking. "I can't believe you hooked up with Beau," I say, the words coming out quick. I look up right into the sun, which burns in a good way. "You knew how much he triggered me. And I never said anything, but he took nude photos of me without my consent." I'm deciding to weaponize this fact despite that it really never bothered me.

"Wait, what?"

I remove my hands from my face and Nina is looking right in my eyes and it's intense and uncomfortable.

"I mean," I say, "it's not exactly, um, confirmed, but I'm pretty sure he took advantage of me in Palm Springs. Jake Perez found the photos online."

"Wait," Nina says. "The photos of you by the pool?"

I nod, confused.

"Prue," she says. "You don't remember?"

I shrug and mumble something about "light addiction issues" under my breath.

"Oh my god." She looks down at her boots. "I'm a predator."

"You're not a predator," I say. "Wait, you took them?" I feel relief, then something approaching delight.

She shakes her head. "I feel awful."

"Honestly, I'm thrilled." I feel silly for not realizing. The photos were too tasteful to have been taken by Beau. Knowing the truth makes me feel better than I felt before, despite that I was keeping myself in the dark to avoid feeling bad. I don't say any of this out loud.

Nina laughs, then puts her hands on her face. When she removes them, her cheeks are splotchy and her eyes are red. She opens and closes her mouth, then says, "I took advantage of you."

"It's fine, honestly," I say. I try to take stock of how I feel, like my therapist has been teaching me. I can't detect any feeling, but I do notice the breeze hitting my skin, which reminds me I have arms. "We're all taking advantage of each other all the time. Isn't that, like, the human condition?"

Nina kicks some dust with her boot. "That's pretty depressing."

"Welcome to me," I say, then put my hand under my chin like I'm on a billboard, trying to make my face all cute, like I used to do with Ellie. "Maybe catch me when my Celexa kicks back in."

Nina tugs on a curl by her temple, then releases it, and it bounces up toward her crown. "You seemed so into it." Her expression is tense, different from the unflappable Nina I remember from the Kingdom. "You were writhing around on the concrete, your body was making these amazing shapes..."

My cheeks heat.

Nina stares at the ground, then looks up. "But I didn't put the photos online."

"Oh," I say. "My friend Jake Perez found them on a Tumblr called 'Island Princessa,' with x's instead of s's and c's..."

Nina rolls her eyes, then her entire upper body. "Fucking Beau," she says. "He borrowed my laptop right after Palm Springs.

He's so shady I could kill him." She kicks some dirt with her boot—aggressively—and I remember having sex with her.

I take stock of how I feel: turned on, but also jealous. "Do you feel homicidal about everyone you hook up with?" I ask. "Should I be concerned?"

She looks right into my eyes again. "I really did like you."

My stomach does a little flip.

"I guess I wanted to make you jealous." She looks down at her boots and I look down at mine.

I laugh. "You bitch," I say, even though I want to kiss her.

"I know," she says. "I'm not even poly..."

I want to yell or hit her. Instead I laugh. "Poly folly," I say in my seductive alien voice, like I'm being autotuned on the spot. Then I say, "I'm not even queer." The word is too embarrassing to me now. *Lesbian* is more glamorous.

Nina smiles, then tugs another curl. "You promise you aren't upset with me?" she asks. "About the photos?"

"Yes!" My voice is spastic and it echoes. A woman on the other edge of the grove glares. I remind myself I don't care what she thinks. "I was born to be photographed in an alcoholic black-out."

Nina laughs.

My cheeks heat again, then a welcome breeze rushes through the grove. "Do you feel better now?" I ask.

"A little."

She grins, then stands up. I follow her lead. We're facing each other, and my gaze floats to the pale section of skin between the top of her jeans and the bottom of her crop top. For reasons unclear to me, I reach out to shake her hand. It's so dorky, but she rolls with it, and so do I. Our handshake is cool and damp, and I can't tell whether her palms are sweating or mine.

ACKNOWLEDGMENTS

Thank you to my agent, Sarah Phair, for believing in me when no one else did. To Olivia Taylor Smith and Unnamed Press for bringing my dreams to life. And Jaya Nicely for this absolutely perfect cover.

Thanks to my early and insightful readers: Catie Disabato, Rachel Dempsey, Lauren Strasnick, Becca Wild, Mary Bowers, Lauren Kinney, Ana Reyes, and Chelsea Hodson. To my incredible writing group, Shitty First Drafts—KK, Maggie, and Robin. And to my most impactful writing teachers: Francesca Lia Block and Claire Pettengill.

Thanks to Eric Fulcher, the hype man of my dreams.

To Catie Disabato, for her unparalleled kindness.

To my mom, Palmer, for her eternal elegance, for listening to all my dumb ideas, and for loving me even though I never became an accountant.

To my sister, Maimai, for forcing me to smoke weed and being my best friend. To my granny, the original icon. To my brother, Joe, for being very cool for a boy. To my dad, for not cutting me off.

To Abby Kohlman, for being friends with me since before I waxed my eyebrows.

To Aaron Alexander, Nicola Fumo, Harrison Jobe, Aubrey Bellamy, Kenzy El-Mohandes, Mary Russ, Alana Kopke, Kentaro Ikegami, Chris Martin, Alex Rose, Lindsay O'Brien, Andrew Extein, Alex Kreger, Molly Coyne, Nat Shelness, Ria Fulton,

Cassie Spodak, Liz Constantinou, and Christie Bahna, for being the most inspiring friends and for dealing with *moi*.

To my muses: Mary-Kate Olsen, Lana Del Rey, Maria Wyeth, Little Edie Beale, Sonja Morgan, Azealia Banks, the Red Scare ladies, and Kanye West.

And to *you* for reading. Thank you.

ABOUT THE AUTHOR

Anna Dorn is a writer living in Los Angeles. A former criminal defense attorney, she regularly writes about legal issues for *Justia* and *Medium*. She has written about culture for *Los Angeles Review of Books*, *The Hairpin*, and *Vice Magazine*. Anna has a JD from UC Berkeley Law School, an MFA from Antioch University-Los Angeles, and a BA from UNC-Chapel Hill.